COOL.
AWKWARD.
BLACK.

EDITED BY **KAREN STRONG**

VIKING

For Black teens who shatter expectations
and make their own realities

VIKING

An imprint of Penguin Random House LLC, New York

First published in the United States of America by Viking,
an imprint of Penguin Random House LLC, 2023

Library of Congress Cataloging-in-Publication Data is available.

Book manufactured in Canada

ISBN 9780593525098

1 3 5 7 9 10 8 6 4 2

FRI

Edited by Liza Kaplan
Design by Opal Roengchai
Text set in MT Garamond Std

CONTENTS

Editor Introduction by Karen Strong v

"Our Joy, Our Power" by Julian Winters 1

"The Book Club" by Shari B. Pennant 19

"Nina Evans, in the Round" by Kalynn Bayron 33

"Earth Is Ghetto" by Ibi Zoboi 50

"Initiative Check" by K. Arsenault Rivera 69

"Corner Booth" by Leah Johnson 89

"Betty's Best Craft" by Elise Bryant 107

"The Panel Shows the Girl" by Amanda Joy 123

"Spirit-Filled" by Jordan Ifueko 141

"Cole's Cruise Blues" by Isaac Fitzsimons 157

"High Strangeness" by Desiree S. Evans 174

"Catalyst Rising" by Tracy Deonn 192

"Requiem of Souls" by Terry J. Benton-Walker 211

"Honor Code" by Kwame Mbalia 231

"Drive Time" by Lamar Giles 243

"Wolf Tracks" by Roseanne A. Brown 264

"The Hero's Journey" by Tochi Onyebuchi 284

"Abyss" by Amerie 301

COOL. AWKWARD. BLACK.
EDITOR INTRODUCTION

I was a quiet girl who read comics and fantasy. A Star Wars fan who cosplayed Princess Leia with huge afro puffs. A Black girl living beyond what others envisioned for her; a studious teen who loved coding and astronomy, an artistic daydreamer who danced on pointe shoes and composed music. None of these spaces seemed to truly cater to a Black girl from the American South. I didn't see many dark-skinned girls who had adventures or superpowers in the pages of the comics and novels I read. Nobody taught me about the Black women scientists making vital discoveries. Where were all the brown girls who performed onstage or wrote film scores? The scarcity of Black people in these spaces made it easy to believe that what I loved maybe couldn't love me back.

I wasn't proud of myself when I won an academic award during my freshman year of high school—I was ashamed. It didn't help that my nerdy interests and straight As had already made me a target for bullying. But then my father told me something that I still remember to this day: *Your brain is the most beautiful thing about you.* Knowledge was an asset, and if I kept feeding my brain everything it loved, then it would take me anyplace I wanted to go—much farther than the country dirt roads of my small town. My father's words convinced me that the labels other people gave me were wrong, because they were too small to contain me. I began to understand that I was the only one who could define my identity.

The good news is that I eventually found my people. Black geeks who loved to code. Blerds with epic comic-book collections, and brown bookworms with library cards. Black girls who embraced science and math, and Black boys who were passionate about the arts and music. With our shared interests and passions, we created communities that thrived, and I embraced the truth that my Blackness has no boundaries.

I believe stories are important. Black teens deserve to see themselves at the center of storytelling. But just as importantly, I believe everyone can benefit from reading about Black teens who push past the limitations set upon them. We all need to see Black teens celebrating their passions, embracing their magic, falling in love, and saving the world (or themselves). These eighteen stories from bestselling, critically acclaimed Black authors span many genres and introduce an exciting new voice, Shari B. Pennant. I chose this rising star from an open submission call of over one hundred fifty stories.

In the pages of this anthology, you'll meet a girl invited to a secret magical book club, a boy who can summon souls of the dead with music, and a group of teens searching for UFOs on their last summer trip before college. You'll find stories of sweet romance, dark magic, self-discovery, fledgling superpowers, and geeky shenanigans.

Cool. Awkward. Black. is a celebration of Blackness beyond the mainstream. A shout-out to the lovers of manga and anime. A head nod to the cosplayers and gamers. An homage to the book nerds and STEM geeks. An invitation to the devotees of the arts and the stars. As a teen, it would have meant everything to have a book like this. It's a gift to see a reflection of yourself on the page and realize the true power of your identity.

I hope these stories can reveal that truth and beauty for you.

OUR JOY, OUR POWER
BY JULIAN WINTERS

To absolutely nobody's surprise, Jasmine is late.

It's kind of my best friend's thing—being fashionably unpunctual to events. Usually, I don't mind. It's part of what makes our friendship work. She rolls up late, we bicker about it, then she ensures I will have the most memorable time ever in a sincere attempt to apologize. It typically works. By the end of our hangouts, I've long forgotten her poor excuse for keeping me waiting in the first place.

But why'd it have to be tonight? The one time where I want—no, *need*—to be somewhere other than inside my own head.

I check my phone: 7:56 p.m.

The ball started almost thirty minutes ago.

Minutes before the sun sets, the city is bursting with nerdiness. I love downtown this time of year. When, at any moment, sidewalks are teeming with mini parades of people in costumes. Anime characters to all the best sci-fi creatures. Harley Quinns talking to Ewoks. Peter Parker holding hands with Miles Morales. Everyone braving the insufferable heat to show off their craftsmanship.

Infinity Con brings out that loud, proud geek we rarely show off the other fifty-one weekends a year.

Outside the Rosa Parks Freedom Museum, kids who don't look much older than me excitedly climb the stone steps toward the annual Geeks in the Night teen ball. As always, Infinity Con has gone all out for this evening's spectacle. Moving spotlights. A long red carpet leading inside. All my favorite music pouring into the late-summer air like a siren's song.

My heart races with anticipation. It's like that first kick on a skateboard where you're unsure if you'll fall or glide.

I can't wait to dance the evening away with my people.

Well, I *think* they're still my people. I'm not too sure anymore.

Somewhere in my head, the announcer's voice from earlier today repeats:

"And in fourth place . . . Jalen Harding!"

Fourth place. Not even runner-up. I wasn't good enough to stand with winners.

"No, no," I whisper while pacing the sidewalk outside the museum. "You're fine. Remember Gramps's words."

"Don't you dare let them dim your shine."

Easier said than done, I think.

Maybe I would be fine if Jasmine were here. Especially because this isn't just any Infinity Con. It's our first adult-less Infinity Con. An entire *ball* for teen geeks like us.

Yet, here I am, alone.

I pull out my phone again. Since the Geeks ball has a strict "no reentry" rule, I can't pop into the museum's bathroom to check my appearance without leaving Jasmine behind. Both our tickets are in my jacket pocket.

I open the camera on my phone—ignoring all the passersby shooting me annoyed looks because I'm in their way—to angle the lens up high and inspect my fit.

My naturally black curl twists are temporarily dyed dark green. The crimson tie looks sharp against my white button-up. My gray suit jacket fits a little big. I did the best I could tailoring it. At least I found a pair of hunter-green slacks at a thrift store along with some fire-red Air Jordan Retro 11s that I'll spend the rest of my life paying Gramps back for.

Totally worth it.

I look just like my favorite anime character, Deku. Mostly. We're both sixteen. He doesn't have my rich brown skin or dark eyes. The thick Harding eyebrows. Plus, at the rate I'm growing, none of these clothes will fit in a year.

Deku also doesn't sweat like he just ran a marathon in the middle of July. My face is glowing with perspiration.

Self-consciously, I scan my surroundings. No one's paying attention to me anymore. Just like when I lost that cosplay contest.

There you go again.

On the second to last step, I spot a handkerchief. Perfect. It looks clean, freshly dropped. The silky, expensive material is royal purple with the initials PCW stitched into a corner.

"Sorry to this man." I chuckle softly, wiping all the sweat from my face.

When I go to check my face one last time, I realize I'm not standing alone anymore. There's a boy in a suit behind me. I almost drop my phone.

"Whoa. Sorry, sorry!"

His voice is gentle, a little deep. He throws his hands up, palms out like he means no harm. Yeah, creeping behind someone doesn't leave that kind of impression.

"If you were trying to take a selfie, I was gonna offer to take a photo for you?" He scratches at the side of his neck. "Y'know, so you could get a full shot of your dope costume?"

"I wasn't," I reply, still slightly breathless. "Trying to take a selfie, I mean."

Wait. Did he say my cosplay was . . . *dope?*

"Oh. Sorry again." He's backing away, shyly rubbing his forehead.

I take him in. Somewhat taller than me. Short, tight brown curls. Fair gold-brown skin with features that are simultaneously soft and sharp at once. He's wearing one of those cheap black domino masks that's been bejeweled with violet stones around the edges. The perfect juxtaposition to his tailored black suit with purple accents.

To be honest, *beautiful* is too understated for this boy.

"Should I—maybe I'll just go wait over there." He points toward a corner of the street where I suppose he came from. The top button of his shirt is undone. Pinkish blush rapidly spreads from his collarbones to his jaw.

I bite on a smile. "Are you waiting on someone?"

"My best friend. *Ex*–best friend. He's dead to me for being late."

He's still walking backward, almost tripping on his own feet.

A snort-giggle I'll never forgive myself for escapes my body. "Same," I say. "Late is my bestie's default."

"Sorry about that."

I shrug, unable to loosen the hold this ridiculous grin has on my cheeks. "Not your fault."

Another group of teens dressed as the Avengers marches past us, up the steps to the ball.

"So. I'll wait." He anxiously brushes a hand over his curls. "Over there."

There's a hesitance in his backward steps. Almost like he doesn't want to go. I don't think I want him to leave either. Only because I enjoy company at these things. I like talking to strangers in line, waiting for autographs from our favorite actors. Or, like backstage today, when I struck up a chill conversation with two girls about music.

Minutes before my disastrous contest finish.

"Find somewhere else to get your happiness," Jasmine told me this afternoon while brushing disappointed tears from my face. "We'll plan for next year later. Right now? Let's focus on having the time of our lives."

And maybe you'll meet a cute boy, is something Jasmine didn't say, but knowing her, it was implied.

"I liked your cosplay earlier, by the way." He stops walking. "I thought it was great."

I'm snapped back to reality by that deep, timid voice.

I blink hard. "You saw me?"

He nods like he's unsure if he said the wrong thing. And he kind of did. But only because I'm embarrassed that he witnessed what happened.

"Guess it doesn't matter if I lost," I struggle to say against the dejectedness in my voice.

The guy shrugs. "They got it wrong."

Despite hearing those same words from Gramps and Jasmine and all my online followers after posting behind-the-scenes photos, it sounds more genuine coming from this stranger.

"I'm Jalen!" I say.

His lips twitch into a smile that reveals a pair of dimples. "Carter. My name, I mean. Er, Carter."

Another snort-giggle. Seriously, this is the worst.

"We can wait together if you want?" I offer.

Crinkles form in his brow. He's thinking. And what's wrong with me? Number one rule of being an adult-less teen at a convention: Don't agree to hang out alone with a complete stranger. Always in groups. Always with a friend one text away.

Carter checks his phone. He nods, smiling while strolling back toward me.

"Sounds like a plan."

Thank Cyborg, Jasmine's not around to see me. I'd never hear the end of the way my entire face lights up at those four words.

■ ■ ■

Actually, this was a pretty bad plan.

Carter and I do nothing but stand around, drowning in our silence. Two awkward Black boys on a sidewalk.

More and more teens scramble up the steps to the ball. In the distance, the sky melts from blue to a peach-lilac as the sun gradually sinks behind the cityscape. The heat fades just enough that my pits aren't damp anymore. Yes, that's what I'm focusing on: perspiration issues rather than the fact that my best friend is possibly standing me up.

"So." I turn to Carter.

His eyebrows raise but he doesn't follow up on my obviously poor conversation starter.

"Uh. Never mind."

Back to the quiet we go.

I bob my head to the music roaring from the museum every time those golden-glass doors swing open. It's a mix of old pop-rock and classic hip-hop. I can only imagine the okayish-to-cringeworthy dancing being showcased inside.

In my peripheral, I can see Carter checking his phone. It's the third time he's done that in the last ten minutes.

"Something wrong?" I ask.

"N-No. It's nothing."

"You sure?"

I notice his hands are shaking as he pockets the phone.

He nods quickly, then winces when more music blares into the streets.

"Sorry. Not a fan of loud places."

"But you came to . . . a ball?" I say.

"I like irony?"

Once again, I can't resist the snort that tickles my nose. To be fair,

Carter's funny when he's not, you know, looking like a nervous squirrel. Then there's the dimples. Jasmine would approve. So would Gramps.

"Whoever he is betta make you laugh and not cry," Gramps always warns me whenever the topic of potential boyfriends comes up. "Life's too short to let anyone steal your joy."

Especially if you're Black, queer, or both, I always want to add, but I think Gramps already knows that part.

"Do you want to, maybe, go for a walk?" Carter asks.

"A walk?"

"Just around the block?" He makes a circular gesture with his index finger. "Unless you think your friend's gonna be here soon?"

I wrinkle my nose. The way today's been going? Highly doubtful. But leaving a very public place with a somewhat stranger is still questionable. I text Jasmine. A few choice emojis should do the trick.

"Okay," I reply.

"Okay?" Carter looks surprised.

I squint at him. "Do you not want to—?"

"No!" He waves both hands around. "I'd love that."

I can't fight the smile that pushes my cheeks higher.

I forget how pretty this city is at night. Mainly because I live in the suburbs with Mom and Gramps. And I'm sixteen with a strict curfew. Streetlights on? I better be inside or somewhere with an adult chaperone.

Around us, darkened glass buildings reflect the purplish sky. Neon signs paint the sidewalks in rainbow hues. Restaurants heave breaths of freshly cooked food in our faces. Honking cars can't compete with a Hard Rock Café's jazz soundtrack. Adult cosplayers hang out on street corners, waiting for the After-Dark Prom to start once the ball concludes.

Tomorrow, they'll all be hungover and still up early for the Infinity Con parade.

It's my favorite part of the weekend.

Since I was knee-high, Gramps has brought me downtown to watch the Sunday morning parade. He'd hold my hand while we wiggled through the massive crowds. Show off all his favorite heroes. Rant for hours about the dozens of big-budget movies they made before he finally got to see his *first* with a Black main character in theaters.

He's too old to do all the con things now. It's kind of cool he wants me to carry on the tradition.

I point out all my favorite costumes to Carter as we walk. He nods and smiles, tight shoulders gradually relaxing. "Still not as good as your look today," he comments, nudging my elbow.

Is he flirting with me? Or did he really love my costume? Both? Nah. It couldn't be that.

Another voice enters my head. An older white woman who, even when being kind, still looked like she smelled a fart:

"We didn't think you embodied your character as well as the others . . ."

It takes a second to shake off the memory of those words.

"Thanks," I say as we pause at a crosswalk. I want to remind Carter I still lost.

It's my own fault. I was too confident. After the months I put into designing and creating my costume, I really thought the judges would see a determined boy dressed as Spike from *Cowboy Bebop*, another one of my favorite anime characters, and think he was worthy of first place.

But all they saw was a Black boy who didn't cosplay as a Black character, and it was an instant "No."

"We just think," another judge tried to explain, *"if you'd maybe gone in a*

different direction—like Black Lightning! Static Shock! Black Panther! Maybe . . ."

I don't even remember the third judge's comments before I walked off the stage.

They'd made their point.

Unexpectedly, the side of Carter's hand brushes mine. Like he's trying to get my attention. Because I'm drifting. Mom says I do that a lot. Get lost in my head.

Carter smiles crookedly. "They clearly didn't see your greatness."

I roll my eyes. "Okay, sure."

He beams like he's so right and I'm so wrong about myself.

It's the same way Gramps was earlier. Our conversation hits me like a cold splash of water in the winter.

"With great power comes great responsibility . . ."

"Gramps, I have no power." I was slouching in the passenger seat of his old SUV as we sat parked outside the convention center. "The judges practically said it to my face."

"Jae, our *joy* is our power," he insisted, gently grabbing my chin until I stared him in the eyes. "They can't have it. It's yours. Don't you dare let them dim your shine. You never know how your light might brighten someone else's darkness."

The crosswalk signal changes. Carter and I shuffle with the small crowd. We take a left. I'm not thinking as much about the ball. Only him as his shoulder grazes mine. He smells sweet. Like kiwi and honey and deodorant.

I gravitate toward him.

"It's not like I'm not used to it," I say, shrugging half-heartedly. "It happens all the time to us."

I'm not bitter. It's just facts.

The moment someone finds out you're Black in a high-profile fandom, they always ask, "What're you doing here?" or "Shouldn't you be in a different space?" Or they say, "I didn't think you would be into this." As if liking things like anime or comics or freaking Star Trek is revolutionary. A concept beyond a sixteen-year-old queer Black boy.

Breaking news: It isn't. Kindly dump your micro- and macroaggressions to the left.

"That doesn't mean things can't change," offers Carter.

I laugh dryly. "Pretty sure that same group of judges have done this for years."

I remember at least two of those faces from last year when I was in the audience.

"Infinity Con's one big flaw," I sigh.

As much as I love the con, I recognize it's an institution that resists change. The same organizers and venues. Same judges and hosts, all the way down to who does and doesn't get invited. But it's my only option here.

"They're changing CEOs, though," says Carter as we pass Coretta Scott King Park. From the entrance, I can see the memorial fountain lit in blues and greens. It's Jasmine's and my favorite spot to chill between con events.

"He's one of us!" Carter grins.

"I've heard."

Justin Washington, former comic bookshop owner turned movie director and now CEO of Infinity Con. Not gonna lie—it's nice to have someone who looks like me at the top. Brown skin with dreads and the kind of smile you can trust. But who knows if it will actually make a difference.

"Let's just hope he doesn't become another puppet for the corporate gods keeping us on the outside looking in," I grumble.

"He's not," Carter says almost confidently. When I flick up an eyebrow, he corrects, "From what I've read online."

Again, I shrug lazily. Carter's pinkie almost hooks with mine, then falls away. Heat rushes to my cheeks thinking about holding his hand.

He nods earnestly. "It's gonna get better."

As nauseating as it is to admit, his optimism is contagious.

I find myself telling him about all my favorite bands with Black lead singers. How I almost came to Infinity Con dressed as Prodigy, another queer Black hero from the X-Men books. We talk TV shows. Favorite movies. Make faces at each other while scrolling through past Halloween costumes on our phones.

"I don't know about you, but I made a handsome Gambit," he insists.

I crinkle my nose to soften my smile as we round another corner.

"Have you ever thought about going into costume design?" he asks when I'm quiet for a few steps. "Your looks are next level."

My frown is inevitable. All I can picture are the judges' confused expressions as I walked to center stage.

Carter must notice my face. "Or . . ." he starts, "maybe acting? Like, be *in* the movies?"

I've considered it. Jasmine always says I'm too dramatic about everything. There's a side of me that wants to star in a reboot of one of the classic superheroes. Batman or Spider-Man. But I also want to play an original character. Be the first time a kid like me sees a hero they can relate to on the big screen.

I don't want to wait decades for that to happen like Gramps did.

"Maybe," I reply.

"You have the face for it." Carter bites his lip but doesn't look like he wants to take it back.

This time, our hands brushing *isn't* accidental.

"What about you?" I ask, tapping into my deflection skills like a pro.

A brown-skinned girl dressed as Jubilee hoverboards past us.

We stand on a corner. The stars in the sky sluggishly blink awake. I peek at Carter. His left dimple flexes. Enthusiastically, he says, "Nah. No acting for me. I want to be behind-the-scenes. I like to write. Maybe I'll draft an epic screenplay. Start a writers' room filled with people like us. Be that guy who makes space for all of us in fandom."

He cues up a video on his phone. A trailer for an upcoming TV series I haven't heard about. It's a majority Black and brown cast, centering a family of superheroes like the Incredibles.

Endorphins explode inside my chest.

"This is *sick*," I say, refusing to hide the awe in my voice.

"My dad says we all deserve a win," Carter whispers. "That's how I want to make us feel."

There's so much certainty behind his words. Nothing like that stammering, jittery boy I met outside the ball.

"But not right now. I'm only sixteen," he announces, pocketing his phone, "I've got time."

I like that too. The way he's in no rush. Like every single thing he does won't make it or break it for all of us. He's not carrying the weight of everyone else's dreams on his shoulders. Just his own.

Carter rubs the back of his head, that nervousness returning. Like he's said too much.

I want to tell him he hasn't said enough. I could listen to him talk all night.

Instead, we follow the pavement back toward the museum. I can already hear the music. See the latecomers in their last-minute costumes high-stepping toward the lights.

Now would be a good time to ask for his number. Or his social media handles. Is it too soon to slide into his DMs?

Does that almost-hand-holding moment mean we could have an almost-kiss too?

"Hey, Carter, would—"

"Jalen, where the hell have you been?! You said you'd be gone *ten minutes*."

It's Jasmine, rushing up to me as best as she can in a full-on Valkyrie-from-the-Thor-movies-inspired outfit, blue cape flapping wildly. By her side is a dark-skinned boy with a low fade, light brown eyes, and a black T-shirt that reads THIS IS MY COSTUME in bold white print.

He shoots a smug grin Carter's way.

Jasmine smacks my arm hard. "Answer my question!"

"Me?" I reel on her, incredulous. "Where've you been? You're late, late, *late*."

"I was . . ." Jasmine trails off. She has all the features to pull off this look—round face, expressive mouth, kill-you-with-a-glare eyes. Her curly hair is teased big and messy. Her gaze flits in the other boy's direction and even the gold and ivory battle armor she's wearing can't hide the way my best friend's *blushing*. "Preoccupied."

"Seriously?" I gasp, scandalized. "You ghosted me for—"

I cut myself off to size up the cheesing boy. "And you are?"

Before he can answer, Carter says, "Landon, my best friend."

Oh, you have got to be kidding me.

"Look at you!" Landon jostles Carter. "Meeting someone. Wandering off to—"

"Shut up," Carter hisses, his face screwed up.

I spin back toward Jasmine, trying not to overanalyze what Landon was about to say. "Explain. Now."

Sighing, Jasmine gives a brief synopsis of her disappearance: She and Landon met in the Starbucks line today while I was suffering a painful dismemberment via those racist cosplay judges. He commented on her

Tomb Raider costume. She snarked about his lack of fandom-inspired outfit in the middle of a convention.

"Not really my thing," says Landon, shrugging nonchalantly as if he wasn't eavesdropping on our conversation. "I do it all for Carter."

This guy is all charisma, no indecision. A.k.a. Jasmine's type.

"We hit it off," whispers Jasmine, like she's in that stage of pretending this is nothing when we both know it's *something*. "We texted all day. Met at a café for bubble tea. And—"

"Forgot your best friend was waiting to go to the most important party of the weekend?" I provide. "His one chance to forget what happened to him during that nightmare cosplay contest?"

"Technically, yes, but not as brutal." Jasmine peeks past me at Carter. "Besides, I'd say you found someone else to help you forget things."

She leans closer to whisper, "He's hot."

I almost mouth, *I know*, but I can feel Carter's embarrassment reaching nuclear levels from here.

"You're deflecting," I tell her.

"I'm giving you facts and facts only."

Landon's "Mm-hmm" doesn't go unnoticed, but I don't get to call him out too.

A tall woman in a sleek onyx suit with an umber complexion, skin fade, and all the badass energy of the Dora Milaje from *Black Panther* walks up to us. Her eyes fix on one person.

"Prince Washington, I've been texting you. Your father is waiting!"

"Damn, we're busted," Landon says, then quickly throws a hand over his mouth.

The woman is seconds away from unleashing fury on him when Carter stammers, "Hi, Toya. Sorry about that. I got lost?"

She *pfft*s. Carter's an unconvincing liar.

"I'm really sorry." He inhales deeply. "And I'll explain." Over his shoulder, his eyes flicker toward me. "If you'll give me five minutes."

"Two," replies Toya, stiffly. Her mouth curls at me and my organs dissolve. "Hurry. Mr. Washington needs you by his side when they announce him."

"Okay," grumbles Carter. He turns to me, motioning a few feet away. I blink at him, confused. He swallows, wincing. "Can we, uh . . . ?"

"Go talk to him," Jasmine whispers to me in the least discreet voice.

I close my eyes, sighing. "Sure."

When we're away from everyone, I say, "So, what—you're a prince? Like con royalty?"

"No." He laughs shakily. "Prince is my first name. Carter's my middle name. It's easier than explaining that my dad was obsessed with the singer growing up."

I nod slowly, trying to process all of that.

"And your dad is . . ."

"Justin Washington, the new CEO of Infinity Con," he replies. His face reddens.

So, he *is* con royalty. Kind of.

I'd seen pictures of Mr. Washington before. His wife too. But they've done a good job of not thrusting Carter into the spotlight. The online news blitzes never even mentioned a son.

"All of that—back there?" I jerk my head in the direction we walked. "Was that for PR? To hype up your dad?"

"No, no, no." Carter steps closer.

I edge back.

He frowns. "I said it because it's *true*. My dad's always wanted to build something that our community could be proud of. That other Black nerds like me could aspire to."

Like Gramps.

"Things are changing. And not just because the con finally recognizes that a person of color should lead them into the future." Carter scrubs a hand over his curls. "Because of people like you and me."

"People like you and me?"

He smiles, dimples activated. "Yeah. The ones who never half-step. Who are great even though others keep reminding us that great is only *one thing* we have to be."

I swallow, heart climbing closer to my throat.

"The ones who exist when, sometimes, that's the hardest thing for us to do," he says quietly. For the first time, his fingers find mine. They twist and twine and it takes everything inside me to stand still.

"We're better than fourth-place finishes," he continues. "You believe that, right?"

My lips part. Nothing comes out. I'm . . . confused. I want to be everything Carter just said, even when people like those judges tell me I'm not. But it's difficult.

"Prince!" Toya's voice booms from the steps. "Time to go."

It's not me who breaks our fingers apart. It's Carter. Or maybe it is me. Because I haven't said anything. I haven't done anything but breathe and stare. He gives me a reluctant grin, then walks in Toya's direction.

Just as quick as he appeared, Carter's gone.

"Jalen Anthony!"

I'm not prepared for Jasmine's thump to my shoulder, but I should be. More than once, I've been on the wrong side of her left hook. But this one feels particularly ruthless.

"Ow!" I stumble back.

"Why did you let him *leave?*"

I wave a hand to where Toya was standing thirty seconds ago. "What was I supposed to do?"

"Look, I know we just met," says Landon, "but knowing my bro Carter, it's best you say what's on your mind." I notice he is still attached to Jasmine's side. "He's always lived in his parents' shadow, so he kind of needs to be pulled into his own light sometimes."

As much as I want to inform Landon he can keep his unsolicited advice to himself since, in fact, we *don't* know each other, my brain drifts back to what Gramps said.

"You never know how your light might brighten someone else's darkness."

Was I—did I do that for Carter?

Tug him out of his own darkness? Remind him how remarkable we are as just queer Black geeky boys?

I shove my hands into my pockets, defeated again. My fingers catch on something velvety. The handkerchief. My throat goes dry as I outline the initials. pcw.

Prince Carter Washington.

I spent most of the ball wandering around the city with a prince.

My gaze falls on the steps. I wish he was there. I wish I would've said—

"One more thing!"

I blink three times. It's Carter, almost falling down the steps with an annoyed Toya following behind. He's breathless when he reaches me. Bright eyes and dimples and domino mask removed. Even the imprints it left behind on his face are charming.

"I know I'm going out on a limb, but hear me out," he pleads, gasping. "There's an annual spotlight dance in five minutes. A Geeks ball tradition."

His fingers wiggle at his sides like he might grab mine again. He doesn't. But his eyes search mine. A hopeful smile pushes at his lips. "I'm a really bad dancer. I get so nervous around others . . . except with you tonight, Jalen."

I lick my lips, still unsure what to say.

"Would you like to—join me?"

My eyebrows lower. "This isn't to impress anyone, right? To make your dad look—"

"Jalen, I like you!" he shouts, startling both of us. He briefly grimaces but doesn't shy away from me. "I want to spend tonight and tomorrow at the parade and *whenever* talking to you."

We inhale together.

"If that's cool with you?"

Behind Carter, Landon's gesticulating wildly. Jasmine's staring me down in that you-better-not-overthink-this way she's mastered.

And I'm not.

Because I've done that enough.

Because I can't let one more person take away who I am.

I take his hand. "On a scale from one to ten, how bad is your dancing?"

"Negative two. All this melanin and no rhythm. It's tragic."

I sputter a laugh that fills my whole chest. His fingers squeeze around mine. Then he relaxes, beaming as he leads me up the steps and into the ball.

We don't look back to see if anyone's watching.

We know they are.

How could you not look at us shine?

THE BOOK CLUB
BY SHARI B. PENNANT

The bookstore was unbearably loud. Not the loud of the wild house parties that Amara rarely attended—all pounding bass and gossiping teens, the crunching of a hundred red Solo cups. Nor was it the loud of the school homecoming game with its packed stands and screaming fans.

No, this was the kind of loud that only stillness could provide.

The blow of icy air-conditioning. The sizzle of ghostly fluorescent lights. The faint whistle of wind whenever a new patron walked through the door.

And, of course, there was also the sound of magic.

To Amara Crane, magic sounded like a rushing of blood between her ears. Or a heavy heartbeat, like her entire body had become a percussion instrument. That, combined with the sound of a thousand thoughts crashing into one another in her head.

But today, tucked away in a lone corner of Corvus Books, the city's oldest bookstore, Amara tried her hardest to drown her magic out. The store itself was pretty empty—probably because of what her brother claimed were "weird vibes"—and Amara had picked the farthest, most secluded spot possible to do her research. The last thing she needed was someone poking their head into her business—or witnessing any of the strange things she could do.

Mountains of books surrounded her on all sides. A handful hovered in the air above her head, a shifting cloud of novels plucked from every genre from every corner of the store. From fiction to nonfiction, sci-fi to mythology, religion to urban fantasy. From aliens to witches to mutants and metahumans—and everything in between.

Just like every other moment in her life, good or bad, she turned to books. Each one was a brand-new world to lose herself in. One where she didn't have to worry about losing control in front of her classmates. Again. Or freaking her mom out with another accidental display of power. Again. Where the unspoken words on the page drowned out the sound of magic in her blood. Books always held an escape. But now, she needed them to have an answer.

A stack of Zatanna comics wobbled by her ankle. The superhero sorceress's shining face smiled up at her. Amara had already thumbed through that entire collection of issues. Not that they satisfied any of her burning questions.

She needed to know what made her different from all the other kids. The normal ones. Was she born this way, like a demigod princess from one of those classic TV shows? Or was she made this way, pumped full of spliced genes or vials of super serum? What gave her the power that flowed through her veins, the magic that vibrated from her limbs?

Why me?

Amara jumped to her feet and knocked her head on the Ferris wheel of books above her. She hissed and then quietly thanked the universe for the cloud of kinks and coils piled on top of her head. With a wave of her hand, the books floated back down to earth, joining their equally unhelpful brothers on the ground. She turned her attention to the cluttered shelves behind her. She ran a finger along each of the spines, tracing every embossed letter, as if she could somehow absorb all of their knowledge from touch alone. Wouldn't that be nice?

She kept going, until her hand felt soft leather. This one had no title, no author. The spine was bare. Just the smooth, uncracked edge of a book rarely opened.

That's weird.

She moved to pull it from the shelf. But, as if it had sensed her thoughts, the book shimmied out of its slot and jumped into her outstretched hand.

The sounds came as soon as the aged leather met her skin.

Blood rushing. Wind howling. A whisper.

You . . .

Amara jumped so hard, her thick glasses almost fell off her nose. She turned the book over. The cover was worn and sun-bleached, like it had been sitting around for a thousand years. A man's silhouette was crudely etched into the front.

It's you . . . The voice came again. *We need you.*

"Me?" she asked.

"Yes, you!" someone snapped from behind.

"Eek!" Amara squeaked and jumped, instinctively hiding the strange book behind the pleats of her skirt. She whirled around to face the person who spoke.

It was a girl, maybe around Amara's age. Neon blue streaks were woven into her box braids, which fell across her face and barely hid an annoyed scowl. There was a sharpness to her that sent every hair on Amara's arms on end. The crackle of the lights got louder.

The girl's arms were crossed tight over her leather jacket, which was covered in patches and pins. The largest pin—an ebony bird in flight—sat next to a name tag with *Olive* scrawled in spiky cursive.

Amara let out a breath and tried to steady her pounding heart. The girl must work here.

"I've been trying to get your attention forever," Olive said. "We close in five minutes."

"Oh, sorry," Amara tumbled over her words. "I was, uh, lost in thought."

"So are you actually going to buy any of these?" Olive pointed to the dozens of books that littered the floor.

Amara glanced down at the mess. Her earlier picks were still settled on the ground, without any trace of gravity-defying magic. They looked as normal as possible. A twinge of guilt gnawed at her. It would be so easy to wave her hands, push her intentions into these inanimate objects, and watch them fly back to their respective homes in the store. She shook the thought from her mind. It was good that she had stopped using her magic when she did. If Olive had seen her, who knows what the other girl would have done? When Amara first started trying to understand her powers, she'd spent hours reading about the Salem witch trials. The things that happened to people who were different. Like her.

She didn't sleep for weeks.

And there was still more research to do. She grabbed the closest three books she could and piled them on top of the nameless one. "I'll take these."

Olive waved her hands toward the cash register, as if to say, "Lead the way." They weaved through displays of old manga and collectible Funko Pops. Amara dropped her stack onto the cashier's desk. New Age self-help, a classic science fiction novel, and a board book. And, of course, the nameless one. Olive marched behind the counter and stared at the mismatched assortment. Her eyebrow quirked upward.

Heat rose in Amara's cheeks, and she shuffled her feet under the girl's intense gaze. "Just a little light reading."

"Right."

Olive pulled each book toward her. But when she got to the nameless leather one, her whole body tensed. The cashier's eyes widened a fraction, but her expression returned to normal so quickly that Amara almost missed it.

"This one's not for sale," she snapped.

Amara jerked back. It had been on the shelf. Why would it be out there if someone wasn't meant to find it? If *she* wasn't meant to find it?

"But I need this one," she insisted.

"Sorry," Olive said, not sounding sorry at all. She shrugged and pushed the other three forward.

"Wait a minute—" Amara made for the nameless book, but Olive slammed a hand down on it so hard, the table rattled. Her palm covered the carving of the man on the front.

"I said *no*."

Amara yanked her hand back and her shoulders fell. "Okay! Sorry. I thought it could help me understand something. It was like it was . . . calling to me. Like it needed my help or something."

Olive stared at her again, incredulous. Her dark eyes turned stormy. "A *book* asked for your help?"

"No, of course not!" Amara tried not to swear. How could she let something like that slip? "Never mind."

She grabbed some manga volumes from the closest display, desperate for something else to focus on. Olive tucked the nameless book beneath the desk, far from sight. She stacked the manga on top of the others and rang up the pile in silence.

Amara could still feel the other girl's eyes on her, analyzing her every move. Her cheeks warmed again.

"Your total is $42.98."

Amara handed her a stack of cash and made to grab the pile of books when the other girl called out.

"Hey, hold on a second."

Olive flicked her wrist and a long tasseled bookmark appeared in her hand. Amara blinked hard, twice. It was as if it had materialized out of thin air. The bookmark was trimmed in gold and had a holographic finish, shimmering in the white fluorescent lights that hung above. Like the nameless book, it had no words.

A picture of a blackbird sat in the middle. Its dark wings were outstretched, surrounded by swirls of glittering gold. When Olive tilted the bookmark, the bird seemed to come alive, like it was about to leap off the paper and head right for her. It was the same as the pin on Olive's patched jacket.

"There's a, um, book club that meets here every week. You can come hang with us if you want." Olive's sharp voice cut into her thoughts. "Maybe we can help you find the answers you're looking for."

She pushed the bookmark toward Amara, impatient. As soon as Amara touched it, power rushed through her. The whispers returned.

It's time . . .

Amara gasped. She glanced up at Olive, expecting her to be just as shocked as Amara was. But the cashier was still watching her, unmoved. Olive must not have heard the voice.

Amara snatched the bookmark out of the other girl's hand and quickly stuffed it into one of the books. She shoved the teetering pile into her bag, whipped around, and pushed for the front door. In her rush, her elbow accidentally knocked into the display shelf, sending novels and collectibles flying in every direction.

Panic seized her. Without thinking, Amara threw her hands up into the air. Everything froze. The falling items stopped in their tracks, still several feet above the ground.

A cold dread washed over her. Slowly, she turned to face Olive, not sure what would happen. She half expected the other girl to have her phone out, ready to blast Amara's frightened face all over social media. Or to be calling 911, like her dad had the first time she used her powers. Or FaceTiming an exorcist. Something.

But Olive just stood behind the cash register, watching the scene unfold. Her eyes danced with amusement.

"Well," she said. "That's interesting."

Amara didn't—*couldn't*—respond. Her arms dropped, and with them, so did everything else. Books and toys hit the ground with a heavy clatter. Without another word, Amara grabbed her fallen bag and bolted for the door. She ran outside so swiftly that she almost missed Olive's words.

"See you next week."

Amara sprinted out of Corvus Books, feet pounding hard against the cracked gray concrete. The Crane family brownstone was only a few blocks away, so it didn't take very long for her to reach home.

Amara skidded to a stop at the front steps, her lungs aching and begging for air. She tried to smooth out her rustled skirt and pat down her wind-troubled curls. Her hands still trembled with anxiety and residual magic. She reached out for the brass doorknob.

One . . . two . . . three . . .

The door pushed open and a cool breeze welcomed her inside. But where she was expecting a cacophony of voices—excited news anchors or soccer refs blaring out match scores—she was met with nothing. Her parents were out again.

Thank goodness.

Normally, their absence bugged her. But today, it was a blessing. Her parents didn't need to see her like this. They already thought she was out of her mind. Not that she could blame them.

"Yo," her little brother's voice echoed through the hall. He must have heard her walk in.

Amara held the bag of books close and made her way to his bedroom. Omar was sitting cross-legged on his unmade bed, surrounded by video game controls and half-eaten bags of chips. He waved an orange-encrusted hand, beckoning her inside.

"'Sup nerd? Where've you been?"

"Nothing. Nowhere," she answered too quickly.

Omar's bushy eyebrows went up and Amara wanted to kick herself. He paused his game and moved his headset off one ear, skewing his afro.

"Really," he drawled. His eyes roamed over her—spooked, disheveled, and out of breath—before landing on the bag she was cradling. Amara shuffled her brown arms, trying to hide the bookstore's outdated logo from her brother's view.

Omar ran a hand down his face. Flakes of cheese dust stuck to his cheek. "Please tell me you didn't go back to that weird old place."

Amara rolled her eyes. "It's a bookstore. Not a cemetery."

"You know Mom and Dad would kill you if they knew you were out doing 'research' again." He added air quotes to the word *research*, and said it like she was planning a hostile government takeover.

Amara bit the inside of her cheek, barely holding back a frustrated sigh. It wasn't as if he didn't know how important this was to her. Or like it was the first time he caught her obsessing over strange texts to try and find some answers. Their parents might've preferred to pretend Amara's weird abilities didn't exist. To ignore her and all the things that made her "abnormal." But that didn't mean that she was okay living without her truth.

"Just don't tell them," she snapped.

"What's in it for me?"

Wow. Jackass.

She waved her hands, summoning the manga she'd bought. These were supposed to be a treat for herself, not a bargaining chip. But hey, whatever got her brother off her back and let her get back to her reading. They flew across the room and landed on the bed, where they scattered crumbs in every direction.

Omar's mouth fell open. Not in fear at her magic, but at the limited editions she'd snagged. "Deal!"

She started to walk away when her brother called her back.

"Y'know," he said as he sucked at his fingers. "For what it's worth, I think Mom and Dad are wrong. Your powers are pretty cool. Wherever they came from."

"Thanks, O. At least someone thinks so." Amara sighed and smiled back at him. He may have been a jerk, but he was her jerk. "That means a lot."

When Amara finally made it back to her room, she all but collapsed onto her bed. She snapped her fingers twice—once to shut the door behind her and again to light the dust-littered floor lamp in the corner. The books followed obediently behind, never more than a few feet away, before settling down at her feet. Her mind drifted back to the nameless book missing from her pile. The way that it called to her. Between that and Olive's weird invitation, Amara felt closer to the truth than ever before. And yet, somehow, further away from it too.

She flopped over and screamed into her pillow, until her voice felt scratchy and hoarse. She pulled herself back up and focused instead on the book closest to her, and willed its pages to life. The book hovered over, each of its covers flapping like an owl's wings. Feathered pages ruffled in the imagined wind. It began its descent, but before it landed, a flash of light streaked from its pages.

The holographic bookmark fluttered down. Light caught the reflective paper, bathing it in shades of silvery blue and shimmering gold. The blackbird in the center beat its wings as it fell. Amara plucked it out of the air. As soon as she did, power surged through her body just like before. And as if ignited by her touch, words appeared on the paper, written by an invisible hand.

Dear Ms. Amara Alexandria Crane . . .

Amara froze. What in the world?

We would like to present you with an exclusive invitation to The Society. If you accept, please join us this Wednesday at 11:59 p.m. at Corvus Books. Tell no one.

Amara shook her head, tossing her already tousled hair in every direction. This must be some kind of joke. Or a mistake. A hallucination. She had spent too many sleepless nights and breakfast-less mornings poring over books. And now it was all catching up to her.

A new hope threatened to blossom in her. She blinked hard, scared the words would fade away as quickly as they came. But the writing stayed.

Amara's mind flew back to Olive, the mysterious and weirdly intense cashier. What had she said? *"Maybe we can help you find the answers you're looking for"?*

Could this be it? Could this be the moment she'd been waiting for her whole life?

Goose bumps trickled along her skin. A giddy excitement began to build and breathless words tumbled from her lips. "Do you know what I am?" she asked the bookmark.

New words appeared, shimmering in the faint lamplight.

You are the one we have been waiting for.

Wednesday night couldn't come fast enough. Amara had been a nervous wreck all day—a restless ball of energy who couldn't even handle her mom's pot of curry without setting the whole thing on fire. It took every ounce of restraint to wait until her family had gone to bed. Then she snuck out the back window and went straight to the bookstore.

She finally reached the store's steps, winded and buzzing. She glanced down at her phone. 11:59 p.m. Right on time. Corvus Books was dark and empty, without a soul or flicker of light in sight. In the shop window hung a sign with Olive's familiar spiky handwriting.

Closed.

"You've gotta be kidding me," Amara huffed. Maybe this was all some sick prank. There never had been a secret book club. She would never discover her truth. After everything, she was going back home, empty-handed.

Amara's shoulders fell and she turned her back on the store. Her purse slipped down her slumped arm. She glared down at the bookmark, clutched hard in her hand. Harsh wrinkles streaked through the blackbird's feathers.

But when she looked back up, three sets of eyes were staring back at her.

"You came," Olive said. "Welcome back."

Olive had appeared, seemingly out of nowhere. As if she had melted from the shadows. Her blue streaked braids whipped around her head, carried by a sudden gust of wind. She was flanked by two girls. The girl on the left towered over them all with locs piled high on her head and bright purple lipstick framed around a permanent sneer. The purple glimmered and shifted—to sizzling red to acid green to midnight black and back. The girl on the right didn't even look up at Amara. Her face was buried in a graphic novel, while her purse, keys, and Starbucks cup floated high above her space buns.

Amara's jaw dropped. She scanned the streets, praying nobody would appear and see such a casual—*careless*—display of power. But even if anybody had noticed the strange girls and their strange magic, these three didn't seem to care.

The tall one stepped closer and the streetlights sputtered. She folded her arms tight across her chest. "This is her? She doesn't look like much. She looks . . . *plain*."

"Hey!" Amara flushed. She tugged at the hem of her skirt and adjusted her glasses, feeling awkward under this girl's gaze. To tell the truth, Amara wasn't sure what she was expecting either. Maybe a cult of hooded weirdos. Or a squad of alien body snatchers.

Definitely not a team of snarky magical girls.

"She's the real deal," Olive said. "Trust me."

"Be nice, Jelani," the other girl said in a singsong voice, still not looking up from her novel. She had a dreamy air about her and seemed to glide across the sidewalk. In fact, her feet never even touched the ground, instead, hovering a few inches over the pavement. "Besides, the blackbird wouldn't have summoned her if she wasn't one of us."

At that, she tapped a pin that was stuck to her frilly blouse. It was the same as Olive's. They all had one.

"Exactly," Olive said. She gestured to the keys twirling above the spacey girl's head. "Willow, can you pass those?"

Willow nodded and the bundle of keys zoomed through the air. Olive caught them one-handed and unlocked the store's front door. While the others filed inside, Amara wavered by the front steps. Her head spun. What the hell had Willow meant by "one of us"?

"Are you coming or not?" Jelani's voice cut through her thoughts. Behind Jelani, Olive snapped her fingers and the lights of Corvus Books came to life. Then she disappeared behind the cashier's desk.

Amara walked forward, but her foot caught on the top step and she almost tumbled right to the floor. Jelani's soft snickers echoed throughout the store's foyer and Amara's face got hot. She was surprised, though, to see Jelani's outstretched hand. She grabbed onto it, grateful, and let the tall girl pull her to her feet.

"Uh, thanks?"

Jelani shrugged. "Girls like us gotta look out for one another."

There was that word again. Us.

Amara smoothed out her clothes. She glanced down at the crumpled bookmark in her hand and then up at the glittering flying bird on Jelani's pin. "Can someone please explain what's going on!"

Nobody responded. Instead, Olive silently reemerged from behind the desk. She cradled an oversized tome in her arms. The brown leather of its cover was battered and the edges were frayed. An etching of a man peeked through her sleeves. The nameless book.

A terrible breeze flew through the store, ruffling pages and shuddering shelves. The whispers began again. Amara slammed her hands over her ears.

"You hear it, don't you?" Willow whispered. She leaned forward, looking into Amara's eyes for the first time. Her gaze was piercing and unsettling, like she could see straight into Amara's soul. Maybe she could. "He's coming."

"Who?" Amara demanded. "Who's coming?"

Olive waved her hands again, and hundreds of books flew out of the store's shaking shelves. The pages inside tore from their seams. One by one, they folded like origami—into shapes, people, buildings. A skeletal paper man fell from the air right into Olive's waiting hand. The other figures surrounded them, dancing around the room. A story coming to life.

"Thousands of years ago," Olive began, "there was a magician. His power was great. And terrible. He put darkness in men's hearts, rampaging and threatening to use them to destroy the world. The Society was formed to stop him."

Four paper warriors appeared, diving from the air and surrounding the figure in Olive's hand. They fought hard. The sounds of rips and tears filled Amara's ears.

"They created this book and trapped him in here." She set the nameless book down in the middle of the floor and took a large step back. "It was the only way to keep the world safe from his machinations. But even they knew that this would not hold him forever."

"The three of us," she pointed to herself and her friends, "have been trying to keep him at bay. But without a fourth, we just aren't strong enough. Our powers can't reach their full potential."

"I think we've been doing okay," Jelani scoffed.

Willow hit her arm. *"Shh!"*

"Every generation, four are born with the power to keep him locked away in his prison, until the day comes that the wards finally break. Today is that day."

The tattered book on the ground trembled. Faint whispers turned to breathy chatter. Breathy chatter turned to wretched screams.

"You were right, Amara. The book's magic really did call out to you." Olive turned to her, and so did the others. "We need your help to reseal him and to keep our world safe. Everything about your life—everything about your powers—has been leading up to this moment."

The tattered nameless book blew open with such force, the origami storytellers scattered, flying across the room. The wind howled again. A tornado of pages and ink erupted in the middle of the store. A hand, carved of torn ribbons of paper, reached from inside. A face, anguished and angry, ripped from the ancient book's seams.

Olive, Jelani, and Willow stepped around the screaming book. They left a space open in their circle. A space for Amara.

"Do you see now?"

She did. All the years of questioning herself. All the years of wondering about her role in this world. This was where she belonged. *This* was where she was meant to be. Amara stepped forward, taking her place.

The Paper Man climbed from his book. A chill ran up Amara's spine. The breeze bit against her skin. But the cold faded away as a warm hand wrapped around hers. Olive looked at her.

"Are you ready to begin?"

NINA EVANS, IN THE ROUND
BY KALYNN BAYRON

I sat on the edge of my bed, clutching the flyer announcing the auditions for the Filmore High production of *The Sound of Music*. It was going to be the biggest event of the '74–'75 theater season and I only had two weeks to get ready. That wasn't a lot of time.

I could sing. That was a given. My mama told me once that I didn't speak my first words as much as sang them. Daddy knew it too. I was hoping when I showed them the flyer, they'd understand that this was something I had to do.

I'd been involved in six Filmore High productions in the four years I'd been in the theater program. I knew the theater rigging, the lighting, back-stage, and behind-the-scenes stuff. My junior year I auditioned and got a small role in *Cabaret*. Mama told me she couldn't make it. There was a part of me that knew she didn't really want to be there and it killed me. But Daddy got off early and took the train all the way from Queens to Brooklyn in the dead of winter to see me.

He sat way in the back, but he waved his arms around so I could see him. His theater etiquette was terrible, but it made me feel good, even if all I did was walk across the stage in a few scenes.

I gripped the flyer. Auditions for ensemble were open to everyone, but I didn't want to be in the background—or backstage—for this production. Mr. Kelvin, the acting coach from the rec center, told me I had what it takes to be right up front, and I wanted the lead role of Maria.

I went to find Daddy in the front room where he was watching the news and sat down on the couch next to him.

"What you up to, baby girl?" he asked, patting me on the leg.

I slipped the flyer into his hand and he read it.

"You helping out with the set design again, baby? You did such a good job on the last one—what was it? *Pippy?*"

I laughed. "*Pippin*, Daddy. The last production was *Pippin*."

I'd helped design the entire set and he was right, it did look good. But that wasn't what I wanted to do this time around.

"Auditions are coming up," I said quietly. "I was thinking about trying out for the lead."

Daddy angled his head and glanced at me. "You sure that's something you want to do? You know your mama won't be happy about it."

I tried to keep the expression on my face unchanged. "I know, but this is important to me."

"I don't know," he said. "You could be studying up on nursing. That's where you're heading after you graduate anyway. Maybe focus on that?"

Mama and Daddy's plan for me was nursing school and then a good, steady job. They made me feel like that was the best choice—the only choice if I was being honest.

"But I love music, Daddy," I said. "It makes me feel—" I pressed my hand to my chest. It was hard to explain. Even with my parents steering me away from it, I kept finding my way back because of the way it made me feel inside. Singing was like breathing. I needed it to be whole. To live.

"I know you love it," Daddy said. "I love music too, baby. Don't forget I went to church with David Ruffin. Taught him everything he knows."

I didn't roll my eyes, but I wanted to. When Daddy got to talking about singing in the choir at Mount Salem Methodist Church with David, former member of The Temptations, he never left out the part where he supposedly taught him to sing. It wasn't true. Everybody knew that. But it was Daddy's way of letting me know that he had a sweet spot for music too.

"Music is a hobby," Daddy said. "It's not for paying bills and it sure ain't for us when it comes to the theater. I know that where you wanna be, baby. But that just ain't for us."

"Okay, Daddy," I said. I got up and walked into the kitchen. I leaned against the fridge and tried my hardest not to cry.

The door to our apartment creaked open and Mama came into the kitchen before I could fix my face.

"You okay?" She set her purse on the table and came over to me. She looked at me like she could see inside my head. "What's going on?"

"I was just talking to Daddy," I said.

"About?" She eyed the flyer in my hand, then stretched out her own. "Let me see."

I handed it to her and braced myself for what I knew was coming. I studied her face as she read it over. She sighed like she hadn't taken a breath all day. It was deep, almost mournful.

She crumpled the paper and tossed it in the trash, then tied on her apron and started pulling pots and pans out of the cabinet. "Baby, I need you to season that meat for me while I wash up. Can you do that?"

"Yes, ma'am. But I—"

"Aht. Aht," she shushed me. "Not now, Nina. Dinner first." She left the kitchen without another word.

The only sound at dinner was the scraping of our forks across the plates. The dead silence was my fault. Daddy kept trying to lighten the mood, cracking jokes, talking mess about our downstairs neighbor who was always fighting with his roommate.

"The food is really good, Mama," I said.

"Thank you, baby," she said. "You cooking this weekend, right? What are you planning?"

At least I got her talking. That was a start.

"Greens, porkchops," I said. "Then next week Daddy's doing ribs on the grill."

"As long as I don't have to cook, it all sounds wonderful to me." Mama smiled warmly. "Nina, baby, you need me to help you press your hair this weekend too, right?"

"I can do it," I said.

Mama waved her hand in the air. "I'll help. You never bump the ends. It looks so nice like that."

A little piece of me died every time I went to school with my ends bumped under. Mama thought it was cute. I thought it made me look like a cuter version of James Brown.

My heart crashed in my chest as I worked up the nerve to bring up the audition again.

"The auditions for the school production of *The Sound of Music* are in two weeks."

Silence swallowed the room again. Daddy looked down into his plate and Mama just stared at me across the table. "I was really hoping I could audition . . . for a lead role."

"I thought we were done talking about this," Mama said.

"We didn't talk about it. Not really," I said as I toed the line between back talk and telling Mama how I felt.

"I'll help you clear the table," Mama said, standing up and stacking her plate on top of Daddy's.

A knot grew in my throat. "Mama, please."

Mama set her stack of dishes down a little too hard and they rattled together. "No."

"You used to sing," I said. It's why all of this made me so upset. Mama had parts in all kinds of musicals from the time she was in high school. She even had done some off-Broadway stuff. She knew what it felt like to want to be onstage and still, every time I brought it up, she treated it like it was taboo.

Mama was the type of person who would show up to my school when teachers weren't treating me right. She was the type to let me know she was there for me when I needed a shoulder to cry on, when I needed advice. She had always been my biggest cheerleader but not about this. Never about this. She tried to keep me from it, and she made it seem like it was for my own good. What did she think she was protecting me from?

Mama put our dishes on the kitchen counter and went to her room, closing the door behind her.

Daddy sighed. "I don't know, baby. Maybe it's time to put all that aside. At least until you get into nursing school."

A nurse. A really good job but one that put me in the role of a caregiver. Nothing wrong with that, but while I was pouring into everybody else who was gonna pour into me? Who was gonna make sure I was tended to?

"Can I be excused?" I asked.

Daddy patted the back of my hand and nodded.

At lunch the next day, I sat with Tre and Lena and had to listen to them argue about which one of them was going to use their mom's car on Friday night.

"I'm technically older," Tre said. "So I have seniority."

"You're older by three minutes," Lena said. "And I have priority because I have to go to work. Where you taking it to?"

"That's my business." Tre knew he was in the wrong and there was no way their mom was gonna let him take the car when Lena had to work late.

"The sign-up sheet for auditions is up," I said, trying to change the subject. "All I have to do is pick a time."

They both looked at me like I'd lost my mind.

Tre leaned across the table. "Does your mom know?"

I looked down into my paper bag of leftovers. "I mean, I showed her the flyer."

"So no then," Lena said. "You think she's not gonna find out?"

"Y'all act like I'm telling her I want to drop out of school and join the Peace Corps or something. All I wanna do is be onstage."

Lena reached over and squeezed my hand. She looked me in the eye and a devious little smile spread across her face.

"What?" I asked.

"A part of me thinks you should go on and do it."

"Lena!" Tre said. "You tryna get her in trouble? Her mom will flip."

Lena shrugged. "I know it's not the smart thing to do because your mama don't play, but she can't stay mad at you forever, right?"

I actually thought it was a real possibility.

Tre raised his eyebrows. "Oh, okay. We're acting like we don't care what Mama Evans thinks. Okay, fine." He threw his hands up. "I will not be involved."

"Hush," said Lena. "She gotta follow her dreams and we all know Nina is not cut out to be a nurse. She passed smooth out in biology last year, remember?"

I grimaced. "Don't remind me."

Lena grabbed my hand. "Come on. Let's go see what time slots are still open."

She pulled me out of the cafeteria and down the hall. And as much junk as Tre was talking, he was still right behind us.

We rounded the corner and almost ran right into Madeline Sayer. If high school was a musical, Maddie Sayer would have been the main villain and her troupe of tagalongs would have been her supporting cast. She was popular, her parents had money, and she had been the lead in nearly every school play we'd ever had. The thing was, she was also supremely untalented. She held notes the way a sieve held water, but she somehow managed to edge her way in even when it was clear she wasn't the best person for the role. Maybe she had an in with somebody in charge, maybe she knew my chances of getting the part were already dead in the water and she enjoyed watching me prepare for nothing. Whatever it was, she seemed to revel in making me feel like I didn't belong.

"You must be joking," Maddie said as Lena and I came sliding around the corner. "Stage crew don't sign up for auditions. Just meet the rest of the help backstage."

She and her minions laughed like she was the funniest person in existence.

"What role did you sign up for?" Lena asked Maddie. "This play doesn't have a family dog."

A girl standing over Maddie's right shoulder gasped so loud she almost choked.

Maddie only smiled, pushing her long blond hair over her shoulder. "Even if I was the dog, I'd be better than you. At least most people love dogs."

Tre sucked his teeth and rolled his eyes.

The implication was clear, but I wasn't interested in arguing, or coming to blows with Maddie. I sidestepped her, picked up the pen that was attached to the sign-up sheet with a string, and printed my name on the line next to 1 p.m. Saturday. The next line asked for the name of the role I'd be auditioning for. I hesitated for a moment, then scrawled the word *Maria*.

Maddie stifled a laugh and narrowed her piercing blue eyes at me. "Why do you do this to yourself, Nina? You're never gonna get the role." She smirked. "Besides, nobody wants to see a Black Maria. It'll never happen."

I knew it was coming. Maddie was nothing if not predictable. It still stung because in a way she was right. I knew I could sing. I knew I could act. But sometimes that didn't matter. I had to be twice as good, work three times as hard, and still watch someone as uniquely unqualified as Maddie Sayer get the part.

"Don't nobody wanna hear all that yodeling you call singing," Tre said. He'd heard enough. "Sounds like somebody is strangling a cat every time you're up there." Tre looped his arm under mine and pulled me away from a shocked Maddie and her friends. "My ears were bleeding, Maddie," Tre called back. "I'll send you my doctor's bill!"

We rushed off, laughing so hard I thought I'd piss my pants. Tre and Lena headed off to class but I had a free period and went to the empty music room to practice scales like I did whenever I had time.

When I went inside, Mr. Purnell was at the piano.

"Sorry!" I said. "I didn't know you were in here."

"It's fine," he said smiling warmly. "Come on in."

Mr. Purnell reminded me of my grandpa. He was an older guy with a balding head, and his fingers were knotted at the knuckles. His voice had a deep rasp that told me he probably used to smoke or maybe he still did. I wasn't sure. But that didn't stop him from playing the piano like his life depended on it. He said he learned to play like that in church, but Daddy said he'd seen him at this jazz joint in Harlem when he was younger. He had a regular gig there but he didn't want anybody to know. Mr. Purnell was full of secrets.

"You need some accompaniment?" he asked.

"Sure. Could you help me warm me up?" I asked.

He smiled and gave me a middle C to start, then walked me up and down the piano until the notes slipped past my lips effortlessly. When I felt my vocal cords strain a little too much, he walked me back down. Mr. Purnell always said the voice was like any other musical instrument—you had to take care of it, and that meant knowing when to ease up. He clearly didn't take his own advice, but I did, and my voice was better for it.

After I was warmed up, Mr. Purnell sat back on the bench and grinned at me.

"What's that look for?" I asked him.

"You got a voice like I've never heard," he said. "Your tone, your resonance. It's amazing."

"Amazing enough to get me the part of Maria?"

Mr. Purnell's expression dimmed. "It should be, yes. You run circles around everybody here. Hell, maybe run circles around some of these folks making a living on the stage."

"But that's not enough, is it?" I asked.

Mr. Purnell closed the piano and folded his hands on top. "I don't have to tell you that white folks already think we're taking something away from them by asking for equal treatment, equal opportunities. You see how mad they are when we're here sitting in the same classes as them. I got students not allowed in my class because they mama or daddy don't think I can teach them. Don't matter if I got a degree from Howard or been playing music longer than they been alive."

"No, I know," I said. "But if it's me or Maddie Sayer—"

"Maddie auditioning too?" He looked genuinely troubled. "Lord, we all need that role to go to you, Nina. We can't listen to her for two whole hours."

I smiled, but the weight of everything he'd said pressed down on me. "So there's no chance?"

"There's always a chance," he said. "But like I was saying, they already mad. What happens when they see you excelling?"

I shook my head and sighed. "I'll still try out."

"That's the spirit," Mr. Purnell said. "Eventually they'll see. We not going nowhere so they might as well get used to it."

I gathered up my bag and walked to the door.

"Miss Nina," Mr. Purnell called.

I looked back over my shoulder.

"I think you'd make a very good Maria."

At home, I slung my bag down and washed up. Daddy wasn't home yet, but I could hear the record player skipping in Mama's room. Must have had a scratch, or maybe the needle needed changing.

I went to her door and found it ajar. I could see her fast asleep on top of the covers. I went in and gently pulled a knitted throw over her, then sat at the foot of the bed.

Mama's room was an ode to music, to theater. She had playbills tacked to the walls. Some of them even had her name in small print at the bottom. She'd had a career, gone to school for it and everything. The music degree had been parlayed into a teaching career when she'd left the stage, but it haunted her. It's why she was so against me getting into it, but she never wanted to talk about why she left.

"I wish I could make you see," I said quietly as she slumbered. I stood and adjusted the needle on her record player. Nina Simone's balmy vocals flowed from the speaker, wrapping me up like a warm embrace. I was named after her. That's how much Mama loved her. I swayed back and forth as she sang about the ripples in the stream and how tomorrow is never promised.

Mama's love of music had made ripples, and they washed over me every time I heard the chords of a familiar song. Music made me feel alive.

I hummed along and then, because I couldn't help myself, I let the lyrics flow out of me. I knew every word. Every note. Every breath. If this wasn't what I was supposed to do, why did it have such a hold on me? Why couldn't I set it aside the way she wanted me to?

Is Mama right? I asked myself.

Mama cleared her throat and I spun around to find her leaned up on her elbow.

"I'm sorry," I said quickly. "I—I didn't mean to wake you up."

She wiped tears from her eyes and patted the bed next to her. I crawled in and she put her arms around me, holding me tight.

"Why are you crying?" I asked as I rested my head on her chest.

"You know, I can be stubborn as a mule," she said against my hair. "I had to be like that because it kept me safe. That's all I've ever tried to do for you. Just keep you safe."

"I know, Mama."

She pulled back and looked me in the eye. "I know what music means to you and I understand better than anybody the way it calls to you. But that's why I'm afraid. You think I don't know you can sing?" She huffed playfully. "You got me crying after the tail end of that Nina Simone record. I know you got it, baby." She sighed and rested her head against the pillow.

"You remind me of me. I'd been playing bit parts for years. Always got on the crew, always got to be a part of the supporting cast, but, baby, I wanted that lead role. I wanted to be Cinderella in an off-Broadway production of Rodgers and Hammerstein's version."

I stared at her. "Mama. You would've been the perfect Cinderella."

She stuck her chin up and smirked. "Oh, I know, baby. I went to the audition, and I was the only Black woman there. I'm biased but I thought I was top two, easy. I got a callback but they lied about the time. Good thing I showed up an hour early to practice; otherwise I would've missed it completely."

"They tried to get over," I said.

She nodded. "I did my bit, knocked it out the park, but the director took me aside and told me something I already knew—that even though I had aced my audition, even though I was clearly the right choice, audiences just weren't ready for a Black Cinderella."

My heart sank. I figured it had to have been something like that, but hearing Mama confirm it, imagining all the work she had put in, all the schooling, all the practicing, just to get told she couldn't do it because the world wasn't ready . . . it was all so unfair.

"The theater community prides itself on being this place where people from all walks of life, people who maybe march to the beat of their own drum, can find community. But racism is funny that way—come one, come all, but not if you're Black and talented, then you can come in only if we allow it. They want you to wait until they're ready to accept it and, in case you hadn't noticed, they're taking their sweet time learning to do better."

I pressed my cheek against Mama's chest and heard the hitch in her breathing. She was trying very hard not to cry.

"Imagine seeing you," she said. "How talented you are, knowing from the time you could speak that music was going to run you the same way it did me. I just didn't want you to be hurt. But I feel like I hurt you even more by not letting you find your own way. I'm sorry, baby."

I couldn't hold back the tears. I didn't want to. Mama was scared, and now I understood exactly why. I was scared too, but now it felt like I had someone in my corner that not even the likes of Maddie Sayer would want to mess with.

"I love you," I said.

"I love you too." She readjusted her arms around me. "I want you to go to that audition and I want you to sing down the house, you understand?"

"Yes, ma'am."

The days leading up to the audition were chaos. Lena and Tre came over to help me practice almost every day. Daddy went into full-blown choir director mode. He even tried to make me wear his old choir robes. He said it'd be good luck since the last person he taught to sing was good ol' David Ruffin. Tre teased him about it, asking if he taught him how to dance too. Daddy's old robes smelled like moth balls; I don't think he washed them after the last time he wore them so I declined, and he was just happy to call himself "helping."

Four days before the audition, I went home after school and lay across my bed. Maddie had gone out of her way to make sure I saw her practicing Maria's lines in the music room earlier. She was already acting like she'd been given the part and a stifling doubt crept in. As I lay in my bed the door crept open and I was surprised to see Mama standing there, home early from work. In her right hand was a little white envelope and she was dressed like she was going someplace fancy.

"You're all dressed up," I said.

"You should be too." She handed me the envelope. "Put on something nice. Make sure your face is washed and your hair is pulled up."

She left the room before I had a chance to ask questions. I opened the envelope and two tickets fell into my hand. Emblazoned across the top were two words in bold type. *The Wiz.*

We took the train to Broadway and stood outside the Majestic Theatre in the bitter cold until it was time to file in. I'd never been inside the Majestic, and when we finally made our way to the seating area, I couldn't believe what I saw.

The Spanish brick interior and the arched windows made it feel like we'd been transported to another time and place. I could feel the electricity of a thousand performances; the anticipation of hundreds of performers past and present hung in the air. I looked up at the mezzanine level, wondering how we'd get up there.

Mama squeezed my hand. "No, baby. We're right here."

She pulled me down the aisle, showed our tickets to an usher, and walked me to row B. We were in the third row of seats, orchestra level, right behind the pit. I sank into the seat and Mama took hold of my trembling hand.

"We're in for a very special treat," she said.

Music wafted out of the pit as the musicians warmed up. The program in my hand said the role of Dorothy would be played by Stephanie Mills—Mama had a record with her singing on it. Evillene was going to be played by Mabel King—she was Maria in the national touring play of *Porgy and Bess*.

I turned to Mama. "This is an all-Black cast."

Mama took a deep breath and nodded as her eyes misted over. "Watch what we can do, baby."

The low rumble of voices grew quieter until finally the lights went down and the curtain went up.

The *ooh*s and *ahh*s of the opening notes gave way to the lively jazz piano. Dorothy and her Aunt Em came out hanging clothes on a line, and for the next two hours, I watched as an all-Black cast danced and sang their way to Oz. The music reverberated through the floor and into the soles of my feet; I could hardly keep them still. I wanted to jump up and sing and shout. There were moments when it took everything I had to stay in my seat. When the curtain closed and the crowd erupted in thunderous applause, I sat still, barely breathing. Nothing would ever be the same for me.

When me and Mama left the theater, I didn't even want to go home. I wanted to stand in the street and look up at the blazing marquee above the Majestic just so that I'd never forget the feeling. As I breathed in the cold evening air, Mama stood next to me.

"It's been done before," Mama said. "An all-Black cast. They don't want you to know that. They don't want us to know that we belong here as much as everyone else. *A Raisin in the Sun, Shuffle Along,* Pearl Bailey's all-Black *Hello, Dolly!*—we've *been* here." She closed her eyes for a moment. "Now we have this, and this is gonna change things, baby. I can feel it in my bones. It's building off everything that's happened before." She tilted her head up and the lights glinted in her eyes.

We made our way home and I knew nothing would be the same for me. I'd seen with my own two eyes what was possible for us up there onstage. For the first time ever, I felt like there was a place for me in this world.

"You ready?" Mr. Purnell asked as I paced in the hallway outside the school's auditorium.

"No," I said, clutching my sheet music. "But if I let these nerves get the best of me, I won't do it."

He smiled. "You're the last audition of the day."

"I signed up for the one o'clock slot," I said. "I got here right on time, but they keep telling me to wait. I guess they're running behind."

"I think they was hoping you'd get bored and go home."

I huffed. "I bet they were." I thought of Mama and of the way her audition times were changed without her knowledge with the hope of discouraging her enough to walk away. "I'm not going nowhere, Mr. Purnell."

He tipped his chin up and gave me a grin. "Well, all right. Now, listen, I could see that they were being a little funny. Maddie already did her audition and my ears ain't never gon' be the same, but what's important is that we let everybody know how good you are. Sometimes people act up because they think nobody's watching. Sometimes we need a witness. So I took it upon myself to invite a few folks. Hope you not shy, Miss Nina."

"What do you mean?" I asked as my heart cartwheeled in my chest.

"You'll see," he said as he opened the door to the theater.

"Nina Simone Evans!" someone called from up front. "You're up."

"I'll explain later," Mr. Purnell said as he ushered me inside.

I went through the doors and climbed the stairs in the darkened theater. I stood center stage as Mr. Purnell took his seat at the piano. I handed him my sheet music.

"Let's just get on with it," said Mr. Hayes, head of our school's music department as he sat, legs crossed, in the front row.

I could tell he already had his mind made up. I wasn't getting the part of Maria, and for a moment, I considered walking out. But then I stared into the darkened auditorium. The seats were nearly all full. Students and teachers sat quietly, waiting. And in the second row, right behind Mr. Hayes, was Mama and Daddy. I glanced at Mr. Purnell and he winked.

I closed my eyes. Took a deep breath and nodded at Mr. Purnell. He played the opening chords. It wasn't the song I rehearsed with Lena and Tre and Daddy. Mama and I had found a better song last minute: "Home" from *The Wiz*.

In my mind, I saw that stage at the Majestic. I saw myself up there. I sang about home, which for me was on the stage, about knowing where I belonged and how when everything was telling me to run away, what I needed to do was slow down and give myself a minute to take it all in.

When I finished singing, the auditorium was dead silent for a split second before Mama and Daddy stood up and started clapping and hollering.

Soon the entire place lit up. Lena and Tre shouted and jumped up and down; Maddie stormed out, but some of her minions stayed behind to join in the cheering. If that was as far as I got in my bid to be my school's first Black leading lady, it was enough.

Four months later

The orchestra warmed up and their notes floated through the auditorium, making their way to the backstage area. I stood in the wings checking my reflection in a floor-length mirror. I could feel my nerves threaten to get the better of me, so I reached in my pocket, felt the rumpled ticket stub from my trip to *The Wiz*, and let a sense of calm wash over. I was right where I belonged.

Mr. Purnell came up beside me and gently put his hand on my shoulder.

"House lights go down in five," he said. "You ready?"

I stared at my reflection. The students in the costume department had made Maria's signature blue apron fit me just right. My wig could have been a little better, but Mama helped me make the most of it and I wasn't complaining.

The world may not have been ready for me, but I was done waiting for them to tell me it was my time.

"Yes," I said. "I'm ready."

EARTH IS GHETTO
BY IBI ZOBOI

By the time Ingrid Jesula Pierre started the eleventh grade, Frederick Douglass High School had received a bunch of money from some rich scientist and investor to launch a brand new astronomy department. It was housed in the musty old basement where the janitor's office used to be, and there was one desktop (not even a twenty-one-inch iMac), one telescope (not even the Celestron Omni XLT), and a poster of the solar system (not even a single orrery or a 3D-model science project). So what was supposed to be a whole science department was just an astronomy *club*.

"For people who understand what Neil deGrasse Tyson be talking about," the girl standing in the doorway said. Her name was Lauren Marcus—lashes for days, edges laid, weave down her back, and wearing white creaseless Air Force 1s. Ingrid stared down at the girl with her piercing, judgmental eyes, and for anyone who really knew her, that was a sign Ingrid was about to throw some serious shade, enough to rival a rare total eclipse.

She cleared her throat and, with her slight Haitian accent, said, "Do you mean, this *club* is only for those who would like to further understand and investigate the cosmos outside of the corporate cult of personalities where high-brow science is fed to the masses in the form of a McDonald's Happy Meal?"

Ingrid hated bad grammar. She had to do all this work to learn English as a third language just for other people to speak in double negatives and misuse verbs.

The girl crossed her arms and cocked her head. "My mama said that rudeness is a sign of inner turmoil and childhood trauma. Or maybe you're just an Aries, a Gemini, or a Scorpio. Am I right?"

"You are wrong," Ingrid said, knowing that she was indeed a Gemini, but she wasn't going to give that girl the satisfaction of being right.

Ingrid had seen her around before. Loquacious, restless eyes, and short. She pushed past the girl and walked into the classroom where there were only two other kids hogging the computer playing some video game. An older woman had her head behind her own laptop, typing away, so Ingrid blurted out, "Spaceship is landing tomorrow! I need to communicate with the captain!"

What planet are you from? was a frequently asked question since the seventh grade when she first came to this country. It was a fair question. After all, everything about her neighborhood and her school seemed light-years away from her small town in Haiti.

The older woman, Ms. Sandler, looked up from her laptop and said, "This is the astronomy department, Ms. Pierre. Not Comic-Con."

Ingrid ignored the teacher and made a beeline for the boys hogging the computer. "Move, or you will be moved!"

One of the boys turned around with a huge smile, pointed to her, and said, "*Captain America: Civil War.* 2016. The first introduction to the Dora Milaje in the Marvel Cinematic Universe."

Ingrid froze where she stood and her belly did something weird. She'd never seen this boy, and maybe it was because he looked like a middle schooler—wiry thin, wearing glasses like her, and with a headful of thick, tightly curled hair. "Florence Kasumba as Ayo," was all Ingrid said, and her voice cracked a little. "And you still have to move."

The boy turned back and mumbled, "I don't have to do anything. I don't care how tall you are. You're not a Dora Milaje."

The boy was right and this made Ingrid's belly flutter a little. He seemed to have his own mind and was not like everyone else at that school calling her Okoye or Ayo because of her height and short-cropped hair. Ingrid was not a warrior and she wasn't trying to be. Her strength was in her wit and intelligence, so she knew nothing about throwing hands. Extemporaneous, classy insults were her brand. But here at Frederick Douglass High School, a beat down, a stomp squad, and a mouth straight out of the gutter would've earned Ingrid enough respect to demand a couple of pimply-faced pubescent boys to give up the computer because she was about to make history and save herself (not the world).

"I need the computer," she pleaded. "I was told to be at a device at exactly sixteen hundred hours. My cell phone is not charged and I will not have enough time to get home. What better place to communicate with alien life than from the astronomy . . . *department*?" No one would believe her, anyway, so why not tell the truth?

"Alien life-form?" the boy turned around and asked.

But before Ingrid could respond, the door to the classroom swung open and Mr. Braithwaite, the principal, barged in with a bunch of other students behind him. "Oh good, y'all have enough seats in here. Ms. Sandler, this'll be the detention room for today."

Ms. Sandler looked up from her laptop again and said, "This is the astronomy department, Mr. Braithwaite. Not a correctional facility."

"Even better!" the principal said. "Guys, you can learn about the cosmos. The day they abolish prisons will be the day all the rich leave for Mars."

In seconds, what was supposed to be a whole astronomy department was now the after-school detention room, and Ingrid felt the weight of the universe crash down on her. The kids bumped into her, moved past her, and ignored her. Even though she was as tall as a tree, she was invisible, just like in all her other classes at this school. No matter how smart, how well-read, and how good her vocabulary was, Ingrid felt like an abandoned building—everyone knew it was there, but no one cared about how it got to be so broken in the first place.

Ingrid checked her watch. She had ten minutes to get to a computer.

"Hey, everybody!" the girl who'd been standing in the doorway called out, waving her colorful acrylic nails in the air. "For twenty bucks, I can read your horoscope. For a hundred, I can read your birth chart. North and South Nodes extra. I take all forms of payment, including cold, hard cash!"

Ms. Sandler looked up from her laptop a third time and said, "This is the astronomy department, Ms. Marcus. Not Miss Cleo's Psychic Readers Network."

"Who's Miss Cleo?" several of the kids asked at the same time.

Ms. Sandler did not respond, of course, choosing instead to return to her typing while Mr. Braithwaite brought in the last of the remaining detention students. "All right, y'all. One hour. I'll be back to make sure that each of you are still in here."

Five minutes left.

Ingrid was a keen observer of human behavior. So she pushed up her glasses and watched her peers divide themselves into small tribes: the class clowns, the gamers, the manga geeks, the influencers, and the ballers. She deduced that her peers believed that they were the center of the universe, and therefore, not much different from invading alien life-forms, or this country. When she'd criticize America for its culture of dominance in her APUSH (Advanced Placement United States History) class, someone would retort under their breath, "Then go back to where you came from!" Or worse, someone would repeat what they'd heard an American president call her home: a shithole country.

Ingrid's saving grace in those moments were her height, her complexion, and her short-cropped hair. She'd been compared to a Dora Milaje, so

Ingrid went around pontificating that Haiti was at one point like Wakanda. Its reign as the sugar capital of the colonial world (read: Vibranium) ended when they annihilated Napoleon (read: Thanos) and their enslavers during the Haitian Revolution (read: Infinity War). It made for a great comic-book story, and she could share this with the two boys hogging the computer. But only as payment after they'd let her use it.

So Ingrid went back to the boy and tapped him on the shoulder. "Please. I need to log onto the dark web to communicate with the captain of an alien spaceship."

The boy turned around and said, "Yeah, *right*. Why would aliens want to talk to you, anyway?"

"Because I was the first to make contact," Ingrid said plainly.

Both boys narrowed their eyes at her for a long second. Then the first boy extended his hand toward her. "I'm Tobi. Tobi Chineke."

Ingrid told him her name and that she had three minutes to make contact, but before Tobi could even get up from the chair, someone smacked him upside the head.

"Get up, stupid!" another boy said.

Ingrid looked over at him and her stomach sank. She didn't have to look down at him like she did with everyone else because Kyle Henderson was the point guard for the basketball team and stood a whole two inches taller than her.

"Sorry," Tobi whispered as he and his friend cowered, walked over to a corner, and became invisible like Ingrid.

"You're going to let him bully you like that?" Ingrid exclaimed, but to no avail. Tobi sat on a table in an opposite corner of the room, cowering and averting his eyes. Octavia Butler was right. Ingrid had read all her books and essays, listened to every interview, and watched every adaptation of her novels. "Human beings really are hierarchical," Ingrid said out loud, shaking her head, looking at Kyle with disgust.

Kyle Henderson glanced up at her from his seat as the rest of his friends gathered around to finish the game Tobi had started. "Wanna play?"

Ingrid froze. While her wit would disarm any dig about her looks, accent, or hair, she was rendered silent in that moment because this was an invitation, very much like that coded invitation she had received a month ago when she hacked into a top secret website. But still, there was no time to consider whether or not Kyle Henderson—her vertical equal with a face chiseled by ancient African gods—was interested in her. Whatever. He was mean to everybody, anyway.

"Did you know that these game designers are subconsciously preparing you for world war? Meanwhile, aliens are going to take over our planet once we've managed to destroy it."

"Damn," Kyle said as his friends laughed. "It's not that deep."

"Yes, it is!" Ingrid said. "Let me show you."

Kyle wouldn't budge, but Ingrid reached over him, stroked a few keys, and she was in. With his eyes glued to the screen, Kyle hesitantly gave his seat to Ingrid as she logged onto website after website, provided cryptic passwords, answered questions relegated to brain surgeons and rocket scientists, and decoded symbols that were a mix of Sanskrit, Egyptian hieroglyphs, and some complex ancient African language that anthropologists had ignored.

"Yo, she just hacked into NASA!" Kyle blurted out, and everyone rushed to surround Ingrid and the computer.

Ms. Sandler looked up from her laptop a fourth time and said, "This is the astronomy department, students. Not the set of *Tron*."

"What's *Tron*?" a few kids asked.

Ms. Sandler tossed her salt-and-pepper locs over her shoulders and started, "A 1982 sci-fi cult classic. A programmer gets uploaded as a digital version of himself into a software invention and has to battle other—"

"How will I know it's you?" Ingrid asked out loud, and the kids were suddenly distracted by something on Ingrid's screen.

The computer screen quickly flashed an image of the captain.

"Oh, shit!" some of the kids exclaimed, while others stepped back, startled by what they'd just seen.

Green (more like a fern green) with giant, black shiny eyes and a tiny hole for what should be lips. It was a quick second. And everyone saw it. The screen fizzled and flickered, and there it was. Like one of those pranks where everyone is watching something else and a bogeyman pops into the frame making your heart jump out of your chest.

The classroom couldn't quiet down. "That shit was fake!" someone said.

But Ingrid didn't care. Soon, they would all find out. She didn't have to boast or make proclamations that Roswell in 1947 was real, that the government knew all along, that NASA had been keeping secret their knowledge of extraterrestrial life, and that the best way to hide the truth from people is to put it right in front of them.

Green aliens were real. They were coming to visit Earth for the umpteenth time. And this time, Ingrid was going to leave with them.

"I suggest that you stay away from Ronald McNair Park at exactly seven hundred hours tomorrow morning," was all Ingrid said as she left the astronomy *club*, what was supposed to be a whole astronomy department, where she learned nothing about the cosmos and its potential for life and death, war and peace, endings and new beginnings. As Ingrid walked down the hall, the ruckus continued as if nothing had ever happened; as if the world would keep spinning as it always did—broken, fractured, and full of egotistical human beings trying to outdo each other.

"So hierarchical," she said out loud, shaking her head in disgust, and walked out of the school. For good.

The next day, as promised, at seven hundred hours in the morning, a giant spaceship landed in the hood. Right in the middle of the Ronald McNair playground. It messed up the basketball courts, the monkey bars, the handball wall, and even the bench with all the flowers and balloons where that little boy got hit by a stray bullet. The Vazquez bodega across the street got its front door knocked down with space debris. The notorious Washington Projects on the other side of the street were still standing. And some of the guys who lived there were either slinging dope or playing ball right in that park. They ran out of the way just in time.

First, it was something that lit up the night sky so bright, everyone thought it was the Second Coming; that Jesus himself was descending from heaven right where he was needed most. With all that praying and hollering going on over at Calvary Baptist Church around the corner, it was inevitable. Jesus had a huge fan base in the hood, so he just had to roll up in heaven's version of a Bugatti. That's the story that made the most sense around here.

But only one person knew the truth.

It was the sound that woke up Ingrid—a rumbling, cracking, screeching, and splitting that made it feel as if her ears were about to explode. Ingrid thought it was a nightmare. Or a memory. Or that *it* was happening again, even though she was far, far away from what used to be home.

Ten years ago, the ground in her town of Les Cayes, Haiti, opened up to swallow just about everything and everyone she loved. The world crumbled around her as she slept in her rickety bed that was pushed up against the load-bearing wall in her father's house. She had screamed until her little throat burned. She held on to her pillow, the sheets, and the mattress as if that bed was the one thing in the world that would save her. In the end, it actually did. The middle of the floor to her small bedroom had crashed down to the first level, but she was protected by another wall with its cinder block and exposed rebar. It was as though Jesus himself had said, *I got you.* But Ingrid believed otherwise because where was God all those other times the world had crumbled around her and took her friends and family? Alien life-forms were a more practical explanation for so much suffering. So she went looking into the dark web for the source of all things explainable; all things science, algorithms, and coded messages, and not magic or belief. Alien life in outer space was purely scientific. So she believed.

Here in America, in the hood, where her apartment was five floors aboveground, earthquakes were not supposed to happen, and Ingrid didn't believe in the Second Coming despite her middle name being Jesula, which means "Jesus is here." She knew exactly what had landed in the middle of Ronald McNair Park that night and she couldn't wait to see it for herself.

When the noise from the spaceship stopped, the screaming and shouting and cursing began. Then the sirens. Who knew what the cops would do once they saw what they'd actually have to deal with. They'd assume that just because it landed in the hood, everything about that spaceship and whatever was inside would be Black and guilty, and they would respond accordingly. So Ingrid had to act fast. The first thing she reached for was her phone. The message was there, encrypted in a code she'd been learning for the past month: *We are here!*

"Yes!" she exclaimed. Dressed in gray sweats, she grabbed some books and comics and wondered if she needed hair products on an alien spaceship.

"Jesula! We have to pray!" her mother shouted as she barged into Ingrid's bedroom. She rushed to grab Ingrid and pulled her into the living room where there was a small statue of Jesus.

"Ajénu!" her mother shouted in creole. "Kneel and beg for Jesus's mercy. He is here. He is risen again!"

Ingrid's mother was a devout born-again, so much so that she would preach in the subway telling people to get ready for the Second Coming. Of course, all the signs were there. Disease, earthquakes, flooding, murder, and mayhem. Little did she know that her daughter was communicating with the Antichrist itself: aliens from another galaxy.

Ingrid's blue suitcase was packed and hidden behind a pile of coats near the apartment's door. The suitcase she'd come to this country with; the one that held her things for three years as she and her mother begged for asylum, moved from shelter to shelter, and finally landed in this tiny apartment in a broken and forgotten part of the city. She kept her eyes on the door as her mother recited verses from the books of Psalms and Revelation. Then, Ingrid hugged her mother long and tight, and they cried together.

"I love you, Mummy," was all Ingrid said.

The screams and shouts and sirens continued outside, and time was running out. The aliens had let her know in their encoded message that Ingrid had exactly ten minutes to get to the spaceship.

She quickly slipped away during her mother's long and passionate prayer to Jesus, quietly pulled out her suitcase from the closet, and tiptoed out of the apartment just as her mother began to sing a hymn from *Chants D'Esperance*.

Ingrid bolted down the block faster than the Flash. Cop cars and firetrucks had beat her to it, but she had firm instructions. The north side of the ship was where she would be beamed up, just like on Star Trek.

The police were roping off the entrance to the park, so Ingrid discreetly made her way to the back where the fence was down. The ship was exactly like the ones in movies—shiny steel with blinking lights that could be a fancy, state-of-the-art circular airplane. It emanated a magnetic pull, and the deep, humming sound let Ingrid know that the engine—or whatever it was that made that thing work—was probably still running.

"I am here!" she called out. "It is me, Ingrid Jesula Pierre. Please take me with you!"

She felt the tingling in her feet at first. Then the sensation rose up to her legs, her body, and to her head. All those movies, UFO sightings, and conspiracy theories had not provided enough evidence for what it would actually be like for this Black girl to be uploaded onto a spaceship in the middle of the hood. So Ingrid with her suitcase and tall, Black immigrant body hovered up into the spaceship where there was nothing but white space and zero gravity. And right before her was a humongous hologram of the captain—a green, bug-eyed alien like the ones in Roswell in 1947. The captain had been serious and terse in its communications. So, now, it wasted no time asking, *Why do you want to come with us?*

"Oh, no!" Ingrid exclaimed. "Why is a white man's voice the default for how an alien sounds? I can't even escape white supremacy on another planet?"

From our study of your planet, this is the voice of reason and power, the captain explained.

Ingrid sighed and rolled her eyes. "No," she said. "You got it all wrong. The voice of reason and power on this planet is Oprah." She looked around at the deathly white nothingness and wondered if she'd made a mistake, if she should go back. She would miss her mother and her Haitian meals, but nothing else. Here, there was freedom. There was opportunity. There was a future. After all, her cosmic mother, Octavia Butler, once said, "There is nothing new under the sun, but there are new suns." "Take me to your new suns!" Ingrid exclaimed. "Take me to this new world."

But you have to tell us why you want to come with us. We already know why we want you.

"Don't you see how they are treating one another like trash and destroying the planet? Will I always be running away to find peace somewhere else, huh, alien? Migrating from here to there and begging for freedom when not even the school I attend can offer a little bit of respite. I hope you have nice, comfortable, soft things on your planet, captain."

We need others, the captain said. *You, queen of the revolution, must bring us two of each.*

Ingrid spun around. Her feet and hands dangled in the zero gravity atmosphere as if she were a lightweight doll. This was definitely the hull of the spaceship. There was no steering or communications system, no motherboard. "Queen of the revolution?" she asked.

Yes! Your ancestors started a revolution and formed the first truly free nation. You are tall and intelligent. You learn quickly and read voraciously. These are traits we admire and need on this planet. That is why we want you!

"You mean the Haitian Revolution? Well, you should see us now. Thanks to the French monarchy and their ninety-million-dollar bill for property damage, global embargoes, and American greed. So, Uncle Sam, if you think so highly of me, why can't I come alone?"

Humans are not capable of asexual reproduction. You have evolved from microbes, the earliest form of life on Earth. Or rather, devolved.

"Um, wait a damn minute. Reproduction? You want me to make babies on this new planet?'

We need humans.

"Didn't I just tell you we're messed up? Didn't you see it in your research?"

You humans are so innovative. We can teach you a new way of life. You can adapt. There can be peace, love, and harmony. No need for a revolution. No need for war. No need for famine and drought. You will have all that you need.

"But, alien! Human beings are hierarchical. I see it in high school. I saw it in middle school. I even saw it in Haiti. Everybody's trying to outdo each other and they'll repeat those same patterns on your planet. No matter how good they have it. Let me come alone, please! I deserve nice things!" Ingrid pleaded and whined, bringing her hands together as if praying to a god.

While we are indeed a planet outside of your galaxy, we cannot grant you eternal life. You will die, and we will have no humans.

Ingrid was disarmed. The truth hit her like a gush of hot air. She was so desperate to leave this planet that she hadn't thought about her own mortality. "That's okay, though," she said, not fully believing her own words. "I don't want to die here, anyway."

That is selfish, the captain said. *You are just like every human on this planet.*

"Wait a damn minute. I'm special. I'm different. Everyone treats me like I don't belong here. And I don't."

There are others like you. Find them. One other female. Two males. In time, four will be eight, eight will be sixteen, sixteen will be thirty-two. And you will be the queen. You can name yourself and your queendom.

"But, alien, that is the *definition* of hierarchical!"

But, human, someone will have to lead them. How will they know otherwise?

Ingrid felt a wave of something warm and bright come over her. It was either an epiphany or she'd been given superpowers. She hadn't considered it before, but she could rule her own planet! Her ideas and vision would influence an entire galaxy. But at what cost? "So two females, two males? So, basically, you guys are the Garden of Eden?"

Ah, yes. One of your creation myths. However, there will be no rib or serpent or apple. Not even God. Just Eden.

"Alien, what about gays, and trans and nonbinary people? What about those of us who do not want to reproduce?"

Choose wisely, was all the captain said. *You must return at sixteen hundred hours today. Two females, including you. Two males. Ripe and fertile and ready to make a new world. That is our deal. We will wait for you. But if you do not arrive, we will find others.*

Before Ingrid could even respond or protest, she was yanked right out of the spaceship's hull and dropped down to the ground so hard, her whole body hurt. Her suitcase landed on her lap and she wanted nothing more than to sit there and cry and yell at the sky.

Police were scouring the area, and before they could spot her, Ingrid rushed out of the park and headed straight for school. If she was going to populate a new planet, it'd better be with people she actually knew. Whether she liked them or not was a whole other question.

A spaceship that landed in Ronald McNair Park, just five blocks from Frederick Douglass High School, was not a big enough event to shut down the building for the day. But still, no one got any work done. Ingrid bit her nails down to their nubs and she couldn't sit still, which made her very visible. Everyone was talking about the spaceship. The teachers let the students watch the news. There were open discussions and debates about whether or not the government had anything to do with it.

So when Tobi Chineke, Kyle Anderson, and Lauren Marcus confronted Ingrid in the astronomy club, she had to fess up.

"We didn't expect to see you back here," Lauren said. "I watched you type all that stuff into the computer and I believed you. The stars were aligned. Mercury was in Gemini. Mars was in Aries. Venus was in Taurus. Perfect timing for an alien invasion. Why are you still here?"

Tobi narrowed his eyes at Lauren. "This is the astronomy department, not *astrology*!"

"It's the same thing!" Lauren said. "Astro, astro . . . *duh*!"

Ingrid sighed. "Astronomy is a science while astrology is a belief system.

Not the same." Were these her options for planetary cohabitants, staring at her?

Lauren shook her head and clicked her acrylic nail tips as she spoke. "Don't you know we're made of stardust? We're connected to the movement of the planets and stars. So those aliens on that spaceship are our friends. We're all connected."

Ms. Sandler walked in carrying a stack of books. Ingrid recognized some of the authors. H. G. Wells, Philip K. Dick, Robert Heinlein, Ursula Le Guin, Samuel Delany, and her favorite, Octavia Butler. "I suggest y'all get ready for what's to come. Canned foods, bottled water, cash on hand, a generator, and a bunch of these books," Ms. Sandler said as she set up her laptop so everyone could watch the livestream footage of the spaceship.

Cop cars and helicopters were swarming the area. Yellow tape around the perimeter of the playground kept bystanders away as they held out their phones and waited to pose for selfies with aliens.

"I'm not reading books during an invasion!" Kyle blurted out. "I'm gonna need protection."

"Their weapons will be far more advanced," Tobi said. "We'll have to strategize and outsmart them."

"Impossible," Ingrid said. "Besides, they are not here for you. They are here for me. I need to take three more with me onto the spaceship."

The room was suddenly abuzz with chatter. More students had come in after hearing rumors about that girl from Haiti having made contact with the aliens. The other kids closed in on Ingrid, each demanding that she take them with her.

"Why on earth would any one of you voluntarily leave with aliens?" Ms. Sandler asked.

Everyone went silent and stared at the teacher as if she'd asked the stupidest question in the world.

Ingrid was getting annoyed and impatient, so she pushed the kids away and stood on top of one of the desks. "Here is the deal. They want more humans. I am not enough. I will die and they'd have to keep coming to Earth to replenish their human population. That is not feasible. So they will need two of each to create a new human world."

Someone raised their hand and so did another, and another, each wanting to plead their case as to why they were the best choice to build a new world away from this planet. Ms. Sandler shook her head at the students, and Ingrid realized that this was harder than she thought. She couldn't take everyone with her.

"Two of each what?" Tobi asked quietly.

"Male and female," Ingrid responded.

A few of the kids dropped their heads, and Ingrid's heart sank.

"Do they want one Black and one white too?" Lauren asked. "I get it. Same shit, different planet."

"I hear that! Let me see who I'm gonna bring," Kyle said, scrolling through his phone.

"Selective breeding," Ms. Sandler interjected. "This all sounds like planetary imperialism, if you ask me."

"That was not one of their demands," Ingrid said. "I have the power to choose who I want."

"So you'll be like God?" Kyle asked.

Ingrid's heart sank a little deeper and she stepped down from the desk. God was never an aspiration. Being left alone was the dream. She had asked the captain for all the things necessary for her survival: oxygen, food, water, shelter, and sun. Nowhere on that list was people. Aliens, in whatever form they presented, would've provided the company she thought she needed. Not once did she think that she could mold and shape the world of her dreams. She believed that it was already there waiting for her, fully formed and created. As Ingrid Jesula Pierre looked down at her eager and inquisitive classmates with their dreams of a new and different world, she wondered where it had all gone wrong that so many of them wanted to leave it all behind, like she did.

So she asked Ms. Sandler, "Do you want to go with the aliens?"

"And leave this beautifully flawed world behind? No thanks, honey. The most wonderful thing about being human are these." She pointed to the stack of science-fiction novels. "If whatever you want doesn't exist, you can create it in whatever way you like. Books, movies, a painting, or . . . a whole *department*. I keep telling you all that this is the astronomy department, but you don't want to believe me."

Ingrid checked her phone and glanced down at the suitcase she'd been dragging around the school all day, waiting until it was time to leave. She had just ten minutes to bring three other people with her. One more female, two males. Girl and boy. Man, woman, and the word of an alien. Back to square one. As it was in the beginning.

"I'll make it easier for you," Tobi said as he stepped closer to Ingrid. "I can't come. That new world isn't for kids like me."

"But we can make it the world we want!" Ingrid said, realizing that her options had been staring at her all along. Lauren, Tobi, and—for the sake of time and good looks being high on the list—Kyle.

"Well, you're gonna have to get other people to make other people," Tobi said. "Selective breeding. I don't want anything to do with that. No matter how bad it gets on Earth."

Ingrid's belly twisted into something small and tight and painful. She watched Tobi as he and his friend removed themselves from the group of eager wannabe migrants and hogged the computer to play some video game, lost in its hypnotizing, synthetic world. She scanned the room for other possible cohabitants, but there was no way to pick the best. Maybe everyone was necessary; each person was enough to replicate over and over again in the new world.

The clock ticked, and the world spun. All the kids in the astronomy department presented an argument as to why they should be the one to leave, the one to be heard, the one to be seen, the one to be given special treatment because this planet had made them invisible in one way or another. And even in their invisibility, they fought for a spot in the light.

Then, in that moment, in the buzzy chatter of the room and the chaos out there in the world, Ingrid watched her fellow humans simply be . . . human. Flawed, complex, beautiful, intelligent, and yup, hierarchical.

The clock struck sixteen hundred hours and Ingrid had not left the classroom or the school with anyone or anything.

"The spaceship is leaving!" someone called out. "You're not going?"

Ms. Sandler displayed her laptop's screen where the livestream showed that the spaceship was now surrounded by more police cars and firetrucks, SWAT teams and cannons, the National Guard and the FBI as it hovered and then slowly lifted higher and higher up into the sky. Within nanoseconds, it blinked out of existence. And then, nothing.

The kids stared at the screen as news reports replayed the moment over and over again. Scientists and clergy, eyewitnesses, and nonbelievers all weaved their own stories of the day's events. The moment would live forever in history—looped videos, photos, movies, books, memories, tall tales, legends, and myths.

So Ingrid cleared her throat and asked her classmates in almost one breath, "Does anyone want to help me dismantle capitalism so corporate greed and human ignorance will not continue to deplete the Earth's resources and force humans to migrate to walled and bordered places where they are not welcome, which in turn leads to refugee crises and apathy for human life and clarion calls for war and genocide? Anyone?"

Ms. Sandler looked up from her laptop one last time and said, "This is the astronomy department, Ms. Pierre."

Ingrid and everyone else waited for her to continue, but that was all she said.

"I know. Astronomy means the law of the stars. How constellations, planets, and celestial bodies move around each other—one outshining the next, destructive, creative, and existing as they are. Science and magic at the same time. We are stardust!" Ingrid exclaimed as something warm washed over her—an epiphany, or superpowers maybe. "You were right, Lauren. Astronomy and astrology are the same. We are the aliens and the aliens are us."

Ingrid looked around the room for Lauren. She was not there. Then she scanned the room for who would've been her cohabitants. Kyle and Tobi. Kyle was gone too. Then she spotted a note on her suitcase. She unfolded it and read the scribbled words: *Thanks for letting me peek over your shoulder. Got my queen. Got two friends. I'm about to be king of a new world! —KH*

Ingrid ran out of the classroom and raced down the hall. There was no use. The spaceship was gone and it would be hours before everyone learned that Lauren and Kyle had gone with it, along with two quiet kids who'd been watching this all go down and planning their escape. Somewhere out there in another galaxy, there'd be another planet full of ballers and astrologers. Another imperfect world. This made her smile a little. And maybe this was the hope that she needed all along. This was the new sun she'd been looking for. Right there in that astronomy department with its one desktop, telescope, and solar system poster were perfectly imperfect humans destroying the world and building it back up, over and over again.

INITIATIVE CHECK
BY K. ARSENAULT RIVERA

"So you haven't talked to her in months," said Gabe, "but you saw fit to grant her a seat at our most sacred gathering of gamers."

I rolled my eyes. "It's not like we're inviting people to the Round Table."

"You're right. The Round Table was less exclusive. They had *dozens* of knights. We only have four," Gabe countered. He was one hundred percent serious. "But to continue with that metaphor, this woman you once cast aside may well prove to be our Mordred. Doesn't that worry you?"

I mean, a lot of things worried me about it. First of all, I kind of hadn't planned it. Last week, for the first time in two months, I'd bumped into Leah Baptiste in the hall. Leah had everything: she was super popular, captain of the city's champion soccer team, already being scouted for colleges, and always busy on Friday nights. But Leah was also my first crush, and one of my oldest friends. We hadn't spoken in months after she flaked on my birthday party. I was so nervous when I saw her that I just . . . blurted out an invitation to my tabletop gaming night. Like nothing had ever changed between us, and like she hadn't hurt me.

I didn't expect her to say yes.

We'd always talked about maybe playing together someday, and I guess part of me still wanted to have that chance.

"Man, could you not? It's already weird. Don't make it weirder," I said. "Besides, Leah's cool."

"Hmm. She is." The deep, rumbly voice came from Gabe's boyfriend, Adonis. Adonis was about six feet tall and bear shaped, which could have earned him a spot on the football team—but he liked attention even less than I did. In real life he loved cooking, rolling lots of dice, and Gabe, in that order. "Took home ec with her one year. Chill."

Leah could coast on being a good athlete to get into college, and her parents were pretty well off. My mom was a nurse, and it was just the two of us. I spent every second I could studying or working on extracurriculars— except the seconds I spent here.

At the center of the table was a stack of Adonis's steaming hot home-made pasteles. I wanted to grab one—but you can't just go snatching food before everyone's at the table.

"Please don't be weird, Gabe," said Chris, our gamemaster. "I'm begging you not to be weird."

"What if *she's* weird?" he shot back.

"I don't think she has a weird bone in her body," I said.

"False. If that were true, she wouldn't be here with us. There's got to be something else."

"Like what?"

"He's going to say she has a crush on you," said Adonis.

"Hey! Hey! That was my revelation to make!" protested Gabe.

I leaned back and sighed. Gabe was . . . a lot. But without him, we wouldn't have a group. He was the one who talked Chris into GMing. Invited me, too, once he saw me reading old *Dragonlance* novels. But man . . . could he be annoying.

Besides, he didn't understand. That wasn't possible. I mean, maybe it was, back in the day. Maybe my fingers laced together with hers a couple times in the dark of Leah's basement, the light from her computer screen flickering on our faces. Maybe I had worn a whole new outfit and got my hair done for my birthday party months ago just so she could see.

But she never showed up, and someone who had a crush on me totally would have . . .

Before I could think of something to say in argument, the doorbell rang. The sound of chanclas shuffling rang through the apartment as Adonis's mom went to get the door. All eyes were on me again. I wanted to melt into my seat.

And then his mom called out: "Mijo, un varón esta diciendo que vas a jugar algo con el? Se ve medio raro . . ."

Leah kept her long hair in cornrows for soccer, dressed like a hypebeast, and was mad tall. It was an easy enough mistake to make. Didn't feel great though. Me and Adonis both winced.

"Let her in, Ma," he called.

Five or six latches all got undone at once. Leah's voice carried—"Nice to meet you, your apartment's looking great. And it smells so good in here!"

Adonis looked to me, then tilted his head toward Leah. I got the message—I had to go get her.

Adonis's mom was smiling and nodding politely at everything Leah said without an idea of what was going on—but when I walked in, Leah started smiling too. At me. "Hey! Just who I was lookin' for."

How could she be so chill about this? Maybe it was my fault. Maybe because I hadn't made a big deal of stuff when I asked her, she didn't want to make it weird. I had about a dozen questions for her, but . . .

Maybe I could put them aside for just a little while. Maybe if the game went well, we could talk about it after.

She spread her arms for a hug and I went for it. A quick hug, you know, nothing serious.

I walked her back to the table. Adonis had laid out the rest of the food: yellow rice with peas, a couple of bottles of soda, and a bag of Takis emptied into a commemorative bowl. Gabe and the others had their sheets out and ready.

"This is Leah, everybody," I announced. "Please don't be weird."

Leah took her seat and started piling food onto her plate. Adonis frowned—usually he said grace before we started—but didn't say anything. I mouthed a thank-you to him as she took her first bite.

"Man, this is good," she said. "You guys eat like this every week?"

"Adonis spoils us," I said. "His druid's the same way."

"Chris lets me use *goodberry* to make whatever food I want in game. We always eat good."

Gabe pushed his glasses up his nose. "Right. So did you remember to bring a sheet?"

Leah dabbed her hands clean, nodded, and pulled out her tablet. A couple of swipes and her sheet was on display. "So who you guys playing?" she asked. "Y'all been at this awhile, right?"

Though she asked everyone, she looked at me. *Keep it cool, Jas. Don't be weird.* "M-My character's a bard. Halfling bard. She plays the trumpet, and her goal's popularizing jazz, but no one really likes it so far, especially no one at her old magic school, except one—her old friend Izkahar, who she had to stop talking to for story reasons; she hasn't seen him in forever. Anyway, she left the academy, and now she's trying to put together a band. On her off time. When she isn't . . . adventuring."

"Jas. You're playing a jazz-playing halfling."

That . . . definitely was weirder than I wanted it to be, wasn't it? "Y-Yeah. She's pretty good at it . . ."

I didn't have time to react to that disappointed look on her face before Adonis cut in. "I'm Saul Colmillogrande. Druid. Half-orc. He likes bears."

"He likes bears, huh," said Leah. "That the whole backstory?"

"Our group's pretty relaxed," said Chris. "But don't worry, everyone's kind of underselling themselves. They didn't get to level 12 goofing around."

Leah raised a brow. "Right, it's just I thought—"

"Your spell slots are wrong," said Gabe. Why was he going in on this now? Spell slots determined how many spells you could cast every day, but Chris was never too strict on them. It was total nitpicking.

"What?"

"You have the wrong number of spell slots. A level 12 paladin has four, three, and three slots. You have two on the last one."

"Don't talk to me like I'm a kid," Leah said. "It's just one spell, man, this my first time playing."

"Details are important," he said. "Especially if you're here as a *serious* player."

She'd never played before and she still said yes? Why? I mean, she had so many friends . . .

Leah's face screwed up in disbelief. She waved around a hand at the table. "Really? Because it don't sound too serious so far. You don't know me or my character." She looked to me again. "Jas, you hang out with this guy?"

"She doesn't think we're serious. And you invited her?" Gabe asked.

Words stopped up my throat. *He isn't that bad, he's just really attached to rules*, I wanted to tell Leah. *He's bad with people.*

But he *was* being rude. Shouldn't I say something? But maybe this whole thing was weird already, inviting someone as cool as Leah to hang out with guys whose only idea of social skills comes from talking to Chris's made-up townspeople in games. Maybe this was all my bad.

No matter what I said, it was gonna be a problem.

"Maybe it'll be easier if we get things rolling?" said Chris. "Me and Leah worked out a great backstory for her, and we're all here to have fun, so . . ."

He sounded desperate, and I was desperate for things to relax too. Swallowing down my discomfort, I nodded.

Leah rolled her shoulders. "Right, yeah. My bad. Let's just see how things go. We need anything to start?"

Chris cleared away the now-empty plates. He laid out his homemade map in the center of the table, then set down his giant robot model kits to the side. Looked like we were going to have a big fight ahead of us if those guys were meant to be the baddies.

"So, the party's coming up to Castle Fractal Shine," he said. "You guys can position yourselves wherever you like. Leah, do you have a token?"

She pulled out a tiny unpainted paladin mini. "Right here."

"Cool. Don't put it down just yet—these guys have to spot you, first. But you can think about where your character would be. From the rest of you, can I get a Perception check to start things off?"

I picked up my dice—a custom set my mom got me for my birthday with quarter notes in the center. I rolled right onto the map.

Nat 20.

"Nice! Roll that again. If you get another twenty, there might be some extra information in it for you," Chris said. He sounded oddly smug about that, and I had a weird feeling, but I rolled anyway.

Another nat 20.

Hold up. Did someone mess with my dice? I rolled again, only to see another 20.

I looked up to stunt on my friends, but that was when I realized something was . . . different.

For one thing, they were all a lot taller than me. For another, they didn't look anything like themselves anymore. In front of me was an elf in embroidered robes and a huge half-orc wearing a bearskin cloak. I was staring at them; they were staring at me. Another second and I realized we weren't even in Adonis's house anymore. Looming behind the half-orc was Castle Fractal Shine.

"Are you guys here too?" said the elf. No—that was Gabe, I'd know his voice anywhere. And he played a lost Elven prince in game too. A wizard who had a spell for just about every occasion.

Adonis, the half-orc, shrugged. "Looks like it. Pretty cool."

Gabe gawked. "Pretty cool? Are you serious, babe? You're a half-orc and it's just *pretty cool*?! This is the best thing that's ever happened to us!"

"I don't have pasteles anymore," he pointed out.

I laughed. It came out high, squeaky, not like my laugh at all—but exactly like the laugh I always did for Waffle in character. That . . . would explain why I was shorter. And why I had a miniature trumpet strapped to my front. "You got magic now, right? Try making some."

A dim glow surrounded Adonis's hands for a second and then—*plop*. A steaming hot pastel. He grinned and scarfed it down. "Sweet."

I slapped myself to make sure I wasn't dreaming. No dice. I stayed Waffle, and Waffle stayed me.

"So what do we do now?" asked Adonis.

"World domination," Gabe answered without missing a beat. "With our spell lists, and without a *gamemaster* in the way, we're invincible. Come on!"

"Shouldn't we look for Chris and Leah?" I asked, but it didn't seem like they heard me. And besides, if Chris was the GM, that meant he didn't have any set character. Maybe he was looking down on all of us or something.

But Gabe grabbed Adonis's hand and pulled him toward the wilderness surrounding the castle, never mind what I said. They only made it a few steps before they beefed it on a pair of metal rails. Then came a booming voice: THIS IS THE RAILROAD OPERATOR. HEROES MUST COMPLETE THE DUNGEON BEFORE VENTURING FORTH.

"You have *got* to be kidding me," Gabe whined. "I'm finally a *real* wizard and I can't take over the world?!"

Think, Jasmine, think. What would Waffle do?

Chris had told us a little about our destination, Castle Fractal Shine, last session. A powerful wizard named Isricht built it. Society had rejected Isricht, so he rejected society, that sort of thing. Trouble was that the castle was on a ley line and drawing tons of energy. That meant this whole area was prone to earthquakes, random hailstorms, even raining fireballs. The townspeople had had enough—so they hired Waffle and her backup band to go take a look.

"We're in game, right? Let's do what our characters would do and check out the castle," I said.

I was about to make a joke when I walked straight into a brick wall. A wall that then laughed and patted me on the shoulder. "You gotta keep an eye out, Jas."

That was Leah's voice. I heard sirens in my head. Leah was in the game? Leah, who was already kind of the best at everything she did? My heart was hammering. She was so cool in real life—would her character be too?

When I turned toward her, it was hard to keep my jaw off the floor. I thought she looked cute in her soccer uniform? This was next level. Level thirteen. A whole suit of mithral plate, bright as the moon even in the dark of the night; a cloak of velvety crimson; that cocky grin on her face? Talk about charm effects.

"I, uh . . . You . . . look . . ."

"I know," she said, smiling. She knelt down to my height. "Gotta say, wasn't expecting this. I ain't complaining, though. This always happen?"

"Nah, first time," I said. "Gabe tried going out on some colonizer nonsense, but this wall stopped him. I think we're supposed to clear the castle."

"That's what my paladin Seyorah's here to do," Leah said. She stood up. "I got an old friend in there. Came all the way out from the Marches to save him. You all down to come along?"

Gabe cleared his throat and put on a higher voice. "Matters of friendship are of utmost importance to elvenkind; as such, even a trifling matter like this might attract—"

"You don't gotta say all that," Leah said.

"He says sure," said Adonis. Right before he straight up became a bear in front of our eyes. One second he was a huge dude and the next he was a bear.

The whole thing was . . . I couldn't stop laughing. Maybe I should've been more afraid, but how could I be? This was the life I'd dreamed of for years. In the regular world, I had to deal with talking, job applications, college applications, studying, capitalism . . . But here, in the fantasy world, I could be whatever I wanted.

I didn't hesitate. Went straight for the gate. I jumped up to the demonic doorknob—only for somebody to grab me by my patchwork hood. I dangled above the ground, kicking my feet as my captor lifted me to eye level. Leah tapped her temple. "Remember: keep an eye out. That door's trapped as hell."

She turned me to face the door. Was it trapped? Waffle had a level in rogue, so she had trapfinding. That meant she could spot a trap a mile away. But I was just in her body, so how was I supposed to know? I wasn't actually Waffle, I didn't know much about—

But then I saw it: A mechanism visible in the keyhole. A string of twine attached to the knobs. If I'd turned them, the wire would have snapped. A dozen different traps scrolled through my head until, at last, the image settled on one in particular. Noxious gas. I was sure of it.

"You don't have trap sense," Gabe said.

"Don't need it. Seyorah helped the evil wizard Isricht build this tower, back when they was cool. Course, then he stopped talking to her," Leah explained. She set me down. "Jas, think you can crack it for us?"

And the way she was looking at me then, like I was the only person in the world—I didn't care that I'd almost died via poisoning. I wanted to do my best. God, I forgot what being around her was like.

Waffle kept her lock-picking tools in her trumpet case. I opened it up and got to work. Turned out, my hands knew what to do, even if I didn't. Trapfinding must have transferred to me too.

After I got the door open and we walked into the castle, I understood why they'd called in professionals. We got maybe five steps in before the ground started to rumble. Gabe fell backward onto Adonis's bear-back.

"What'd I just say? Watch out!" Leah called. But she needed to take her own advice: all that shaking loosened a beam above her head. It came swinging down like the hammer of god, and she was right in its path.

I couldn't just stand there. I threw myself at her, no plan to it except to get her out of the way. We tumbled to the ground a second before the beam swung over us. Leah looked down at me with a smirk. "You got me back for the trap, huh?"

"You're the one who said to watch out," I answered.

"Fair enough, fair enough," she said. She helped me up. "If I remember this place right, we gotta head up those stairs over there."

"I don't suppose you know what's up those stairs, noble knight?" asked Gabe.

"Fight pit."

That was a joke, right? "Fight pit"?

Leah shrugged. "Isricht's running some kinda experiment. Said he'd have a bunch of different golems fight. Whichever wins out is the best golem. Then he takes that one and makes a whole bunch of new versions, then they all fight . . . you get it."

"That . . . sounds pretty sick, actually," I said.

"Right?" said Leah. She smiled. "Knew you'd get it. Anyway, we gonna have to fight our way through all that, so follow my lead and let me take the heat."

It ended up being Leah on point, then Gabe and me, and Adonis at our back. Climbing the spiral staircase, hearing the distant crackle of magic, the thumps of a fight up ahead . . . I felt like my heart was truly about to burst.

It got even better when we reached the pit itself. First of all, it had no reason to be this big. This place was the size of our school's gym, except round, with cages lining the walls. And these weren't regular golems, oh, no. They were the giant robots I'd seen earlier, except this time they really were giant. Every single one was twelve feet tall with a laser sword. The door we needed was on the other side of the room.

Lightning crackled between Gabe's fingers. "You said golems."

"Chris said golems in the message he sent me," Leah confirmed.

She didn't wait to explain before running right into the middle of things, shield raised. An aura flared to life around her—I felt braver being close to her, but I had to run to keep up.

"*Lightning bolt!*" Gabe shouted, as happy as he was afraid. And maybe magic was that easy: a flash of light sent one of the golems flying into the wall.

Leah caught a laser sword swing against her shield. Behind me, Adonis was in a slugfest with one of the other golems, leaving huge claw marks across its waist.

Waffle wasn't all that big on fighting—she liked magic, stealing things, and music. But she was always happy to help a friend. The right thing to do felt obvious.

I put the trumpet to my lips and started to blow.

Music and light flowed from the bell. A twisting golden music staff wrapped around my friends, with notes scrolling by as I played them. I'd never played a trumpet before, but the music I was playing felt . . . like me. Like the me I wanted to be: warm and fuzzy, but confident at the same time; hopping fast, kinda complicated, but you'd understand the soul of what I was saying even if you only heard it once.

And even better than all that, it was working. The notes steadied Leah's shield arm, protected Adonis from the golem's counter swings, and sent Gabe's bolts faster and farther.

"Thanks, Jas!" Leah shouted. She hurled the golem's sword away and barreled ahead. The others followed, and so did I, playing for everything I was worth. By the time we hit the stairs, I was out of breath but the happiest I'd been in months.

"Wait, has Waffle always played that well?" Gabe asked. "You sounded better than *our* trumpet. And the way you integrated the spell with the music!"

"I mean, I don't know, I didn't . . ." I answered. "Man, that was sick, though."

"That's Jas for you, always acting modest," Leah said. "We wouldn't have made it out of that without your help."

"Thanks," I said. She really thought that? "Do we, uh . . . What's on the next floor?"

"Puzzle trap," Leah said. She thought for a second. "One of those things, looks kinda like a skelly board? You gotta step on the tiles in the right order."

"Or . . . ?" Gabe ventured.

"It's the gas, isn't it," I said.

She nodded. "Isricht's not creative with traps. Too busy doing wizard stuff."

"Did Chris tell you that too?" I asked.

"Yeah. He told me all sorts of stuff about this place so my character could tell you guys. Said it was gonna be a really special session, but I didn't expect all this."

A thought came to mind. "Wait. Let's get up there, I want to take a look."

It didn't take long to make it to the next floor—you never have any fights on the stairs. The room was long and narrow, with five-colored tiles lining the floor. The nozzles up near the ceiling must be where the gas would come from. With Waffle's eyes, I saw that the trap's mechanism was tied to the keyhole on the other side again.

"Gabe, you have *feather fall* ready?"

"I always have *feather fall* ready," he said. "But only one, so—"

"Let me have it," I said.

He tilted his head at me, which, fair. I didn't usually ask for stuff like this.

It felt weird, asking. Part of me wanted to go back on it when he stared at me like that—but I didn't. And, eventually, with a sigh, he cast the spell.

Magic tingled against my skin. Felt like pins and needles. When I took my first moon-man steps onto the tiles—yeah, I was a little worried. But only a little. The tiles didn't sink when I stepped on them. Behind me, I heard Gabe let out a sigh of relief. It didn't take long to undo the trap either.

Nothing could wipe away the grin on my face as the others made their way across. Especially not when I caught Leah smiling too. "All right, all right," she said. "Lookin' good out here."

"Thanks," I said. "Whatever's up next, I bet we got it handled."

She laughed. "Oh, word? You sure?"

We heard a roar from the other side of the hall. A really, *really* big roar.

"Was that . . . a dragon?"

"Yeah, a young one," Leah said. "Isricht uses its blood for ink. And it's a good guard too."

Adonis bear-laughed. He loped on ahead of us. We followed. If the druid wasn't worried, maybe there wasn't anything to be worried about.

But we knew different the second we set foot in there. A cone of fire threatened to scorch us up. Would have killed us if it wasn't for Leah blocking some of it, and the rest of us dropping to the ground. Once the fire cleared, we were staring at something ancient, terrifying, and pissed off. The dragon took up most of the room, with shackles around its neck and arms. It couldn't even rise to its full height in a place like this.

I didn't have much time to feel sorry for it before another cone of fire came our way. Behind me, Gabe was screaming.

"That . . . That's supposed to have a cooldown!"

He was right. A dragon's breath had a 1d6-turn cooldown, and given a round represented only six seconds of real lifetime . . .

"Maybe he rolled well," I said. "But we're going to have to get past him—"

The fire stopped.

I looked up again.

Adonis, still a bear, held out a paw to the dragon. On it was one of his homemade pasteles.

"Oh my god," I whispered.

"Let him work, let him work," said Leah.

But Gabe went dead quiet. I could feel the anxiety coming off him in waves as he watched his boyfriend wave meat in front of a hungry dragon.

A tongue darted from its lips to snap up the pastel. It let out a satisfied sound—and then flashed white. Huh. Adonis had . . . enchanted . . . that?

The dragon rolled over and started snoring.

Yeah. Yeah, he had. Like it was the easiest thing in the world, he broke down the next door and stared back at us, then tilted his head. *Come in*, he seemed to say.

All of us tiptoed past the sleeping dragon toward the door. Another long hallway awaited us, but at the end of it was something that looked like the heavy doors to a fancy library. The evil wizard's lair, without a doubt. I could feel the magic in the air the closer we got.

A second later, I heard boots against the ground, weapons clattering, the distinct hooting laugh of . . .

"Gnolls?!" I shouted.

"Yeah, uh, he got guards," Leah answered. "My bad. I forgot about them."

A company of gnolls was flooding into the room—and their leader was waking the dragon.

"You forgot?" Gabe said. "There's, like, a dozen of them, and you forgot?"

"Lotta stuff to remember, stuff slips by," she answered. "Form up. We can bottleneck them here."

I looked between the two doors—the one to the den, and the one up ahead. We could hold off a couple of them, but the whole group . . . In situations like this, you needed to deal with the boss first. And something about the inscription on the door was familiar. A step closer and I realized why: there was a musical staff there, too, and the tune written on it . . .

. . . was that the song I'd been playing?

"Guys . . ." I started.

But Adonis and Leah were already swinging back at the gnolls, already in the thick of it. Only Gabe turned toward me. I pointed to the door.

"I think I have to go through here," I said. "Waffle must know this dude. If I talk to him, maybe he'll get the guards to chill."

Gabe's elf-ears twitched. An arrow flew over his head. He turned back toward the melee—then sighed. "All right. Leah, you go with Jas."

"What?" she answered.

"Seyorah and Waffle both know Isricht," he said. "You two have the best odds of talking sense into him. A half-orc druid and an elven wizard can handle most things together, if they try."

Adonis roared, taking down two of the gnolls with a mighty swipe of his claws.

Leah looked from Gabe to Adonis. Fending off another hit, she shook her head and sighed. ". . . All right. I appreciate it."

She took off like a bolt. Instead of waiting to unlock the door or to see if it was trapped, she broke it down with the pure force of her charge. There, just past the splinters, was Isricht.

"I've been waiting for the two of you," he said.

He looked like Chris, and I knew he was, deep down in my heart. It made sense—he had no character, but he'd put a ton of work into his villains. And just like Isricht had set up all these traps in the game world, Chris had set them up in the real world. I was happy to see him, but something was off.

"Happy to see you too," said Leah. She offered up a hand to him—only for a magic missile to knock it away.

"After all this time, Seyorah, that's what you have to say for yourself?" The wizard stood. Light blared from his eyes. "Like nothing happened?!"

Another missile flew toward her—she barely got her shield up in time to deflect it. Not that that was much help. The missile shattered a nearby alembic full of glowing liquid. The second that stuff hit the ground, it went up in blue-green flame. Sweat was already dripping into my eyes. Everything in the study was filled with that liquid.

No way we could keep fighting here.

But homie was starting the monologue, so we weren't getting out of this any time soon. When I took Leah's hand to pull her out of this place, the workshop flooded with violet light. Runes on the floor sparked as they activated; magic bolted our feet to the ground.

We locked eyes as the flames rose around us. "How'd Seyorah know him?" I asked.

"Old friends," Leah said. She was frowning, the muscles in her neck flexing as she tried to get free of the spell. "He got kicked out of . . . this magical academy . . ."

All of a sudden, the spell holding us in place went heavy as iron. We sank to our knees.

"I trusted you. Confided in you," said the wizard. "The Academy didn't like the way I did things. I told you that."

Up above us the ceiling opened up, as if someone was peeling away a sticker, revealing stars and swirling infinity. The flames leaped higher.

"And what did you do? You brought *her* here!"

Wait a second. I looked at him again—Waffle looked at him again. Hatred and pain distorted the features, but she could see the boy Izkahar in the wizard Isricht. Years ago Waffle found him in the middle of forging demonic pacts. She'd had to report him, what else was she going to do? His soul was at stake. But after that, they'd never spoken again. Whenever she reached out, he'd only pushed me away.

This was the guy from Waffle's backstory. The only one who had ever liked her music.

"This . . . is all . . . your fault!" he screamed.

The lights beneath my feet went out. I realized in horror that he'd released the spell—which meant the only thing keeping me attached to the ground was gone too. Before I could take off, the vortex yanked me up into its clutches.

Staring into the dark, cold infinity, I thought I was gone for sure.

But a howl of pain and a pull backward said otherwise. I looked down to see Leah's hand wrapped around my ankle. Determination was burning in her eyes. "I let go of you once," she said. "I'm not letting go again!"

My heart was hammering, the wind of the void was whistling in my ears. Isricht's hand glowed deathly violet, his mouth started shaping the syllables to something old and dark.

Power word kill.

If I didn't act fast, Seyorah was going to die. And what did that mean for Leah? I didn't want to find out.

What was I going to do? Think. He said he hated Waffle, but what if that was the demonic pact talking? What if I could remind him of who he was?

I put the trumpet to my lips and blew. Golden music cut through the maelstrom's din. From the first note, he was transfixed, his lips falling silent.

Waffle knows how to speak music, how to play, but all I could do was feel. So I felt as hard as I could. All the things I missed: old inside jokes, 3 a.m. memories. The clothes she lent me and never picked up, the ones that made me feel like I was her girl when I wore them around the house. Her mom's cooking, her dad's bad jokes. Months without talking, months of quiet hurt—and months spent yearning for us to be cool again.

That was the song I played.

What spell was it? Man, I don't know. *Fascinate person*, maybe. What I do know is that it worked. Isricht couldn't concentrate on his spells anymore. One by one they flickered out of existence, until I tumbled back to the ground, and Leah caught me, then set me down. "You did the hard part. Leave this to me," she said. She leveled her sword at Isricht.

"Don't—" I shouted.

The sword blared white. I had to cover my eyes—I couldn't watch her kill him, not when he finally looked like he understood what he'd done. I braced myself for the scream.

It never came.

When the light faded, the fires were gone, and it was just Chris there—in his hoodie and jeans. He looked at his hands and laughed. "Huh. Guess that's one way to clear a curse," he said. Then, he turned his attention to us and cleared his throat. "Izkahar runs to his old companions and throws his arms around them. The sky outside clears. With the town safe, you're free to take a breath . . . End session."

When I blinked, we were back at the table, like nothing had happened. Gabe and Adonis were hugging. Everything was normal.

Except my hand was in Leah's.

As the others talked, I had to ask, "Did you . . . Did you make all this happen?"

She pulled her hand away—but only so that she could wrap her arm around my shoulders. "Nah," she said. "Wish I did, though. Been a minute since I seen you that happy. Never knew you could play like that."

"I didn't either," I said. It all seemed so impossible, but . . . she smelled nice, and after all we'd been through, it felt natural to lay my head on her shoulder. "So . . . you really wanted to see me?"

"Wanted to talk with you awhile now. Just didn't know how to start," she said. "When I hit up Chris, he was so excited to give us a space where we could talk again without it being weird. Didn't know he'd go *that* ham on it, though."

I glanced at him. Unlike everyone else, he had this knowing glint in his eye. He'd gotten us into the game, but how? Maybe I'd have to take another look at the dice mat afterward. Maybe he'd gotten a magic one somewhere.

And if he had, I wanted one too. Because I wanted Waffle and Seyorah to hang out together as much as I wanted to hang out with Leah.

Yeah, she'd hurt me. But I could forgive her for that if she'd put in all this effort to learn about my nerdy hobby and make up for it.

"You could have said sorry," I said.

"You're right. But I just felt so bad missing the party, it was like . . . my brain made it a bigger deal to say sorry than it was, you feel me? And then there was this energy like I knew I was wrong, it got harder and harder, and . . . you were still doing you, and I thought you were probably happier without me." She shook her head. "It's my bad. I should have apologized earlier. But then when you asked me—you know, I'd been trying to get a game off the ground with my squad for months. Felt meant to be."

The words settled in my chest. It was a lot to take in, a lot to talk about, but we didn't have to do all that right now.

For now . . .

"I missed you," I said.

She nuzzled against me. "I missed you too."

CORNER BOOTH
BY LEAH JOHNSON

What people don't understand about competitive spelling is that it doesn't require genius. You don't have to be a prodigy, born a savant and destined for greatness. It's much simpler than that. Once you know that a word is only as good as the sum of its parts, you can cobble together almost anything. It's not about having an endless catalog of words. It's about having the *roots*. But therein lies the problem.

When you're born with roots, you don't spend your life searching for them. Not like I have.

"What's the score tonight, honeypie?"

CiCi pours a fresh pot of hot coffee into my almost-empty mug and looks over my shoulder at my phone. She's the only person I talk to on nights like these. And even though her sweet, syrup-slow drawl distracts me from my mission, I flash a smile up at her. It lasts less than half a second, but it's enough. She places a hand on my shoulder and squeezes.

"825 with one move to go," I answer. For the first time ever, I have the letters to hit 850 on the nose—the highest score in Dictionary Dynamo history. From there, it's only a matter of time until I surpass it. My knee bounces under the table nervously. "If this person would just hurry up and take their turn."

I'm not an impatient person, but I've been waiting on my opponent to go for the past three minutes. Technically, each turn allows for six minutes before you forfeit, but people never take that long. Once you reach this level—the Dictionary Wizard distinction is only given to players who consistently score 700 points or higher per game—either you have it or you don't.

You either know what it takes to maximize your score with the seven letters you've been provided and the existing words on the board, or you don't.

I *always* know. I never miss a word. And that's why I'm one of the best to ever play.

"Well." CiCi purses her lips and raises her eyebrows. I'm always impressed by the way her red lipstick is perfectly applied, even at four in the morning. "One of these days you're gonna break that record and we're gonna shut this whole place down for a party."

I roll my eyes and try not to let the superstition creep in. If you say you want something, if you put it out in the universe, that makes it real. And the minute it's real, there are expectations. And expectations mean disappointment. So, I nudge CiCi with my elbow and say, "Don't you have a wayward trucker you need to listen to complain over a plate of runny eggs or something?"

She looks back over her shoulder as the bell over the door chimes, and two men in worn sneakers and heavy Carhartt jackets push through the door as if on cue. She laughs as she notices the new rigs parked outside, just like clockwork.

"Okay, little miss smarty." She pokes my temple with her carefully painted acrylic nail and turns to greet the truckers with a grin and a *Hey, sugar, what can I do ya for?*—really laying on the accent thick like it makes the whole diner experience more authentic or something.

Just as I look back down at my phone, the other player, RegionKidd's, letter chips appear on our board.

I gasp as they block the exact row I was planning on using and pretty much close off the entire top right-hand corner of the board. And with a double letter, triple word, bringing their turn score to 93 points and their game score to 847.

Shit.

The word taunts me as it sits on the board: SYZYGY.

I puzzle through the word like that'll help unravel the move somehow. Like I haven't been playing against this person for two hours now, fighting them every step of the way to eke out a win. Like they haven't surprised me with their plays at every turn, undermining my every move so I have to use the backup to my backup.

As always, I start with the root. *Syzygos*. From the Latin? No, the Greek, *-zygon*. Which means to yoke. And *-syn*, which means together. God. I should have thought of that.

I take a big gulp of my coffee as I survey what's left of the board and barely even notice how it burns my tongue going down.

All I need are 26 points. 26 points and I can stop. 26 points and it'll be done. I'll—I can quit.

Instead of soothing me, the thought just makes my hands sweat and my throat tighten. So many nights and early mornings in this diner, doing this exact same thing, working toward this singular goal. Waiting, plotting, *working*. Three years of this game being the one buoy I have, keeping me afloat, keeping me from being sucked under, lost.

26 points.

L-O-S-R. I rearrange it to the word part *-sol*, from the Latin *solari*. To console. Like a father might do to his daughter after she's cried herself sick because she's placed in her fifth foster home in as many months. Like a mother holding her daughter after watching her scream herself awake through her fifth nightmare of the week.

I tap my screen to place my word on the board. My time is almost up.

SOLACE. Triple word score. Play total: 24 points. Final score: 849 to 847.

The confetti pops across the screen, signaling my barely there win. *Congrats, DinerGirl05! Better luck next time, RegionKidd!* blinks back at me amidst the too-gleeful digital celebration. It doesn't fill me with the same type of satisfaction as usual, though. I drop my head into my hands and try to ignore the way they shake as I think about the *R* I'd abandoned. Not because of the mortal sin of leaving a letter unplayed or because I didn't know what to do with it.

But because I *always* know.

SOLACER. Triple word score. Play total: 27 points. Final score: 852 to 847.

So close. To winning. To beating the record. To having nothing left to reach for.

I lock my phone and shove it into my pocket before waving goodbye to CiCi, who is flirting hard with one of the truckers. I drop a five-dollar bill on the table to cover my coffee and a small tip and flip my hood up over my head. I breathe in the icy early morning chill and try to bite back a shiver as my fingers fumble with the freezing lock on my bike.

Tomorrow, I promise myself as I swing my leg over and kick up the stand. I repeat it like a mantra. *Tomorrow I'll do it. Tomorrow I'll do it. Tomorrow I'll do it.*

As I ride, I can almost convince myself I mean it.

The area I'm currently staying in is what my dad used to call *saditty* (African American Vernacular English, origins in the 1940s, meaning to affect an air of superiority or affluence). My foster parents, Paul and Margaret, own one of the fancy colonial-style houses downtown—the kind of place where real estate agents on TV brag about how "the original heart pine flooring maintains the integrity of the structure" and other frivolity like that. I've been bounced around enough to recognize that some homes are infinitely better than others—nicer, certainly, on paper—but that doesn't mean shit in the grand scheme of things.

Not when the people inside aren't your people. Not when everything you own can fit in a trash bag.

All things considered, this isn't a bad place to bide my time until I get booted from the system in two months when I turn eighteen. Margaret is spread thin by the number of kids in her care, and that's ideal. If she doesn't pay attention to me, she won't notice when I disappear. And I disappear with alarming regularity. So.

I hike my backpack up on my shoulders and slip out the front door, pulling it shut behind me with a *click*. I grab my bike from the side of the house, then roll down the sidewalk, and I'm gone.

I can breathe easier when I escape the twelve-block radius of the Lockerbie Square neighborhood. When the streetlights flicker more and the broken glass in the streets takes maneuvering around, I know I'm almost there. The faster I pedal toward the diner, the looser my shoulders get, and the more the tension in my chest abates. It's not safe to be a teenage girl pedaling the streets of the city after-hours, I know, but these are *my* streets. These are my people.

Even if he's gone, I'll always be Darryl Ferguson's daughter, and that still means something out here.

I lock my bike up outside the diner and blow into my hands to get rid of the chill as I step into the heat. The diner is always summer-warm, no matter the season, and it's that type of consistency that makes it my favorite place on earth. I slip into my usual booth in the back—red leather seats cracked with age, Formica table perpetually sticky, perfect view of every corner of the diner—and pull out my phone.

This time of night, I'm usually playing with other insomniacs or people

on the other side of the world. But Dictionary Dynamo is the great equal-
izer. The board is the board, and the letter tiles are the letter tiles no matter
the time of day or the time zone.

I check my matches, the people currently online and at my level who
have requested to play me recently. Their highest scores are next to their
screen names and none of them are above 700. I usually choose whoever is
first on the list—it doesn't matter who I play, my win is already a foregone
conclusion as far as I'm concerned—but this time I stop to examine my
options. Last night was a closer call than I'm used to. I haven't lost in two
years and nearly 450 games—haven't even come close, honestly. Not until
RegionKidd.

But there was a sort of thrill, too, in having to work for every point,
every word. I wasn't just playing against myself for the high score. I had a
real, honest-to-God challenger. My dad would chuck me on the chin and
say, "A little squeeze is good for you," when I was a little kid scared of an
obstacle. But I haven't been a kid in a long time, and he was smart enough
to stop giving me advice even longer ago than that, so I select an unfamiliar
name out of spite.

CiCi drops off my mug of coffee with a pinch to my cheek before zip-
ping off to take care of other customers. I tune out the buzz and focus on
my screen.

The game is over before it begins. I have no idea how the person I'm
playing managed to reach this level of competition. Sloppy placements,
low-point-yielding words, a general waste of my time. They don't even have
the courtesy of not muddying up the board so I can make some stellar
plays. My best play of the night is MAXIMIZE. Only 78 points. Truly embarrassing on my part.

An hour later and the diner has mostly cleared out, the dull roar of a
busy kitchen and dining room mostly dimmed to a soft hum. CiCi has re-

filled my mug once and I'm killing time listening to *Merriam-Webster's Word of the Day* podcast until some new matches appear for me to play.

I close my eyes and mouth along as the host pronounces the word *fulminate*. Even as I roll the vowels around on my tongue and test out the heaviness of the Latin root, *fulminare*, I can't help but calculate what it would be worth in a game of Dictionary Dynamo. Aside from the *F* and the *M*, they're all low-yield letters, so not a super impressive play. But you never know. If you get a triple letter, you could—

"Hey!"

My eyes snap open at the sudden proximity and volume of the voice outside of my headphones. Some boy is standing next to my table, frowning down at me curiously, his caseless phone dangling from his long fingers like he couldn't care less if he drops it. I pull the cheap earbuds out of my ears and paint on my most impressive scowl. I don't know where this boy came from or why he's in my diner, looming over my table, but I need him to go. Now.

"Good, you're alive," he says, smile growing gradually across his face. He bumps his skateboard against the table on accident and winces when my coffee spills over the top of my mug, but the smile returns almost instantly.

He has dimples set deep into his brown skin, and one of his eyes is bright blue while the other is nearly black. *Heterochromia*, my brain supplies. 23 points. High yield but would require building blocks that are unlikely. Maybe if someone played *hetero*, but even then, the likelihood that you'd have all seven letters necessary for—

"What?" I'm so distracted by my own train of thought that I miss the fact that he's still talking. To me. While waving his hands around like he's trying to signal the landing for a fighter jet. "Why are you speaking to me?"

I know I sound gruff. Some of that is just my nature, or the way I've been nurtured, maybe. But the rest of it is that I'm out of practice. It's been a long time since I spoke to anyone who wasn't CiCi, and even those interactions usually last no longer than five minutes.

"Oh, um." He scratches the back of his neck and points over his shoulder toward the door. "I came in, like I just said like two seconds ago, and saw you over here and you just looked . . . dead? Or possessed, maybe? It was a toss-up to be honest. Anyway, I wanted to make sure nothing unsavory was happening in this fine dining establishment before I imbibed, so I came over to suss out the situation."

Imbibed. 14 points.

I don't respond. The boy stands there smiling down at me like he's just said something unbelievably funny or clever, hands stuffed into the pockets of jeans that are skinnier than skinny jeans should reasonably be, and I don't have time for whatever little game he's playing. I don't come to the diner to be on the receiving end of half-baked flirtations. This is the only place I can exist without everything extra. The hapless apologies, the empty promises, the cutting insults that are waiting outside those doors.

His smile starts to slip when I put my headphones back in my ears and close my eyes again. I try to ignore the squeak of his beat-up Vans as he walks away, but I can't help but crack one eye open to watch. He flops down at a table on the other side of the tiny diner, long legs and arms sprawled everywhere like the booth isn't big enough to contain all of him. He's not wearing a coat, even though it's pushing thirty degrees outside, but he seems content reading a worn library copy of *Go Tell It on the Mountain* and clicking around on his phone between pages.

It's incredible how fast I decide I want CiCi to go full bodyguard and haul him out of here.

I open the Dictionary Dynamo app and try to focus on another matchup instead of the way the boy is wiggling around in his seat like he's hearing music no one else can. The old jukebox has Willie Nelson crooning over the speakers, but he's not anywhere near the beat of "Always on My Mind." I decide right then that there's little else more unbearable than a man who doesn't know how to move on the two and the four.

I don't know if it's the sudden appearance of this infuriating stranger, or if it's the lackluster game from earlier, but I want to play. *Really* play. I want to be drawn into a game so deeply that nothing else exists besides word parts and letter tiles. So when I tap through my matchups and see that RegionKidd has just logged on and wants a rematch, I almost allow myself a smile.

Game on.

My knee bounces under the table, and I chew at my thumbnail until I can taste the copper tang of blood every time I bring it to my mouth. I won last night, but it was another close call. It feels like all I am these days is a collection of *almosts*.

The game I've *almost* beaten.

The phone call from my dad this morning saying he *almost* made parole.

The boy is back across the diner, and I'm half convinced he's being unbearably annoying on purpose. I'm playing RegionKidd again and my lead in the game is narrow—unbearably so. The boy with the dimples shovels a mountain of pancakes into his mouth and consumes a truly unconscionable amount of pork products, drawing my attention his direction every few seconds. By the time my match reaches its last few plays, he's playing music from his phone speakers instead of having the decency to plug in some headphones, and the tinny, mumbled voice of whatever rapper he's blasting sets my teeth on edge.

I shake my head. I've never been this far behind in a game. And this time, RegionKidd isn't letting up. It's triple word after triple word. Double letter on a *Z*. Bonus points for using all seven letters in their hand.

It's a bloodbath.

I only have thirty seconds to make a play that will close the hundred-point gap between us, and I just don't see it. The board starts to blur, and the letter tiles begin to jumble themselves in my head. This has never happened to me before, and I'm not sure what's going on tonight, but I feel like I'm going to be sick.

I play the best word I can, JETTY, on a double word for 30 points total.

RegionKidd counters with CARABINE, using my *E*, on a triple word, for 36 points. Final score: 848. And before I know it, the game is over. For the first time in over two years, I've lost a matchup of Dictionary Dynamo. And I didn't lose by a little, I lost handily. Humiliatingly. Definitively.

I don't wait to see the congratulations message pop up for RegionKidd, I lock my phone and slam it down on the table so hard my mug rattles. The burning feeling in my chest is untamable, wild, and it's growing by the second. It's like shame, but worse. It's a feeling that I've kept locked up and tucked away since the day my dad got sentenced and my mom left town in the middle of the night without so much as a note. It's *rage*.

I don't even bother being subtle as I stomp my way across the diner. There's only one explanation for my poor play—only one variable between this night and every other night that I've sat in the same seat, drank the same stale coffee, and played against the same nameless, faceless, incompetent opponents. Him.

"Listen, asshole," I press my hands against the table and pitch my voice so low that every word drips with malice. "I don't know where the hell you came from, or why you decided to set up shop here, but this is the last night you're gonna spend in this diner."

The boy looks up from his book like he's surprised to see me, but not at all unnerved.

"You've got a lot of pent-up aggression, you know." He cocks his head to the side like I'm a puzzle he hasn't quite figured out yet. "Drinking coffee this late probably isn't helping. Why are you up at this hour anyway?"

I clench my hands into fists and the bitter taste of my fourth cup in three hours becomes even more pronounced on my tongue. How dare he lecture me? Who does he think he is? Not even my fath— Nobody lectures me. Nobody.

"It's none of your fucking business," I snap. "You shouldn't be here. You don't *deserve* to be here. Don't you get it? This is my place."

I sound like a petulant kindergartener whining over a stolen swing at recess and yet I can't stop myself. I don't want him here. I don't want him invading my space, distracting me, speaking to me, smiling at me. Distracting me from my game. Not at my diner.

"*Your* place?" He quirks up one side of his mouth in a slight smile. "No offense, but I don't think you can claim a whole diner. I just want somewhere to eat some bacon at the witching hour and screw around on my phone in peace." He shrugs. "That's all."

I can't do this. I know I'm having a disproportionately huge reaction, but I can't seem to stop myself. Something about his nonchalance, his stupid smile, his ridiculous entitlement to my space overwhelms me. I look at the half-full glass of water on the table and smack it so it splashes all over the green hoodie he's wearing. He frowns and CiCi gasps from across the room, and when the glass crashes to the ground and shatters all over the floor that CiCi just mopped an hour ago, I feel like I'm the one that's been doused.

Everything suddenly feels like so *much*. So I do what I learned to do a long time ago: I leave. Instead of responding, I spin around and walk back to my table. I throw a five down for the coffee, grab my backpack, and practically run out the door.

And if the tear tracks on my cheeks sting against the cold as I attempt to unlock my bike and peddle back to the house, then I guess nobody has to know but me.

The next few nights, all I can feel are the dueling sensations of mortification and exhaustion when I so much as think about going back to the diner. Not just each play of the game—every opportunity for a high-yield word I missed, every disappointing play, all of it—but also the way I confronted the boy.

I've been good about concealing my emotions my entire life. I've made a sport of it, almost: How much weight can Fergie bear without revealing any of the cracks in the surface? It was a necessary tool in a house with a mom who was just as likely to fly off the handle at the drop of a dime as she was to spend a week in bed, and a dad whose kindness toward me was only matched by his bloodlust for the people who ever had the audacity to wrong him and his.

Later, it was to protect myself from the foster parents who wielded words the way some people wield fists—hitting harder and harder at your weakest points until you crumbled in front of them. If they didn't know your weak points, though; if you gave no indication of how much it hurt to hear them call your parents *a good for nothing junky* and *nothing but a thug*, then they'd bypass it. They'd find a different chink in the armor—one that wasn't much of a chink at all.

I leave every unsaid word to Dictionary Dynamo. Maybe I don't know how to articulate myself in the world without some sort of damage. In the game, though, I have no shortage of language.

But I allowed my emotions to get the best of me. I lashed out at someone who didn't deserve it, not really, and my words were too similar to the people I'd rather forget. So when I finally walk in three days later and see the boy has already taken up residence at what I guess he's claimed as his table, I roll my shoulders back, take a deep breath, and slide into the bench across from him.

His dimples come out in full force almost immediately, like he's happy to see me somehow despite what I said and how I acted when I last saw him here.

"Hey, Diner Girl!" He practically inhales the piece of French toast on his plate as he speaks. I try not to wince as pieces of it fly everywhere. "You're back."

My heart catches in my throat at the name. How does he know my Dictionary Dynamo screen name? Nobody knows that.

He swallows and takes a huge gulp of orange juice. As if reading my mind, he amends, "Sorry. I mean, I don't know your real name, but this is 'your diner,' so. You know. That's what I've been calling you in my head."

"Oh." I breathe. "Good."

I wait a beat in silence. I don't know how to start this apology.

"Not that I don't appreciate the company, but, you know, is there a reason why you're looking at me like I drowned your puppy?" he asks.

I sigh and decide to just be honest, even though I can't bring myself to meet his eyes.

"I shouldn't have done what I did the other night. Any of it. It was unbelievably childish of me." I swallow. "I'm sorry."

The boy doesn't speak for a second. He sets his fork down and leans forward on his elbows. When I finally look up at him, I feel struck by that one blue eye. It's piercing, the way he looks at me without any trace of harshness dotting his features.

"What's your name?" he asks suddenly.

"Huh?"

He smiles and leans back. "What's your name, Diner Girl? I figure if we're going to be friends, we should at least exchange names."

I shake my head. "I don't get it. What about—"

"You had a bad day," he interrupts. "We all have bad days. And my loud music probably didn't help any while you were getting in your zone or whatever." He waves his hand in the air like he can brush the interaction out of the way. "I forgive you. So what's your name?"

"Um, Rose Ferguson," I answer. "Or, um, call me Fergie. It's a nickname."

"Okay, Fergie," he says my name like it's a pair of new shoes he's trying on, slowly, with just a hint of satisfaction. "I'm Wes."

He holds out his hand for me to shake and I take it gingerly. His palm is a little calloused, but warm and strong as it grips mine. When we pull apart, he raises his eyebrows.

"Wanna split some sausage links?"

Wes comes to the diner every night for a week, and soon, it's Christmas break. I show up a little after midnight and try to convince myself each night that I'm not hoping Wes will already be there waiting for me. I'm unsuccessful in that endeavor, but I try anyway.

Not that it matters, because each night, Wes *is* there, in the corner booth that used to be mine alone but now seems to belong to both of us, reading his copy of each new library book he's checked out, clicking away at his phone, and bobbing his head offbeat to whatever is playing over the jukebox speakers.

Sometimes we talk. Or, well, he talks, and I listen, because even though I don't find him completely intolerable anymore, my initial assessment was correct, he does have a big mouth. But I like it. I find that I don't mind asking questions about his take on formal education ("I'm taking a gap year next year before college so I know it's what I really want to do") or veganism ("It's honorable, but I don't think I could give up breakfast foods") or his hometown ("I'm from up north, but I think I'm here to stay").

But I never ask him why a seventeen-year-old skater with no coat and an appetite like he hasn't eaten in days comes to a shithole diner at two in the morning every day, and he never asks me back. It's an unspoken agreement between us.

Still, most of the time, we sit together silently. He does whatever he does on his phone, and I play Dictionary Dynamo on mine. Every day I inch closer to the high score, but I never hit the number from the first night I played RegionKidd. The night I threw the game.

"Hey."

I nudge Wes's foot under the table with my boot. He's wearing a Santa hat because tomorrow is Christmas Eve, and he looks cuter than he has any right to look. It's disarming.

"Hey yourself." He smiles that smile from the first day—90 percent dimple—and it makes me feel sort of . . . floaty. I would kick myself for using such a low-yield word if I had any dignity left at all.

"Do you ever feel like you're afraid to move on?" I don't know if I have the words to express what I'm feeling, but I keep going. The thought has sat in my stomach like a rock since that first game. Since I came so close to the end but backed out before I could reach it. "Like, if you cross a finish line of something you've been working toward, there won't be anything waiting on the other side?"

Wes tilts his head to the side and narrows his eyes like he often does when he's thinking. The first time he did it, I felt scrutinized, under a microscope. But now it's reassuring. Like he's taking what I'm saying so seriously that he has to completely dissect it to respond appropriately.

"Yeah, for sure. But, Ferg." He stops to tap his fingers against the tabletop. "We're not supposed to run forever. You gotta get to the other side so you can finally rest."

He slides his hand across the sticky surface until just his pinkie rests on top of mine. His smile is so soft it makes me want to combust. This simple press of fingers is the closest we've ever been, and every nerve ending in my body stands at attention. I smile down at where our fingers are touching and pull out my phone with my other hand.

I don't know what's on the other side, but I decide that maybe he's right; maybe I'm long overdue for a break.

On Christmas morning, Wes and I sit in our usual booth and order CiCi's gingerbread pancake special to split. It's the only time we've ever seen each other in the daylight, and it's almost too much to bear. His eyelashes shine with melted snow droplets and his smile is so gleeful it's almost childlike, and I'm suddenly more aware of the fact that he's the most beautiful boy I've ever seen that I can barely handle it. I didn't get any gifts this morning, but when I look at him and feel his leg pressed up against mine under the table, I think maybe I did. Here. Now.

Wes pulls his phone out like he usually does, and I settle in for our usual routine. Companionable silence and my secret competition. As close to perfect as things have been in a long time.

"I have a confession to make," he says. His head snaps up from his phone and he scratches his neck, suddenly the picture of nerves.

My heart lurches in my chest. This is the moment where he tells me something drastic, like the reason he comes to the diner every night is because of some heinous living situation or that he's moving away, and we'll never see each other again. His face is so serious, I brace myself for the worst.

I swallow around the lump in my throat. I cross my arms over my chest. "What is it?"

"The reason I come to the diner every night is because . . ." He shakes his head and shoves his phone in my direction. "Here. Just look."

On the screen is the home page of the Dictionary Dynamo app. I look between the phone and Wes and back again while I try to catch my breath. A hundred different possibilities run through my head for why he'd be showing me this, and none of them feel good.

"Wes . . ."

"I'm a giant nerd, okay? I play this game every night because I'm trying to beat the high score." He looks out the window and crosses his arms. It's the first time I've ever seen him look self-conscious or even vaguely fearful. I don't get it. Why would this be some big confessional unless he knows that I'm—"It's, like, my biggest obsession. And I sit here every night with you, and all I want to do is talk to you and look at you and, I don't know, like, hold your hand, but I've gotta beat this freaking game first."

I shake my head, but he doesn't stop.

"I like you, Ferg. Like, a stupid amount. I don't want you to think I don't just because I'm always into my phone." He grabs my hands and squeezes them. His face looks nervous as he adds, "The minute I beat this chump who keeps knocking me out of the number one slot, I wanna take you on a real date. At a place with tablecloths and a chef instead of just CiCi slinging pancakes and waiting tables. But I gotta do this first. I just—I have to."

Oh my God.

The strangely colorful vocabulary. The fact that he's from northwest Indiana—otherwise known as the Region. The fact that RegionKidd is always online at the same time as me.

"Wes?"

"Yeah?"

"What would you say if I told you that the word *syzygy* comes from the Latin root -*zygon*?"

It's a strange, almost out-of-the-blue question, but I want him to put the pieces together himself. I want him to remember that first game and just know, the way I did, that he's finally met his match.

"I'd say you know I hate to call you out, Ferg, but the root is actually Greek, so—" He stops. He leans back. His mouth drops open. "Oh my God. You really are Diner Girl."

I smile and shrug. "In the flesh."

I want to add that I think he's brilliant, that his vision for the possibilities on the board is better than any opponent I've ever had, that I've never felt more alive than I do sitting with him at our table every night talking about everything, as we hold each other's fears and joys over plates of lukewarm hash browns, and simultaneously push each other to think harder, more critically, every night on the app. But before I can get the words out, he leans over the table, and cups my cheeks in his hands. I nod once, a silent permission, and he presses our lips together.

Everything in my body is attuned to him, to this moment, to every point we're connected. And when we pull away, we both smile at each other dopily, trying to catch our breath.

Wes picks up his phone and raises his eyebrows in my direction.

"Best two out of three?" he asks.

He smiles and I swear there will never be a word adequate enough to describe how it makes me feel, but I try them all anyway. *Transcendent*. 15 points. *Ebullient*. 11 points. *Loved*. 9 points.

It's beyond words, this sensation blooming in my chest. And for the first time in my life, I'm okay with that.

"I thought you'd never ask."

BETTY'S BEST CRAFT
BY ELISE BRYANT

Here is a list of ten things that I hate:

1. Hot glue gun strings hanging from a finished project

2. When Lois is working the cash register at Craft Cabin and won't let me stack coupons—feeding me some mess about company policy even though Darryl lets me do it all the time!

3. The way my mom always says she'll be home for dinner even though we both know she's never home for dinner

4. How Craft Cabin changed the formula on their store-brand acrylic paint and just expected no one to notice

5. Jhamir Watson

And you know what, I can just stop this list right here because numbers six through ten are all related to number five. Like, Jhamir Watson's stupid fake smile. Or how everyone at Tom Bradley Charter High School fawns over Jhamir Watson as if he's perfect even though he's *definitely not*. In fact, I could probably get all the way to one hundred, listing all the ways that Jhamir Watson is the worst—if I was willing to waste my time like that.

So, when Mr. Richards, my African American history teacher, starts assigning partners for our final project and says that incredibly infuriating name right after mine, I immediately stand up. My chair clatters to the ground and I wince. I wasn't trying to be all dramatic like that, but maybe it was necessary to get this very important point across.

"I can't."

"Excuse me, Miss Green?" Mr. Richards asks, looking up from his list. His thick Bert-and-Ernie eyebrows press together.

"I can't—I can't work—" I sputter out. *"With him!"*

Laughter explodes behind me, and I turn to see Jhamir's friends in the back row covering their faces and falling over in their seats. Jhamir stares at the ground like it's the most interesting thing in the world.

"What did you do, bro? Steal her knitting needles?" Nick Martin calls out, slapping the table. Which is ridiculous because I keep my knitting needles stored in a special carrying case when not in use, and I would *never* tell Jhamir the combination code.

Next to him, Jhamir looks up and just shrugs and gives that fake smile. I know it's fake because his lips are pressed together, hiding the gap between his two front teeth. He's self-conscious about it, so you always know he's really happy when it's on full display, his smile wide and unrestrained. Unfortunately, I know a lot of things about Jhamir.

"The partner list is final, Miss Green," Mr. Richards says, fixing me with one of those scary teacher looks. I swear they take a class on them in teacher school. "Unless you have a serious reason you'd like to share?"

Should I tell him about the Mission-Project Destruction of 2018? Or that this Jhamir sitting behind me is *so different* from the scrawny, silly boy who used to ride up to my house on his scooter that I'm not even convinced it's the same person? No, I can't actually say any of that out loud. Better to quit while I'm ahead and still look mildly rational.

I pick up my chair, sit down, and mumble, "Never mind."

"And, Mr. Martin, we'll talk more about your comments after class today," Mr. Richards says, giving Nick a scary teacher look of his own. There's a chorus of *ooooh*s, and inside I die a little bit. Teachers always think this kind of thing helps the person being bullied, but really it makes it all so much worse.

"As I was saying, this final project is your chance to demonstrate all that you've learned this year about the important, and often overlooked, figures in African American history. It will take the place of your final exam—"

Liana Garrick, who always sits front and center, raises her hand, but doesn't wait for him to call on her. "Can we still take a final exam if we prefer?"

"No, I'm not making one." Mr. Richards smiles. "This is your chance to be creative, to think outside the box. Instead of a traditional exam or essay or PowerPoint, I want you to create something exciting, innovative."

Liana raises her hand again.

"Yes, Miss Garrick?"

"But we can still write an essay? Or make a PowerPoint? Right?"

Mr. Richards' smile gets a lot more strained. "Well, I guess you can, but—"

"Good." Liana locks eyes with her partner, Brandon, and nods with finality.

"While that is an option," Mr. Richards continues, "I'd much rather see you express yourselves creatively. Write a song or a short story, make a short film or a painting. The options are endless. Craft something that only you can!"

My frustration over having to work with Jhamir is still making my chest all hot and tight, but that loosens it, just a bit. *Craft.* I get to craft!

I'm only an average student. If my mom remembered to check my report cards, they'd probably get a "meh" and a shrug before being tossed in the trash. But when it comes to crafting, I've perfected the ultimate papier-mâché recipe, see cross-stitch patterns in my dreams, and could give a presentation on the pros and cons of the top five acrylic paint brands at a moment's notice. Maybe this is my chance to finally shine at school too.

I shoot my hand up. "Will the project rubric assess our craftsmanship? And, like, the overall creativity?"

"Yes, definitely, but it's also about fully representing the person who—"

"Okay, thanks."

I know exactly who I'm going to do my project on. Well, who *we* are going to do our project on, I guess. Jhamir is going to have to just get on board.

"Me and Justin call dibs on Kobe!" Nick calls out. "So all y'all better get ready to lose!"

"This is not a compe—you know what, why don't y'all just get started on this for the last few minutes of class?" Mr. Richards says, pinching the bridge of his nose and walking back to his desk. "I need to take a Tylenol."

I pull out my craft-ideas notebook—not to be confused with my sketching notebook or supply-list notebook—and start brainstorming. It's only been a couple minutes when I feel the presence of someone standing next to me. I don't look up.

"Listen, Betty, I know this isn't ideal," Jhamir starts. His voice is low and solid now, completely absent of the staccato squeaks that used to explode without warning from him when his voice was changing. "But I really need to do well on this assignment. Coach looks at the final semester grades to determine who can play in the fall, and uh . . . I'm not doing so hot right now."

Maybe it wouldn't be the worst thing if he didn't play football anymore. Maybe he would go back to the kid who held my glue gun when applying the finishing touches to our Halloween costumes and thought I was worthy of hanging out with him—instead of the nerd that he barely acknowledges now.

But of course, I'm not going to let *his* issues affect the assessment of *my* crafting ability. I've basically been training for this my whole life.

"We're doing our project on Faith Ringgold," I say, snapping my idea notebook shut. "Can you still sew?"

"Uh, maybe?"

I sigh, shake my head. "Hmmm."

The bell rings, and I stand up, bringing us face-to-face. So much is the same: his deep-set dark brown eyes, the slightly crooked bridge of his wide nose where he broke it trying to do tricks on his scooter. But so much is different too: sparkling studs in his pierced ears, a tiny cut on his chin from shaving (even though this boy has no business shaving).

"Meet me at my house tomorrow after school. I'm assuming you still remember where that is."

He gives me that same closed-mouth smile he gives everyone else, but his eyes are crinkly, warm. I might actually believe it if I hadn't made that mistake before.

Jhamir didn't go from being the person I knew best in the world to my worst enemy overnight. It started out small. It started out with "other plans."

We always went to my house after school. That's just the way it was. It began as a nanny-share between our two, single workaholic parents—law for my mom, investment banking for his dad. But by the time we hit third grade, they said see ya to Gina and decided that we were old enough to lock the doors and fend for ourselves. We struggled through long division. We cooked feasts of pizza bagels. We worked on whatever my latest craft project was. Alone, but together.

Our five days a week went down to four, though, when Jhamir joined the youth football league at the park down the street and had to go to practices. Sometimes he had two practices a week or had to skip hanging out on Fridays for games. And then he started making other plans: beach days with the team, all shuttled in some mom's minivan. Hanging out at Quentin Baxter's huge pool, behind the gates of his fancy neighborhood.

When he *did* come to my house, he was always on his phone. He wasn't as into winding my yarn while I knit scarves for all the residents of the assisted living center on Atlantic Avenue anymore. He barely helped when I decided I wanted to cross-stitch inspirational Ruth Bader Ginsburg quotes.

And then there was the Mission-Project Destruction of 2018.

In California, fourth graders are required to make a model of one of the Spanish missions, these churches that stretch up El Camino Real from one end of the state to another. I don't know why they focus on *that* part of the state's history when there was so much going on here before the Spaniards showed up, but I leaned in. It was a craft challenge. I *live* for craft challenges. And I figured, why make one mission when I could make all twenty-one.

I spent weeks getting every detail just right: researching floor plans, cutting and staining balsa wood, dying moss the perfect shade of green, testing out mixtures of paint and Mod Podge and sand until I had the exact consistency of stucco.

It was a lot, but it's not like I had anything else to do—Mom was working later and later and I couldn't count on Jhamir to show up anymore.

When I walked into school with the finished project in my arms, shining in a sea of Styrofoam and Popsicle sticks, I was proud. But that lasted all of five minutes. Jhamir was tossing a ball back and forth with his friends in the class line, their barely done projects sitting on the ground, and he missed a pass.

Because of him, the football landed right on top of Mission San Juan Capistrano.

The project wobbled in my arms and fell to the ground. I screamed. And then Jhamir fell backward—right on top of the other twenty missions.

Destroyed. Completely.

"Hey, chill. It's not a big deal, Betty," he said as the first tear fell down my cheek. "You can just do one of those premade sets from Craft Cabin tonight. Mrs. Combs won't care as long as you turn something in."

Next to him, his football friends giggled behind their hands. Quentin Baxter didn't even try to hide how he rolled his eyes and mouthed, "Nerd."

I was embarrassed. I was devastated. I felt stupid for caring too much, being too much.

So, I cut Jhamir out of my life completely. He stopped by my house after school. He tried to apologize, lying about how he didn't really mean it like that, how it was all a misunderstanding. But in my head, all I could hear was him saying "chill" as weeks and weeks of my work lay broken on the ground. All I could see was him checking his phone when we were together, looking for something better to do. I wasn't going to give him the chance to hurt me again.

Here is a list of things I made instead of wasting my time with Jhamir Watson:
1. A papier-mâché mask of my own face
2. Approximately one billion yarn pom-poms
3. Felted dolls of the cast of The Fresh Prince of Bel-Air while I binge-watched every single episode
4. An entirely new tie-dyed wardrobe
5. A quilt out of the cut up tie-dyed wardrobe that I was never actually going to wear

I watch Jhamir as he walks up the path to my house.

Five years ago, he was a tumble of lanky limbs, like one of those inflatable guys outside of a car dealership, but now as a freshman, he's solid, sturdy. He looks in the window, making direct eye contact, and I fall backward off the couch, nearly knocking my head on the coffee table. When he rings the doorbell, I count to fifteen before I answer.

"Hi," I say, taking him in. He's wearing gym shorts and socks with his black-and-white Adidas slides. Which makes me self-conscious because after school I changed into a lavender tank dress with a scalloped collar that I crocheted myself. Not because of *him*, just because I wanted to. And I don't want him to think that I care.

"Hey, Betty." He smiles with his teeth. "Your house looks exactly the same."

Is that a compliment? Or, more likely, a subtle insult. Like, we couldn't bother to do anything all these years. But you know what? It doesn't even matter because, *again*, I don't even care.

"Okay."

I turn and walk back into the house. I hear the door gently close behind me and his footsteps as he follows.

"Like, that's the same couch where we'd sit and watch all the new Disney shows on Fridays," he says, not taking a hint. "Gina would always burn the popcorn. Why did she always burn the popcorn?"

"I don't know."

"And, oh man, that's the same stove!" he continues as we walk through the kitchen. "You know that day when you wanted to melt wax to make your own candles, even though we weren't supposed to use the stove? We turned off the alarm, like, milliseconds after it went off. And we thought we were so slick until the fire department showed up and then your mom—oh, she was screaming! Do you remember that?"

I don't get why he's bringing all this up, trying to highlight our shared history. It's not like it matters anymore.

"I remember," I say, staring at the table in the family room instead of him. "So I was thinking we could work here. I don't know if you did any research on Faith Ringgold on your own, but I have a few of her books, to give you an idea of her style—"

"Will your mom be home soon?" He sits down and leans back in the chair, all comfortable. "Or is she still 'making sacrifices in order to give you a better life.'" He holds up his fingers, making air quotes.

I can't help but smile as he drops the standard line both of our parents would use, to justify making us nanny kids, and then later, latchkey kids.

"No, she still works crazy hours, probably worse now since she made partner at the firm." I shrug. "But it's okay. It's her credit card on my Postmates account."

He laughs, showing the gap between his teeth. "Right? I mean, I still love me some pizza bagels, but it's nice to mix it up with some pho or tacos now."

"So your dad's work is the same too?"

"Yep. Like you said, maybe even worse now that he's not worried I'll burn the house down or get kidnapped." He grimaces. "Pretty much the only time I see him for sure is at my games, or the scrimmages in the off-season. He's always front and center for those."

Of course, football. His dad is the one who pushed him to join. I remember his dad used to play, too, in college, before something happened with his knee. I'm glad football brought them together, but it's hard not to think about the fact that it's also what changed everything between me and Jhamir. It's what made him too busy, too cool for me.

"Well, we better get to work," I say, pulling out my idea notebook. "We're wasting a lot of time."

He blinks and cocks his head to the side, examining me in a way that I don't like. Finally, he says, "Okay. What do you have in mind, Betty?"

"Yeah, so, like I said, we're going to do our project on the artist Faith Ringgold. She was pretty prolific—she painted and she made these really beautiful masks too. But she's really well-known for her quilts. She used them to tell stories, about herself and about the Black experience. So, I was thinking we could recreate one of her most famous quilts, like the *Street Story Quilt* or *Tar Beach*."

"The whole Woman on a Bridge series is so dope. I love how you almost feel like you're up there flying with Cassie."

Wait . . . what?

"You looked her up?"

"Of course I did. This is my project too, right? I actually checked out the *Tar Beach* book from the library." He ducks down, pulling it out of his back-pack. "And I'm so down with this idea of making a quilt. But what if—just hear me out here—we make one that tells the story of her life instead of recreating one of hers? Each panel could be something significant . . . like, did you know she got arrested for her art in the seventies? For desecrating the flag, or some shit. It's wild."

I feel my chest getting tight, as all my plans for this project shift and change. It's not that his idea isn't good—I can admit, begrudgingly, that it is. But that just makes me feel even worse. This is supposed to be my chance to shine. To show that this thing that is so nerdy about me, so uncool, has some value after all. Now he's coming around, though, after years away, and stepping in like it's nothing.

"You okay?" he asks, reaching out to touch my arm. So, I guess my existential crafting crisis is all over my face. "Hey, Betty, chill. We can do whatever you want."

Chill. That word has the opposite effect and I feel like my hair is bursting into flames and smoke is shooting out of my ears. Jhamir leans back, as if he can feel the heat coming off me.

"This may not be a *big deal* to you, but it is to me," I whisper, staring at my idea notebook so intently that it's likely to incinerate.

It's so quiet. I don't know if he gets the reference to our fallout. I don't know if he even hears me.

Finally, he says, "We can do it your way, Betty. We always do."

My way? He's the one who left. He's the one who moved on to something cooler.

We work in silence for the next hour, pouring over Faith Ringgold's work to select the perfect piece. But his words are blasting in my head on a loop as I try to figure out exactly what they mean.

Late that night, I'm still thinking about what Jhamir said, even after Mom comes home. I can hear her switch on the Bravo shows she uses to decompress, but they don't drown out his words either. And I'm still thinking of them the next day, through the pop quiz in geometry and Ms. Grundy's dramatic read-aloud of *The House on Mango Street* in Freshman Lit.

So when we meet up at Craft Cabin on Saturday morning, I march right up to Jhamir and launch the question without hesitation. "What did you mean by that? When you said we always do it my way?"

"Are you wearing an apron?" he asks, grinning at me.

"Yeah, this is my Craft Cabin shopping outfit, but—"

"You have a specific outfit for shopping here?"

"It has a lot of pockets. I need to have my hands free so I can properly consider the materials." I cross my arms over my perfectly normal apron. "Now answer the question."

Jhamir lets out a long sigh and runs his hands over his head.

"It's not like I'm still holding onto this or whatever. It's just that, when we were kids . . . I was kinda like your assistant, right? We were at your house every day. We did what you wanted to do. You know, all the knitting and painting and hot glue gunning. And that all was fun. We made some really dope stuff. But also, it would have been nice if we could have done what I was into sometimes too."

"Like football?" I ask.

"Like football," he repeats. "But also, I don't know—just riding around on our scooters or climbing that big-ass tree in your backyard. Not all the time, just sometimes."

I nod, looking down at the ground. It's true that I always picked our activities. And my cheeks get red, remembering so clearly all of a sudden how I would quickly shoot down Jhamir's suggestions, sure that what I had in mind was better. That probably didn't make him feel great. Is that the reason he started looking around for other friends?

"I'm sorry," I say, finally.

And he waves that away. "It's fine. It's old news, and that was kinda low, me bringing it up like that on Thursday."

"It wasn't. I needed to hear it." I clear my throat, stick my hands in my apron pockets. And then take them out real quick, self-conscious. "Should we . . . ?" I motion toward the double doors of Craft Cabin.

"Sure, let's go."

We're greeted by the cool breeze of AC and tinny soft rock drifting from the speakers. This usually brings me immediate peace, like I'm coming home. But I don't feel like I usually do. I can barely even muster a smile in return when Darryl, my stacked-coupon-savior, waves at me from the cash register and points excitedly to the half-off silk flowers in the front.

Jhamir and I trudge over to the fabric aisle, and we consider the options in silence, reaching out to touch the yards of soft fleece and sturdy cotton blends.

He holds up a particularly ugly flannel. "Do you think this—"

"Look. I know I was pushy," I blurt out. "But—but . . . that still doesn't excuse what you did!"

Jhamir blinks, presses his lips together. And I'm thinking I need to explain exactly what I'm talking about because, okay, maybe it's not so normal to be holding onto a five-year-old craft-destruction grudge. But then he nods.

"I know. The missions. I'm so sorry."

"I spent so long on them. I sourced those tiny brass bells from a specialty shop in Barcelona! The shipping alone cost my allowance for a month!"

"I know. It was an accident, but . . . you're right."

"And the worst thing about it, the thing that made me feel so stupid, was that you—you told me to chill! You told me it wasn't a big deal! That no one would care!"

"I was such a dick."

Darryl peeks his head in at the end of the aisle, his face creased with worry, and I realize I'm making a scene but I don't care. I shoo him away and he scatters.

"So then, why? Because there was everything that happened with the project, but . . ." My voice cracks and I hate it. "But you started moving on from me . . . from *us*, way before that. Why did you ditch me just to—to be cool?"

He steps toward me. "It's not an excuse, but I wasn't having the easiest time with the other guys in school. I mean, we were some of the only Black kids there, and I don't know . . . sometimes it's easier to be who they expect you to be. Like the things they expect you to like. In order to survive."

"So football instead of knitting at recess?"

"Yeah, football instead of knitting at recess."

It's true, there were very few Black kids in our elementary and middle schools. It's one of the reasons our parents first bonded and did a nanny-share, setting us up to be friends. And I always felt it—the pressure, the eyes—but still—

"I didn't do that. I didn't—I *don't* care what other people think."

"You don't," he says. "But I wasn't as brave as you."

I've never thought of myself as brave before. Different, yes—and maybe just a tad overzealous. But not brave.

"And your dad liked you playing football," I say, putting it all together. "He came to your games. You saw him more. I guess that must have helped too, huh?"

"Yes, I saw my dad more, but regardless—" He waves that away. "I know it was wrong, how I treated you. I tried to apologize, but . . . I gave up too fast. And I always regretted it. I—I lost my best friend." He reaches forward and takes my hand. "I hope you know how sorry I am, Betty."

I squeeze his hand back. "I'm sorry too. For letting you go so easily."

I look into Jhamir's big brown eyes, and I see the kid I used to know so well—the one who always said yes to my big ideas, who made me feel less alone when my mom had to be somewhere else. But I also see the guy he's become now—who can own up to his mistakes, who can be honest with me when I need it. And then there's the guy he could be—who *we* could be.

"Do you need me to cut some fabric?" asks a gravelly voice. Lois appears out of nowhere in her Craft Cabin polo shirt, wielding sharp scissors and a yardstick like she's going to battle. Jhamir and I drop hands and jump apart, making me realize just how close we were standing.

Jhamir clears his throat. I can't see the blush on his deep brown cheeks, but I can *feel* it. My cheeks are flaming too.

"Um, yeah," he says, reaching forward to brush his fingers across a red-and-yellow Hawaiian print. "I think maybe this one? It's a good match for the border, if we're still gonna remake the first quilt in Woman on a Bridge."

Lois raises her scissors, and panic builds in my chest. "Wait!"

Jhamir and Lois both stare at me with wide eyes.

"I don't think we should recreate that quilt."

"Well, I'm not, like, tied to that one," Jhamir starts, but I cut him off.

"I don't think we should recreate *any* of her quilts. I want to do your original idea. Making our *own* quilt, one that shows all of Faith Ringgold's life. It's a better idea. That's why I had such a hard time accepting it, because I didn't think of it on my own. But I can't let my pride get in the way of us creating the best craft possible. And I think we can make that, Jhamir . . . together."

Jhamir's whole face lights up, smiling so big that the gap between his teeth is on full display. "I know that was hard for you."

"Yes, very out of character. Don't expect it going forward." I press my lips together to hold in my grin.

"Oh, so we're hanging out again?"

"Well, first we have to finish this quilt." I step forward and take his hand again. "And then let's see what happens."

He squeezes mine back. "Okay."

Lois looks between us and then lets out a long and dramatic sigh. "So do you want the fabric or not?"

Here is a list of ten things that I really, really like:

1. *Cutting and arranging fabric, while Jhamir expertly uses my sewing machine like no time has passed*

2. *Letting someone else take the lead for once and having everything, surprisingly, turn out okay*

3. *The view from the top of the tree in my backyard*

4. *The impressed look on Mr. Richards's face when we present our finished project to the class*

5. *Nick Martin's crimson cheeks and gaping mouth when he interrupts our presentation and I tell him to shut up*

6. Going to football games. Who knew there were so many crafting opportunities? Knit beanies in school colors, pennants, hot-chocolate cozies . . . the possibilities are endless!

7. Finally getting the courage to ask my mom to come home for dinner on Fridays, and the way she hugs me and promises to really try

8. Walking hand in hand, with Jhamir, through the Faith Ringgold exhibit at the museum downtown

9. Feeling truly seen and accepted by someone, just the way I am

10. Jhamir Watson

THE PANEL SHOWS THE GIRL
BY AMANDA JOY

[The panel shows the girl (16), hovering above the earth. Her fists are clenched; her mouth stretched wide in a feral yell, calling the strength of an ancient alien bloodline. Her hair is an angry storm of coils, each strand perfectly attenuated, defying gravity and crackling with the electricity racing around her form.]

Three minutes left and still nothing.

I discretely slide my phone into my desk and return to the sketch eating up half my physics notes. I barely make it another fifteen seconds without glancing at the screen again. If Dvorkin catches me texting again this week, there's no way I'm escaping without a detention. However, this is an emergency. Real cataclysmic shit.

I left my sketchbook in my last class. At first I hadn't been too worried about someone looking inside. My friend Jhela has AP English after me, and I sent her approximately fifteen SOS texts begging for a rescue. It's been nearly an entire block period and she hasn't replied yet.

I count to sixty and pull out my phone again. I resist the urge to cheer as an alert pops up.

Jhela: 911. Naomi found it before I got here. :(

That little emoji does nothing to convey the seriousness of the situation. Naomi's name settles like a brick on my chest, snuffing out the relief and leaving only heavy panic.

I cuss loud enough to draw Dvorkin's attention. "Ms. Daniels, your lang—"

The shrill ring of the bell cuts him. I'm at the door before anyone else reacts. Behind me, Dvorkin calls, "I dismiss the class, Ms. Daniels. Not the bell."

I pause at the threshold for a second, debating whether Naomi with my sketchbook is worth a write-up and possible Saturday detention. I decide yes. I'm not going to give Naomi the rest of the day to catalog every embarrassing detail those pages reveal.

I walk as fast as I dare down the hall and up the outdoor path to the English wing. I shove my way through the deluge of bodies hurrying to their next class.

Naturally, Naomi is the first person I see. My heart, which was already throwing itself against my ribs, gives a desperate lurch at the sight of her holding my sketchbook up to her face.

We used to be close. Like, sleepovers-on-a-school-night close. Nothing truly disastrous happened between us. Freshman year she got a girlfriend and I was still too much of a coward to admit my feelings and we grew apart. (Note: my full-tilt sprint to this hallway may or may not indicate I am still a great big coward.)

Coward or not, with time apart, I could finally see the more toxic aspects of our friendship. Like the way she subtly adjusted her personality and interests depending on who was around. Naomi would clown something she knew I loved right in front of me if it meant bonding with some random classmate. When we were alone, we were intensely in sync, sharing entire conversations with a glance. But whenever someone else was introduced to our dynamic, Naomi suddenly deferred to their interests and their sense of humor. It wasn't entirely her fault. I shrink around new people and Naomi blossoms. I would always feel like her sidekick. When she and the girlfriend broke up, I ignored her texts and DMs like she'd ignored mine. Eventually, they stopped coming, and by then, I'd met Jhela and Bevan.

Things have stayed tense between us. Possibly because I can't stop drawing her infuriating face. Blessedly, this year we only share gym and the same lunch period, which hasn't at all influenced my decision to have lunch in the library. (The library has books *and* Ms. Bennet lets us use her microwave and eat in one of the study rooms in the back. Why *wouldn't* I choose the library?)

If not for the small issue of my sketchbook, I would turn on my heel and flee. But as it is, I stare. Naomi's dark braids are piled atop her head in a giant bun, a few strands hanging down to artfully brush her shoulders. A pleated denim skirt falls perfectly on her. She's paired it with a vintage Nike windbreaker, a dangling gold chain with her name in Gothic script, and Jordans the exact same powder blue as the jacket.

Vanessa "Nes" Hawkins, my current crush, stands next to her. Her chin-length cap of curls is inky blue today. Nes's outfit looks like she got it at the same vintage shop as Naomi, but if Naomi's outfit was in the display window, Nes had pulled hers from the $2 bin in the back: stonewashed jeans two sizes too big and a Wu-Tang shirt with a scattering of holes around the bottom.

Before this moment, I would've said Naomi has no idea about my thing for Nes. Now I get the feeling she's well aware. Nes—who barely comes up to Naomi's shoulder—rises up on her toes to see better. Naomi leans into her and tilts the battered sketchbook down so the other girl can see. All while Naomi's eyes are on me.

Thankfully Nes's eyes are glued to the page. She looks almost impressed.

Jhela, dependably late to any gathering, finally makes her appearance a few feet behind Naomi and Nes. She's very Nancy Drew today, in a kelly green plaid skirt and a cream sweater vest.

Jhela's eyes meet mine over Nes's shoulder. She grins and darts forward. She reaches between them and snatches the sketchbook out of Naomi's hand.

"Thanks for this," Jhela says cheerfully. She steps wide around the two, passes the sketchbook to me, and loops an arm through mine. She blinks innocently up at Naomi, whose expression is somewhere between pissed and impressed.

Naomi's eyes narrow, but her smile doesn't waver. "We were admiring your scribblings. How long have you had this one—not since freshman year?"

I shrug, like that *scribbling* dig means nothing. "Something like that."

Jhela lifts her chin. "Amaya's illustrations are amazing."

"Yeah," Nes says, her dark eyes snag mine. "You're really talented."

"Um, thanks, it, uh, passes the time," I say. *Ah yes, completely misrepresent your interests when complimented—that'll get the girl.* "I mean," I add quickly, "I've always loved animation."

"Me too," Nes beams up at me. "That drawing of Principal Rosen as Frieza? In the hover pod? Sick. Maybe you can draw me, I mean, if you have time."

I grin and bite the inside of my cheek to ward off a verifiable swoon. "Sure, I can—"

Naomi cuts in, "What was that show you used to love? *Sailor Moon*? I think you made us watch every episode five times. I was like, you know there are *other* anime to watch . . . but that's how Amaya is with her obsessions. Nothing else exists."

I'm about to remind Naomi of the hundred-thousand-word Tuxedo Mask fanfic she demanded we read aloud and record our own audiobook of one summer, but Jhela says, "Uh, can we go now? Bevan's waiting."

"Sure," I say. "See you in AP Euro, Nes. Later, Omi."

Her eyes widen at the nickname, but she shakes off her surprise. "Wait. Amaya, can you draw me like her? Sailor Moon?"

"I—uh—sure," I manage to stutter out a response. What I really want to know is *why,* but Naomi hooks her arm through Nes's and gives me a wink and a flirty grin. The combined power of the wink and the dimples in each of her cheeks scrambles my thoughts for a good ten seconds.

When I catch up to Jhela, she blows out a sigh. "Ugh, what is with you and Naomi? The energy between y'all is weird and . . . intense! I don't even know how you two were so close without ripping each other's faces off or . . . like angrily making out?"

"Gross, J. Don't put that image in my head!" I mutter. The less time I spend thinking about Naomi, the better.

Bevan's already settled in one of the study rooms in the back of the library. Behind their full lunch tray, sticker-covered laptop, and two stacks of books, all I can see of Bevan is their hair. It's buzzed low and dyed a peachy pink already fading into not-quite rose gold.

"Sorry we're late," Jhela says as she drops into the chair across from Bevan. "Amaya had drama with Naomi."

"Good to know you can still be counted on to exaggerate a single conversation, J," I snort, sitting in the other chair between them.

Bevan looks up from their book and raises a single brow.

"It wasn't drama," I say, then flip open the sketchbook, while Jhela explains what happened. It takes three pages to find the first drawing of Naomi.

At first glance, you wouldn't know it's her, what with the antlers I drew growing from her forehead. A strand of roses is woven through the jutting bones, prongs sticking out like thorns. I can't even remember when I did it. I use my sketchbook anytime staying focused on a lesson alone becomes impossible, which is pretty often. Otherwise time slows to a crawl, and I get caught up in elaborate daydreams until the bell rings and I've missed whatever homework was assigned.

Some of my teachers tolerate it once I've explained; others don't. Maybe if I'd gotten my ADHD diagnosis when I was a kid and not during the terrible summer between freshman and sophomore year, it would be easier to get accommodations. My mom tried, but to the admin, my past grades are proof I don't need them. You'd think a brief period of inpatient treatment for major depressive disorder would be proof against that sort of logic, but nope.

Jhela and Bevan's conversation fades into background noise as I consider the pages. Most are filled with our classmates, a few I've known since kindergarten. Warmth spreads up my neck and my head feels light as I count the twenty-plus sketches of Naomi. She probably thinks I still have a thing for her. Which I very much do not.

Bevan senses my rising panic. "So are you going to do it? You've been waiting for an opportunity with Nes."

Their expectant looks make me glad I never told them specifics about Naomi and me. They'd pounce on it like wolves. It's a relief to think about Nes's upturned nose and green-gray eyes. Nes who liked my Principal Frieza drawing and didn't cringe at watching hours of *Sailor Moon*. Nes who I at least hope wouldn't drop me as soon as someone shinier came along.

I try to project confidence. "I'll draw Nes, definitely. Naomi . . . I'll have to find a way to put her off. If I avoid her for a while, she'll forget."

Because no matter what, I'm never drawing Naomi Davidson again.

It's with great shame that I slide the envelope across the—regrettably sticky—lunch table two days later to Naomi. "There."

She looks up, shocked at my sudden appearance. "Wow, so you finally remembered where the lunchroom is?" she snorts, though the insult lacks her usual bite. She spots the envelope and her smirk turns impish. "A gift? For me?"

I roll my eyes. The one with Nes's name scrawled across the top remains in my back pocket. I'd decided to get Naomi over with first, but now I wish I'd gone straight to the library.

Naomi reaches for it, but Elijah Priest, sitting across from her, gets there first.

"Hey! Eli!" Naomi protests, but he ignores her and pulls out my drawing of Naomi as Sailor Venus—not Sailor Moon as she'd requested—with long ombré box braids, her legs stretched across a bright yellow motorcycle.

Elijah whistles, "Ay, Daniels, this is sick. Naomi said you could draw! I didn't know you were raw like this. Can you make one for me? I'll Venmo you!"

"Naomi said—what?" I glare at her. The smugness rolls off her like noxious fumes.

"Yeah, do one for me like you did Naomi—only, you know *Death Note*, right? That frog-demon looking MF?"

Out the corner of my eye, I see Naomi's smirk, pleased to find me at a loss. But the rest of it doesn't track: Why would Naomi brag about *me*?

Elijah gets drowned out by a second request and then a third. Time goes funny again, because before I can process everyone's sudden interest, I'm sitting next to Elijah, who pulls out his phone and starts taking down the requests. And it's Elijah, not me, who determines my rate: twenty-five bucks a pop. When I try to lower the price, Elijah reassures me that we should keep it high, seeing as, if the demand continues, he plans to start charging me a small finder's fee. Naomi rarely joins the conversation, but I can tell she's listening.

By the time I extricate myself, I have a list of a dozen commissions.

I shove open the door to our meeting room in the library. Jhela and Bevan are already packing their bags. "What are you doing, we still have like fifteen minutes of lunch?"

Bevan glances at their watch. "Twelve minutes actually. And you know we have to get to North Campus."

"Shit, you're right, I'm sorry. I had to stop by the lunchroom and—"

Jhela cuts in, "More Naomi drama, I'm assuming?"

"I mean, not drama but—"

"You can tell us in gym later, then," she says, hiking her backpack over one shoulder.

Bevan offers me a quick smile. "Any luck with Nes? Did she like it?"

I cover my face with my hands. I completely forgot about Nes. I retrace my steps and head back to the cafeteria. I find Nes by her blue hair, which is picked out and in two fluffy pigtails today. The gold studs in her ears gleam beneath the lunchroom's atrium ceiling. I take the envelope from my back pocket and resist the urge to smooth it between my palms.

"Hey, famous," she says as she takes it. "Thought you forgot about me. Seems like Eli has you booked for months."

"I doubt everyone will actually want or pay for one. They'll move on as soon as Naomi does." I don't add, *hopefully by tomorrow.*

"Well, looks like you're in trouble then," says Nes. "She hasn't stopped talking about you since she saw your sketches."

I shake my head because that can't be right. Naomi clearly hasn't told Nes our history. Naomi's the one who dropped me. Even if my sketchbook made her reconsider, it won't last.

"Don't worry, she'll go back to ignoring me soon."

Nes cocks her head and citrusy perfume rolls off her skin. "What do you mean? Naomi really likes you."

"Er, no, trust me, Naomi can't stand me."

Nes stares hard at me, like she's waiting for a punch line. When I say nothing, she laughs. "No, trust *me*, Amaya. I would know." She peers into the envelope and pulls out the drawing of her as San from *Princess Mononoke.*

"Thanks for this." She gives my hand a squeeze before skipping down the hallway.

I barely notice, stuck on her words. *Naomi really likes you.*

A week has passed since I left my sketchbook in AP English and I'm already looking forward to early retirement. In the days since, I've done five commissions; meanwhile, I missed two more library lunches, and last night, I completely spaced on group therapy with Bevan.

Seventh-period gym is the best class on my schedule this year because it's the only class I have with Bevan and Jhela and because the final period is always reserved for Mrs. O'Keefe's Outdoor Ed class. Last week we all aced our assessments on building fires and Mrs. O'Keefe is finally letting us take canoes out onto the BioPond.

"Bevan Thorne, Naomi Davidson, Vanessa Hawkins, and Amaya Daniels, you're up next. Wait for my whistle!"

I groan. Hearing my name in the same group as Naomi makes me strongly consider asking to go to the nurse. But O'Keefe's a spry, gray-blond sexagenarian marathon runner with a gimlet eye for attempts to skip her class.

Naomi strides ahead of us, Nes trailing half a step behind. I try to meet Bevan's eyes, but they're looking back at Jhela, probably sending SOS brainwaves.

When we reach the canoes, Naomi starts directing us, which is typical. The canoes hang atop a half-rotted wooden structure.

"All right, let's go under," Naomi says after she picks out our boat. No one argues; Bevan and I take one end, lifting it above our heads, while Nes and Naomi take the other.

Nes and Bevan sit inside, while Naomi and I push them out into the shallow, muddy water. Unlike me, in sodden Keds, Naomi's wearing knee-high neon-green rain boots and another one of those mini-backpacks of the exact same hue. If I were drawing her, I'd make her box braids chartreuse and weave daisies through them so they looked like flowering vines.

We're nearly up to our knees when Naomi announces, "I'm coming in." She hops gracefully into the boat. I attempt a similar move, only when I clutch the edge and throw my legs over the side, the canoe heaves back and forth, my momentum carrying us further out into the pond. Water laps over the edge, soaking our feet.

"Sorry, shit, sorry!" I blurt when the canoe settles. "I didn't mean to—to nearly dunk us. I'm sorry, I'm terrible on land, so I don't know why I thought water would be any better. I'm so sorry!"

"It's fine," Nes says. "Really."

"I know, but still, I'm so—"

Naomi finally turns to me. "Relax, Amaya. We get it, you're sorry. Try not to jump again, you know, since we're in a boat and who knows what's in this water."

Bevan looks up, glaring. "No need to be rude."

"I'm not being rude," Naomi fires back. "I'm telling her we get it. She'll guilt-trip herself for hours, or don't you know that? Aren't y'all supposed to be friends?"

"Um, let's not fight," Nes says, looking between Bevan and Naomi.

Bevan ignores her and cocks their head at Naomi. "Yeah, we are friends. What, are you jealous now?"

"What do I have to be jealous of, Bevan?" Naomi asks. "Lunch in the library? Psh."

"See, it's weird you know that. Maybe jealous isn't the right word. I'm thinking *obsessed* fits better?"

Naomi lets out an actual growl and lunges toward Bevan.

I grab the back of her shirt and manage to yank her back down. I raise my voice, trying to head off any more arguing. "Er, since we're talking about *me*, can I say I don't think any of us are obsessed with *anyone* present—and we should probably get rowing—"

"I am not," Naomi grinds out, "obsessed. I was being *nice* to make up for what I said the other day. I know that Sailor Moon comment pissed you off. But the sketches were good, so I mentioned them to a few people."

I laugh, but there's no joy in it. "Next time apologize instead of telling *everyone* about something I didn't even freely share with you."

She rears back, hurt. A rosy glow begins to radiate from her skin. "Thanks for reminding me why I stopped trying with you at all. I knew you'd act like this."

"How, Naomi? You don't know me anymore. You haven't known me for two years."

"Exactly." Her hands, balled into fists, shake at her sides. She looks at me and when her eyes begin to glow, I feel the first stirrings of true fear. Nothing could have prepared me for what comes next: the scattered clouds overhead *part*. Literal sunbeams wrap around Naomi's body like a glittery shroud. When one of her hands shoots up into the air, and Naomi's neat, short nails lengthen and begin glittering iridescent light, I know exactly what's happening.

I've seen it a hundred times. I've seen every episode of *Sailor Moon*, in Japanese and dubbed in English. I know an instant before it materializes in her hand; the glowing item she's clutching is Venus's wand.

"Venus Crystal Power Makeup," Naomi cries.

We've drifted almost to the center of the pond, and overhead, Naomi twists through the air, her braids cast out in an arc behind her as they turn from black to wheat blond. I yell at Nes and Bevan, "Start rowing, we need to get off the water. Now!"

"What the hell is happening," Bevan says.

An odd sense of calm washes over me. "It's hard to explain and we need to *go*. Now."

Nes adds, "Amaya drew a picture of Naomi as Sailor Venus and I'm pretty sure somehow she's turning into her? Or maybe we all *did* fall into the pond and the afterlife is one big ponderous hallucination?"

I'm about to ask why I am the only one thinking of an exit strategy when Naomi shouts, "Venus Love-Me Chain."

"Seriously?" Nes mutters. "She knows the attacks?"

What looks like a glowing whip of yellow heart emojis lashes out, snapping the side of the boat. We go tilting again but hunker low to stay in the boat.

"The drawing," Bevan asks, a frantic edge to their voice. "Do you think she still has it?"

"What?" I gasp, trying to keep a hand on each side of the hull.

Bevan crouches, scuttling through the canoe's watery interior, until they find Naomi's neon backpack. Nes and I duck at the cry of wind overhead, signaling the chain's impending arrival.

"Get down, Bevan!" A second later, the chain wraps around my arm. My hand feels like it's been dunked in boiling water.

I scream as the chain grows taut, lifting me until my toes dangle a foot in the air above the canoe. Then Bevan, a look of pure triumph in their eyes, pulls a neatly folded piece of paper out of Naomi's bag. They unfold it and Nes gasps, "The drawing! Of course!"

I hear the sound of paper ripping. Instantly, the pressure and heat on my arm disappears. I crash to my knees; the pain of bone striking steel makes everything go white for a second.

When my vision clears, Naomi's splashing in the BioPond and she no longer glows with planetary power.

I could kiss Bevan for that.

Nes must think the same thing, because she throws her arms around

Bevan's neck, and plants several kisses on their cheeks. "Genius. You saved us."

Spots of pink appear on Bevan's golden brown face.

"What the hell happened? How did I get in the water?" Naomi asks.

Only once we help her back onto the boat do we hear the alarms coming from the nearest building.

Mrs. O'Keefe has screamed her throat raw by the time we make it back to shore.

She holds up her radio. "I don't know what's going on inside, but they're evacuating everyone to the north parking lot." She claps her hands. "Make haste!"

Jhela, who'd been standing a few feet back with all of our bags, immediately starts grilling us as soon as O'Keefe is out of earshot. "What happened with you all out there? All I could see was the four of you arguing, then all this sunlight started beaming through the clouds at the same moment the alarms went off. Next thing I could see was Naomi wading in the damn BioPond—what the hell went down?"

I let Bevan fill her in and tune out the rest of their whispered conversation, not wanting to relive it. Though I do notice Naomi listening in with wide eyes.

We trail O'Keefe back up the hill. The doors to the nearest building are open, and a steady tide of students and teachers all stream out toward the long path to the north end of campus.

We keep walking, until I realize—

And I stop, fear rooting me in place. "I did five commissions."

Bevan looks at me. "You don't think?"

"Maybe what happened with Naomi is happening to others?" I say.

"That's probably why the whole school is being evacuated! I need to go inside and stop it."

Naomi shakes her head. "No way, it's too dangerous. Didn't you draw Jared riding Shenron? How do you propose we slay a wish-granting, all-powerful god-dragon?"

We all turn to gape at her.

"I know some things." She shrugs, looking uncomfortable.

"We have to destroy the drawings," Bevan says. "We can do that, at least."

"Well, what we *should* do," Jhela says, "is call up the firefighters probably on their way here and tell *them* how to vanquish the bad guys."

"You know they won't believe us. Let's go," I say, though I want to throw up. When Naomi's eyes meet mine, she gives me a tight nod, like she gets it. We did this, and we're going to fix it.

The sounds of battle cries and loud crashes lead us to the cafeteria. We nearly jump out of our skin when see it—a seven-foot-tall monster with bulging eyes and a nondescript black notebook in its clawed hand. Jhela lets out a piercing shout, and grasps my arm, trying to pull me backward. Once my heart is back in my throat, I notice finer details, the way his skin is brown and not deathly white, and the topknot of locs bleached nearly white.

"Elijah?"

He grins. "Finally someone recognizes me, though it'd be better you ran screaming. I swear Darius is going to bring the building down. I've been running through the halls, trying to scare off anyone left. You should go, by the way."

"Uh, about that. Naomi kind of got transformed into Sailor Venus—but Bevan ripped up the drawing and she changed back! So we need to find the other five sketches. Crisis averted, school saved, rah-rah?"

Everyone turns to gape at me. Finally, Elijah/Ryuk says, "Ah, I'm not sure that'll work. Once you get a look inside, you'll see why."

Elijah/Ryuk checks if it's clear. After a second, he waves us forward.

Aside from the row of lunch tables turned over on their sides, it barely looks like the cafeteria. Piles of rubble blanket the floor and a cloud of dust hangs in the air, coating my mouth in chalky bitterness.

"What the heck?" I whisper-yell. "Who did all this?"

"Ah, well. It started before I got here, a big fight in the lunchroom. I was in the hallway and decided to check it out. I tried to force my way in, and someone hit me. All I remember after that is being pissed and suddenly I've grown taller by two feet. That's when I spotted the real fight. Angelica Valez was friggin' earthbending, grabbing bricks off the walls, and flinging them at Darius. Course, I wouldn't have even known it was him if she hadn't been yelling at him to calm down."

"Where is he now?" I breathe. Darius, who I drew as Naruto at his most overpowered—Six Paths Sage Mode. Enough power to annihilate a small planet. Great.

The crunch of gravel underfoot is our only warning before a swirling energy blast flies right above our heads and strikes the wall, making a hole three feet wide. We sprint toward the nearest overturned lunch table and crouch behind it.

"So, you see," Elijah whispers, "that plan y'all have isn't going to work. We go out there and start searching, he'll take us out, one by one."

"What if you draw something new? Someone who can beat him, some weapon that can help us," Bevan suggests, breathless.

It's not a bad idea, but . . . "Anyone who can beat Darius will bring the building down on our heads." Still, I look inside my bag for the sketchbook, because what other options do we have?

Another blast whizzes overhead, but this time, it strikes, catching the edge of the table Bevan and Nes lean against. Bevan grits their teeth and shakes it off, but Nes jumps to her feet with a vicious yell. We stare as a wolf pelt materializes on her back. She slams the butt of a spear into the ground and holds up a dagger in the opposite hand. "Come and fight me then," she screams, with all the wild confidence of the wolf-reared princess whose guise she wore. She looks truly fierce with the mask resting atop her head, pelt on her shoulders, and bloodstained spear cast out behind her.

Guilt knifes through me. They can't fix my mess because it isn't fixable. The solution strikes me then. This problem, this day, is too complex to be solved by one omnipotent character. That'll only create new problems. Today has to be erased completely, like it never happened.

I know what I need: time. A memory tugs at me from a movie I've seen just once, *The Girl Who Leapt Through Time.* I turn to one of the last untouched pages in the sketchbook and press my pencil to it.

Every time an image comes to mind, Darius/Naruto lets out a wordless yell and my pencil jumps across the paper.

"I can't concentrate in here," I groan, ripping out a failed attempt. I close my eyes and try to visualize what I need to draw, but another attack whizzes past and yanks me from my reverie.

"Nes, do you have your headphones hidden somewhere in that furthing?" Naomi asks.

Nes, busy hovering protectively over Bevan and Jhela, blinks at Naomi, uncomprehending. "Headphones!" Naomi repeats, voice going shrill as another blast passes overhead.

The fog clears from Nes's eyes, and after rummaging through her "furthing," she pulls out her headphones, the cord connected to her phone. Naomi hands me the headphones and scrolls for a minute before the opening notes of the soundtrack to my favorite movie, *Howl's Moving Castle,* begin to play. It's so familiar, so bright and cheery, and so unlike our current disaster; I immediately sink into it. My panic recedes bit by bit, until I can breathe. Until the pencil in my hand steadies and my vague memory of the movie begins to fill out.

I know what I must do; dread churns in my stomach. In the movie, the main character masters time through a brush with death. If this strange ability to turn my drawings into reality, if it misinterprets my intentions, if, if—I shake my head and turn up the music, drowning out my spiraling thoughts. Better not to think too long on accidentally killing myself. Naomi's warm shoulder presses into mine and it's exactly the reminder I need.

I don't know how much time passes as I fall into the drawing. It could be two minutes or two hours. When I feel the rumbling from Darius/Naruto flinging out attacks, I work even faster, knowing Bevan, Naomi, Nes, and Jhela won't be safe until I do this.

Finally, I yank out the headphones and stare down at the page, thankful for the spare mid-2000s style.

[The panel shows a girl (me), brown-skinned, long-limbed, and thick around the waist, on a bicycle, the brakes of no use, as she flies straight into the path of an oncoming train. The second panel shows her tossed from the bike, while the train heads straight for her, a tragic death imminent.]

I climb to my feet. "Whatever you see, don't try to stop me."

Before anyone can offer a word of protest, I run through the maze of overturned lunch tables, around smoldering lunch trays and rubble strewn across the floor.

I spin around at the sight of movement in one corner in time to see Darius/Naruto forming a whirling ball of air between his hands. His coat looks woven of the brightest, hottest fire and his eyes show no recognition. As it flies from his fingers, his eyes burn with orange-red fire, and from his expression, you'd think I'm a resurrected evil shinobi come to destroy his village.

Something between sobbing and laughter escapes me and then the blast hits.

Three more minutes.

I look down at my phone screen. Memories from a week that haven't even happened yet crash into me. I nearly jump to my feet, adrenaline still pumping. I take a deep breath before raising my hand. I ask to be dismissed early. Dvorkin writes me a pass.

When I reach my English class, Ms. Dellaria waves me in. "Did you forget something, Ms. Daniels?"

"Yes, sorry to interrupt." She shrugs and gestures as if to say, *By all means, go ahead.* Naomi sits at my desk, the sketchbook open in front of her. She shuts it as soon as I get to the desk and hands it to me. I note the warmth high on her cheeks and hold the image in my mind so I can draw her the moment I'm alone.

"Thanks, Omi!" I retrieve the sketchbook and give her a smile and a wink, not unlike the one she gave me on a very different version of this day. Nes, at the desk behind her, waves.

I leave the room, still a few minutes before lunch begins. The rush of relief leaves my eyes burning. If anyone sees me crying on my walk to the library, I don't notice. Moving on autopilot, I settle down at the table in our study room, wipe my face, sharpen my pencil, and turn to a fresh page.

SPIRIT-FILLED
BY JORDAN IFUEKO

When Romilly Agboro imagined the Almighty, she never saw a face. Just a brown forehead that smoothed in approval or deepened with disappointment, depending on how her daily deeds added up. Her job, she had known from a young age, was to banish even the smallest wrinkle from that forehead. Her whispered prayers and *Sorry, Mom*s and worship songs pressed up, up, like fingers to God's sagging brow, and when it worked, she felt him beaming—warmth rushing over her like the heat from her mother's ionic blow-dryer.

She would make God smile later. She really would, but—

This novel was getting really good.

As Romilly read a feminist fantasy tome in the Sunday school supply closet, she clung stubbornly to the comfort that she hadn't told a lie. Not technically. Lies saddened God, followed closely by crop tops, and pop music, and evolution—so she'd been told. The tears of a depressed God scared Romilly much more than the threats of an angry one. Hellfire warnings from her Nigerian parents had lost their sting after fifteen years: God's wrath synced suspiciously often with parental bad moods. But under the lectures of sandy-haired Youth Pastor Brett, his pale sunburnt neck flushing with pathos, Romilly's fantasies of a God who *wasn't angry, just disappointed* sprouted weeds of guilt in her stomach, strangling every worldly temptation.

The benevolent maker of the universe, suffering? Because of *Romilly*?

The idea made her wilt, like the roses outside her family's condo, beaten by the dry SoCal sun.

She had checked out *I, Adaline: Peasant Queen* almost two weeks ago, smuggling it home like a bomb strapped to her chest. Her crossed arms had held it in place beneath her sweater, laminate binding clammy against her bare skin as her mom picked her up from the library. Today, she had carried it to church the same way, a plan that wouldn't have worked on a Sunday. Her mother still insisted she wear dresses to Sunday Morning Worship, and books didn't lie flat beneath Target jersey maxis. But today was Tuesday Morning Women's Prayer, and when she'd tagged along to church, watching her mother disappear into one of the Scripture-muraled meditation rooms, Romilly's overalls had hidden her contraband just fine.

Precariously stacked shelves pressed into Romilly's back as she sat on the threadbare closet floor, devouring the pages of *I, Adaline*. The Sunday school supply closet was safer than her room at home, where her seventy-year-old Auntie Eghosa could burst in any moment. The room smelled of stale goldfish crackers and old apple juice, the sickly sweet scent of her childhood. She had decided against closing the door completely. That would look suspicious if anyone walked in on her, and so she'd jammed a rubber wedge in the doorframe, letting the faint pulse of a drum set waft in from the ThisLyfe Church's sanctuary, rooms away. Romilly chewed absently on the end of one of her black Kanekalon braids. It was a habit, she knew, that she was too old for at fifteen, but the plastic crunch of extensions between her teeth could calm her when nothing else did.

God wouldn't be super bummed about *I, Adaline*. Right?

She hadn't told her parents that she *wouldn't* read in the supply closet. And while, technically, Mom and Dad would forbid her from reading *Adaline* . . . they didn't know it existed. So there: lying and disobedience avoided.

Please don't be sad, she thought to her beloved Great Forehead. Surely this was mild-wrinkle-only material.

The content of *Adaline* was harder to justify. Impossible, really, but

Romilly knew how to appease the acid guilt in her stomach. She only had to acknowledge the bad parts. It was a ritual she had mastered with her contraband library books, plucking out the dangerous parts and arranging them into neatly labeled piles, like a deconstructed salad bar of sin. If she named them, then God would know she knew better, and indulge the rest of the good bits—the melancholy adventures of Adaline, with her dragons and torturers and star-crossed love affairs. Adaline *did* things. Her life had meaning beyond the walls of her parents' house, or the white, sun-wrinkled faces of a suburban SoCal community.

I am undone, the latest chapter began. *Annieve's herb garden has been trampled. In the twilight, forest sprites float among the ruins, silver light waxing and waning, as though trembling in mourning. Only the juniperwort and gazelle's fern remain unharmed—the herbs my sister uses for conjuring the future. "Tell me," I whisper into their twisting leaves, "who violates my sister's garden, her only joy? Who in the name of Mother Earth could hate her so?"*

Witchcraft, Romilly labeled dutifully. Annieve was practicing magic, and magic was demonic. With practiced discipline, Romilly shut out the part of her heart that ached for shy Annieve, a girl who sang to plants and whispered secrets into the ground, surrounded always by her silent, sprouting friends.

Who in the village would betray my sister so savagely? The other villagers, in their ignorance? The duke and his men feed lies to the people, keeping us weak and ignorant. Now I know I must defy him. Praise the Mother—I'll ride before his tower with my head held high, rallying the people to rise, rise against ignorance. Against tyranny.

People should submit to authority, Romilly paraphrased. Romans 13:1. Only—

This one had always confused her. Rick Santo-Garcia, the head pastor of ThisLyfe Church, quoted this verse when Black people were on the news with picket signs, flashing slogans like NO JUSTICE, NO PEACE and

ALL COPS ARE BASTARDS—or when headlines described migrants on the border—men, women, and children being marched through barbed wire fences, their hands up.

But if it was wrong to defy power with picket signs and border-crossing, Romilly wondered . . . why did Pastor Rick hold Men's Practice at the shooting range every Saturday?

"Gotta be ready, saints," he always said, flashing his square, stadium-floodlight smile. "The folks up there in the liberal government? Well, they're always trying to disarm us believers. You know why they want our guns, right? 'Cause they want us helpless. Sitting ducks they can keep in line. Well, if they think that . . . they've got another think coming!"

Once, she'd brought up the contradiction to her parents. They had merely shrugged. Despite being staunch Republicans, the Agboros' stance on patriotism leaned toward apathy. Much to Romilly's relief, they held no desire to defend American honor with a gun. Her family had immigrated for McMansions, gold-trimmed cars, and consistent electricity—not a love affair with the stars and stripes. But they also seemed to think that most problems that plagued the average Black American could be solved if they just "pulled their pants up" and "stayed in school."

Ironically, the Bible didn't have much to say on pants or school. But it had a lot to say about tyrants. And so, incidentally, did *I, Adaline.*

Only Mother and Grandfather know of Annieve's gift. The only other person is . . . My breath catches. It couldn't be Brennan. He would never trample my Annieve's garden, not days after kissing me on the castle wall. My breath catches when I think of his lips on my collarbone, his strong, calloused hands running down my—

Premarital sex, Romilly noted, feeling lightheaded as her eyes ran over the steamy paragraph. Reading about *silky skin* and *wet ecstasy* mere rooms away from the church sanctuary might be enough to crease the Divine

Forehead forever. *Adaline and Brennan shouldn't be doing that*, Romilly thought, and hungrily read on.

Brennan would never betray me so, I decide at last. Perhaps I will wed him, someday, so long as he realizes I will have no master. I will never curtsy to any lord, be he king or husband.

Wives should submit to husbands, Romilly thought automatically. But this idea, too, always pricked uneasily, like tights straight out of the dryer, pills itching on her thighs. Maybe that just meant she wasn't ready. Someday, she'd *like* submitting to a husband—or at least, that's what Heather, Youth Pastor Brett's pixie-faced wife, always said.

"It's just how God made us," Heather had said on the Girls Purity Retreat this summer.

The youth group girls sat in a circle on the cabin floor, hugging pillows and scooping up fistfuls of popcorn. Every night, they had read from a book called *God's Perfect Fairytale*. On the cover, a white man in a fedora offered his hand to a beaming white woman with wavy yellow hair. According to the Christian publishers of North America, godly women were often blond. They also liked holding mugs of coffee, and stood laughing in a lot of wheat fields.

"Men were made to lead, and women were made to follow. That doesn't mean you don't have a voice, of course!" Heather laughed, straightening her golden ponytail. She had dyed it with bright blue streaks, to show she *wasn't afraid to have fun*. "But the happiest marriages—the ones that last—are ones where the woman lets the man be the leader he's meant to be."

Romilly had raised her hand. "Not to be mean. But. What if the man's . . . well. Stupid?"

The cabin burst into gasps and giggles. Her face burned. Romilly couldn't help but compare this evening to the one she had spent at another retreat—

a teen camp hosted by her county library. No one had giggled when she spoke then. Instead, faces glowed like hers, rapt as she read passages aloud from the week's chosen fantasy epic. And the camp had been sponsored by Mount Conejo University, which had one of the fanciest writing programs in SoCal—the only reason Romilly's parents had allowed her to attend.

"Not to be mean," she repeated. "But what if he isn't good at his job? Or if he's a crappy dad, or just doesn't know as much as you do? How do you, uh, submit then?"

"That," Heather said, raising a knowing finger, "is when you pray. Build him up. You make sure you're his number one cheerleader. And when he comes out on top? Your marriage is that much stronger."

Romilly had nodded quickly, though her eyebrows inched together. Her hand shot up again, as though with a life of its own. "Sorry. Um—but what if he can't admit that he's done anything wrong? What if he keeps screwing up, over and over again?"

For a moment, Heather's lips had thinned into a pink glossy line, as though Romilly was being difficult. Then she had exhaled and smiled.

"Great question, Romilly. And that's why it's so, *so* important for us ladies to pick a man who loves the Lord," she said, staring seriously around the circle. "It's so sad when we get ourselves into situations that hurt the heart of God."

Romilly wondered why men, if God's chosen leaders, depended so heavily on the virtue of women to make good choices themselves. She had asked God why but had never received a true answer. Only a strange, listening warmth, like a sigh at her ear. Sometimes, between waking and dreaming, she could have sworn the sigh held a word, rolling over and over like a leaf on the wind.

Ask.

Ask.

Ask.

But then again, she'd always had an overactive imagination.

Footsteps sounded outside the supply closet, making Romilly jump. The drawling surfer voice of Youth Pastor Brett floated through the closet door—he was standing outside, just a few feet away on his cell phone. Romilly froze, sweat trickling down the starched Peter Pan collar of her blouse . . . until she realized he hadn't seen her.

"So we're good for the weekend?" murmured Pastor Brett. His voice was low and intimate, and so Romilly knew he was talking to Heather, his "smokin' hot" wife. "I told you babe, Palm Springs. Unbelievable weather . . ."

Romilly bounced the book on her knee, frowning. She couldn't focus while he stood there, and she had to finish *I, Adaline* by Wednesday: tomorrow. Wednesdays were when Romilly's mother dropped her off at the Las Ranas City Library, allowing Romilly to pick out new books and, more importantly, return books without her mother seeing what she'd borrowed.

Once, on a non-Wednesday, she'd made the mistake of telling her mother that a book would soon be due.

"Just give it to me," Patience Agboro had said, her Yoruba accent clipping the words. "I'll drop it off on my way to the hair supply store." Romilly had turned to stone. She imagined the cover of her due book, *Isn't It Necromantic,* which featured a beautiful Black teen girl bracing a dagger in one hand and reaching up with the other to receive a cup of bubbling green liquid from a shirtless boy in a crimson skull mask. Forget necromancing—the look of fearful disgust that would disfigure her mother's face would send any undead army straight back into its grave.

Romilly had mumbled some excuse about mistaking the due date. Then she'd smuggled the book back the following Wednesday, narrowly avoiding losing her library card to the holy fervor of Patience Agboro.

Until Romilly turned sixteen, her library card maintained Youth Patron status. So on certain cursed occasions—such as an unreturned book—her mother received emails on Romilly's behalf. If Romilly didn't return *I, Adaline* to the library tomorrow, then at 8 a.m. on Thursday morning, Patience Agboro would receive a chillingly detailed email containing Romilly's borrowing history. If that happened, she could kiss her library card—her lone portal to worlds like Adaline's, with revolutions, and adventures, and girls who lived beyond their roles to other people—goodbye.

So Pastor Brett needed to finish this stupid phone call. Now.

"Look," he continued, his voice still tentative. "I know, I know. But we need this. I need *you*." He paused, then his voice cheered up. "Great. You're gonna love it. Thursday night. Uh-huh. Yup. All weekend. Okay. See you there."

Romilly sagged with relief as the conversation ended . . . only for terror to race up her spine when steps approached the supply closet.

She flung the book behind a box of felt puppets, springing to her feet with the practiced agility of a homeschooled teen with West African parents. When Pastor Brett pushed open the closet door, Romilly was busily adjusting the dusty plastic boxes, hoping the thud of her heartbeat didn't echo down the church halls.

She purposely took a moment to turn around, as though she'd been so absorbed in her task, she couldn't possibly have been eavesdropping . . . or reading sin-tillating novels.

"Oh. Hey there, Roms," Pastor Brett said. He had stiffened in the doorway, then softened, choosing to believe Romilly's distant, totally-wasn't-paying-attention-to-your-phone-call smile.

"Hey," she chirped. "Just, um, getting candy to give the littles. Prizes for the Bible Quiz Fair. Have you seen the box? I've looked everywhere but I can't . . ."

He seemed to relax the longer she prattled, running a hand though his short, sun-bleached hair. "Ah. No problem-o," he said, reaching to pull a box down from a shelf and placing it in her arms. "Thanks for helping out the kiddos. God sees that servant heart of yours." He winked at her, and she nodded a few too many times before fleeing the closet, box of Jolly Ranchers in tow.

Only then did Romilly remember *I, Adaline: Peasant Queen* . . . right when Pastor Brett exited the supply closet, locking the door firmly behind him.

So what I'm not going to do, Romilly lied, *is panic.*

She dried her sweaty palms on her overalls. Okay. Keys. She knew where to find spares: the front office, just past the meditation rooms . . . where her mother currently sat in Tuesday Morning Women's Prayer.

But as Romilly neared the office, a rising swell of murmurs and low, guttural wails made her shoes turn to lead. The meditation room door where her mother prayed was open—and before Romilly could sneak past, several curious heads peered out at her.

"It's Rommie!" gasped a kind, wavering voice. "Just in time to lift up the youth in prayer. Won't you come and join us, dear?"

The speaker was Mrs. Hazimoto, a gray-haired Japanese woman who hunched over a walker, and who had attended ThisLyfe Church for as long as Romilly could remember. On one side of Mrs. Hazimoto sat Romilly's mother, her pristinely braided hair veiled by the blue sheer cloth she called a *shawl of intercession*. On the other, a young woman named Zoe nursed her infant as her lips moved in fervent, unintelligible whispers. Around the circle, some women rocked and even moaned.

"Um. Sorry," said Romilly, quailing beneath her mother's scrutiny. "I don't want to interrupt—"

"Little Rommie is very good with the children," cooed Mrs. Hazimoto, rheumy eyes going soft. "Remember the Christmas Praise Bonanza? Romilly had the second graders. She whipped those sugar-fueled little gremlins into a flock of caroling angels."

"She should have attended this prayer group from the beginning," said a husky-voiced white woman named Mrs. Palmer. "Goodness knows these young girls need more prayer than anyone."

Late mornings on weekdays, according to ThisLyfe, was the holiest time for feminine gatherings. The question "What if women have work?" didn't appear to have occurred to anyone. Neither did the question "What if Romilly has school?" The answer to both was cheerfully unspoken: godly women didn't work full time, and godly girls were homeschooled.

"She had homework," Patience Agboro said defensively. "I assigned her an essay on the Ephesians. She was supposed to be writing it." Patience raised an eyebrow. "I suppose she's done now, if she's wandering around with nothing to do."

"Not nothing," Romilly countered, pulse racing. "I'm—um. Having my own prayer time. For—" Her eyes raked the hall for inspiration. "The building," she blurted. "The church. You know, so it's . . . sturdy. And safe. From—uh. You know . . ." But before she could start spouting terms like *drywall rot* and *improper drainage,* Mrs. Palmer mercifully butted in.

"From assignments of the Devil," Mrs. Palmer asserted, her expression steeling with interest. "Well, thank the Lord. I'm glad *some* young people take spiritual warfare seriously."

"Churches who follow the *whole* Bible are always targeted," observed another middle-aged white woman. Her name was Miss Rose; her fuchsia-stained cheeks made it easy to remember. On her lap, she balanced a pile of cotton squares Romilly recognized as anointing cloths—handkerchiefs doused with oil, offered to the sick to induce miraculous healing. Miss Rose appeared to have made Mrs. Hazimoto her project, waving the scraps of cotton over the older woman's walker as if to make it disappear.

Mrs. Hazimoto—who in fact seemed very fond of her walker, which she had painted teal with yellow stars—ignored Miss Rose, smiling dreamily around at the Scripture-muraled walls. "I remember when this building was a vacuum-cleaner warehouse," she mused. "Back in the eighties. The factory motto used to be in the sanctuary. What was it? *Come one, come all at Ernesto's Lil Suckers?* Or was it, *If you need sucking, Ernesto's your—*"

"You don't usually go on prayer walks, Romilly," interrupted Patience, her tone laced with suspicion. "Why this one?"

Romilly fidgeted. "A feeling, I guess," she mumbled. "Um. A conviction?"

"Divine assignment," hummed Mrs. Palmer, rocking with stern approval. "A scrimmage with dark principalities of this world—"

"I'm getting a word," said Zoe, jostling her baby as she perked up. Her voice trilled with excitement. "Hedge. A hedge around the church, protecting us from all the attacks of the evil one."

Happy murmurs rippled through the circle. Words of Knowledge, like faith healing and speaking in tongues, were taken very seriously at ThisLyfe. Romilly's stomach turned. Lying about a word would surely sadden God more than anything else she'd done. She had to come clean—and now.

But where would she even begin? The closet? *I, Adaline?*

"Show us the way," demanded Mrs. Palmer.

Romilly blinked. "What?"

She watched, frozen, as Mrs. Palmer stood, shook out her lurid LuLaRoe skirts, and stepped into the hall, causing the others to follow her lead. Romilly stammered, "Sh-show you what?"

"Where we need to intercede, of course," said Mrs. Palmer. "For every place in this building where the evil one has left his assignments."

Romilly opened her mouth. Closed it. "Office," she said at last. "The word I'm getting. It's . . . office."

So down the hall the ladies went, a whispering, humming, and occasionally wailing parade with Romilly at its head. She sent prayers of repentance heavenward, like shots of Botox to what she now imagined was a *deeply* wrinkled forehead.

She cast her eyes over the gray industrial walls of the church, now brightened with swaths of fabric and framed Scripture calligraphy. If demons *did* linger in the nooks and crannies of ThisLyfe, she wondered if they had been there since the days of *Ernesto's Lil Suckers*. A sudden vision of possessed vacuum cleaners, evilly mowing pentagrams into carpets, choked Romilly with manic laughter. She held it in, knowing if she started, she wouldn't stop.

When she actually thought about it, Romilly liked that a church could spring up anywhere, like a stubborn yellow dandelion, fighting its way up between cracks of asphalt. Still, it was hard to romanticize *being in the world but not of it* in such unromantic surroundings.

Sometimes, during worship, she imagined her box braids covered with a deep satin hood, like priestesses wore in the bootleg fantasy films she streamed in secret. She replaced her denim overalls with a sweeping robe, and a gratifyingly severe neckline that grazed her dark brown chin. She wished away the refurbished warehouse-turned-sanctuary and pretended to sing in a hall of lacy stone, her eyes cast solemnly on the ground as suitors gazed after her, moved to sensual adoration by her holiness.

The fantasy always vanished, though, when Pastor Brett launched into the fifth chorus of his original piece, "God, You Really Get Me, You Do It All, My Guy"—electric guitar competing with the howl of the exposed AC piping.

It was like the worst part of being a nun, Romilly decided. All the strict rules, and none of the lovely stained glass windows.

When Romilly and her entourage arrived at the front office, it was deserted except for Heather, Youth Pastor Brett's wife. The blue streaks in her hair had faded since the Girls Purity Retreat, falling around her face in frazzled wisps as she rooted through the pastor's desk.

"Oh!" Heather jumped, sending papers flying around her shoulders. "Hi, ladies."

"Sorry," Romilly said. "We didn't mean to startle you."

Heather panted, blue eyes hunted. She smiled in confusion. "What's going on?"

"We're covering this office in prayer," said Zoe with great importance, bouncing her baby. "Romilly had a word."

Romilly's eyes locked on the rack near the back of the office, hungrily reading the labels above each key-laden hook. *Sanctuary. Youth Rec Room. Nursery* . . . and her heart sank to her sneakers.

Beneath the label marked *Sunday School Supply* . . . the hook lay empty.

"It's not here," Romilly said, causing a lull in the prayer group's hubbub. Even Miss Rose, who had begun daubing pieces of furniture with oil, paused mid-anointing, bottle dribbling into some poor secretary's keyboard.

"What?" demanded Patience. "What's not here?"

Romilly didn't bother replying. Her throat burned with tears.

Her chance of returning *I, Adaline: Peasant Queen* was gone. At least, until the next time Romilly could get into the supply closet, which probably wouldn't be until Sunday. Five days too late. And by then it wouldn't matter, because Romilly's mother would know everything—and she would never let her daughter set foot in the Las Ranas City Library again.

And what if that wasn't the end of it? Romilly's breath quickened with the beginning of a panic attack. What if her mother checked all of her borrowing history? What if she was so horrified by Romilly's sinful taste in media, she wouldn't let Romilly go back to book camp, either—the only place Romilly had ever felt understood?

Mrs. Palmer cupped Romilly's chin, misinterpreting her lost expression. "What do you see?" Mrs. Palmer asked reverently. "Are you having a vision? Another word?"

Something inside Romilly snapped. She laughed, throwing up her hands. What did anything matter now? She had disappointed God beyond repair, and after tomorrow, she'd be grounded for a thousand years. So she glanced around the office, eyes falling on Pastor Brett's nameplate, and said the first words that came to mind.

"Palm. Springs. Thursday. Unbelievable weather." She rattled them off in a monotone, nearly descending into giggling at Mrs. Palmer's stunned features. Then Romilly noticed Heather. The youth pastor's wife was frozen, mouth slack with horror. She started to sob.

"I knew it," she screeched. "I *knew* he wasn't going on a damn mission trip to skid row. I saw the hotel receipts, but I never thought he'd go back to her—to that *slut*. Brett, you two-faced piece of *shit*—"

And then Heather stormed from the office, sobs and expletives echoing down the hallway in her wake.

"Language," Mrs. Palmer scolded weakly to no one in particular. Then the room erupted into gossip, faces gleeful with wonder and horror.

Romilly realized very, very quickly where the focus of the conversation would soon lead. Deftly, she backed out of the office . . . and ran straight into Mrs. Hazimoto, who had hung back in the prayer parade, slowed by her walker.

"Sorry," Romilly said, trying to retreat the other way. But before she could, Mrs. Hazimoto put a hand on her arm.

"Not so fast, Rommie dear," said the old lady. "I've had a Word of Knowledge myself."

Romilly wanted to scream. "I don't have time for another word," she said through clenched teeth, but waited anyway, crumpling under Mrs. Hazimoto's kindly gaze.

"I don't know if Rose's anointing cloths heal anyone," said Mrs. Hazimoto, reaching into her cardigan pocket and retrieving a crumpled handkerchief. Her gaze was distant. Wistful. "But I think sickness doesn't always look like a cold, or a walker. They call God the Great Doctor, did you know that? And there are as many medicines, I suspect, as there are people."

Her gnarled hand pressed the anointing cloth into Romilly's palm. To Romilly's surprise, there was something hard inside the cloth. When she turned it over, a key winked in the fluorescent hall light. Her hand closed around it.

"Ah," Mrs. Hazimoto said in a strange monotone. "Would you look at that. Must have forgotten to put that back after teaching the littles last Sunday. Well. Oops-a-daisy. Put it back for me, won't you, Rommie?"

"I—" Romilly's voice was barely a whisper. "Did . . . did you know?"

"Know what, dear?" Mrs. Hazimoto murmured, carefully avoiding Romilly's gaze as she hobbled back down the hall, gazing up at the industrial scaffolding. "Now that I've had time to think about it, I'm pretty sure it *was* 'Come one, come all at Ernesto's.' Quite catchy, if you ask me. I would have trusted that salesman with all my sucking needs"—and Romilly collapsed against the wall, laughing until her sides ached.

Romilly rode home from church, *I, Adaline* cradled safely beneath her shirt, and placed the anointing cloth between her cheek and the cool glass of the car window.

"Are all stories medicine?" she said as the California hills whipped by in great ridged backs of brown. The question fogged the glass. First of many, she knew, some scarier than others. But when she looked up at the spotless coastal sky, it stretched above her like a broad, lineless forehead, sun flares winking, whispers on glass.

Ask.

Ask.

Ask.

COLE'S CRUISE BLUES
BY ISAAC FITZSIMONS

If it weren't for Dad's chronic lateness, I probably wouldn't have seen the boy on the gangway as we board the ship. He looks about fourteen, my age, and he's wearing a starched pink polo, crisply ironed khaki shorts, and boat shoes. A woman I'm hoping is his mom licks her fingers and flattens his eyebrows as he squirms away.

I can't wait to tell Sage about him. He's the type of guy we'd laugh about back home. But thinking about Sage wipes the smile off my face because next year there will be nobody to laugh with anymore. Sage is going to be homeschooled so that her family can travel, meaning I'm going to high school without my best friend.

With Sage, everything is an adventure. She's always snipping off chunks of her hair with blunt art room scissors to give herself crooked bangs in direct violation of Section C, Paragraph 2 of our school's dress code ("Hair must not be worn in an extreme or inappropriate style"). I only know this because her parents waged a war against the school, arguing they had no right to "stifle her creative expression." #HairPolice trended for days.

Being her friend is great, don't get me wrong, but she's the kind of person who takes up a lot of space. Mostly, I'm nervous about what's going to happen next year. A small part of me, though—a part I'd never tell anyone about—is also kind of curious to see who I am without Sage. That's why this cruise is so important. A chance to be myself.

Before today, I hadn't seen Dad in four years. This is the first time he gets to see the real me. I want to make sure he gets the best version, even though I'm not sure who that is yet. If everything goes to plan, by the end of the cruise, I'll know.

We finally make it to our cabins and my stepsister Hailey flops facedown on her bed, not bothering to take her shoes off. When Dad picked me up at baggage claim, he told me how excited Hailey was to see me, but she's pretty much been glued to her phone since we left the airport. I sit on the edge of my bed and take my own phone out.

Beth pokes her head in through the door that connects our cabins. "No, absolutely not." She comes into our cabin with her hand stretched out. "Both of you, give me your phones. We didn't pay all this money to have you two hunched over a screen like zombies."

I like Beth all right. I mean, she's not an evil stepmom or anything. But I don't think she's ever forgiven me for what happened at the wedding. She'd wanted me and Hailey to wear matching flower-girl dresses. It was humiliating enough having to share an outfit with a six-year-old, and the idea of wearing a dress made me want to scratch my skin off. I threw such a big tantrum that I was allowed to wear a suit.

Not wanting to get on Beth's bad side the very first day, I power off my phone and give it to her. Hailey sighs heavily and does the same.

Beth opens the door to the hallway. "There's a kids clubhouse on board. Why don't you check it out? We'll meet for dinner at six thirty." She shoos us out the cabin before calling after us, "And stay together, you two." I groan inwardly. One thing for sure is that playing babysitter to a ten-year-old I barely know is *not* part of my plan to discover the new and improved Cole.

At the clubhouse, we're greeted by a woman in a white polo with STAFF stitched on the pocket just above a rainbow flag pin.

"Hi, I'm Anna. Are you checking in?"

I nod. Anna shows us how to scan our wristbands, which we got before boarding, to print a name tag. Hailey goes first. The printer spits out her name tag and she slaps it on her shirt before going inside. When it's my turn, the printer whirs, then my name tag pops out. Except . . . it's not my name. I mean, it *was* my name, but not anymore. I snatch it from the printer before Anna sees. I begin to ask if I can just write my own, but she's already moved on to help someone else. I gulp when I see who it is. It's the boy from the gangway with the unruly eyebrows.

"Excuse me." He reaches across to pick up his name tag from the printer and carefully unpeels and sticks it on his pink polo. He leans over again to toss his trash away and I can smell his sunscreen.

"Hi, I'm Evan." His left eyebrow is still sticking up, and I have the urge to smooth it down. I see him searching for my name tag and realize I'm supposed to introduce myself, but I don't want to, not with this name.

I open my mouth to say something, but what comes out is, "Hi. I'm . . . leaving." I hurry out the clubhouse, crushing the name tag in my fist.

Unlike most people, I got to name myself. Well, Mom helped. We chose Cole. See, for thirteen years, everyone thought I was a girl until I came out as trans last year. Most people have been pretty cool about it, using the right name and pronouns. Dad and Beth even invited me on this cruise, which they totally didn't have to do. I expected some awkwardness, like Dad not recognizing me at the airport. I mean, I had trouble recognizing him too. A person can change a lot in four years. But if I can't be Cole, then I don't want to be here at all.

I spend the next few hours wandering the ship, which is like its own little city at sea. When it's time for dinner, I head to the main dining room and search for Dad, Beth, and Hailey in the crowd.

I spot Dad at a round table and pull out a chair. His face falls when he sees me. "Where were you?"

I frown. "What do you mean?"

"Hailey said you weren't at the clubhouse with her."

"Oh," I say, remembering that Beth did ask us to stay together. I don't want to bring up the issue with my name at the table, so I apologize instead. "Sorry."

"You should've been there, Cole," says Hailey. "The clubhouse is awesome. They've got video games with a gigantic screen and a fridge filled with soda and candy and stuff. Also, there's going to be a talent show on the last night!"

"Cool," I say. And it does sound cool. But I don't know if I'll be able to enjoy any of it if I have to use the wrong name all week. "Dad," I say, quietly, not wanting Hailey and Beth to hear.

"What is it?" Dad starts cutting through his chicken.

"What name did you use to register me?" I ask.

He puts his knife down. "Oh. Sorry, kiddo, I had to use the name on your passport."

"Oh." I push away my plate. Suddenly I'm not hungry.

After dinner I ask Beth for my phone so I can message my mom. Before I left, Mom bought me the basic Wi-Fi package to keep in touch. I send her a quick text letting her know I made it, then write a longer one to Sage about the issue with my name tag.

It takes a while for her to respond and when she does, my heart drops.

It could be worse, right? Some kids get kicked out of their house when they come out. Your dad invited you on a cruise, so I don't see why you're complaining.

I turn my phone off without responding. If she asks, I'll blame it on the Wi-Fi. Believe me, I know how lucky I am, but if my best friend isn't on my side, who will be?

The next morning, I dig through my suitcase to find the perfect outfit. Since I'm not sure which Cole I want to be yet, I start with who I *don't* want to be, and after what she said last night, I try to find the least Sage-approved clothes I own, and the person who comes to mind when I think about the exact opposite of Sage is that boy from the gangway: Evan.

I don't have a pink polo, but I do have one in navy and a pair of coral-red khaki shorts. Hailey bangs on the bathroom door.

"Come on, I want to go to the clubhouse!"

I grab a sweater and wrap it around my shoulders. But when I see myself in the mirror, I toss it back in my bag. There are limits to how preppy I'm willing to be.

Hailey skips ahead to the clubhouse. My plan is to drop her off then find somewhere else to hang out before picking her up for lunch. Hailey swipes her wristband and goes in. I'm about to leave when I hear someone call my name.

"Cole, right?" It's Evan. Gone are the polo and khakis. Instead, he has on a blue rash guard and swim shorts. His hair, which was combed neatly yesterday, resembles straw. Suddenly I feel completely overdressed.

"How do you know my name?"

"Your sister told me." He nods at Hailey who's already talking to a couple younger kids inside.

I like how he doesn't hesitate over the word "sister," considering Hailey's white, like Beth, and I'm Black, like Dad.

"We need another person for foosball. Want to play?"

I hesitate. "Um . . ."

Then Anna comes up to the check-in desk. "He'll be there in a moment." Anna waits until Evan gets back to the foosball table then smiles at me. "You know, if there's a name you'd prefer to go by, I can put it in the system," she says.

"Really?"

"Yeah, it's no problem." I swipe in and Anna hands me a name tag with "Cole" written on it.

"Thanks."

"Don't mention it." She gives me a look that I've seen a few times since coming out. Like from that cashier with the pierced nose when I bought my first boys bathing suit for this trip. *You're not alone*, the look says. *We've got you.*

I join Evan at the foosball table. He introduces me to two others who are also playing. Someone named Liv and her brother, Sander.

"You're on my team," says Evan. "You can play defense."

I grab the handles and Sander drops the ball in. Evan and I make a great team and soon win the game.

"Nice!" he raises his hand for a high five. It's soft and warm against my own.

"I'm bored," says Liv. "Let's go to the pool."

"You in?" asks Evan, eyes bright.

I look down at my outfit, not pool ready. "Um, I have to stay here and look after Hailey," I say, grateful, for the first time, to have a little sister I can use as an excuse.

Hailey's head pops up from where she's playing video games nearby. "I want to go to the pool too." I wish I were an only child again.

I use the cruise messaging app to send Dad a quick text letting him know where we're going, and reluctantly follow the others to the pool.

The rest of them wade right in, but I find a beach chair and lie down. Hailey, who was obviously much smarter than me, takes off her shorts and T-shirt to reveal a bathing suit, and heads in as well.

Evan dips his foot in then turns back to me. "Coming?"

"Nah, I'll just watch." I keep an eye on Hailey in the water. After a few minutes Evan wades out of the pool and collapses on a beach chair next to me. He peels off his rash guard. Even though he's about my height, he's got a lot more muscle than I do.

Evan shakes his head, sprinkling water everywhere. "The slide is awesome. You should try it."

I glance at the plastic slide that towers over us. It's an orange monster that winds around the deck like a serpent. At one point, it curves to the side and hangs over the open water. "I'm good."

"Why? Are you scared?" he teases.

"No," I say, a defensive tone to my voice. "I don't have my bathing suit." Which is true. "I love waterslides." That is not. Just thinking about it is making me sweat through my polo. Then again, maybe Preppy Cole wouldn't like waterslides, but a different Cole might.

"Yeah, I'm a total adrenaline junkie," I continue.

"Really?" asks Evan.

I nod enthusiastically. "The more extreme, the better." I don't know why I say that. I'm the person who grips onto the railing when I go down the stairs because I'm afraid of falling. It's not that I don't like sports, I just don't have the build or coordination that some others have. But that could change.

"If you think this slide's intense, wait till we get to the island tomorrow. There's a wave pool, and roller coasters and a huge zip line."

"Yeah, sounds awesome," I mumble. My attention is torn away from Evan when I hear sobbing. I jump out of my chair and see Hailey staggering toward me. Tears mingle with the water on her face. I run to her and grab her shoulders.

"What's wrong?"

Hailey's body shudders as she sucks in a ragged breath. "I was going down the slide really fast and I reached the bottom and I fell out of my tube!" she wails. A snot bubble pops on her face. And I'm embarrassed.

Not because of her meltdown. I'm embarrassed that a ten-year-old was braver than me, and I'm ashamed that I hadn't even noticed her tip over. I'd been too distracted with Evan.

I wrap my arms around her and feel her tremble against me. "But you're okay now, right?"

Her chin wobbles as she nods.

I take her hand. "Come on, let's go chill out."

We start walking to our cabin, but Hailey is still pretty worked up. Then I remember how disappointed Dad was last night when I'd left Hailey alone. Imagine if he finds out that she'd nearly drowned on my watch. Instead, I take her to the clubhouse to see if I can get her to calm down first.

After scanning in, we collapse onto a couple beanbags. She's mostly stopped crying and is just hiccupping.

I look around the room for something to distract her with and spy a deck of cards. An idea comes to me.

"Hey, want to see a magic trick?"

Hailey's face brightens. When I was younger, I was obsessed with magic, until Sage told me I was appropriating Wiccan culture and should stop. But I still remember a few simple tricks. I begin shuffling the deck.

"This trick is called 'The Whispering Queen.' First, pick a queen."

"The queen of diamonds."

"Good choice." I flip through and find the queen of diamonds, removing it from the deck. "How it works is you're going to pick a card and the queen of diamonds is going to tell me which card you chose. First, let's put her over there so she can't peek." I push the queen to the side and place the deck back on the table. "Cut the deck into thirds." Hailey takes a few cards off the top and puts them in a pile next to the original deck. "And again."

Now, this is where the trick gets good.

"Point to one of the stacks." Like most people, Hailey points to the center stack. Perfect. "Great. Pick up the top card and look at it, then stick it anywhere in the stack."

Hailey examines the card and puts it back. If she had pointed at any other stack, I would have said, "Okay, we'll get rid of that one," and ask her to pick again until only the middle stack was left. That's the genius of this trick: Hailey thinks she made the choice, but *I'm* the one in control.

"Shuffle the cards." Hailey shuffles them clumsily and puts them back on the table. I close my eyes suddenly.

"What is it?"

"Shh." I put my fingers to my lips theatrically. "The queen is speaking to me." I pick up the queen of diamonds, put it to my ear, and nod, pretending like I can hear. "The queen is telling me that the card you chose was the three of clubs. Is that right?"

Hailey's mouth drops open in surprise. "How did you know?" she asks.

I open my eyes and grin. The truth is that when I was taking out the queen of diamonds, I peeked at the first card, which became the bottom card when I put the deck facedown, and the top card of the center stack after Hailey cut the deck into thirds.

"A magician never reveals his secrets."

■ ■ ■

By dinnertime, Hailey's back to her usual self and I'm spared having to tell Dad and Beth about her accident at the pool. She's chatting excitedly while stuffing her face with spaghetti.

"Guess what? I signed Cole and me up for the talent show."

A meatball drops off my fork onto my plate. "What?" I say.

"That's great," says Beth.

"We're going to do a magic trick. Cole's the magician and I'm his assistant."

"Nice, Cole. I'm glad to see you two spending time together." Dad squeezes my arm.

I want to tell them, *No, I did not agree to perform a magic trick with my little sister in front of a crowd.* That's not the Cole I want to be. Sure, Preppy Cole was a bust, and even if Adrenaline-Junkie Cole might be better, I'm pretty sure he doesn't do magic tricks. But then I see how Dad's looking at me and remember how he and Beth shelled out money for my flight and cruise ticket.

"We'll need to practice. The talent show is the day after tomorrow," says Hailey.

"Yeah, can't wait," I lie.

Adrenaline-Junkie Cole wears a bathing suit bottom and a rash guard. I think about putting on a headband like athletes do but decide that's too much.

The disembarkation process lasts just as long as the embarkation process, but at least this time, white sand and crystal clear water are waiting for us on the other side. Beth leads us to the beach. The sand is a fine powder between my toes.

"This is beautiful," says Beth, collapsing into a beach chair. Dad joins her and Hailey spreads out her towel and says, "We should practice our trick."

"Um, I was thinking about going to the water park for a bit," I say.

"Why don't you take Hailey?" says Dad.

"Actually, I was going to hang out with my friend Evan." He found me last night after dinner, and we made a plan to meet up. "We're probably going on some of the more extreme rides. I don't know if Hailey wants to come."

"Cole . . ." begins Dad.

"Oh, let him go," says Beth. "Hailey and I can have a girls' day."

"Thanks, Beth! We'll rehearse later, I promise." Before Dad can object, I take off to meet Evan. He's already in line to board the shuttle bus that loops the island.

"Ready?" he asks.

"Let's do this!" The voice that comes out of my mouth doesn't even sound like mine. It's bold, confident, and I'm here for it. I'm here for the wave pool. I'm here for the snacks at the cabana. I'm here for a whole morning hanging with Evan in his navy swim shorts with lobsters on them. I'm here for it all.

And then we reach the zip line.

My mouth grows dry, like I've just eaten sand, and I want to tell Evan that maybe we should try the lazy river instead, but he's already getting fitted for a harness.

I fight to control my breathing as I get strapped into my own harness and helmet. Adrenaline-Junkie Cole can do this. *I* can do this. Our instructor goes over safety protocols but I'm only half paying attention. Then, before I know it, I'm following Evan up the rickety wooden structure to the first platform.

Before we even get to the zip line of doom, we have to carry ourselves across a wire stretching between our platform to another in the distance.

Evan flits across the wire bridge effortlessly, then it's my turn. The smelly gloves they're making me wear grow damp with sweat as I step onto the wire. Keeping my eyes trained directly ahead of me, I make good progress at first. In fact, I'm almost enjoying myself, until I reach the middle and the shaking starts. Whether it's the wire or my legs, I'm not sure. All I know is that if I move, I will fall.

"Come on, keep it moving," yells the zip-line instructor. "One foot in front of the other." I'm too afraid to turn around but I can imagine the growing line of frustrated people behind me.

The wire shudders even more violently.

"Cole!" calls Evan from up ahead. "Whatever you do, don't look down!"

Why would he tell me that? Because immediately, I look down. My legs shake more violently. My heart pounds and I can hear blood in my ears. That's the last thing I remember before my feet slip off the wire and I drop.

I don't die. Not physically. The harness stops me from crashing to the ground. But emotionally, I'm dead. Perished. Deceased.

They need to bring in an emergency crew to fetch me. While I'm dangling there like a piece of overripe fruit ready to fall off a branch, I decide that Adrenaline-Junkie Cole is probably my worst Cole yet.

Even now, safely on solid ground, I'm still on edge. I spent the rest of yesterday and most of today holed up in my cabin on the ship. I can't face Evan, not after what happened.

I jump when Hailey bursts out of the bathroom. "Ta-da!" She's wearing an ivory dress and her hair is in braids. Then she sees me still in bed. "Why aren't you ready? The talent show is tonight."

"I'm sorry, Hailey. I can't do it."

Her face falls. "Why not?"

"I just can't," I say, not wanting to explain how mortifying it is to plummet off a highwire bridge on the way to a zip line in front of a really cute boy.

My bed dips as she sits down. "But I can't do it myself. Every time I asked you to teach me you said you'd do it later."

I roll away from her. "YouTube it."

"Mom has my phone." She shakes my shoulder. "Please, Cole?"

I shrug her off. "Leave me alone." I curl up into a tight ball.

"Fine."

She slams the door shut behind her. A few moments later the door opens.

"I said I'm not doing the show, Hailey."

"You don't have to do the show."

It's not Hailey, it's Dad.

The bed dips even lower when he sits down. "You know, when your mom told me about the new you, I have to admit I was worried that you'd be a completely different person. But I know you, Cole, and you're the same caring and generous person you've always been, if not more so. I love that you've gotten to spend time with Hailey. And I'm sorry if it feels like I've been pushing you two together this week, but you both mean so much to me and I want you to feel like you have each other to lean on. So, you don't have to do the show if you really don't want to, but I know Hailey would appreciate it if you were at least there to support her." He shrugs. "It's your choice."

The mattress shifts again, and he's gone. I sit up and rub my eyes. It doesn't happen often, but in this case, Dad's right. The least I can do is support her.

■ ■ ■

The talent show is already in full swing when I get there. I catch the last off-key verse of a song from *Moana* and then a boy with bleached tips does a TikTok dance before Anna announces Hailey.

Hailey runs to the front brimming with energy. Man, I wish I had the self-confidence of a ten-year-old.

"For this trick I'm going to need a volunteer." A few hands go up. "How about you?" She points directly at Evan, and he joins her at the front.

Hailey starts off strong, introducing the trick and having Evan choose the queen. But then after she's removed the queen, the deck slips out of her hands and the cards fan across the floor.

"Oops," she says, as Evan helps her scoop them up. I have no idea if they're in the right order for the trick.

"Okay, now cut the deck into thirds." She waits while Evan follows her directions. "And now choose a pile."

I let out an inaudible, "No," under my breath when he chooses the pile to the right.

"Um, not that one," she whispers, loud enough for everyone in the audience to hear. They laugh. Eventually Evan picks the middle pile.

Hailey gets really into pretending she can hear the queen, which makes the audience laugh harder, but then it's time for the reveal, and that's the part I'm most worried about.

She waves her hand in a dramatic flourish. "Your card is the two of spades, right?"

Evan chuckles awkwardly. "Uh, no."

Instead of running off like I would've done, Hailey holds the queen to her ear again. The card trembles slightly in her hand.

"Um, was it the three of spades?" she asks in a wavering voice.

Evan looks just as embarrassed as I feel. "It was not. Sorry."

"Oh." Hailey looks down at the floor, blinking back tears. I'm hoping that Anna will come to her rescue, but she's setting up the music for the next act and doesn't seem to realize how badly Hailey is tanking.

Here's the thing, magic might not be cool, but what's even less cool is watching your little sister choke onstage.

Before I realize what I'm doing, I'm at the front of the room. I look out across the audience, thinking fast on how to save this trick.

"Sometimes the queen doesn't answer to us peasants," I say, which gets a light chuckle from the audience. "What was your card?" I ask Evan.

"It was the eight of diamonds," he says.

I flip through the deck and pull out the eight of diamonds. I show it to the audience and then give it to Evan.

"If my assistant would be so kind as to get me a pen," I say, putting on my magician voice.

"Dad, can I borrow a pen?" asks Hailey. At this, the audience starts cracking up. Dad tosses us a pen, which I give to Evan.

"Could you please draw a picture on that card. Don't show it to me, just hold it up so the audience can see."

I turn around while Evan draws a picture, then holds it up. "I'm done," he says.

"Now, put the card back in the deck facedown." Evan shoves the card into the deck. The toughest part about doing magic is that you have to distract the audience while you're doing it, which for me means making small talk with the cute guy I completely humiliated myself in front of thirty-six hours earlier.

I lift up the deck slightly and peek at the bottom card, which, with a quick sleight of hand, I can see is the card that Evan has drawn on. When I see what he drew, I almost lose my train of thought. I shake my head and continue the trick. "So, your card is somewhere in the middle, right?"

Evan nods.

"All right, I need complete silence because the queen is going to tell me what you drew." I put my finger to my temple and close my eyes as if I'm concentrating. I know I look ridiculous, but if I'm going to salvage the trick, I have to go all in.

"Assistant, please bring me the queen."

Hailey hands over the queen. "She's ready to reveal what you drew." I take the pen from Evan and sketch the drawing on the queen. When I'm finished, I show it to him. "Is this what you drew?"

Evan's eyes widen. "Yeah, it is!"

I show the card to the audience. "Is this what he drew?"

There are a few shocked gasps and applause. "Thank you, everyone. And a special thanks to our volunteer, and my wonderful assistant, Hailey."

I grab hold of both of their hands, and we bow together.

Later that evening, I'm standing on the deck inhaling the salt air and listening as the waves lap against the ship. This cruise has flown by, and while I'm excited to get back on dry land, I'm actually going to miss spending time with Dad, Beth, and Hailey.

I hear footsteps behind me.

"That was a pretty cool trick," a voice says.

It's Evan. I feel, more than hear, him come stand next to me. "I'm sorry about yesterday," he says.

I turn to look at him. "Why are you sorry?"

"If I'd known you were afraid of heights, I never would've suggested the zip line."

"To be fair, I didn't know I'd be that afraid until I got up there."

He laughs. "But seriously, I didn't care what we did. I just wanted to hang out with you." Pink dots appear on his cheeks. "You didn't have to pretend to be someone you're not."

He's right. The past four days I've been playing several parts, trying to find the right fit, but now I'm ready to be me. I stick out my hand. "Hi, I'm Cole. I hate wearing polos, and I'm terrified of heights, but I love magic."

He takes my hand. "I'm Evan. I also hate polos, but I love heights." He pauses. "I'm really glad you were on the cruise."

"Me too." And I mean it. Obviously, four days is hardly any time, but who knows what could happen in the future.

"Before we leave, I wanted to give you this." He hands me the eight of diamonds that he drew a small heart on earlier. I take out the queen from my pocket with the heart that I drew and give it to him.

We turn back to the railing, his arm resting against mine, and watch the sun set across the twinkling water.

HIGH STRANGENESS
BY DESIREE S. EVANS

I. [CLOSE ENCOUNTERS]

Hey, you, look up.

There are strange lights in the skies over West Texas. There are people vanishing into the high grassy plains. *Poof*, gone without a trace. A statewide mystery. A puzzle for the ages.

Yet, I know the truth.

"Aliens," I state the obvious. "You know, the child-sized grays with big black eyes and long knobby fingers." I suspect they are leading people away, zapping them up into their little alien spaceships. *Zap, zap, zap!*

Sure, the news says it's just a bout of heat madness. With the summers so hot from global warming, people can't help but wander off sometimes, get confused and lost in all the wide-open spaces of the world. I kind of get that idea; sometimes I just want to get lost too.

This is what I'm thinking about as I curve my body into the shotgun seat and listen to the drowsy breathing of my friends. I'm thinking of what it would mean to get lost out here, in this middle of nowhere, in this wide-open space. Texas. America. Earth. The universe. To just disappear into some tractor beam of greater extraterrestrial machination. *Zap, zap, zap!*

I smile, very pleased at the thought, and in the middle row of seats behind me, my best friend Rhee sighs because she's a sigher. I know Rhee believes in aliens too, but her idea of aliens is closer to that of algae and sea sponges.

"It has to be experimental government spy planes," Rhee explains, as if that is the more obvious answer.

"If it's just high-tech spy planes, how do you explain all the disappearances?" Vivian, my other best friend, calls out from the last row of seats in the very back of the van. "Why, exactly, is the government kidnapping people?"

Rhee sighs again. I hum, turn to look at them both, and say, "Good question, my dear Viv."

Vivian is the more pragmatic of my two best friends. While Vivian is also a true believer in the weird, as we all are, having been dubbed our high school's "Trio of Weird," Vivian has a tendency to ask questions and to think on things for a long time before coming to a conclusion.

I, on the other hand, love throwing guesses at the wall in hopes something will stick. That's why I repeat, "Aliens make the most sense," because, obviously they do. Sure, one might say this is all a bit out there. I get it. But this kind of stuff is sort of *my thing*. I'm Lola Pierce, age sixteen (as of tomorrow). Myers–Briggs type: INTP. D&D alignment: chaotic neutral. Occupation: Academic Decathlon dropout and part-time UFO hunter.

My particular obsession with hunting UFOs is the reason I'm out here in the middle of nowhere contemplating the vastness of space with my two best friends and our new classmate, Makayla. This little adventure to the middle of Texas to see the mystery lights is actually their birthday present to me. Every year, tons of people come out this way to do exactly what we're doing right now—follow the trail of the mystery lights that haunt the dusty town of Shine, Texas, a backwater locale known for its high number of energy vortexes and eerie encounters.

I've been dreaming of coming out this way since I was old enough to spell Geordi La Forge. So . . . a long time. (According to my mama, I was already binging episodes of *Star Trek* at the age of two). Needless to say, I love out-of-this-world conspiracies, I always keep an ever-watchful eye on the night sky, and I dream of making first contact. I also write a blog called *Waiting for Halley's Comet*, where I collect, and comment on, weird stories I find on the internet. Lizard people, chemtrails, alien sightings, psychic pandas, you name it.

If it's strange, I tell the world all about it.

"Sorry, did you actually just say aliens make the most sense?" Rhee asks, bringing me back to our current conversation. She sticks her face between the two front seats and looks at me with something akin to bewilderment. "Our government is shady as fuck, and we all know that. In point of fact: MK-Ultra."

"Okay, okay," I laugh, sit up straighter, and begin the difficult task of un-sticking myself from the vinyl passenger seat. I'm not winning on the topic of government conspiracies tonight. Rhee is our government-conspiracy expert.

From the driver's seat, a startling laugh shakes me to the core, fills me with light and warmth.

Makayla Jackson. The new girl. The latest addition to our unicorn crew. Rhee and Vivian constantly tease me about my crush. It's not a crush, okay, it's just . . . scientific curiosity. I am a curious person. And Makayla and I hit it off when she first arrived in town last month. We chat sometimes in gym and AP Bio, and always Black-girl nod to each other when walking down Shadrock High's dizzying fluorescent hallways. Our budding friend-ship feels like the beginning of something pretty cool, so when Makayla offered to use her parents' van to transport me, Rhee, and Viv on this little adventure of ours, I couldn't say no. Even if it feels like there's some big and fierce thing vibrating beneath my skin now.

I flick a glance in Makayla's direction, noting how she carefully navigates the dark ribbon of highway. I sit up straighter in my seat, hands in my lap, tattered paperback between my thighs, and try not to make it obvious I'm watching her. If I'm honest, I've been sneaking peeks her way since we got in the car three hours ago. We somehow managed to fit ourselves and our bags into Makayla's parents' lime-green classic VW van without a hitch, departing from our hometown of Shadrock, Texas, just after 7 p.m.

I take a deep breath and purposely direct my gaze out of the van's bug-splattered windshield. Outside, fields of tall grass sway in the headlights. Towns come and go, bumpy silhouettes on the horizon that fade as fast as they appear. In the distance I see the first sign of hills, such a shift from the flatness of Central Texas.

It feels weird to be traveling without our parents. We're four Black girls braving the dark back roads alone. It's scary, it's thrilling. The world could end and we'd never even know it, out here in all this strange country. Honestly, it took a hell of a lot to convince our parents to let us do this trip. We actually had to say we were staying with Rhee's relatives in Salt Springs. But the truth is, we'll make camp outside of Shine, our ultimate destination, the last in a rather long list of small towns we've passed today that barely justify a dot on the map.

I rest my head against the passenger-side window, close my eyes, imagine the four of us floating out into space.

"Lola," Makayla wakes me from my daydreaming, her fingers brushing my shoulder. Such a light, respectful touch. I open my eyes, turn to look at her. Her lips curve into a hypnotic smile.

"Hey," I say, a bit dazed.

"We're getting close," Makayla says, nodding toward the dark highway.

"Where are we?" I ask, full of goose bumps.

"Somewhere between," Rhee pipes up. "A definite liminal space."

Rhee flaps open her large *Rand McNally Road Atlas*. She refuses to solely use the GPS on our cell phones, says paper maps are pieces of forever. "We finish out this stretch of I-85 South, then hook a left onto State Highway 1 heading west all the way to Shine. Fifty more miles."

I nod, my eyes tracing the tiny lines that represent our chosen route. We're in the middle, the betwixt and between. I take a look at the empty spill of dark road ahead of us, the long line of shadowed trees. For a moment, I wonder if this is all some kind of dream. I wonder if I'll wake up to the reality of my twin bed, my stack of geometry homework, the niggling fear of always letting my parents down.

I tilt my head back, feel the cool vinyl against the nape of my neck. Count to five. Breathe in, out. *Relax, Lola.*

From the back seat, Vivian says, "It's our first time in an area of high strangeness."

"What do you mean?" Makayla asks, glancing at Viv in the rearview mirror.

"Shine, Texas, is a vortex of weirdness," Rhee explains. "It's considered the Roswell of the Lone Star State. A place where the veil is thin, where UFOs and mystery lights are seen on a regular basis."

"So," Makayla begins, brow arching, "we're definitely going to get abducted, right? Actually, I've never heard of Black people getting abducted."

"Sadly, we Black folk are a very small percentage of folks who report seeing UFOs or being visited by little green men," I admit with a disappointed sigh.

"Maybe that's 'cause *we* are the aliens," Makayla says, giving me a soft, private smile.

My heart beats wondrously. I say, "Very likely." We both laugh.

"Here it is!" Vivian exclaims, and I glance toward the back of the van where she's waving a tattered copy of her favorite book, *The UFO Encounter*. She leafs through the pages very quickly and pauses to read out loud:

high strangeness

n.—(of a UFO). Being unexplainable, bizarre, peculiar, and highly absurdist in nature.

I smile at the definition, and then turn to Makayla to explain it better. "It was a term invented back in the day by some of the scientists who first studied UFOs. It was a way to measure the . . . shall we say, weirdness of some UFO sightings and reports. Like a scale. Some things were low on the scale, and some things were high. Over the years it became a catchall term for all the really weird phenomena that occurs in tandem with some UFO sightings and alien abductions. Some places are just full-on weirdness hot spots."

"What do you mean by *weirdness* exactly?" Makayla asks.

"I'm talking Shine-level weirdness," I say, getting in my groove. "Paranormal hot spots with a deep history of folklore, strange sightings, and mysterious disappearances."

I pause to take my scrapbook out of my backpack at my feet. I toss several sci-fi paperbacks to the van floor, and pick up my thick, overstuffed binder. I open it up to the newspaper clippings at the very beginning. Makayla glances over, eyes widening as I point to the first page.

"These are dozens of news stories from the town's history," I explain. "Paranormal activity of all kinds, not just the spook lights. Poltergeists, hauntings. Cryptid sightings like bigfoot, thunderbirds. Time slips."

Vivian joins in from the back. "Places like Shine have a high level of UFO activity, missing people, crop circles, strange humanoid creatures stalking the farmland, cattle mutilations. Men in black."

"It's *Twilight Zone*–level weird," I say.

"*Doo di doo doo, doo di doo doo*," Rhee, helpful as always, singsongs the *Twilight Zone* theme music.

Makayla turns wide eyes on me, and I close my scrapbook, suddenly aware of having revealed to her my own level of strangeness. Scale: *high*. I give her a sheepish look and ask, "So, um . . . you regret offering to drive us yet?"

"Y'all are real freaky, that's true," Makayla says, chuckling softly. She glances at me for a moment, and her lips quirk a bit when she adds, "But I *like* it."

I preen. I float. I feel high as a kite. I rejoice in the momentary chaos of being out here surrounded by a bunch of freaky sophomores ready to solve the secrets of the universe. I turn to watch the black night blur around us. Nobody else is out here with us. Most folks are home, tucked safely in bed, streaming movies, sipping beer, hooking up. But I'm out here chasing stories. Trying to figure things out by being right in the middle of it all.

Most days, I feel like I'm just waiting, you know? Waiting to graduate and leave Shadrock. Waiting to fall in love. Waiting to be rid of the tight fist around my heart, the panic underneath my skin, the constant fear of being too much and not enough all at once. Waiting and waiting. To go on adventures. To find magic. To dance with fairies. To follow the rainbow. To do something, *anything*. Sometimes I just want to explode like a supernova.

"Lola."

I blink, shake off my cosmic ambitions. Outside: the van's headlights pick out trees, the collapsed remains of a barn near the side of the road. Inside: the radio blends with the hum of the engine. I turn to look at Makayla.

"Thank you," she tells me.

"For what?" I ask, a frog stuck in my throat.

"For welcoming me into your weird little circle," Makayla says with a teasing huff of breath. "Moving from Houston, I was worried I wouldn't find my people."

I don't know how to respond to that. I feel a little winded by it, honestly. *We're her people.* I want to look at her face, but I'm too shy, so I look at the soft brown of her hands, catalog the firm way she grips the steering wheel. The sparkling gemstone rings on her slender fingers, the black nail polish that fashions her fingernails. I listen to the low, steady sound of her breathing this close to me. Everything, in all of space-time, comes down to this. Moments like this where we just exist with one another. Our faces lit by the dashboard's amber glow. The miles rolling beneath us.

After a time, Makayla changes the radio station to a classic R&B one, still keeping the volume low. Something settles around me then like a gentle hug, makes me wonder if the closer we get to Shine, the more everything will feel this *liminal*, like Rhee pointed out earlier. Like we're on the verge of something new, becoming something more.

When I finally find words, I speak. But my voice is still a bit unsteady. "Makayla, I want to thank you too. For coming along. For driving us, for doing all of this." I take a breath, count to three. We're just bodies floating in the dark of space after all. "It means a lot . . . *to me.*"

"I wanted to help. You're good people, Lola Pierce," Makayla says quietly. "And you know what? I definitely feel like we're traveling through another dimension, a dimension not only of sight and sound but of mind . . ."

I can't help but to continue, because, hello, this is my thing. "A journey into a wondrous land whose boundaries are that of imagination!" I recite. "That's the signpost just up ahead—our next stop, the Twilight Zone!"

Makayla and I both laugh, giddy and full. All around us, the night spins on.

II. [COMMUNION]

We stop for the night on the outskirts of Shine, next to an open field located behind an abandoned, ivy-covered gas station. The spot is well hidden, surrounded by a cluster of tall hardwoods that we've been taking turns peeing behind. The van is ticking off heat as I lean against the hood, waiting for the others to finish. I breathe deeply, rolling my shoulders against the muscle cramps garnered from the four-hour drive. I turn sixteen in fifty minutes. I shiver.

Nights this time of the year are typically cool and dry. I've come prepared for the chill though, wearing my favorite black skinny jeans with their artistically holey knees, and my red-and-black anarchy-symbol hoodie over my well-worn SMUGGLE ME, LANDO CALRISSIAN! T-shirt. My teeny-weeny afro, which I'm wearing in a twist-out for my birthday, is tucked halfway under a black beanie. Vivian said I looked skater-boy chic, and Rhee said I looked like I wasn't even trying at all, and that basically sums up my personal style.

"We're ready for your mystery lights, Shine!"

I glance over at the sound of Rhee's booming voice. She and Viv are running around the moonlit clearing, twirling each other in circles until they're dizzy. Sometimes I think they might be in love, and it makes me happy because they are two of the best people I know.

Makayla suddenly pops out from behind a nearby tree, and I jump. I open my mouth to speak to her, close it again. I waver uncertainly. We're alone, and I'm feeling out of sorts.

Damn.

"So," Makayla says. She must notice I've gone silent. "Excited about what we might find?"

"I am," I say, rocking forward on my feet. "It's like I'm buzzing."

"I get you," Makayla says, nodding. "It's like when I'm working on a new song, when I feel like I'm on the verge of figuring out how everything comes together. We're in the mystery."

I grin. The first conversation we ever had was in the girls bathroom. Bonded over my alien cell phone case cover. That's when she told me she fronts an all-girl experimental art-punk band called the Psychophants, and how she once wrote a song called "Little Green Men Come and Save Me." I can see it now: with her black fishnets and voice like a wild banshee, Makayla will one day rock the Afropunk and Coachella stages. I want to be there.

Makayla taps me on the arm, alerting me once again to my silent gazing. "Why don't you go set up while I look for more snacks?" she suggests.

I nod, because that sounds completely doable, and a perfectly good excuse for me to run away. When I reach Rhee and Viv, they've already settled down on a picnic blanket in the middle of the field. There's a battery-powered lantern throwing light onto the food display, an array of junk food from our last gas station stop: cold hotdogs with buns that have gone stale, three packs of chocolate cupcakes that they plan to stick candles in, Twinkies, HoHos, and a bag of Reese's Peanut Butter Cups. Plus a bottle of sparkling grape juice because we are feeling pretty grown and fancy tonight.

Viv's waist-length dreadlocks have come undone from her bun, falling down around her shoulders. Rhee has taken off her shoes and is lying on her back, knees splayed. She smiles up at me with a dopey little smile, her dimples popping, as she hands me a cup of juice.

"To the moon and stars, to Lola and Makayla sitting in a tree," Rhee toasts.

Viv snickers beside her, and I roll my eyes at the both of them before taking a sip.

"Where's Makayla anyway?" Viv asks before biting into a Reese's cup.

"Grabbing more snacks," I say, pointing back at the van.

Vivian and Rhee both pause in their snacking and drinking. They arch their heads simultaneously and give me a long, withering look. I stare in awe at them. They truly are urban-legend material.

"Why aren't you with her?!" Rhee demands in a harsh whisper.

I swallow, shrugging, helpless. "Because." *I ran away* is the part I don't say.

"We left you two alone for a reason," Rhee says pointedly. "Go get your girl."

Vivian gives a sharp nod in agreement. "You don't want her nabbed by Texas hill folk. Or a chupacabra."

Rhee laughs, and says in a more teasing tone, "You are the only scary thing she needs to see tonight."

"Okay, okay," I say, glancing back across the clearing. "I'll go help her. Or something."

"You're hopeless, babe," Rhee tells me, not for the first time. I look down at my friend and with all the gentleness and grace afforded to me, give her the finger.

Rhee has the nerve to laugh at me and then say, "Viv and I just think it's funny that Makayla volunteered to drive us out here."

I cross my arms in a defensive gesture. "Look, none of us have access to road-trip-ready cars," I explain, reasonably. "And she volunteered because she's, like, a nice person."

"You're the only person she really talks to at school," Vivian points out.

"That's not true," I say, even though, yeah, it kind of is true. Makayla is your textbook loner-misanthrope type. "Look, she and I have a couple classes together. She heard me talking on the phone to y'all about my dream birthday trip, and how the dream couldn't happen without a vehicle, and she offered to drive us."

"She offered to make your dream come true," Vivian says, pronouncing each word slowly, her eyes going wide as if this is all some sudden, unbelievable realization on her part. "Wow, Lola, that is pretty sweet."

"Super sweet sixteen," Rhee says with way too much glee. "The cute goth girl you've been crushing on since she moved here agreed to drive your butt to the middle of the state. Lola, darling, you believe in everything, but you don't believe this girl is into you?"

"Whatever. I'm going," I announce, throwing my hands in the air and turning around with a forcible twist of my hips because my best friends are . . . a lot.

I walk quickly back to the van, where I find Makayla juggling an armful of road-trip snacks.

"Hey, you're back already," she says as I approach.

"I'm back already," I repeat with a guilty huff, and Makayla's expression tips into something soft, something chastening, and I become very aware of the unsteadiness of my heartbeat.

"So . . . I got Twizzlers," she says, jumping down from the van, her boots making a loud clomp on the broken pavement.

"Cool," I say because, yeah, snacks are cool. Makayla closes the distance between us, coming to stand right in front of me as she plops the giant bag of candy into my hands. "Thanks," I say.

Anxiety is like this constant, steady hum underneath my skin that flares up at Makayla's too-close proximity. I gaze up into her kohl-rimmed brown eyes. Honestly, I might be shivering just a little bit—and not from the cold. I meet her gaze for a long, tense moment because this is a thing we've done a couple of times before in class, the *look look look just keep looking* game, until I inevitably have to look away. I always look away first. So what if I'm a coward?

To distract myself from the awkward hotness of everything, I open the bag of Twizzlers, stuff one into my mouth, chew forcefully at the rubbery texture, and settle my view on the dark trees lining the station. I imagine the red eyes of the Mothman looking back at me. Truthfully, cryptids are far less scary than Makayla Jackson.

I chew harder and think about how Makayla dressed up for the trip in this gorgeous Gothic-looking velvet black dress trimmed by black lace, which rests nicely against her dark brown skin. She's even shaped her thick afro into a braided Mohawk style, the curly tips of the fro-hawk bleached platinum blond. Her silver septum piercing matches the seven silver hoops that adorn the rim of her left ear.

Makayla is beautiful and weird, and weirdly beautiful, like some kind of mysterious alien planet. More than the beautiful thing, there's this strange sharpness about her that pulls at something equally sharp in me. The kind of sharp edge that probably comes from living in our skin the way we often have to—our defenses always up, our eyes ever wary. The way the world spins differently for girls like us.

"Ground control to Major Tom," Makayla sings in a soft whisper, and I startle, realizing once again that I've been staring off into the void for far too long. Makayla is smiling knowingly down at me like she sees all my inner weirdness. I like that Makayla seems to get me. I like a lot of things about this girl. Not just the dark nail polish, dark eyeliner, skull rings, and goth-punk accessories. Not just the fact that Makayla stares at me from across a crowded gymnasium like I'm actually somebody worth looking at.

Sometimes it seems like Makayla is this parallel universe only I can access. In these moments when we're looking at each other, I feel like nothing can get at me. It excites me, and it scares me. It leaves me floating in zero gravity far above the world. A total space oddity.

"I . . ." I begin, but drift off because what even are words?

Makayla smirks. "*You . . . ?*"

I make a big deal out of straightening out the Twizzlers bag, and then I make an attempt at a normal face. "Want to, um, go for a walk?"

Makayla turns the kind of smile on me that I should really be used to by now, blinding and uninhibited. Though it always manages to catch me off guard, makes me go breathless.

"Lead the way," Makayla says. Taking a deep, fortifying inhale, I gather my strength and lead us toward the edge of the clearing. Makayla falls into step on my left, humming a tune beneath her breath. We leave the snacks behind.

I love this time of night—the witching hour—when the world feels so huge—expansive and full of dimension. Everything is sensational. I can feel the rocky terrain though the soles of my worn-out Vans. For almost ten whole minutes, I manage to somehow put one foot in front of the other without embarrassment. That is, until I trip on a big-ass rock that appears out of nowhere, and Makayla is there to grab me by the arm, to keep me from falling flat on my face.

There's this moment when the world stops, and Makayla's tight grip on me feels real and affirming. Life changing, almost. I am completely undone.

"Thanks," I say, breathless, weightless.

When I flutter back down to Earth, I'm a little awed by the fact that I can still feel the warm imprint of Makayla's hand on my arm, even though the grip lasted mere seconds.

"Sure thing," Makayla responds, all easy smile. "I packed an extra pair of boots if you want to use them tonight."

I smile up at her, momentarily caught off guard by the dark rim of lace encircling her collarbone, and the paint smear of a birthmark on her right cheek. I clear my throat and say, "Maybe I can wear them when we hike to the hilltop in the morning."

Tomorrow, as the morning dawns on my sixteenth birthday, we will gather together to visit Shine's biggest hill, the site of one of the earliest alien spaceship crashes in Texas UFO-logical history.

"Absolutely," Makayla says. "For now though, here." She looks down at me and offers me her hand.

My soul is attempting to climb out of my body. Miraculously, I still manage to place a trembling hand in Makayla's soft, willowy one, whispering, "Thank you," again under my breath as we continue walking.

Two Black girls can disappear in the dark. Mostly though, we walk. We bump up against each other, our bodies weaving through the grass. Makayla hums something sweet over the rhythm of her boots. When I almost trip again, Makayla tightens her hand in mine, and I find myself holding on. Gravity has nothing on us. We move hand in hand into the soft night.

III. [FIRST CONTACT]

Before Roswell, there was Shine, Texas. In the mid-1800s a group of settlers, well let's be real, a group of *colonizers*, claimed to have seen a bona fide spaceship crash. While wrangling his cattle, farmer Conrad Williams witnessed a series of mysterious crafts moving in formation in the northwest sky, which the local newspaper dubbed "saucers." One of those saucers crashed on a hill a few miles from his farm. When he gathered enough men to go check it out the following morning, all they found was a strange oval impression seared into the grass. For weeks after, farmer Williams and his family saw dancing lights all along the horizon. The story became one of the many local legends in a town called Shine.

I'm thinking about farmer Williams, that night when his world changed forever. I feel something of that now, the way my hands shake. Whether we're all alone in the universe or not, I'm somehow sitting on a log next to Makayla in the middle of the woods, and our legs are touching. I distract myself by thinking about how our bodies are made of carbon and a handful of other elements. The hydrogen inside of us was formed in the big bang. I'm thinking about this when I see Makayla's tattoo.

Next to the black jelly bracelets on her right wrist, my eyes can make out the tiny inked words wrapping around her wrist. "We are star stuff," I read the tattooed words aloud, smiling wide. "You're a Sagan fangirl, eh?"

"A little," Makayla says, and flashes a surprisingly shy grin. "Sometimes I just need to be reminded. You know. To look up."

I can see something in her eyes, something that leaves me feeling split off from the rest of the world, or maybe just a little bit lost, like I'm stuck between universes. Multiverse theory is all the rage right now, right? The words inside of me disappear, but the worlds inside of me multiply.

"The first time I ever saw you," Makayla says on a soft breath, "you were just standing in the middle of the track during PE, looking up at the sky."

I laugh quietly, shake my head. "I was probably looking for chemtrails."

"Look up," Makayla tells me.

"What?" I ask, confused.

"Look up, Lola."

So I look up. Somewhere in the universe, there are stars exploding, somewhere there are planets forming. Multitudinous comets are being tossed out across the galaxy. But right here, right above us, there are shapes moving across the star-spun night sky, whizzing so fast I almost miss them, till Makayla takes my hand. Then she's pulling me to my feet. She's jumping up and down next to me, pointing and whispering, "Oh my God, oh my God. *Lola, just look!*"

That's when it hits me. This is really happening. Something is actually moving above us, creating strange geometric patterns in the dark, shooting out points of light like falling stars. So I start jumping up and down too, screeching, and pointing, and giggling because *oh my freaking God*! Then hand in hand, Makayla and I run back toward Rhee and Viv, who are standing and jumping and pointing to the sky too.

"What the hell are they?!" Rhee yells in wonder, holding onto Viv as they stare at the bright burning sky. So many of the news reports and blogs about Shine describe bobbing balls of light that glow and move around chaotically, and it's a little like that. But these lights have some formation to them too—some method to all their madness.

Beside me, Makayla is singing and dancing and I join her, swooshing my hips like the energy from the stars is coursing right through me too. We wave our arms in the air and shake our butts, and honestly I've never burned brighter or felt more alive.

A warm wind blows. The trees sway back and forth. We dance. I wonder if everything will feel like a dream later, something we only remember in pieces. Lost time. The stuff of internet legend. No matter, because in this moment, hundreds of miles from home, with wild patterns flitting across the sky, I dance under this alien glow. The light sparks off of our dark skin like fire.

Makayla is a blur before me. Her laugh spins out and catches me in its promise. In every multiverse theory, there are moments when things could go differently, when one decision splits off to create other universes, a hundred different ways for a life to play out. In this moment, Makayla catches me and time stops again, just for a beat. She leans over me, and I'm caught in her orbit. I memorize the sharp angles of her cheekbones, the wide slant of her eyes, the curl of her eyelashes. The gold in her hair shimmers.

Makayla whispers, "Happy birthday." She looks at me, and for the first time, I don't turn away. Instead, I lean in and press my lips softly against hers. She kisses me back then, warm and dizzying and mind-blowing. We kiss until we're breathless, leaning against each other for support, and blinking against the dancing light.

"Look up," she whispers to me.

And I do.

CATALYST RISING
BY TRACY DEONN

> Every colour will appear after blackness, and where thou see thy matter to wax black, then rejoice because it is the beginning of the work.
>
> —*Rosarium Philosophorum*, sixteenth century

My new therapist says that anxiety is caused by *What if*s.

What if I mess up my speech?

What if I fail this test?

What if my father just up and leaves me too?

That last one is my main *What if,* apparently. Carol decides this in our third session. It's eight thirty-five in the morning on a Monday, much too early to, like, make *claims* about people.

I stifle a yawn.

"Petra," says Carol.

"Yep, yep," I mumble. I sit higher in the stiff leather chair in the losing war to wake my body up. I'm not used to having appointments before school. At school, everyone walks into the building half-zombied and nobody asks hard questions or expects you to answer with actual human words. "I'm listening." Sorta. Not really. Carol glances at my hands doing their usual tapping thing on the leather armrests. She says extremities like fingertips can start tingling—even go numb—when anxiety peaks.

Mine don't really do that. They just sort of . . . itch.

"What was the question?" I ask.

Her eyes return to mine with a neutral gaze, but her mouth is a thin, tight wire of a smile. "What do you think about that? The idea that the source of your anxiety is your mom's sudden disappearance?" My hands catch her attention again.

I stare at my fingertips, warm brown against the black leather, and *will* them into stillness. The constant tapping gets annoying, even to me, but it's the only way to stop the itching. When my hands get like this, it's best to keep them busy. I tug at a long thin braid that has fallen out of my ponytail.

"Petra?"

Oh. Right. Mom's disappearance . . . source of my anxiety. "I think that is a . . . hypothesis. Not a fact."

Carol shrugs. "You're right, I can't present this idea as a fact, but I would encourage you to keep it in mind. To consider it as you go through this week at school."

"The only way to consider a hypothesis," I say with a sigh, "is to test it. And there is no way to test this one, so . . ."

"I disagree," Carol replies. "I believe you can hold an idea in your mind for a while, giving it space and room to settle in, and see what comes of that."

"No disrespect," I begin, but I think Carol and I both know I absolutely mean *yes*, disrespect, "but this sounds like social science. I prefer *science* science."

"I am aware." Carol sighs. Lays her pen down on the side table next to her own leather chair. "So, Petra, how would you describe your family dynamic, in scientific terms?"

That's an easy question because I've been writing that equation in my head for weeks now.

I hold my left fist out, fingers curled and facing the floor. "My mom and dad were the fuel. The reactants." I hold out my right hand, fingers wide and open and palm up. "Mom's job change was the oxygen."

"And?"

"Fuel reactants plus oxygen . . ." Carol watches me draw my hands together, fist and palm close, but not touching. "Equals . . ." I spread both hands wide. "Boom."

Carol raises a brow. "'Boom' is a scientific term?"

"No." I drop my hands to my knees and roll my eyes. "That would be 'combustion.' An equation that creates light and heat."

"Is that always true?" Carol asks. "The 'boom' part?"

She's bringing us back to social science again, I can feel it. "Not always." I scowl. "But chemical reactions with specific reactants generate the same product every single time."

"As reliable as that may be, if we are to use your metaphor, I propose that there is an uncertainty about the scale of explosion you've just witnessed," she says, gesturing to the air as she muses. "Was it something massive, like the Hindenburg? Was it the lighting of a match? Or was it a gas lantern, lit to lead you on another path?"

"I don't know," I mutter.

"And when our minds grasp at the unknown on a regular basis . . . ?"

Our time is almost up. I give her the answer she wants because I have a feeling that if I don't, this lady is gonna bring up her bad science all over again next week. "Anxiety."

Carol smiles triumphantly. "Exactly. So we are here to discuss the potential impacts of this family transformation, which may be negatively contributing to your mental wellness."

She's so dang proud of herself. So satisfied. Ugh. She wants me to be satisfied too, I think. But nothing about being in this office could ever give me the same satisfaction of being in a lab because people are . . . messy and volatile. And so are parents.

My fingertips itch. Instead of tapping, I rub them together this time, send them silent promises that soon we'll be somewhere more reliable.

Predictable. Where sense is made from atoms and positive and negative charges. In labs, explosions don't happen out of nowhere.

"Hey, Petra!"

"Hey, Tim." I slide into my lab workstation and set my bag in the cubby under the black counter. Tim West is my lab partner and desk mate. A theater kid, so our worlds don't generally intersect much, but he's grown on me this semester. Tim is lanky and tall, with long brown limbs and expressive eyes. He leans over the countertop, groaning dramatically. "Today's gonna suck."

"Today?" I look around. The rest of the class is filing in. "What's today?"

Tim's head jerks backward in shock. "The midterm? Multiple choice *and* a practical exam?"

I smile. Itchy fingers, tapping on the black marble. "Forgot about that."

He rolls his eyes. "Of *course* you forgot. Don't even know why I ask. You live for this stuff." He wipes a hand down his face. "Give me a timed written English essay any day."

I shudder. "Better you than me."

The bell rings. The last few students hustle down the center aisle in the lab, scurrying in pairs to their open seats at the other two-top lab tables distributed around the room.

"Hey, where's Redmon?" I ask. Small scuffs of metal chair feet echo around the room as other students shift in their seats, asking the same thing. A low murmur rises, then crackles with the sound of hope; if Mr. Redmon isn't here, do we still have a test?

"Oh, man," Tim whispers. "Please let it be a sub, please let it be a sub . . ."

The door closest to the long teacher's table at the front of the classroom opens, and it looks like Tim's wish has come true.

In walks the tweed-suited human embodiment of every high schooler's secret desire, the break that you can't predict, and the busywork you won't complain about: a substitute teacher.

Most of our eleventh-grade-certified subs are generalists, which means they won't even bother with anything in a midyear science unit; the topics are too specialized. Tim drops his forehead to the table with a long sigh. "Thank you, God."

The sub pauses at the front of the classroom to look us over. He is a white man in his forties with gaunt cheekbones and short dark hair combed back.

"Good morning." The substitute's voice rolls over the class like a boulder: low and unavoidable and far, far too confident.

This man doesn't sound like a generic sub. No. He's one of those subject-specific kinds. The kind that shows up *prepared*.

Where that low voice has gone, a cold still dread fills the space.

Tim makes a pained sound beneath his breath. "Oh, no . . ."

"Not sure God heard your prayers," I mutter.

Tim raises his eyes to the ceiling. "Lord, why have you forsaken me?"

"My name is Dr. Leopold," the man says. He puts an *actual* briefcase up on the countertop and, without looking down, cracks it open with both thumbs.

Yikes.

Dr. Leopold lays his case down flat. "I am to understand you have a test today?" A low groan ripples from the back of the room to the front. Dr. Leopold raises a thick, bushy black brow. "Problem?"

Beside me, Tim's hand shoots up. "Any chance we could use the day to review the material, Dr. Leopold?"

I roll my eyes. I was looking forward to the quiet and simplicity of the test. No talking to people, just chemical formulas. Letters and subscripts.

"I'm afraid not," Dr. Leopold murmurs. His eyes roam over the class of grumbling students and then, without warning, land on mine. "We must proceed with the great work, as it were." Dr. Leopold's eyes move to the student behind me, but that heavy boulder feeling remains. Like this man's presence is too much for the room—atomic mass more than standard for sure.

"But perhaps," Dr. Leopold begins, "we can shift today's work from evaluation to demonstration."

Ugh. "Demonstration of what?" I ask.

Dr. Leopold slips his hands into his pockets. Each elbow of his tweed suit has a brown patch on it, just like the pictures in old chemistry textbooks when all the labs were filled with white men in full-ass suits. "How about we demonstrate some magic?"

The class laughs. Tim, ever the performer, perks up. "What kinda magic?"

"Also," I add, "Magic isn't real."

Dr. Leopold holds up a finger. "Have you ever seen a stage magician, Ms. . . . ?"

"Lewis," I frown. "Those shows are just science tricks with a bit of pizzazz."

"Exactly." Leopold lifts a shoulder. "Employing what's in this classroom, let's use science to put on our own show. Debunk the magicians' tricks."

"What are the parameters?" I ask, irritated at losing the midterm—and with it, the peace of routine equations in a silent classroom. "What constitutes a magic trick?"

Tim kicks me under the table and mutters, "Just go with it, Lewis . . ."

Dr. Leopold smiles and lifts a stack of sheets out of his briefcase. "Everything you need to recreate some of these more common scientific entertainments is already in supply in this room. None of the experiments here require more safety equipment than a pair of protective goggles and gloves, and the good sense that I assume a class of juniors has by now?"

The class laughs, but I squirm in my seat. I don't like surprises in science. When teachers try and have "fun" in the lab, it feels like they're turning the whole thing into a joke. Guess I'm the only one who feels that way, since everyone else is grinning at the new activity.

Dr. Leopold strolls down the center aisle, letting students choose sheets at random, and student pairs leap out of their seats to go to the supply cabinets on the perimeter walls to gather their materials. When he gets to our table, instead of allowing one of us to choose my and Tim's "magic trick" demonstration, he pulls out the paper himself and hands it to me.

I look at it. "Genie in a bottle?"

Dr. Leopold eyes me. "A classic."

"It's simple," I complain.

"We'll take it!" Tim snatches the sheet from me before I can hand it back.

Ten minutes later, we're standing at our stations in lab coats, wearing goggles and gloves and, at least in my case, a scowl. "This is basic. Junior-high science-fair-level basic."

All around us is the buzz of other students talking through their own experiments, dressed in similar safety gear and hovering over a variety of supplies.

Tim shakes his head. "Only you would complain that an experiment is too easy."

I sigh and stare down at our lab table. A boiling flask: a glass with a rounded shape, flat bottom for stability, and a narrow open neck. A glass beaker filled with 30 percent hydrogen peroxide filled to the fifty millimeter line. A digital scale holding a small plastic dish, empty and waiting.

"Okay," I murmur. "Hand me the catalyst."

"The what?" Tim asks, leaning over to review our supplies.

"Catalyst," I repeat. "There are a few that will work so just grab which-ever. Potassium iodide, sodium iodide, manganese dioxide."

Tim shakes his head. "Sorry, friend. All out of those particular -ides."

I frown. "Maybe somebody else has some?"

"Y'all got -ides?" Tim asks our neighbors. A sister-and-brother pair named Katherine and Brody. Katherine narrows her eyes at Tim and turns away.

Brody snickers. "Which ones, man?"

Tim rattles off the list after checking in with me. Brody shakes his head. I glance at the clock; we have ten minutes left to prepare for our little "dem-onstration," and I have a reputation to uphold. "Ask around," I order.

Tim makes a loop of the room in search of the compounds we need. He comes back empty-handed. "Sorry, Petra."

I curse under my breath and rub my fingers together. The friction of the glove feels great against the sudden itch. "Substitute teacher handing out assignments when the classroom isn't even *stocked* correctly."

I wish Carol was here so I could point out that this is why her "social" and my "science" don't go together. The science in this room is sound, but people? People make it messy and inconsistent. People don't check supplies before handing out assignments. People forget things and ask you to do without. People leave you standing empty-handed even though you're the best chemistry student in school.

Messy Dr. Leopold claps his hands once to call us to attention. "Time's up, everyone. Let's begin the magic show."

All around us, the other pairs describe their experiment, then demon-strate the so-called magic and the science behind it. Making water "vanish" before your very eyes with sodium polyacrylate. "Nonflammable money" with bills soaked in a salt and alcohol-water solution. Purple smoke from aluminum powder, iodine, and water—thick enough we have to open the overhead emergency vent. Everyone claps after each "trick" and the duos bow as if they've actually done something interesting.

Then the class turns to us.

Dr. Leopold nods. "Genie in a bottle, please, Petra and Tim."

"Well, funny story . . ." Tim begins, spreading his hands wide.

"We're missing a catalyst," I interject, scowling. "The supply cabinet is out of all of the compounds we could have used to speed up the decomposition process."

"Booo . . ." Brody calls. "Where's the genie?" A few of the other boys join in, mostly the ones that I've refused to help with their homework because, to them, "helping" means cheating. I'm sure watching me fail at something delights them to no end.

My fingers honestly feel like they might burn through these gloves. I grab the filled glass and hold it out, glaring at them and Dr. Leopold in turn. "See? No catalyst, no water vapor, no gen—"

"Genie!" Tim cries beside me.

"Wha—" I turn, eyes already rolling, and stop short.

The glass in my hand is spewing water vapor into the air in thick gray streams, and growing warmer by the second against my palm. I'm so shocked I nearly drop it.

The class claps and begins to chant: "Genie! Genie! Genie!"

"Oh my God!" I set the glass down on the countertop and step back as it continues to send a stream of storm-cloud vapor toward the ceiling.

Tim claps my shoulder and leans in. "Sneaky, sneaky, Petra. But a *great* performance."

"What?" I ask, dazedly.

"You know," he says with a grin. "*Misdirection.* Tell the audience you can't *possibly* achieve whatever trick, and then miraculously make it happen. It's good stuff." He turns and bows deeply, theater kid to the bone.

When his head dips low, the vapor disperses enough that I can see the only other person in the classroom who isn't clapping and enjoying the show.

Instead of watching the flask, Dr. Leopold is staring right at me.

The bell rings and students hurry around the room, breaking down their experiments as quickly as they can before the next period begins. I turn away, too, not sure which thing is unsettling me more: Dr. Leopold's assessing, sharp gaze, or the impossible chemical reaction still going before my eyes.

At the beginning of the school year, Mr. Redmon gave me special clearance to set up some of the bigger lab experiments at the end of the school day so that they're ready to go in the morning. Usually those involve a complicated array of labware, each piece giving me a thrill to arrange: beakers and graduated cylinders, flasks and alcohol lamps, test tubes and pipettes.

But after the last bell rings today, I speed-walk to the empty classroom, shut the door behind me, and hope no one else decides to stop by. I don't want anyone here for *this* particular experiment. I move fast and only turn on half of the overhead lights.

I jog between the tables, dashing quickly and quietly from cabinet to cabinet to recreate the genie experiment from the morning.

Everything is set up just as it was, except we seem to be out of the heavy-duty chemical gloves. "Ugh." I stalk to the front of the classroom to find the extra gloves in the cubby beneath Mr. Redmon's desk. When I kneel down to look for the bright orange box, I spot a row of three squat glass jars.

"-*Ides*," I murmur. All three of the catalyst compounds Tim had been looking for are *right here* behind the desk. "What the hell?" This isn't even where supplies are supposed to go, much less the exact ones we needed to do Dr. Leopold's ridiculous genie magic trick.

I grab my preferred compound—the manganese dioxide—and walk back to the table. I don't get it. Why would someone want to keep us from doing a simple reaction in class? Was it one of the guys who laughed at us when we went to present? Maybe one of them heard Tim asking around and decided to get back at me for not tutoring them. I snort. Pretty bold to sabotage an experiment in front of a creepy, unpredictable substitute teacher like Dr. Leopold—

Dr. Leopold.

My breath catches as I remember the way he *specifically* handed me and Tim the genie-in-a-bottle assignment. Other kids being jerks, I can see, but would a teacher set up a couple of kids like that? Hide materials just to see us scramble? Ugh.

As I arrange the experiment again, those questions dissolve into the recesses of my mind. They aren't the important queries here. The important query is: How the heck did that reaction happen without a catalyst? And why was the vapor dark gray, nearly black, not white?

With that in mind, I set the manganese aside and stare at the clear hydrogen peroxide in the clear boiling flask. The liquid and glass are both just sitting there, lifeless, waiting for something to happen.

Well, not totally lifeless. The decomposition to water and oxygen would happen on its own even if I didn't do anything, albeit very, very slowly and without any fanfare. That's the point of a catalyst; it introduces a substance that speeds everything up—and that substance isn't consumed by the reaction. No matter what, catalysts stay put. They don't just up and disappear suddenly. At the end of the equation, the catalyst is still there.

Catalysts persist.

I retrace my steps. The only thing missing here is annoying Tim and my gloves. The *gloves*.

I slip both pairs of gloves on and glance at the glass, then back at my hands. Wrap one palm around the flask while leaning back and . . . nothing happens.

I'm just standing in an empty lab holding a flask in the air, feeling foolish as hell. I tense my fingers and flatten them, try and get as much surface area of the gloves over the glass as possible, but still, nothing happens. I set the flask down.

If everything is set up the right way, your results shouldn't be random and shocking and out of control. Science is supposed to be predictable. Science is supposed to be measurable. Good science is *replicable*.

Standing there, irritated all over again with no Tim to snap at, I feel my fingers start their itching thing, and it hits me.

My fingertips. *They're* the variable.

Well, maybe.

It's a hypothesis, not a fact. The only way to prove a hypothesis . . . is to test it.

I tear the glove off my right hand and take a steadying breath that sounds much louder in my ears in an empty classroom in a near-empty school. I swallow. My mouth is dry.

"It's just a test," I whisper, and extend my hand and prickly fingers to the glass.

A low voice rolls through the room before I make contact. "I thought you might come back here."

I gasp and whip around to see a shadowed figure at the door. "Dr. Leopold."

I must have been so distracted by my fingertip-variable thoughts that

I didn't notice the substitute teacher enter the room behind me. His tall shape is a silhouette against the glass in the door and glaring fluorescents of the hallway.

A cold drip of unease slips down my spine. Why would a substitute teacher be here after school? Most of the time, they hightail it out of the building as fast—if not faster—than the students do.

"S-Sorry," I stammer, dropping both hands to my sides. "I just . . . sometimes I come in here after—Mr. Redmon said it's okay."

Dr. Leopold melts out of his shadow into the light, still in his tweed jacket. Still taking up too much space in the room, in my mind. *Atomic weight.* Mass too large for such a small man. My heart thumps against my rib cage.

"I didn't think there would be any need to come to this town, this school, to follow up on a random tip. In fact, I almost didn't come here at all." He shrugs, eyes roaming the classroom, the building, and beyond.

"Uhh . . . okay?" I murmur.

There's a door behind me that exits out into the other hallway, and I'm half a classroom closer to it than Dr. Leopold is. I don't like it at all that this feels like good information to have.

"The typical response to a Phnutian running off somewhere is, of course, to follow." Dr. Leopold eyes me.

"Phnutian?" I ask. "What's a—"

"But in this case, it seemed like it might be . . . what did that boy say earlier? Misdirection."

"Dr. Leopold," I say, sliding back along the counter lining the wall. "I have no idea what you're talking about." Each time my heart pounds in my chest, my fingertips answer with a wave of heat.

His eyes narrow. "If I hadn't seen your response to the reaction today, I might not believe you. But you have no idea what you're doing, do you? You truly are an untrained alchemist."

I bark a laugh. "Alchemy is not a thing. Not anymore."

"Then how do you explain this morning's reaction?" He tilts his head. "You had no compound to bring about that exothermic reaction, and yet, bring it about you did, Petra."

I swallow against the sudden knot in my throat. "*You* hid those catalysts. It *was* you!"

"Evidently," Dr. Leopold answers, "you didn't need them."

"I—"

The door behind me slams open, revealing another figure. Shorter, this time. A teenage boy with a thick shock wave of short, curly black hair and deep brown skin. "Hello, Rufus."

"Darius's boy?" Dr. Leopold drawls. "Really?"

"Uh . . ." I stammer. Who the hell is *Darius* and who is this—his—boy?! *What the*—I shake my head. A conversation has just sprung up around me, and it's one I have nothing to do with and don't feel *any* need to get stuck in. I press as close to the side wall as I can, looking between the two of them as I edge toward an escape.

"My name is not *Darius's boy*. It's Aten," he answers simply. The boy's dark eyes scan the room and land on the flask sitting on the table between us.

Dr. Leopold's hands had, until now, remained behind his back, but when Aten advances toward the flask, Leopold steps forward, producing a short staff out of nowhere. He snaps it into position, holding it horizontally over the table and flask. "The Zosmos claim this find. I was here first, Aten."

The staff is old, smooth ivory, and wrapped with carved serpents who twist around the center rod and meet one another, mouths wide open and fang-to-fang, at the very top.

Aten raises one hand. "I am not here to argue provenance over the solution."

"What the hell is going on?" I cry.

From behind his back, Aten produces another staff of his own. Short, made of wood, with identical carved serpents wrapped around it and leading to a small wing-tipped ball on one end. But instead of holding it out over the table, Aten holds it upright. "No challenge."

Dr. Leopold's eyes flash. "Good."

"What are those? Who *are* you guys?"

Every part of me wants to sprint from this classroom, but no one seems to be doing anything dangerous. Just creepy. And bizarre. With . . . bad vibes. I think. But whatever I thought I would find here in this lab, it wasn't two people speaking nonsense like they're in some sort of . . . turf war. Then it hits me.

"Are you LARPers?" I gasp. "Is that it?"

Aten snorts. "Oh, that's hilarious."

"Are we *what*?" Leopold sputters.

"LARPers," I repeat. "Live-action role-players?" I gesture to their staffs. "Medieval theater nerds with props and things."

Leopold's lip curls back. "Touch the flask, girl."

I scowl. "I don't want to—"

Leopold's hand tightens around his staff until his knuckles turn white "Touch the flask. Just as you did this morning."

Any humor in the room has evaporated. Fled into nothingness. All that's left behind is the cold look in Dr. Leopold's eyes and the taut line of Aten's shoulders.

"Do it," Aten urges. He is frozen in position, eyes on me. "Touch the flask."

I gulp and step forward. My fingers feel like they're on *fire*. I extend my right hand and wrap my palm around the clear base . . . and the liquid turns dark and bubbly. Black vapor shoots out of the opening and toward the ceiling. Without the overhead emergency vent on, the vapor quickly obscures the classroom lights, sending the room into half-darkness.

"*Negrido* . . ." Leopold hisses. "Impossible!" He rushes forward, and in the split second it takes him to reach me, Aten's staff taps my shoulder.

Just as Dr. Leopold's fingers wrap around my own holding the flask, Aten shouts: "Claimed for the 'Nutians!"

"Keep her!" the older man shouts. He snatches the glass from me and screams immediately. The flask falls onto the hard countertop and shatters. Vapor spreads out in a low mushroom cloud. Dr. Leopold lurches forward, grasping the wrist of his burned hand.

In the smoke and confusion, Aten yanks me back the way he came. He jerks the classroom door open and clutches my hand tight. "Run!"

He doesn't have to tell me twice. We sprint down the now-empty hallway, a straight shot through the science wing that leads into a four-way split. "Fastest way out?" He gasps, releasing my hand to secure his staff back into some sort of strap on his back.

"Foreign language hall!" I point.

"ATEN!"

"Come on!" He grabs my hand, and we're off again. Running footsteps follow us—Dr. Leopold is not far behind.

This hallway is shorter. We hit the double doors' metal crash bars at the same time, pushing out into the late afternoon sun of the teacher's parking lot. I gulp fresh air into burning lungs, wishing suddenly that I'd taken gym class just a little more seriously.

Aten pulls me again, rushing us toward a red sports car already parked facing away from the school. "Get in."

"No way!"

He rolls his eyes. "Get in the car, Petra."

"How do you know my name?"

"Because your mother told me," he shouts.

Breath punches from my lungs. "My mom?"

He opens the door and sprints to the driver's side. "Get in, get in, my *God*!"

"ATEN!" Dr. Leopold roars. He's made his way into the parking lot too now.

I jump in the passenger seat and slam the door, barely buckling in before Aten has us screeching out of the lot and onto the residential road that borders the school.

"Who are you?" I demand. "How do you know my mom?"

Aten's eyes are on the road. They occasionally glance in the rearview mirror to the road behind us, but they're always on the road.

I repeat myself, heart pounding on every word. *"What do you know about my mother?"*

He glances sideways, a split second of recognition flashes in his eyes before they move away. He merges onto a road that leads into downtown—away from the school. We join the rest of traffic, and he finally speaks. "Do you know what the philosopher's stone is?"

My breath is finally slowing down. "My mother—"

"Do you know what it is?" He is dogged. Acts like I haven't spoken at all. It makes me want to scream at him, but I don't get the feeling it will do me any good.

I grit my teeth and answer his question, "The philosopher's stone is made up. Fictional. Turns metal into gold or . . . gives eternal life. Some crap like that."

"For nearly two thousand years, alchemists have been searching for a way to complete the Great Work, the process of creating the stone." He changes lanes. "It is believed that the Great Work has four primary stages, defined by color: black, white, yellow, and red. Negrido is the first."

Negrido. That's what Dr. Leopold said when he saw my experiment. My eyes widen. "The vapor from the genie in a bottle started out dark gray . . . but then just now it was—"

"Black." His eyes narrow. "It was black. The stone's first phase of trans-formation." He blinks. "Wait. The genie in a what now?"

"Never mind," I say. "You don't really expect me to believe that, do you? The black vapor back there—that was a chemical reaction that shouldn't have happened. Dr. Leopold—"

"Belongs to an ancient sect of alchemists, the Zosmos, who believe that the stone is a substance. An actual physical item that must follow the phases of creation." He shakes his head. He eases off the main road now, and turns us down a gravel road. "I belong to a sect that broke off from the Zosmos, led by a woman named Paphnutia. The Phnutians."

"Okay . . ." We pull to a stop in the driveway of a large country house that has only just now become visible through the trees. "And what does that have to do with my experiment?"

"That's just it. We don't care about your experiment. We reject the literal explanation. Which is why I knew not to claim the flask." He smirks against his fist.

"But you . . . you claimed me," I say. "Why?"

He pulls to a stop and kills the engine before turning to me. "Because we don't believe that the stone is an object. We believe the stone is a person." He glances down at my hands, balled into fists in my lap. "Someone who can transform elements at the touch of a fingertip."

I'm shaking my head before he speaks. "Look, Aten . . ." But before I can counter his unscientific, mythical substance nonsense, his words take another lap around in my mind. *We reject, we believe* . . . I suck in a breath. "When you say 'we,' do you mean . . . ?"

"The Phnutians, generally, but also," he takes a slow, steadying breath, "I mean your mother, Petra. She's one of us."

Those words land right in my gut, knocking everything in my world off-balance. My fingers clutch the edge of the car seat, holding on, digging in.

This can't be real.

I don't want it to be real, but . . .

What if? What if this is real? And this Aten boy knows my mother, and my mother sent him to find me.

I turn the *what if* into a hypothesis, then into a query: "What did my mother tell you about me?"

Aten's eyes sparkle, as if I've finally asked the right question. "That the philosopher's stone is someone who doesn't *need* a catalyst to transmute matter . . . because she—*you*—are the catalyst."

REQUIEM OF SOULS
BY TERRY J. BENTON-WALKER

The only time I feel corporeal is when I'm playing music.

Otherwise, I'm a mere spirit, floating through day after day, unable to affect a single thing about my world—which has transformed into a nightmare realm since Dad died.

I dress for school silent as a ghost because I don't want to wake Mom, or worse, her boyfriend, Frank. I rub my spin brush over my thick hair, which is just like Dad's. We had the same dark skin too. He also gave me my name—Rocko Sampson—and my flute, my final gift from him, which I slip into my backpack.

Music has always soothed me in a way that drawing never could (though I love sketching no less)—but especially lately when Mom and Frank are fighting. After their shouts woke me last night, I set up my old wobbly music stand and practiced for the spring concert. Playing distracts my mind and allows my stomach and soul to unwind for a bit.

I grab my jacket and keys and open my bedroom door but almost choke when I run into Mom, her hand raised to knock. She's wearing pajamas and her satin bonnet. Dark circles ring the undersides of her maple-colored eyes. She hasn't always looked like this. Exhausted. Beat down.

"Morning," I mutter.

She narrows her eyes. "I know good and well you weren't trying to run out of here early without speaking to me."

"I need to work on a project." Not a lie. More a convenient truth to avoid discussing the phone call she got from my biology teacher yesterday.

Her face softens. "Okay, but first I'd like to know why Ms. White called me while I was at work last night to tell me you walked out of her class."

"It wasn't my fault," rockets out before I can think.

"Someone held a gun to your head and made you leave class without permission?"

I catch myself mid–eye roll and fake like I'm looking away. "Ms. White tried to take my phone. She sees other people on theirs all the time, but I checked mine *once* near the end of class, and she went ballistic. So, I walked out. She hates me, and you know what? I hate her too."

"Rocko!" Mom exclaims.

I don't know why she's surprised. I've explained the situation to her a thousand times. Ms. White's an old, racist white lady who doesn't understand how a poor Black boy tested into honors biology.

"We don't hate anyone." Mom frowns at me. "And the rules aren't always fair, but we have to abide by them whether we like them or not."

Dear God. I'd rather scuba dive in an active volcano than continue this conversation. I look away again because it's more productive to remain silent than fight.

The shrill whine of Mom's bedroom door opening comes from the end of the hall, introducing Frank. The pungent scent of his musky cologne pours into the hallway before his bulky silhouette slinks out. Frank's so light-skinned I think he forgets he's Black sometimes. He's brushed down his rust-colored hair and donned his blue work coveralls. His gray-green eyes glow in the dim light, like a demon's. A familiar, abusive chill rips through me.

"I can hear your whining all the way in the bedroom," he grumbles. "We already tolerate the gay stuff, but you gotta be a wimp too?" My eyes retreat to the floor. "All you wanna do is hide in this musty room all day and night and blow on that fruity-ass flute. Grow up. Quit bitching and moaning and learn some accountability, boy."

My jaws lock. I'm mute. And numb.

Satisfied with my emotional flogging, Frank huffs and leaves for work. The violent slam of the front door rattles the old walls of our home, making both me and Mom flinch.

"Hate him too," I mutter.

She sighs and massages her temples.

I brush past her into the somber living room. When we first moved here with Dad, everything seemed brighter. But now, the ugly floral couch he dragged all the way from Houston is lumpy and misshapen around what remains of our happy memories. Like me lying on his chest, both of us sobbing unabashedly over Disney movies. But Frank's visceral possession of our lives crushed all that and so much more.

"I'm doing the best I can," Mom laments.

I shrug and head for the front door, but her voice cracks behind me, turning my muscles to stone.

"I sacrificed everything for your dad," she says. "I set my whole life aside to come to this dreary town. And now he's gone. What do you expect me to do?"

"So . . . you're blaming Dad for Frank?"

She groans and grabs both sides of her head, flashing the purpling bruises on the undersides of her wrists. "Don't twist my words. When your dad died . . . I . . ."

Gave up. She just . . . gave up. And then she summoned Frank into our lives and looked the other way while that demon fed on what little happiness we had left after Dad died. I can forgive her for everything else, but I cannot forgive her for Frank.

"I pray often." She glances at the Wooden Jesus on the cross hanging on the wall above the couch. He's trapped in this hell as much as me. "I rely on God to guide me."

Trembling with anger, I open the door and a shock of frigid air blows past me.

"God shouldn't have to tell you to protect your kid," I tell her. "See you tonight." I shut the door softly behind me and head for school.

Spring in Wisconsin resembles the dead of winter anywhere else. The dreary atmosphere seeps through your pores and infects your mood. Frank was born and raised here. I wonder if this place is what turned him into a monster—or maybe he was just born evil.

When I get to the band room, I drop my backpack on the floor outside the door labeled ARCHIVES and head inside. I flip the light switch and the fluorescents flicker to life, dousing the room in sterile light. Each wall has floor-to-ceiling shelves packed with boxes of old sheet music, some dating back nearly a century. I offered to digitize the archives because I find plundering these ancient arrangements exciting, like going on an adventure through time.

I slide the rickety ladder down to the section where I last left off and climb up. I have to stand on my tiptoes to reach the box on the top shelf, which is propped precariously atop something. I can't see on what, exactly, because I'm vertically challenged. I stretch myself as tall as I can and nudge the box, revealing wads of paper wedged underneath. When I yank the papers free, the box tilts over the ledge and smacks me square in the face in a puff of dust. An aggressive sneeze throws me from the ladder onto the tiled floor. Pain jolts up my tailbone.

I rub my throbbing booty, then carefully unfold the wadded, yellowed papers and smooth them out on the floor in front of me.

It's sheet music for a song titled "Requiem of Souls."

The pages ripple, the wrinkles ironing themselves out before settling into "like-new" condition. Blood-red ink glints on the pages as if printed moments ago. I pick up the first page and run a finger across the title, but none of the ink rubs off. The score stretches across several pages, but . . . every staff is blank. I'm not sure what I've found nor why it's set off an anxious buzzing in the pit of my stomach.

I turn back to the first page and gasp, dropping the score. The words "For Flute" appear in small lettering beneath the title as if written by an invisible hand. It's like it *knows* I'm a flutist. The rest of the arrangement bleeds onto each page, and I gingerly pick it up.

The song is in common time, four-four meter, which is simple enough, yet "Requiem of Souls" is the most complex arrangement I've ever seen. It's about fifteen minutes long with no rests longer than a couple beats. And there are *nine* movements, or sections of the song, each with a major key change.

I'm pondering where this music could've come from when the warning bell for homeroom sounds. I shove the score into my backpack and rush out the door.

It's near impossible to focus on anything besides "Requiem of Souls" for the rest of the day. It won't let me go, and I don't want it to. When I'm not wondering about the magic contained in those yellowed pages and how it found me, I spend every period with the music camouflaged alongside my notes, studying each bar and humming the eerie, but gorgeous tune in my head.

When the last bell rings, I jet straight home and breathe a sigh of relief to find the house empty. Mom's still at work and Frank's probably—I don't care where that monster is as long as he's not here. I dig "Requiem of Souls" from my backpack and set it on my stand.

Once my flute's assembled, I sit on the edge of the bed, take a deep breath, and play. The song sounds odd at first, and it takes me a while to master the first few lines, because I keep missing flats, and I almost need an extra set of fingers to hit the series of intricate runs that begin in the tenth bar.

Nightfall finds me in the same spot, perched on my bed, still staggering through the first movement. I stand up and stretch, my joints popping with relief. My stomach rumbles, reminding me I haven't eaten since lunch. But something else tugs at me, like a supernatural hand, holding me back. Meh, I'll grab food later.

I sit and play "Requiem of Souls" again. The melancholy first movement sounds like the wind whistling curses as the song leads me on a path through a gray forest of naked trees. The end of the first movement is rife with foreboding thanks to the low notes and somber trills that make gooseflesh prickle along the bare skin of my arms. I play the final note of the movement and lower my flute, panting.

When I look up, my breath hitches. I drop my flute and inadvertently kick over the stand in a flutter of paper as I scramble backward onto my bed.

There are *people* in here with me. Ghosts.

They were so still and silent, I hadn't noticed them before. Or maybe I was too entranced in the song. Even now, none say a word. I've always believed in ghosts, but actually seeing one was never on my bucket list.

I slide toward the headboard of my bed, quivering so violently I have to clench my jaw to stop my teeth chattering.

In front is a tall Black lady with mahogany skin and sharp eyes. An opulent fur sewn along the collar of her dress douses her neck in shadow. Her elaborate Victorian skirts fan out, keeping the others at a considerable distance.

To her left is a Black man, whose clothing has been torn to ragged strips in all but the most private places. The bright whites of his eyes stand out like two moons set into a sea of blood that covers him from head to bare feet. Somehow, I don't think the blood is his.

A thin, fair-skinned toddler appears from behind the flared skirts of the woman. Their eyes are gaping, blacked-out holes, and they're dressed in a long red velvet floor-length nightgown with black embroidering along the front and the hems of the sleeves.

"Please!" begs the woman, her voice low, brittle. She takes a step closer, and I make out the raging yellow-black bruises plastering her neck, which has been crushed to such an extent I'm surprised she can still hold her head upright.

I leap from the bed, stumble to the nearest window, and snatch it open, ready to dive out and run. I don't know where I'm going, but I have to get the heck out of here.

"Do not stop!" she pleads again.

I glance back to see tears glimmering in her furious eyes.

"Please!" Her voice turns to a hoarse howl that cinches my already nervous stomach.

I turn to climb out the window, but movement outside roots me to the spot. The streetlamp on the corner casts a dim glow over a slanted portion of our backyard. A dark silhouette of someone—or something—quite large climbs over our neighbor's fence and lands on all fours just outside the light. For a split second, I think it's Frank—but that's *definitely* not him.

Cloaked in shadow, it stands at a towering height. Its bulbous head pivots slowly toward me, and I realize—

It's not human.

An invisible blanket of cold wraps around me. I want to look away, but I can't.

Suddenly, the thing outside explodes into curly tendrils of smoke that evaporate into the night.

The thump of my flute hitting the floor startles me. I spin around to find the ghosts gone.

I stagger back to my bed. Once I've caught my breath, I crawl to the edge and retrieve my flute and the "Requiem of Souls" sheet music from the floor. I study the blood-red notes, trying to unriddle what the heck just happened. The ghosts, though scary as heck, seem harmless, though hell-bent on hearing the song out. I wonder if it attracts them. And for what purpose? Who would create something like this?

Too wired to sleep, I pull out my sketchbook and transfer their ghostly images onto the page, scrawling names I've given to each underneath.

Angry Victoria. The scowling Black Victorian lady with the smashed neck.

Bloody Barry. The Black man covered in blood with piercing white eyes.

And Goth Baby. The creepy kid with the blacked-out eyes and the clumsy nightgown.

My heart thumps extra hard when I recall the monster in the backyard.

I don't draw or name that one.

The next day in AP Bio, I pore over each movement of "Requiem of Souls" instead of listening to anything Ms. White says. That is, until she slams a printout of my lab report with a bold red *69* at the top onto my desk. "Huh?! A sixty-nine, though?"

Through her glasses, her ice-blue eyes stare down over her sharp nose and taut, disapproving mouth. "You lost an additional fifteen points for not following instructions on the submission site, Mr. Sampson." Her thin lips spread into a smug smirk.

The bell rings and the other students head out in a chaotic shuffle for lunch hour.

"I couldn't get the formatting to work." Frustration strangles my voice so it comes out high and strained, which humiliates me even more. "I emailed you for help, but you ghosted. The submission was gonna be late if I waited, so what was I supposed to do?"

She tuts under her breath and brushes off the sleeves of her pink cardigan as if ridding herself of the crumbs of my shredded dignity. "I'll remind you that you must maintain a C average to remain on the honors track. Stop looking for handouts and take some initiative."

She turns on her pink kitten heels and clacks out the door with a little extra swagger in her step. I clench my fists on top of the desk, then slam them down hard on it. The irate *thud* echoes in the empty classroom. Ms. White is as much a monster as Frank.

Her and Frank's words sack my brain.

"Take some initiative."

"Learn some accountability, boy."

Fine.

I snatch up my backpack and run out the classroom just in time to see Ms. White enter the stairwell at the end of the hallway. Only a handful of students linger in the corridor and most ignore me as I dart by. When I enter the stairwell, the aggressive taps of Ms. White's heels echo loudly. She has three floors to go and doesn't seem in a hurry, preoccupied with her phone.

I drop my backpack and assemble my flute with record speed. I retrieve the "Requiem of Souls" music, lean it against my backpack, and play.

"Who's there?" Ms. White calls up from somewhere below.

Bloody Barry appears promptly at the second bar, standing close enough for me to see the blood glistening on his skin, plastering his torn clothing to him like morbid wallpaper. I lower my flute, and he growls.

"Don't." His voice is deep, exhausted. Trembling almost. "Please. It soothes me."

"I'll keep playing if you do something for me," I tell him.

He clutches his hands over his chest. "Anything."

Ms. White's already started clacking back downstairs.

I lift my flute. "Give her a scare for me?"

He leaps down the first set of stairs like a bloodthirsty mountain lion after prey.

I play until a skin-crawling shriek resounds from somewhere below. With a grin, I stuff my things into my backpack. Last night, the ghosts disappeared not long after I stopped playing. Should only be a few more seconds before Bloody Barry disappears too. When Ms. White yells again, pleading for help this time, I peer over the railing to get a look at what's going on.

I can't see anything, but the stench of rotten eggs rushes up and makes me gag.

Something slams below, giving my heart a jolt. Ms. White's shouts turn to strangled wheezes. I only meant for Bloody Barry to give her a fright, not kill her.

I race downstairs to the second level. What I see terrifies me so much that I trip over my own feet and crash to the floor of the landing. I push myself upright, my throat too tight to speak.

Ms. White's face has gone completely red. Behind glasses knocked askew, her bloodshot blue eyes focus on the thing holding her by the neck in one dark, clawed hand.

That's not Bloody Barry. It's the monster I saw outside last night.

It stands about eight feet tall with skin covered in black scales that wriggle against one another like a sea of maggots. I throw my forearm across my nose and breathe in the cheap fabric-softener smell of my hoodie. The vaguely humanoid monster's legs are almost canine in composition with expansive shoulders and freakishly long arms ending in razored claws. Instead of ears, two gnarled black antlers sprout from either side of its head, tangling in the air like a demon stag. I'm thankful its back is turned, and maybe the fact that I can't see its eyes is what grants me the courage to speak up.

"St-stop!" I manage to blurt out. "Put her down!"

The monster growls and drops Ms. White, who collapses in a heap at its feet and quickly scrambles on her hands and knees to the opposite corner of the landing.

The monster tenses and begins a slow turn away from her . . . directly toward me!

I press my back against the wall, readying to run. *Sorry, Ms. White, you're about to be on your own.* But before I can see the monster's face, it lets out a grating roar that vibrates the very atmosphere in the stairwell. I clamp my hands over my ears, but the sound still ravages my eardrums.

Then the monster turns to smoke and disappears. All that's left is tense, stifling quiet.

"Are you okay?" I ask Ms. White.

Without a word, she rushes through the exit door.

Whatever.

I sit on the steps for a while and catch my breath. The ghosts might be harmless, but that monster had crept even closer than before, bolder this time than the last. I'll never draw it, but I have to name it now. The Creeper.

I can't let it get any closer to me or anyone else. It's too dangerous.

And now I must destroy "Requiem of Souls" before the Creeper kills someone—namely me.

When I get home from school, I try everything. Ripping. Cutting. Burning. I even stab it with a knife, but the blade breaks. *Nothing* works.

"Requiem of Souls" cannot be destroyed.

But one thing is certain—I can't ever play that song again. I can't risk the Creeper coming for me or anyone else. I wad the score into a ball and shove it to the rear of the top shelf in my closet. It'll be safe there until I can figure out a way to destroy it.

The week following my breakup with the magical score passes without much drama. Ms. White doesn't look me in the face anymore nor does she mention what happened with the Creeper. In fact, she doesn't talk to me much at all anymore, which I prefer—so long as she continues to grade my assignments fairly and leaves me alone. Notwithstanding Frank's usual shenanigans, my life seems to have smoothed out a bit.

Until the night of the storm.

Mom opens the front door and looks up at the sky. Thick, black thunder clouds blot out the sun, and if I didn't know better, I'd have sworn it was midnight.

"Something's brewing out there." She pulls her robe tighter as we both stare out the door at the threatening sky. "I wonder if Frank's okay."

I imagine a massive tornado plucking his raggedy pickup from the highway and flinging it and *him* into oblivion. But I keep that to myself.

Mom closes the door and digs out matches and a box of candles from the pantry, handing me a few to set up in the kitchen. Their muted-orange glow immediately infects the room with a sinister aura. Mom lights candles around the living room, and pretty soon, the whole house has an eerie air to it.

I rub the fresh goose bumps on my arms. "Can you spare one for my room so I can still practice for the spring concert?"

Mom smiles at me. "How about you practice out here? I'd like to hear how those solos are going."

My stomach prunes. Frank should be home soon. I'm always reluctant to spend too much time in common areas, lest he and I have a run-in.

But Mom looks to me with hopeful eyes that hold a glint of something I haven't seen since Dad was alive, and I lose the power to say no.

I set up my stand in the living room while Mom settles onto the couch with a coffee mug of wine. Maybe if I do a quick run-through of the show, she'll let me swipe a candle and evacuate to my room before Frank gets home.

I lift my flute, take a deep breath, and—

THUNK! THUNK! THUNK!

My heart takes off like a racehorse out the stables. Mom sits up with a start, sloshing wine over the rim of her cup onto her lap.

"GODDAMMIT, YVONNE! LET ME IN!!" A voice howls from the other side of the front door.

He kicks the door again. "DID YOU CHANGE THE LOCKS ON ME?"

Frank.

"No!" Mom shouts. "Where are your keys?"

He growls like a feral hell-creature and attacks the door. The frame cracks and splinters as the door bursts open. Lightning sizzles across the sky, silhouetting Frank's figure in the doorway. I want to run to my room, but my feet won't budge.

"Frank!" Mom cries, pleading with her hands. "Please, calm down!"

He steps inside and slams the door, but it just *thwacks* against the broken jamb and sticks. Fury flares his nostrils, making him look like a fleshy version of the Creeper in the lambent orange glow of candlelight.

He clenches his meaty fists at his sides. "Do you think I'm stupid?"

Mom shakes her head. "Frank, please. Go lie down."

Lightning flashes through the curtains, illuminating Frank as he dashes across the room and shoves Mom onto the couch.

I cry out and move to go to her, but he turns his paralyzing gray-green eyes on me. They glow in the low light as if supercharged by the storm. I freeze, and he turns back to Mom, who shifts to the end of the couch farthest from him.

"I know your secret, Yvonne," he sneers.

"Wh-What are you talking about?" Mom doesn't lie well. Never has.

He flings a crumpled slip of paper onto Mom's lap. She unfolds it tentatively, fingers trembling, and takes a shuddering breath when she realizes what it is.

"Yeah . . . I found out about your little 'Fuck Frank' account," he says. "You left the deposit receipt in the car yesterday."

Mom curses under her breath.

Frank's fists twitch anxiously. "You planning to leave me?"

I turn to Mom. I'm just as surprised as Frank.

Mom frowns. "No—"

"Stop lying!" he shouts, making us both flinch. "Why are you researching apartments in Houston?"

Everything clicks into place in my head. Mom has an escape plan.

Her shoulders slump and her eyes slink to the floor.

Panic squeezes my gut. She can't give up. Not again.

"Yeah," Frank coos haughtily, looming over her. "I went through your phone too."

He flicks the sides of his work jacket open to put his hands on his hips. Mom and I both stare at the hunting knife in the worn leather holster clipped to his belt.

"Let's chat in private." Frank gestures toward their bedroom.

At first, the word comes out as a croaky whisper, so I have to repeat it. "No."

Frank rounds on me. "This is between me and your momma, boy."

I clench my fists as I approach him. "L-Leave us alone." Fear rattles my voice, but I harden my stare. "Just g-get out."

A corner of Frank's mouth curls down. "Or what?"

I take out my phone. "I'll call the police."

He snatches my phone and stomps it with his work boot. Mom cries for him to stop, but he ignores her.

"Now what you got?" he asks. "Help. Ain't. Coming."

I hit him.

I'm not tall enough to punch him in the mouth, so his gut'll have to do. It shocks us both.

Frank's fist rockets toward my face. The impact knocks me off my feet, ringing my ears and drowning out Mom's shrieks. She leaps to her feet as I fall to the floor, my nose on fire and my head ringing. A stream of blood washes over my lips and drips down the front of my shirt.

Frank's never hit me before. He's completely unhinged.

He yanks Mom by her arm. She attempts to claw free of his grip, but he drags her down the hallway. Their bedroom door slams.

Mom was trying to free us from Frank. I have to try too.

I run to my room and pull down an avalanche of things in my closet until I get my hands on "Requiem of Souls." I unfold it as I dart back to the living room and place it on the stand.

I take a deep, vengeful breath—and play.

My ghost crew appears promptly. Angry Victoria. Bloody Barry. And Goth Baby. The gang's all here.

Mom's screams draw the ghosts' attention. They turn back to me, and I narrow my eyes and nod permission. I keep playing.

They know exactly what to do.

Angry Victoria stomps down the hall first, her skirts bunching against the walls on either side. Bloody Barry follows, grabbing Goth Baby by the collar of their nightgown, toting them like a sack of groceries.

I begin the second movement of the song as Mom and Frank both scream—with sheer terror. I focus on the music, my fingers pumping along the keys robotically.

Bloody Barry drags a flailing and cursing Frank down the hallway and deposits him in the center of the living room. Mom ducks into the kitchen to crouch behind the counter.

"Rocko," she whispers. "What the heck are you doing?"

I ignore her, and she falls quiet.

Bloody Barry grabs Frank by the back of the neck and shoves him to his knees, forcing him to listen as I reach the end of the third movement and transition into the fourth. Frank attempts to pry Barry's fingers from his neck, but it's no use.

"SOMEONE HELP!" screams Frank.

Barry molly whops him, leaving a thick smattering of blood down Frank's face. Frank's shoulders droop and he resigns to whimpering quietly.

An inhuman roar resounds from outside. Victoria and Goth Baby retreat to the shadows of the hallway and peek around the corner, both unwilling to abandon the music. Barry flinches but doesn't move. They're all afraid of the Creeper too.

But I can't stop playing. Not yet.

The tempo picks up in the fifth movement. More ghosts have appeared to listen, ones I've never seen before, but I ignore them.

"Requiem of Souls" is a lullaby to my own soul. I sink into a supernatural rhythm where I execute every note, every run, every emotion as if I'd composed the piece myself.

The Creeper roars again. It's outside now.

The monster rams its clawed hand through the door's center, sending bits of wood flying into the room, along with the putrid scent of sulfur. It flings the door over its shoulder onto the front lawn.

I'm trembling so hard I can't play a single note without vibrato, but I don't dare pry my eyes away from the music. If I look the Creeper in its face, I'll stop playing, and I cannot stop.

Not until we're free. This is the only way.

The Creeper enters the living room. The sound of its twisted horns scratching against the ceiling prickles my skin. Bloody Barry releases Frank and joins the crowd of other frightened spirits, who're inching farther and farther away.

Frank stumbles to his feet. "Ey!" he shouts at me. "*You're* doing this! Stop playing that goddamned song!"

The song's tone descends into a melancholy realm by the end of the sixth movement.

Frank snatches a nearby candle and throws it at me, slinging hot wax across my arms and the side of my face. It stings but not enough to stop me.

"Listen to me, you little fag—"

The Creeper impales the underside of Frank's chin with its claws and rips Frank's jaw from his head before he can utter another word. Flecks of dark blood splatter my pants. Frank's screams morph into gurgling howls. Mom cries out, then claps her hands over her mouth and peers wide eyed over the counter.

I turn back to the music. I have to see this through.

The Creeper wraps a long-clawed hand around where Frank's mouth used to be and slams him to the floor. It hovers over Frank, pressing its hand against Frank's gaping head to staunch the bleeding—but only to keep Frank alive long enough so it can feed.

At the seventh movement, I pause to take a deep breath and find the air rife with a coppery fragrance that lingers along the edges of the scent of rotten eggs. I continue playing with a vigorous fire I've never experienced before.

Lightning strobes, and thunder cracks and rumbles in the background. Frank is powerless now, lying there, sniveling while the Creeper consumes his intestines like ramen.

I begin the ninth and final movement.

My environment lends a morbid percussion to the song's conclusion. The crunch of bone and wet tearing of flesh as the Creeper feasts. The monster's grunts and smacks of satisfaction. Mom's soft cries. And the gentle murmurs of the collection of spirits packed into our home.

I belt out the song's closing note as the Creeper swallows the last remains of Franklin H. Waters. When it rises again, all signs of Frank's existence are completely gone.

I lower my flute. I'm still trembling and can barely breathe. The ghosts all applaud, startling me.

The Creeper's back stiffens. I pray it disappears before it turns on me or Mom—but it doesn't. None of the spirits fade. Then the realization sinks into the pit of my gut.

I've never finished "Requiem of Souls" before. What happens at the end?

The Creeper lifts its head out of shadow and looks straight at me. The sight of him saps the air from my lungs, knocking me back onto the couch.

The Creeper . . . has my face.

I try to slink away, but the Creeper grabs one end of the couch and flips it over, throwing me to the floor and knocking Wooden Jesus from the wall.

Mom screams and starts for me but flinches back when the Creeper roars at her.

The monster whips out his long arm and clenches chilled, bloodstained claws around my neck. He bares rows of crooked fangs and roars, coating my face with the warm, rotten stench of Frank's blood. Every breath becomes harder to take. I can feel my throat crushing.

Mom snatches Wooden Jesus from the floor, launches from atop the overturned couch onto the Creeper's scaly back, and impales the monster's neck with the cross.

The Creeper releases me, and I drop to the floor. Mom tumbles off his back and crashes in a heap beside me. The monster wails a shrill sound like a million cats shrieking at an eardrum-rupturing pitch.

Then it explodes into wafers of dark dust motes and shadowy smoke. The remnants swirl together and swoosh through the gaping door in a gust that blows out every candle.

In the darkness, Mom tugs me close and wraps her arms around me. Tears trickle down my cheeks and onto her shirt.

Lightning flashes and I catch sight of the ghosts. They turn to me and nod before walking through the walls and out of sight. Thunder rumbles outside.

Mom and I are alone again.

Two months later

I've been practicing for the spring concert almost daily, but I haven't seen a single ghost since the night Mom and I exorcised Frank from our lives. That next morning, I dug a hole so deep in the backyard that it was probably halfway to hell by the time I finished. I put "Requiem of Souls" in an old shoebox and buried it at the bottom of that cursed hole.

I hope no one ever finds it again.

The night of the concert, I play with an intensity I haven't felt since the last time I played "Requiem of Souls." I nail all three of my solos, and at the end of the show, I stand proud and bow with the other soloists.

Mom sits toward the back of the auditorium, grinning and clapping. I never thought I'd see her like this again, her entire face alight—really, *truly* happy.

I smile up at her, but then I squint. Someone's sitting beside her. Someone familiar.

Dad?

I rub my eyes as the applause and cheers grow to a thundering ruckus. When I look again, the seat next to Mom is empty.

HONOR CODE
BY KWAME MBALIA

There's a saying that goes, "Don't bring a knife to a gunfight," but whoever came up with that phrase clearly never took a Buster sword to a LARP.

At 8 a.m., Eastgate Mall's doors opened and a bunch of wizards and knights and paladins and sorcerers and—going by the stuffed wolves taped to their hips—a druid or two all rushed inside. The few mall walkers, who still used the dying carcass of capitalism to get their steps in, eyed the intruders on their space with suspicion, but it was too bad for them because we'd all signed the consent forms and paid the rental fees, so Prancercise was going to have share the floor with foam-sword combat.

My cousin and I were hanging out near what used to be an Express for Men, waiting to be assigned a story quest near the dried-up fountain splitting the walkway. I had my character sheet memorized and the broad outlines of today's adventure written in red sharpie on a notecard in my pocket, both of which I hoped would distract me from the constant vibration of my phone.

I readjusted myself on the wooden bench I was on (plate armor was ridiculously cumbersome, whether it was made from hammered steel or from actual dinner plates from the dollar store) then froze when someone sitting on the other side, behind me, squawked in outrage. Right. The Buster sword.

"Hey!"

"Sorry," I muttered and tried to keep still. Easier said than done when I carried a weapon the size of LeBron, but I managed. Last thing I wanted was to be kicked out of the mall, even a nearly dead mall. Not before the event started. I'd worked so hard.

"Kids playing dress up," the person behind me said, getting up to leave. One of the mall walkers stretching his hammies before toddling off. I shook my head but didn't respond. You heard worse when live-action role-playing, and it was almost a rite of passage (a sick, twisted rite of passage indicative of small-minded folks, but I digress). I ignored them and stared straight even as the mall-walker man came around into my peripheral (*don't make eye contact, it only enrages them, like self-absorbed Chihuahuas*) before loudly talking about weirdos and stalking away. I sighed again and tried to force myself to relax. Just a bit.

I peeked at my phone, dreading the notifications I knew I would see. It was the fifth time since I'd entered the mall, and even though I'd put the phone on vibrate, each little buzz felt like someone taking me by the shoulder and shaking me while screaming "Did you see this?" in my face. Maybe I should've turned it off completely, but I had this morbid fascination with watching the notifications pour in, like having a bird's-eye view to a twenty-car interstate pileup that someone who had my name and my face stood at the center of. Just couldn't look away.

I switched hands, keeping my phone in the left and the hilt of the Buster sword in the right, careful to flex my fingers and rotate my wrists. I didn't want to be physically exhausted before the day even got started (mental exhaustion was a different story). Not today. Today was supposed to be my fresh start. A new beginning. I had a new weapon to fight my battles with.

The giant sword stood as tall as I did, nearly seven feet from hilt to tip, and even though it was made of foam and repurposed plastic lightsaber parts, it was beginning to make my arms ache holding it aloft. But it had to be seen. Visible. Obvious. I had spent too much time in a cramped corner of my cousin's garage, inhaling paint fumes and listening to terrible y'alternative rock (no disrespect to the genre, but all shade to my cousin's taste).

This beauty was going to shine.

And when the sunlight filtered through the mall skylights, through the fake two-story trees stretching past shuttered stores and bare kiosks, over zigzagging string lights that still hung in the air above us even though Christmas was seven months ago, to hit the silver-painted edge of the Buster sword, it all felt worth it.

"You look ridiculous," my cousin said, standing next to me. Tev, who'd spent as much time in his garage as I had working on costumes, was peering into the glass case of another empty kiosk, one of a series that split the mall corridors in half, trying to guess what it had sold based on the dust imprints and bits of old receipts still strewn about inside.

I ignored him (hard to do when his armor was made of recycled lemon-pepper wings takeout containers and Bubble Wrap) and continued surveying the crowd, trying to pick out who I would challenge, who would challenge me, how we could figure out who the mysterious villain pulling the strings behind today's story actually was. It was my fourth LARP, and so far I was actually undefeated in my battles.

"I mean, you're gonna be a target. A Buster sword? Everybody and their Cloud-obsessed grandma is gonna be chasing you. You're gonna be knocked out of the game in thirty minutes. Tops. Your literal final fantasy. Do you even LARP, bro? You're not gonna last an hour."

My phone buzzed again and I jumped, but it was only the alarm I'd set the night before (one of five), and not another Twitter notification.

Triangle NC LARP, 8 a.m.

Nothing related to going viral. I was relieved, and also disappointed. (Was it strange that I felt like a social media masochist?)

Did you know if you mute a tweet, the algorithm can still decide to show you notifications depending on how famous the person is who liked or retweeted it? Like . . . here, protect your mentions, but also we at Twitter dot com want you to know that this famous person saw you at your worst / at your best / at your most vulnerable / at the moment when you were most defenseless and decided to share it with their legions of followers. Congrats!

I kept waiting for the other shoe to drop, and every ding of the phone was a miniature heart attack, but I didn't dare turn it off because my sister was our ride home, and she had the patience of a hungry toddler. And, I don't know, I kinda hoped someone would text me, check on me before the event started. Maybe my parents finally saw the coach's racist tantrum and would call and say they were on their way and we needed to talk, or were already here. Or maybe they did what I'd considered doing but hadn't had the courage to go through with, and had gone to the school and demanded an explanation. I didn't want to leave my phone at home and risk missing all that just so that I could get completely into character. Then again, what self-respecting adventurer/warrior/Mamluk/tansoba brings an iPhone to a LARP? Maybe Tev was right. Maybe . . .

A flutter of white appeared in the distance, just around the next bend, where an Auntie Anne's pretzel stand used to be. A flag.

"C'mon," Tev said, "it's time."

I checked my phone one final time, then slipped it into an inner pocket and pulled on my helmet, a modified LED face mask with a 3D-printed crown painted silver and glued on top. When I made it, I was so excited to wear it into battle, but now it just felt like the Buster sword. Like me. Awkward.

So much for the fresh start.

■ ■ ■

Breakfast earlier that morning had been its normal chaotic festivity. A six-piece of shenanigans. Dad calls it the Struggle Olympics. Four kids, two working parents, not enough milk to go in every cereal bowl. We went through it every morning.

Mom shoveling toast in her mouth before another nonstop twelve-hour shift at WakeMed Hospital.

Dad trying to get the twins to stop blowing bubbles into their milk, and to finish their breakfast while also talking about the upcoming basketball tournament, dropping stats and advice on who I should go one-on-one against, while checking email orders on his tablet for his stationery business.

The baby crying for the sippy cup she just threw on the floor.

And then there was me, writing and erasing and rewriting fourteen thousand variations of a message to the basketball team's group chat.

"Dillon, stop playing with your waffle and eat it," Dad said, trying to wipe syrup off of the baby, who thought she was under mortal attack and defending herself to the death.

"I don't like waffles," my little brother, half of the set of doom, whined.

"You love waffles."

"No, I don't, not anymore!"

"Boy, you asked me to buy these and we got the fifty count from Sam's Club, so you got forty-nine more times to love waffles before you're allowed to hate them. Now eat your food. And you," he said to the baby, a mock frown on his face. "I'm gonna tell the cows you don't like milk if you keep spitting it out."

"Moo," Alara said, flashing a gummy grin before promptly depositing her milk onto Dad's lap.

I fiddled with my own breakfast, stirring soggy cereal around the bowl with my spoon as I stared at the latest draft, thinking about hitting send.

What would they say? They'd been there. They'd seen what happened, and a few even spoke out. But would they support me? The video had started to do some numbers, not quite viral but definitely on the way there. Nobody really wanted to get caught in the crossfire of Hindsight Harrys saying why didn't I do this, or why didn't they do that, or the coach shouldn't have said that, or I should've kept my mouth shut. I didn't blame my teammates for not wading into that mess. That's how you catch strays.

Still, it would've been nice.

Mom walked by in her scrubs and flicked my ear on her way to fill up her water bottle. "Hey, Earth to my oldest, are you okay?"

"Huh? Oh, yeah, sorry. Did you say something?"

"I said, do you need a ride?"

I stared at her blankly for a second before my brain caught up with her question. "Oh! No, Tev's sister is gonna take us."

"Okay, tell them I said 'hi.' And I love the crown." She paused and squinted at me, studying my face. "Are you okay, sweetie? You look stressed."

I didn't answer right away, and luckily, Mom became momentarily distracted by Darren and Dillon arguing over who hated waffles more. I could tell my parents. Just get it off my chest. It's not like they were on Twitter and would've seen the post. I could spit it out now, lob the video into the middle of the chaos and hope for the best.

Yeah right.

The cursor on my phone blinked, as if letting me know that the message on-screen wouldn't get the job done either. I tapped the words in disgust, highlighting and deleting the whole section, then sat back and stared at the table.

"Ew, Dillon!" Darren howled as his twin sneezed, bits of waffle spraying everywhere. The baby shrieked in laughter as everyone started talking at once, Dad holding in his own chuckles as he made Dillon go get paper towels, Mom rolling her eyes and lifting Alara out of her high chair and bouncing the baby on her hip as she wiped her face.

And then a horn honked outside and the opportunity for me to speak was lost.

You have to try really hard *not* to find your people in high school. There are cliques for everyone. *You* get a clique, *you* get a clique, like some weird combination of *Oprah* and *Mean Girls*, and I've tried—at one point or another in the school year—to get into all of them. Seriously.

I tried out for the anime club but couldn't Naruto run the full length of the cafeteria, so I didn't make it. I heard not long after that the club got suspended because someone tried to Shadow Clone Jutsu their way out of a quiz and got caught.

There were fifteen different dance clubs—salsa, jazz, contemporary, crumping, pop locking, electro swing, and tons more—and all of them regretfully declined my awkward two-step as an application. What can I say, my heart beats on the one and the three.

I was *this* close to becoming a theater kid, but when it was my turn to recite my lines from *Romeo and Juliet*, I completely flubbed them. Badly. Honestly, this one wasn't my fault. My dad's favorite movie was this oldie called *Romeo Must Die*, so instead of saying "Let lips do what hands do," I recited Aaliyah's hook to "Try Again." To be fair, it was a killer performance. At least that's what the stagehand kids were telling me as the theater director shouted me off the stage.

All those groups, all of those spaces carved out for similar souls to exist in peace, and I couldn't contort myself, couldn't whittle myself down, couldn't shrink to fit into any of them, until I started LARPing.

Taking your character from a role-playing game and interacting in the real world with other characters. Different groups ran their LARPs in different ways, but each had one thing in common—you had to let go of the real world and pretend. Pretend to be someone else from a different story, a different world, with different challenges that I could pretend I actually had the skills to overcome. I was good at pretending. Pretending to care, pretending not to care, pretending I didn't care about the varsity basketball team, pretending it was important to me instead of just something my Dad wished he did and so wanted me to do. Pretending it didn't matter when the coach, in front of everyone—assistant coaches, students hanging out, other players, their friends and family, anyone with a phone—told me that, and I quote, maybe I just wasn't cut out for basketball despite all the advantages that come with being Black. Pretending he actually used the word Black instead of something completely inappropriate.

I pretended I didn't hear the snickers, or see the stares, or see the girl recording only to send it out later, or feel the sting of those words as I dropped onto the bench in front of my locker and began gathering up my things. Every day is another chance to put on armor that I've fashioned to protect myself, and LARPing helps with that. Like I said, I'm good at pretending.

You can run a LARP in a dozen different ways. Admins, no admins, NPC moderators, and more, but today conflicts were supposed to be left between players. We had to keep track of our own character sheets and our own hit points with no Excel sheet or stat tracker to help. Fight your own battles, tally your own accomplishments, document your own defeats.

In other words, there was supposed to be an honor code.

A wizard had her nose broken by a knight with a mace in the food court sometime around noon, so everyone had to pause while they cleaned up the blood and decided if the LARP would continue. Apparently the two players disagreed about the outcome of an in-game duel and the knight lost her cool. Eventually everyone decided to keep playing, but all duels needed bystanders to count toward character progression. No witness, no experience points. If no one saw it, did it even happen?

"That sucks," Tev grunted as we waited near an out-of-service escalator in the central atrium in the mall. We still hadn't dueled anyone yet, everyone either wary of the Buster sword or of the golden armband tied around my bicep, a symbol of my unbeaten streak. A crowd of people clustered around one of the organizers, a who's who of fantasy cosplay. Paladins and druids chugged Coke Zeroes and took selfies. "We gotta take a number to smite our foes now? We're never going to fight. What's next, making a reservation for dungeon raids?"

"Wrong game, nerd," I said, scanning the crowd.

"You get the reference, goofy. Hey, there's Lana. LANA!"

Two rogues—or maybe they were assassins—separated from the others and walked over. They both had matching bows (the weapon, not ribbons, so I guess they were rogues) and eyeliner and fake scars that stretched across their cheeks. I recognized the taller one from third-period calculus and a few other LARP sessions. She smiled at me in surprise.

"Hey! I didn't you think you'd come."

I hefted the Buster sword and grinned back. "And miss out on dueling you? No way. I need to keep my streak alive."

She laughed. "Dream on. Next time we fight, I'm taking you out. You're going to have to wait, though. Dee and I"—she nodded at the second girl, who was restringing her bow as Tev tried to chat her up—"already tag-teamed a knight earlier. Now they're saying if you already dueled, you have to wait for everyone else to fight before you can go again."

"For real?" Maybe Tev and I would actually get a chance to get some experience points. When I looked at my cousin, he met my eyes and fist pumped, then jogged over to get in line to sign us up to duel.

"I like your armor," Lana said, nodding as she surveyed my costume and the Buster sword. "Though I don't think your lil knife is big enough."

"That sounds like a challenge," I shot back, my smile robbing the words of any venom.

"Settle down, Sephiroth, you're always ready to stab somebody."

I held one hand over my heart. "It's how I communicate. And was that a Final Fantasy reference?"

"That's how *I* communicate," she said, tossing her hair back over her shoulder. "Dated video game references."

We joked around like that for several more minutes, and honestly? It felt like medicine for my soul. This is what I loved. This is where I found my people—people who spent hours, days, and sometimes even months on a single costume, for a single day, for a single event. People who transformed themselves into someone new and tackled problems that, while not easy, weren't insurmountable.

Lana stepped closer, her eyes searching my own. "Hey . . . are you okay? I saw what happened on Twitter."

The grin faded from my face. "Oh."

She shook her head. "I reported it to Twitter Support, if that helps, and they said they'll review it."

That was news to me. "Really?"

"Yep. I'll let you know what they say. And let me know if you need someone to talk to, okay? I know what that's like. Some jerk recorded me burning *my own notebook* for an art project and said I was refusing to learn

US history. Suddenly everyone's mother was about equity in education. Are you going to talk to the school about what happened?"

I shrugged. "Haven't really thought about it."

"Well, if you do, let me know. And if you don't, that's cool too. Screw them," she said. "You don't owe anyone anything. Except for me," she added.

I raised an eyebrow and her face immediately grew red. "A *fight*, you jerk."

Someone called her name and she raised an arm, then smiled apologetically and left with her friend after making me promise to get someone to record my duel. I leaned against the Buster sword. Talking with someone about the viral tweet wasn't as awkward as I thought it would be.

My phone buzzed. I reached for it, then stopped. Suddenly it didn't seem as important. The notifications would still be there at the end of the day if I really wanted to see them. I let my hand drop and let my eyelids droop as the sounds of the LARP washed over me. When everything went all blurry, it was almost as if I was standing in the suites of a gladiator's arena as spectators cheered and booed and bayed for blood. What was life if not a battle? What was high school if not a constant quest to be valid? Snaps and Reels and Stitches and Duets and Retweets were the roses the audience threw, going viral with the acclaim. If the right version of you went viral. You never knew when someone was recording. It's like you had to live the authentic version of yourself and hope everyone recognized it. Even if your most authentic self was you pretending to be a knight/Mamluk/tansoba.

"Hey!" I opened my eyes to Tev rushing over, a slip of paper in his hands. "You're up next!"

"Who am I fighting?" I asked.

"Some paladin, I think. He actually requested to fight you. Said you weren't as tough as you looked."

Tev looked apprehensive, but I smiled. Closed my eyes again. Let the rest of the world fade away once more until it was just me and my Buster sword. I could almost see the battle unfolding before it even began, a clash of foam steel and plastic armor and reputations that only mattered during these eight hours inside a dying mall in central North Carolina. I could almost believe that this was the only thing that would ever matter. All the other stuff was meaningless for the moment. In the now. I'd deal with everything else later—with family, with school, with sports and expectations. That was a promise to myself. A promise only I would know if I kept or if I reneged.

Like I said, an honor code.

DRIVE TIME
BY LAMAR GILES

ANNALISE

Is this the right address?

I checked my phone, checked the number over the building's entrance, checked the street sign on the corner. Everything matched my Groupon, yet . . .

Spinning in a slow circle, I took in the general disrepair of the block. More businesses were boarded up with old plywood than not; a bunch of faded FOR SALE/LEASE signs flapped in the light breeze. Among the establishments that might—maybe, *possibly*—open sometime today were Stan's Pawnbroking, Bargain Knives and Vape, and The Gizzard King.

No Zoom-Zoom Driving School, though.

Incredible.

If this was late night instead of early morning I might have been concerned—particularly about Bargain Knives and Vape, but at 7 a.m. on a Saturday, the most dangerous beings around were the pigeons. I stepped under an ancient awning to avoid a white-hot poop bomb that missed my Jordans by inches.

Hoping she hadn't gotten too far, I called my sister . . . and went straight to voicemail.

The car me and Melanie would share once I got my license was kind of ancient and didn't have fancy Bluetooth connections or whatever that would let her talk hands free, so she might not even see I called until she stopped somewhere. I opted not to leave a message and had no plans on waiting around. *Can't believe I skipped practice for this.*

I'd barely opened my rideshare app when a car displaying the company's logo pulled up. I thought, "Am I magic?" That is, until a confused looking, kind of cute in a big teddy bear way boy rolled down the back window.

"Yo. This the driving school?"

THEO

Damnnnnn.

Who. Is. *She?*

Be cool though, Theo. Be cool.

The Mystery Girl said, "Did you get the Zoom-Zoom Groupon too?"

"You know it. Sis." *Why did you add 'Sis'? It don't even sound right coming out your mouth! Never mind. Don't ruminate.*

Meeting a beautiful girl at my booty-crack-of-dawn driving lesson hadn't been on my radar today, but I ain't complaining! Maybe everything was coming up Theo after all!

I slunk from my ride. Cool. Not too eager, just like my Uncle Ronnie taught me. "Women don't like a hurried man," he'd often said, usually with a strong-smelling red plastic cup in hand.

"Hey!" my driver barked. She was pale, with bluish hair and the scary eyes of someone who swindled children's souls in fairy tales. "That your asthma pump on the seat?"

Oh, God.

I spun on my heels and scrambled back to the car. Hurried. Snatched my pump and thought how I might play this off. No need, though. The girl was staring at the building that better not be the driving school.

"The Groupon's wrong then. Right?" I joined her on the sidewalk.

"It must be."

"Theo, by the way."

"I'm Annalise. Should we walk or something? Maybe it's up the block."

"Cool," I said. Then thought, *Why do she seem familiar?* Like we'd already met even though I *know* we haven't. I definitely would've remembered.

Before we'd taken two steps, the plywood board covering the building's entrance lurched outward and someone inside zombie-groaned.

I nearly peaced out, but Annalise went into some kind of Cobra Kai stance, and I didn't want to seem like a basic bitch so I raised my hands like when I slap boxed my little cousins.

Pale fingers curled around the edge of the board, slid it aside. A scrawny, scruffy dude in sweatpants and a stained Virginia State Fair T-shirt emerged, wincing at the sunlight. "Oh God, it's daytime."

He shielded his right eye with his hand. His left eye was purple and swollen shut. He worked at repositioning the plywood while mumbling over his shoulder. "Y'all looking for Zoom-Zoom Driving School?"

Annalise did not relax her fighting stance. "Do you know where it is?"

Dude faced us with his arms spread like, TA-DA! "*I'm* Zoom-Zoom Driving School. But you can call me Zed."

ANNALISE

This was more sketch than I cared for.

"I'm leaving," I said. Then dropped my tiger stance and dialed Melanie again. It went straight to voicemail. *Again.* Only I couldn't leave a message now. I yelled at the phone, "How is your mailbox full?"

Theo and Mr. Zoom-Zoom Zed stared.

Breathe, Annalise. Control the rage.

"Bro," Theo said to Zed, "where's your car?"

Zed trudged down the steps poking at his swollen eye and wincing. He strolled halfway up the block and waved us along. Me and Theo followed at a safe distance. He passed several suspect parked cars, including one that was recently firebombed, before stopping at an old Hyundai Sonata with gray patches spotting its dull blue paint. He looked up and down the block, then checked the high windows in the surrounding buildings, like he was searching for snipers. He circled to the driver's side tire and exhaled his relief. "No boot yet. Nice."

Zed triggered the locks. The alarm deactivated with a weak horn honk, like the battery needed replacing. I finally noticed the faded STUDENT DRIVER bumper sticker under another that read TRUST ME, THAT SQUIRREL HAD IT COMING!

Zed said, "So y'all have some basic driving knowledge, right? I mean, that was in the Groupon requirement. I'm not teaching you *everything*."

"I'm good," I said.

Theo made a wobbly motion with his hand. "Eh. I'm a big fan of the Fast & Furious movies if that means anything."

"It does not." Zed tossed me the keys. "She's driving first."

As I settled into the driver's seat, the smell made me light-headed. Was the gas tank leaking? I started the engine—we didn't explode—and rolled down my window. The fresh air helped, just not a lot.

Theo climbed into the seat behind me but did a weird arching backbend over the upholstery. "What's this stain?"

Zed said, "You think you'll be more comfortable if you know?"

Ew.

Theo slid to the other seat.

Zed settled into the passenger seat, kicking discarded McDonald's bags and empty cups aside.

"What first?" I asked.

He positioned a cracked phone in a dashboard clamp and opened an app. I squinted as the words INCOMING PICKUP flashed on the screen. Zed pointed at a map that appeared. "Go there."

I read the destination. Reread it. "You want me to go to . . . Breakfast Wingz?"

"It's downtown. We'll see how you do in some light traffic."

"But it seems like . . ."

Theo leaned between our seats. "We doing a MotorMeals delivery? During our driving lesson?"

"Two birds with one stone," Zed said. "Now go. My three-star rating depends on my punctuality."

THEO

WTF? Halfway to the Breakfast Wingz spot, this dude Zed got some sunglasses out the glovebox, cranked his seat back all the way into my knees until I was forced to slide into the stain behind Annalise, and fell asleep. Snoring and everything.

Annalise glared. "He can't be serious."

I shook our instructor awake. "Dude. What we doing?"

He gave a heavy sigh and looked to the sky, like I was the rude one. "Look. Last night was a rough one, and I'm going to make it easy on all of us. You two help me run some errands today, and . . . you pass."

Annalise stopped us at a red light. "Wait. *Just* today? Not fourteen sessions like it says in the driver's manual?"

"You read that manual?" Zed waved off his own question, clearly not caring. "I don't want to do fourteen sessions. Do you?"

I said, "That's legal?"

"The only *illegal* things are the ones you get caught doing."

Annalise said, "That is not how the law works, sir."

I said, "You're for real? No cap?"

"Do I look like a liar?" Zed asked.

"Yes," we said in unison.

Behind us someone leaned on the horn. The light was green.

Annalise put us in motion again, a leisurely crawl through uncrowded weekend streets. The three miles we drove had the buildings changing, growing. The beat-up row houses and abandoned storefronts became skyscrapers. The neon, red OPEN signs for like nine different coffee shops scrolled by. The MotorMeals app said Breakfast Wingz was 1.2 miles ahead on the right.

"So, how many errands do we have to run with you?" Annalise asked.

"Like four. Or seven."

"Not to be that guy," I said, knowing whenever anyone started like that, they were being that guy, "but how we supposed to learn driving stuff if we're just doing this for a day?"

"You'll take turns," Zed said, confident. "Trust me, it's more training than I ever got."

"You mean when you were our age?" said Annalise. "You've had training since, though?"

Zed shrugged and flopped back into his reclined seat.

I met Annalise's gaze in the rearview. Her eyebrows rose. A silent question. We doing this?

The speaker on Zed's cracked phone sounded, "*Your destination is on the right in three hundred feet.*"

"You run in and grab the order," I told Annalise. "I'll take the wheel."

ANNALISE

Theo drove us, slowly. Nervously. I would say *grandmotherly*, but my grandma would've smoked him any day of the week. No shade. Not everyone got to run a pickup truck up and down country roads at the age of twelve like me and Melanie.

We finally made it to a townhouse in the East End where I dropped the MotorMeals order on the doormat, then returned to the back seat. "That's one errand. Three to go."

Zed said, "I never guaranteed four errands."

"*I'm* guaranteeing four errands. Next."

Theo chuckled, and Zed whipped off his sunglasses. "That's funny? Guess what your next task is, buddy. Parallel parking."

"Huh?" Theo wrenched the wheel with both hands, clearly flustered. "Why?"

"For thinking Zed is for play." He thumbed an address into the phone and it calculated a route. "There. That address. When you get there, I want the 'Three *P*s.' Perfect. Parallel. Parking."

Leaning as far forward as my seat belt allowed, I said, "Do people really call it that?"

"You wanna have to execute the 'Three *P*s' too?" Zed snapped.

I raised both hands in surrender. "Carry on."

The address Zed entered on the South Side *should* have been a ten-minute trip in such light traffic. The way Theo drove, though . . . someone passed us on a rental scooter and gave us the finger for holding them up. Theo managed to get us to the edge of downtown, then merged onto the sparsely populated I-95 while frantically checking the lane like it was rush hour.

I said, "I thought you watched *The Fast and the Furious.*"

He said, "*Watched.* In my living room. Stationary."

"Speed limit's sixty out here," I said. In case, maybe, he didn't see the many signs.

"That's an upper limit, though. My Uncle Ronnie says it's best to maintain a safe buffer of three to eight miles."

"I'm pretty sure he meant somewhere between sixty-three and sixty-eight. You're doing fifty-five."

Theo tapped an antsy rhythm on the steering wheel. "You won't get nervous if I went that fast?"

"No."

"Zed, should I go faster?"

At the sound of his name, the comatose instructor pressed his face to the passenger window and farted, a sound like rapid gunfire. Panicked, I tried to get my window down. But it was broken. The rotten eggs smell got me coughing. "Drive, drive! We need the breeze."

Theo stomped the gas and the engine roared like a toy jet. We rocketed forward in the right lane, coming up fast on the bumper of a Ford truck.

"Switch lanes!" I shouted.

Theo jerked the wheel left. Hard. Cutting off an old Mustang. That driver let loose angry horn blares amidst the scream of slammed brakes. Theo, gasping and terrified, managed to get his asthma pump from his pocket to his mouth and sucked down a blast. Our car swerved while he did.

"I'm sorry for teasing you!" I said. "Get back in the right lane and slow down. Please."

Whether it was the medicine, or permission to be a slow ass, he got back in the right lane, dropped below sixty mph, and regained full control of the vehicle.

"See," Theo said, sounding relieved. "Told you this was safer."

THEO

Annalise leaned between the front seats, nudging Zed. "Wake up. We're here."

Here was an old suburb. Small houses with big yards. My granddad had a house like this until his health got bad and he couldn't stay by himself anymore. The specific house pinned on Zed's phone was faded blue with missing shingles and a chain-link fence around the front yard. There were at least three BEWARE OF DOG signs.

Zed let out a snore.

"You can let him sleep," I said. If Zed didn't wake up, maybe I wouldn't have to do the three *P*s. I tried to parallel park my Uncle Ronnie's truck once and still have nightmares about it. Why they make fire hydrants so fragile, I'll never know.

But Zed jerked awake, his bruised face looking like a pirate without the eyepatch as he squinted at the house. He pointed to a wide section of the curb. "Parallel park right there."

Annalise said, "What's he parking between?"

I could barely contain my grin.

"There are no other cars."

But Zed's full focus was on the house, and I began the procedure of parallel parking between big swaths of empty and more empty. Still bumped the curb and had to start over, but Zed didn't seem to mind.

Annalise seemed real salty about it. She pressed back in her seat, arms crossed and mean-mugging. "Unbelievable."

When I was comfortably settled, I shifted the car into park. "Well, coach?"

Zed shouldered his door open, climbed out. "Keep the motor running."

He hopped the chain-link fence and slunk around the back of the house.

Okay.

"You know," Annalise said, "you didn't turn your wheel hard enough on your initial reverse. Had there actually been cars, you'd have clipped one."

"I'll keep that in in mind."

"My turn." Annalise popped out the back and stood by my door. "Give up the seat."

"Fine, fine. You don't have to act like a carjacker." I exited the vehicle and held the door open for her.

Instead of getting in, her head tilted. Her nostrils flared. She leaned toward my neck—which was kinda nice, not gonna lie.

She sniffed. "What is that? It's like citrus. Sandalwood. A hint of the ocean."

"My . . . *cologne?*"

"Yes. Obviously. What's it *called?*"

"I don't know. My Uncle Ronnie gave it to me for my birthday. It's from Japan—or maybe it's from a Japanese guy at the mall. Why?"

She stammered a bit. "I—I just—it's . . . *nice*. Barely there. It's like a . . . a phantom smell."

"My Uncle Ronnie taught me that you put on as little as possible. At the pulse points," I pointed at her neck, then her wrist. "I thought he was tripping, but I guess he know something."

"Sure. Yeah." Annalise slid into the driver's seat and stared straight ahead and didn't say nothing else.

Was she still heated about the parallel parking thing? I hoped not.

Because, otherwise, she seemed real chill.

ANNALISE

Cologne. Worked.

I wasn't a believer until today.

The boys at school who used cologne as a substitute for thorough bathing were like cartoon skunks with visible funk wafting off them. The other boys who did bathe yet coated themselves in it were just as bad as the cartoon skunks and needed an Uncle Ronnie in their lives. Theo, the anxious driver that he was, seems to have cracked the code. The cologne. The goofy grin. It was a whole vibe.

I needed to know more.

I said, "What school do you go to?"

"Byrd. What about you?"

"Harrison Prep."

"Cool." There was an awkward paused before Theo said, "Wait. Harrison. With the real nice girls basketball team. That one guard got those TikTok videos where she's making trick shots. Like throwing the ball off three walls before the swish."

My heart thundered. "That was one of my more difficult shots. Took two attempts."

He snapped his fingers and his head popped through the seat gap. "I knew I'd seen you before!"

"I always enjoy meeting followers."

"That shot where you did a somersault off the trampoline and hit the three midflip. Bananas! How?"

"I used to do gymnastics, but I'm really good in basketball. So one day my sister Melanie had her phone and was like, let's—"

"Go! Go! Go!"

The frantic, terrified sound of Zed's voice snatched our attention toward the house. He emerged from the backyard in a sprint, hugging a gray-haired pit bull that licked his face lovingly despite his screams.

An old woman burst from the front door. She wore a bathrobe, face smeared in so much blue skincare gunk you could only tell she was white by her pale hands. But even that was an extreme afterthought because the freaking medieval mace she was swinging was the most noticeable thing about her. She screamed too. "Bring my dog back, Zed!"

Zed hopped the fence like an Olympic hurdler and fed the dog through the passenger window. It crawled into the back seat, taking up almost as much room as Theo.

The mace-swinging woman bolted toward us, looking like she was going to run through the fence. Zed performed an empty air dropkick to shoot his body through the window and into the passenger seat. "I said go!"

Calmly, coolly, I hit the gas and shot us halfway up the block. That old lady was in the middle of my rearview mirror, still swinging the mace and pumping her fist at the sky. "Zed!"

"Who the hell was that?" I said, navigating the neighborhood.

"My grandma."

Like that explained everything.

Theo probed deeper. "*What* was that?"

"Errand number two, homie."

The I-95 ramp was a half mile away. I got us back on the highway, but I had more questions. "You stole your grandma's dog, Zed?"

"Temporarily borrowed."

The dog placed his snout on my shoulder, like, *This is some crazy shit, isn't it?*

Zed punched a new address into the phone. "Eyes on the road. Now for errand number three."

THEO

Twenty miles outside the city limits, the Navigation Lady said, "Your destination is on the left."

No neighborhood this time. We were in the country where long stretches of land got broken up by churches, gentleman's clubs, and gas stations. Annalise veered into the lot of a strip mall housing five establishments: a hair salon, a dry cleaner, a pack-and-ship store, a pizza place, and the final doing-its-own-thing retailer that made me nervous.

When Annalise slowed to park, Zed said, "You know how to back in?"

"I do," she said.

My Uncle Ronnie always backed into parking spots. He said he knew what was going on when he arrived somewhere, but never knew what could be happening when he left.

"Might need to make a quick getaway!" Ronnie would say, cackling, slapping his knee, and swishing his ever-present cup.

Annalise parked the way Zed instructed, taking the only empty spot in the lot. The rest were crowded with mud-caked dirt bikes leaning on their kickstands three or four deep.

Zed said, "All right. Pop the trunk, then you two switch."

Annalise pulled the lever beside her seat; the trunk popped open on loose hinges. Zed exited, snapped his fingers, and the dog followed. I climbed behind the wheel, but Annalise hesitated getting in back.

"Zed!" she shouted. "The dog made another stain."

He rustled through something in the trunk, distracted. "Get in front for now. I'll handle it later."

Zed slammed the trunk, having donned a vomit-green windbreaker with a nylon badge stenciled over his heart, and a trucker's cap that read ANIMAL CONTROL over the brim.

Me and Annalise's necks craned like meerkats when he and the dog passed us. "Be right back."

They entered the oddball store with the blacked-out windows; deafening rock music spilled into the lot the minute Zed cracked the door. That, and the graffiti-styled signage, told exactly what the place was all about: x-TREME ADRENALINE SPORTS.

Annalise flopped into the passenger seat. "You got a bad feeling about this?"

"Yep."

She nodded. "So what do you like to do for fun?"

ANNALISE

We'd been waiting for Zed for like a half hour, but it felt like no time at all because Theo was a great conversationalist.

"Wait, wait," I said, in disbelief. "You cook?"

Theo nodded heartily and jiggled the steering wheel. "Sure do. It's mostly why I need my license. My Uncle Ronnie got a food truck I want to work in, but he's all like, 'You gotta cook *and* drive to be an executive in my corporation.' So, here I am."

"What's the food truck?"

"The Notorious R. O. N.'s Ready to Fry."

My head almost exploded. "Stop. Playing! My family loves that truck."

"You're messing with me."

"I can't eat it much in-season, but on my cheat days that's where I always want to go."

"What's your favorite on the menu?"

"The Reasonable Kraut Beef Hotdog and the Chillmatic Salted Caramel Shake."

"Very popular choices." He smiled. It was a good smile.

Loud guitar riffs and heavy drums intruded on our talk. I spotted Zed in the rearview, backing through the x-TREME store's door, a paint-ball gun in hand. The pit bull zipped around him and hopped through the open car window while Zed backpedaled toward us.

I twisted in my seat for a better view. "What the hell?"

"The door!" Zed called to me. I tugged the rear door handle as several young, tanned square-jawed dudes in motocross gear exited the shop with their own paintball guns trained on Zed.

"We really didn't want to have to swell your other eye, Cousin Zedrick. You're a slow learner, though," said one of the motocross bros.

Zed fell into the car, his gun still aimed through the open window. "Could've done this the easy way."

"The easy way? You're the weirdo trying to ransom Grandma's dog. Again."

Two motocross dudes shoved forward and a lot of things happened at once.

"Floor it!" Zed said.

Theo did not floor it. He pulled from the space slow and cautious. The motocross goons closed the gap on Zed easily and nearly dragged him from the moving car when he squeezed the trigger on the paintball gun.

FWOOMPF!

THUNK!

Then one goon stumbled backward, coughing and massaging his forehead. There was no paint splatter on him, but a white cloud surrounded the guy's head. Both guys began coughing.

"Drive!" Zed screamed, "Before the PepperBalls get us too."

Theo stomped the gas then. We ran over a shrub, jumped the curb, and were on the road speeding back toward the city. In the lot, the two goons who'd tried to snatch Zed writhed on the ground.

"You loaded a paintball gun with PepperBalls?" I asked, stunned, and perhaps a little impressed.

"Will have those a-holes wheezing and crying for hours."

"Not all of them," I said.

Dirt bikes went airborne behind us, nimbly jumping the curb to take the road. Engines howled like a pack of rabid puppies as they drew closer.

The chase was on.

THEO

I said, "Yo, did that motocross thug back there call you *cousin*?"

"And *Zedrick*?" said Annalise.

"Later! They're gaining!"

They sure were because this trash car with the extra bright Check Engine light flashing at me wasn't going to outrun those bikes. Still, I made the highway and aimed us toward the city. Traffic was light—thank God—so with shaky, sweaty hands I pushed us to the speed limit. The speed limit was sixty-five.

Annalise said, "Dude. They're on our bumper."

"Okay. Right." I hit sixty-eight and the wheel vibrated in my grip.

Zed checked his weapon for readiness and brought it up to his face, ready to aim. "I got something for 'em."

Then we hit a pothole. "Ahhhh! My good eye!" Zed screamed and fell backward in the seat.

The dog whined, as annoyed with Zed as I was.

"Give me that." Annalise grabbed the PepperBall gun and leaned out the window.

"Be careful!" I shouted, slowing down reflexively. My chest tightened. My asthma acted up when I panicked. No way to play this cool. Annalise, though . . .

"Making shots is my thing. I got this," she said.

Annalise propped herself in the passenger window frame like she was

Black Widow and fired PepperBalls in rapid succession. FWOOMPF! FWOOMPF! FWOOMPF!

In the rearview, dirt bikes in pepper clouds swerved, then veered onto the shoulder, their riders then hopping off and coughing all hunched over. Not enough of them though.

"Can you go a little faster now?" Annalise requested in a gentle not-gentle voice.

Fast & Furious, Theo! Let's go!

Despite my struggle to breathe, I got us up to seventy-two.

Three more dirt bikes sped up with me. My breathing got more erratic and I tried wrestling my asthma pump from my pocket.

Annalise's aim was pristine, sending two of the remaining three to the shoulder in PepperBall agony, leaving only the final dirt-bike thug—Zed's cousin—in pursuit.

Annalise took aim as I brought my pump to my lips. I barely noticed the yellow caution sign on my right reading BUMP AHEAD.

Oh no.

I slowed some—but not enough. We hit the uneven pavement, jostling us all. Annalise lurched, in danger of falling from the car completely, so I dumped my pump in the passenger footwell and grabbed her belt.

She stayed in the car but—

WHACK.

"What was that?" I asked, panicked.

"Crap! I accidentally dropped the PepperBall gun on the highway."

She settled back into her seat, secured her seat belt. Zed's cousin pulled up beside us.

My chest was uncomfortably tight and my breath was coming out in squeaks. I pointed toward her feet. "Asthma. Pump."

She brightened. "Good idea."

Annalise grabbed my pump, then threw it at the biker. It bounced off his helmet, never to be seen again. "Didn't work."

Well that wasn't going to help my desperate gasps for oxygen. *Think, think.*

"I need to slow down," I said.

"First we gotta get rid of this dude," said Annalise.

I had an idea.

Wheezing, I said, "You know that one Fast & Furious movie, *Tokyo Drift*, where they're using their brakes to slide the car?"

"Wait," said Annalise. "You barely go over the speed limit, now you want to drift the car?"

"*Want* is a stretch."

Zed spoke through his whimpering, "I can't see shit, but I know that's a bad idea."

"Look, I can't do fast driving like you, but I'm good with deceleration."

Annalise said, "What does that even mean?"

An off-ramp with a caution sign indicating a sharp turn was coming up fast. It was just us and the dirt bike on this stretch of road. I veered for the exit, the adrenaline pumping through me loosening my chest, giving me the air needed for a battle cry. "Get ready to drift!"

The dirt bike kept pace with me onto the ramp where I hit my brake, then pulled the parking brake, then did *not* drift.

Metal screamed, and the cabin filled with the alarming smell of metal grinding metal. Sparks flew like volcanic raindrops. Zed's cousin ran his dirt bike into a guardrail, then was catapulted into a retention pond just off the curve.

Annalise twisted in her seat, horrified.

We shuddered to a stop on the shoulder, smoke and heat spewing from the car's undercarriage. Waiting.

"Oh God," said Annalise. "Did we kill him?"

We sat there, staring in the direction Zed's cousin had flown. Watching.

He exploded from that water waving his middle finger. Shouting, "We're gonna get that dog back, Zed!"

Annalise relaxed. "Oh, he's good. Let's get out of here."

I released the parking brake, surprised and relieved that the car still worked. Got us moving back into the city.

"Are we clear?" Zed asked once we were on our way again.

Annalise confirmed we were.

"Awesome. One more errand, then."

Me and Annalise locked eyes, conferring silently. Then she said, "We don't think so . . ."

ANNALISE

There were several abandoned lots close to the Zoom-Zoom Driving School. Theo picked one randomly, then we switched seats one last time. I sat with my hands at ten and two, with the car in park, the engine idling. Theo pinned Zed on the ground.

"Dude, we're done," Theo said. "Get it?"

The dog sat behind me, wagging his tongue and huffing hot breath on my neck.

Zed said, "We had a deal guys."

I revved the engine.

Theo continued playing the heavy. "If you don't sign off on our completion of this course right now, Annalise is going to run over your face."

"Oh, come on. You're going to do me like that? After all you learned?"

The engine whined as I pressed the gas pedal to the floor.

"All right. All right. Jeez. The more compassionate generation, my ass."

"Dope," Theo said, dragging Zed to his feet.

Not that the shady driving instructor was ever in danger. He'd been no-where near the car tires while we pressed him. Since he was still effectively blind from his swollen eye and PepperBall residue, the fake out worked as intended.

We drove Zed back to his creepy home base, and I parked his car in its original spot. We gathered on the steps of the Zoom-Zoom Driving School; Zed's somewhat-stolen pit bull rested its head in Theo's lap.

Zed gave us his log-in for the state's student driver certification site so we could pass ourselves while his vision slowly returned.

Squinting, he said, "You should get an email."

My phone dinged with the confirmation. A few moments later, Theo had the same completion certificate in his inbox.

"Let's get out of here," I said. "My sister can give you a ride if you want."

"You know, after today, I'm what my Uncle Ronnie would call road weary. Can we walk some?"

"Yes. Of course."

We were halfway down the block when Zed shouted, "Can I count on a five-star rating for the course?"

I lunged in Zed's direction, but Theo slipped an arm around my waist and carried me around the corner.

With Zed safely out of my line of sight, he placed me back on my feet. "Maybe you're a little road weary too."

"I just . . . that guy . . ." *No. Do not let that man trigger you, Annalise!*

Theo raised his hands in surrender. "Hey, I get it. He ain't getting five stars. But I might bless him with two. Maybe three."

I was *appalled.* "Why?"

"Because without him, I wouldn't have met you."

"I—" My mouth snapped shut.

Theo gave a little half grin, the uncertain kind, and walked ahead a few steps. I jogged to catch up and we crossed an intersection to a more vibrant part of the neighborhood. A soul food restaurant that looked way better than The Gizzard King had waiters setting up patio chairs and wiping down tables. A local boutique flipped their window sign to OPEN. Someone strummed a guitar in the one thousandth coffee shop I'd seen today. It was good energy.

"I hope I didn't make whatever this is weird," Theo said. "Even if we never talk again, this was a day to remember."

"Not weird. At all. You really think we wouldn't have met without Zed?"

"I don't know."

"I might've come by your uncle's food truck when you were working. You could've made me that Chillmatic Shake. I probably wouldn't have been able to smell your cologne, though. That would've been problematic."

He made a show of sniffing his collar. "I really gotta thank Ronnie for this stuff."

"You do."

Theo crammed his hands in his pockets, stared into the distance while we walked. "If I asked you to hang out again sometime, would you be into that? Think hard before you answer because Zed's three-star rating depends on you."

"Let's see, this day has resulted in," I began ticking off events on my fingers, "a delivery gig I didn't get paid for. Dognapping. A highway battle with dirt-bike pirates. And meeting you. Not my worst Saturday."

"Oh God, what was your worst Saturday?"

"I'll tell you about it when we hang out again."

Theo chuckled. "Three stars for Zed."

"One thing though," I said. "I'm driving."

WOLF TRACKS
BY ROSEANNE A. BROWN

It's 11:45 a.m. on a Tuesday morning, and I have fur in my butt crack.

This is all because of the person sitting across from me, my best friend Benji. This boy is pee-his-pants, over-the-moon, grinning-like-a-complete-fool-with-that-little-dimple-on-his-cheek-I-pretend-not-to-notice excited. He texted me before school that he had a surprise for me, and now that it's lunchtime, he looks ready to explode from the force of keeping it in all morning.

"Okay, do you want to guess what the surprise is, or do you just want me to tell you?" Benji asks, practically bouncing in his seat.

"The aliens who left you on this planet have finally returned to take you back from whence you came and free me from my misery?" I guess.

"Haha, very funny."

He sticks out his tongue and crosses his eyes in an expression so stupidly cute it should be illegal. The fur climbs up the column of my spine and talons push out against the fabric of my sneakers. On the outside, I grin back, while on the inside, I fight for my life to keep the wolf contained.

No one knows how it began. Granddad claims it's actually a blessing passed on to our line centuries ago by a goddess in West Africa. Uncle Frances swears up and down that it's a punishment for one of our ancestors jilting his witch lover decades ago in Mississippi. Whatever the cause may be, nothing changes the fact that for as long as anyone can remember, any time a Martins man falls in love, he turns into a wolf—claws, fangs, the whole nine yards.

And because Jesus or Zeus or whoever is up there hates me, my wolf is drawn to none other than my best friend.

When I close my eyes, the wolf is there behind my eyelids, clawing against my rib cage and snapping its jaws up my throat. The wolf is ancient—older than anything I've ever known, maybe as old as the world itself.

But the wolf is also me, and like every man in my family, I need to learn how to keep it at bay. I fill my head with the most mundane, borderline repulsive thoughts I can—paper cuts. Half-melted snow that's more mud than water. Fresh cat vomit. Granddad's left bunion.

I fill my mind with so many thoughts, there's no room left for Benji. And without thoughts of the person I love to feed on, the wolf recedes, tail tucked between its legs and lips pulled back in a silent snarl.

"Hey, you all right?" Benji asks, interrupting my mental battle. "You spaced out."

"I'm fine." Poopy baby diapers. Unwashed raccoon butts. Taxes. "All right, what's the big surprise?"

It probably has something to do with Seekers of the Grove, the '60s pulp epic-fantasy series we're both completely obsessed with. Benji saw my Seekers-themed lunch box back in fifth grade, and we have been inseparable ever since. Through all the moments we've been through since—me coming out to my parents, his mom losing her job, racist twats in our town, etc.—we've had each other.

And more importantly, we've had Seekers of the Grove.

Unable to hold his excitement any longer, Benji shoves his phone in my face. "TA-DA!"

My mouth falls open before I've even finished reading the subject on the email:

WELCOME TO GROVECON, PANELIST!

"No way, you got into GroveCon?" I exclaim. "How? I thought they rejected your proposal weeks ago?"

"They did, but apparently the person running the 'International Relations in the Grove Realms' panel caught, like, super salmonella or something, so he pulled out, and my proposal on the history of people of color in the franchise was at the top of the backup list!"

It honestly doesn't surprise me that the organizers would choose Benji as a backup. No one—and I mean *no one*—knows more about Seekers of the Grove than he does.

I'm happy for him, I really, truly am but I guess I just . . . it's stupid, but I had hoped his excitement was over something specifically to do with me—or at least us, together.

"Hang on, how is you getting picked as a panelist a surprise for me though?" I try to keep my voice light even though the wolf lets out a mournful howl that rings only in my ears.

"Isn't it obvious? I get free admission and lodging for one co-panelist and that is obviously going to be you. We're going to GroveCon, bro!"

His joy is infectious, and I can't stop myself from returning the high five he puts up before my brain processes what he just said.

"Free lodging, like they're giving us hotel rooms?"

"They're giving us a hotel room. Singular. It might be a little cramped, but it's better than having to drive in each day."

No, it is not better than having to drive in each day because I have never stayed anywhere overnight with Benji. How do I keep the wolf at bay when we'll be so close together for two days straight, when I'll be uncomfortably aware of every breath and mumble and turn?

When I don't agree right away, Benji nudges me with his shoulder. "Come on, you know I can't do this without you. Don't make me look like some sort of fool up there all on my own."

I should say no. My dad would want me to say no. He claims he didn't let himself spend the night with anyone he was interested in until he got his own wolf under control in his midtwenties. One wrong move, one wrong thought, and all the tens of thousands of people attending GroveCon will be in danger. I'll be just like Uncle Eddie.

"I'll have to check with my parents first. I think we might have a family thing that weekend." Benji's shoulders droop, but he nods.

"Well, let me know. I gotta confirm by tomorrow, and if you can't come, I'll have to beg some rando to join me, and you know how much I hate to beg."

I nod back, fighting the urge to tuck back the strap of the backpack that has fallen off Benji's shoulder. "I'll let you know."

I look like I've lost my mind sprinting from the bus stop to my house, but I don't care. There's only one person on the entire planet who has the range to help me with my little "Should I risk going into a wolfish frenzy over a weekend alone with my crush?" problem, and that is my older sister, Catherine.

"Cat! Where are you?" I barrel through the front door, leap up the stairs three at a time, and collide with a monster.

The wolf standing at the edge of our upstairs landing is easily twice my size, its fur midnight-black spun through with tufts of russet brown. He levels a single golden eye my way, and from the way his claws scuffle against the hardwood floor, I know he isn't happy.

I pause at the foot of the stairs. "Hey, Dad. Have you seen Cat?"

My father lets out a wet huff, then flicks his tail toward her bedroom. Before I can squeeze past him, Mom appears from the room next to Cat's with a yawn.

"Babe, you know I don't like it when you shed all over the landing," she scolds, and Dad's ears flatten against his head in apology. Mom rubs his head affectionately as she pushes past him, then drops a kiss on my forehead, which her tiny five-foot self can only do because she's standing several steps above me. "Everything okay? How was school?"

"Um, it was same old, same old. But I need Cat's help with my English project." The lie flows easily off my tongue. No one in my family reacted badly when I came out last year, but my sister was definitely the least weird about it. To be fair, my parents could have reacted a lot worse. They didn't kick me out; they didn't haul me off to a priest or fake doctor to try to change me.

But we haven't really talked about my sexuality since the Big Convo, and I definitely haven't confided in them about Benji. My mom and dad are a part of that Obama generation that is okay with queer people in the abstract. Pride parades, same-sex marriage, all-gender bathrooms? They love that shit. But a gay son in their own home? That's something their traditional Black upbringings didn't prepare them for.

But this is just how they've always been with big things they don't know how to navigate. We don't talk about me coming out. We don't talk about Uncle Eddie. The silence protects us, keeps everything at a distance where it can't hurt. Silence is better than anger.

I finally get to Cat's room (yes, a man who can turn into a wolf nicknamed his daughter Cat. Ironic, isn't it?) and draw her attention from her Switch by throwing a shoe at her head. "Dad's in a mood. Is everything okay?"

"He just got back from visiting Uncle Eddie," she explains, and I wince. Trips to the prison always put my father on edge. I flop facedown onto Cat's bed.

"Benji got us into GroveCon as panelists, and if I go, I'll be sharing a hotel room with him all weekend," I blurt out.

That gets her attention. She swivels around in her gaming chair so she's straddling the back and facing me. "Are you gonna say yes?" she asks. Cat is both the only person who knows about my crush and is also a diehard romantic, so this whole situation is practically candy to her.

"I want to but I know I shouldn't. I don't think I could keep the wolf at bay for a whole weekend."

"But what if you didn't?" Her eyes go wide. "I can see it now: You and Benji, alone in your hotel room after a long weekend of doing weeb shit. You confess your undying love to each other, he notices you've sprouted ears and a tail, you kiss while an orchestral version of a Lil Nas X song plays in the background."

"First of all, weebs are into anime. Seekers of the Grove has no animated adaptation, save an unfortunate thirty-minute Christmas special from the eighties we don't talk about. Second of all, fuck you. It's not that easy!"

Cat sees the wolf thing as something straight out of a fairy tale. A falling-in-love curse is pretty easy to romanticize when you'll never have to deal with it yourself. Even though the wolf has been plaguing my family for as long as anyone can remember, it only affects the men.

And it's not just a cis man thing either. My cousin P. J. says he saw signs of his own wolf long before he was ready to start transitioning. The curse doesn't care what the world says you are or what you were assigned at birth. If you're a man, you're a man, and if you're a man in my family, you're a wolf.

In the best case scenario, you get my parents, who have been together now for almost three decades without incident. My father can transform back and forth at will, and from the two sets of feet I hear puttering around downstairs, he's shifted back to human mode, likely to help Mom with dinner.

In the worst case, you get Uncle Eddie, who is looking at three decades' jail time over what he did in a jealous rage to the dude his girlfriend was cheating on him with a few years back. Dad's so ashamed, he won't even speak his brother's name even though he still visits the prison a few times a year. "A man who can't control his emotions isn't a man at all," he said to me when it happened. Those words dig into me even now. They're the reason I've never transformed all the way before, because I don't trust I could do so without hurting someone.

Cat's expression softens. "I get it if you turn him down, but you deserve this. You deserve every good thing, and no curse should take that from you."

I smile back at her, and of course, she has to ruin the moment by adding, "But I reserve the right to tell my future kids how their Uncle Daniel fell in love over a janky Lord of the Rings rip-off."

I give her the finger with one hand, and with the other, I text Benji two simple, life-changing words:

I'm in.

The second Benji and I step through the revolving door of the hotel hosting GroveCon, we know we've come home.

There are more Grovies than I've ever seen in one place before—some taking photos in hyperrealistic cosplays that probably cost a thousand a piece, while others are poring over programs to figure out which panels and events to attend. The majority of attendees are white, but there's a fair number of brown ones spread through the crowd. Every now and then, we pass a Black Grovie and give them the obligatory "I see you" nod that all Black people in non-Black spaces have mastered. I'm so excited that Benji has to practically drag me to get our badges.

That excitement dies when we get to our room and see exactly what "free board" meant.

"Um, so that is certainly one bed," I choke out, heat rushing to my face as I survey the soft-looking king-sized bed in our room. We've both read enough fanfic to know the "There's only one bed!" trope and all the shenanigans that occur with it. Cat would call this the "serendipitous nature of the universe in motion." I call it awkward as hell.

Benji breaks the silence by throwing his bags on the mattress. "It's cool, we'll take turns. I'll take the bed tonight, you take the couch, then we'll switch tomorrow night." He tugs on my arm, pulling me toward the door, and the wolf rises in excitement. "Come on, our panel's not till tomorrow, so we gotta get as much done today as we can!"

For the first day of GroveCon, we lose ourselves in the series that raised both of us. We sing our hearts out at the karaoke panel, laugh like hell at the comedy show, take copious notes during the history of the fandom lecture event. To outsiders it's a silly hobby, but this book series quite literally saved my life. Fandom was one of the few places I felt safe growing up. My family might not get that, but Benji does, and that's all that matters.

The only incident happens at a panel with this jerky white dude who keeps interrupting everyone and who Benji and I secretly dub "Con Bro." You know the type. The ones who are always like, "This is more of a comment than a question . . ." during the Q&A and who think being contrary is a personality trait. But aside from him, it's perfect.

Then in the evening, the lady running the cosplay contest invites us to a panelists-only after-party. We miiiiight have lied and said we were college students, so when they bust the alcohol out, nobody misses a beat shoving beer bottles into our hands. Neither Benji and I are big drinkers because he has no one to get it for him, and *you* try stealing from the liquor cabinet when your dad's supernatural sense of smell is so good he can detect a bottle missing from the literal opposite side of the house.

All this is to say

WE.

GET.

SLOSHED.

Sometime after midnight but before dawn, we end up back in our room side by side on the bed. I'm doing my best to keep the wolf at bay, but it's hard to focus on festering wounds with Benji giggling like hell beside me.

"We are going to be . . ." *Hiccup*. ". . . sooooo fucked tomorrow," I moan.

"You are such a sloppy drunk!" Benji howls.

"Like you're any better!" I give him what I'd meant as a playful shove, but a bit of the wolf strength slips through and he goes sailing off the bed. Benji hits the ground with a thud that knocks the lamp over, and suddenly my head is filled with images of blood-streaked walls and the caution tape that surrounded Uncle Eddie's bedroom the day after the attack.

I drop beside Benji, shoving the wolf down as far as I physically can. "I'm so sorry, I didn't mean it, are you all right—"

But this fool is just lying on the ground howling with laughter like his drunk ass doesn't even notice he's on the floor.

"You've been holding out on me! With strength like that, you could be a boxer." He tugs on my sleeve with not nearly enough force to move me, but I pretend it is and sink down so we're facing each other on our sides. He props himself up on his left elbow and looks at me, eyes sparkling with what is probably just alcohol but that my heart desperately hopes is something else. I was so worried about the wolf all day, but I'd kept it contained. Maybe Cat is right and I don't need to be so afraid. Maybe I deserve to live like the wolf isn't a problem.

"Yo, thanks again for being here," he says, and I am hypnotized by the curve of his lips. "It's nice to get out of the house for a few days."

I snap my eyes back up to his. "How's your mom doing?"

"Bad. Just this week she's been rejected for, like, three jobs. She can barely get out of bed most days. Dad's picked up extra shifts at the warehouse, but I heard them arguing about bills the other day, and it's just, I don't know . . ."

Benji puts an arm over his face, shoulders shaking. Suddenly, I don't care about my crush or my curse; my best friend is crying, and nothing else matters.

I don't tell him it's going to be all right, or any other of that feel-good crap people say when they don't know what to say. I just wrap my arms around him and let him cry against me.

At some point, the sniffling stops. Benji looks up at me, face streaked with tears, and I open my mouth to crack a joke to help him feel better.

And that's when he kisses me.

My brain short-circuits. My lips don't work. Benji pulls away, clearly embarrassed. "I'm sorry, I shouldn't have—"

He can't get the rest of the words out because now I'm kissing him.

Kissing Benji is better than acing a test I forgot to study for. It's better than that time I found a limited edition of *SotG Book Seven* for three bucks at a used bookstore. The wolf howls with pure joy, but for once, I'm not scared of it because we want the same exact thing—to never stop kissing this boy. His fingers tangle in my curls, and I wish I could tell my younger self that all those nights spent agonizing over what I was were coming to this. We pull apart and then we're kissing again and again and again.

This moment is perfect. Everything is perfect.

I wake up alone on the floor with my head feeling like it's been stuffed full of cotton. The world spins when I sit up, and it's only when it's finally righted itself that I see Benji sitting on the bed going through his notes for our panel.

"Good you're finally awake. We need to go over the agenda one more time, then grab breakfast, then do a tech check."

I wait for him to say more. He doesn't. What the hell?

When it's clear he's not going to mention the kiss . . . the *kisses* . . . I clear my throat and say, "Sure. And, um, about last night—"

"Yeah, we were wasted!" he says cheerfully. "I don't remember anything. Got a hell of a headache though, but I'll plow through just like Valinor did during the Siege of the Nine Trees in *Book Five*."

The sheets on the bed are crumpled, like he clearly slept in it. But we were both on the ground, weren't we? Did he get up in the middle of the night and leave me?

Or maybe it was all one of those hyperrealistic lucid dreams?

No way. I may not be a make-out master or anything, but even I know the difference between a dream kiss and an actual one. Last night really happened, and even worse, Benji is acting like it didn't.

The next five hours are agony. To outsiders, it probably just looks like Benji is in the zone as he locks in all the final details for the panel. But I can tell from the awkward glances and the way he stumbles nervously from topic to topic that he's avoiding me. Was I a horrible kisser? Did my breath smell bad? The wolf paces beneath my skin in distress, and the more it tries to get out, the harder I fight to shut it deep inside next to my disappointment and embarrassment. Cat was wrong. This isn't a fairy tale—not for someone like me.

All too soon, it's time for the panel. At this point, I'm so on edge it's a miracle I even get my laptop open, but I forget my misery for a second when the audience starts trickling in. Whoa, we have a full house!

Benji realizes it at the same time I do, and we shoot each other grins before we remember Things Are Weird between Us™.

At 3:05 on the dot, my best friend grabs the mic and steps to the front of the room.

"Hi, everyone, my name is Benji Rollins and I'm the host of the podcast *Brown in the Grove*. This is my . . . friend, Daniel Martins. Welcome to our panel 'Black Elves and White Knights: An Analysis on Race within the Seekers of the Grove Franchise.'"

Claws push up beneath my fingernails at the word "friend." I bite the inside of my cheek, make the claws retreat by imagining finding a giant turd under the tree on Christmas, and click to the next slide. It features an official illustration of every named character, human or otherwise, in the Seekers of the Grove franchise. There's easily over two hundred people here, and a quick glance confirms that the vast majority of the human ones are white.

Benji continues, "Seekers of the Grove has been beloved for decades for its nuanced depictions of morality, war, and human nature. However, despite its many accomplishments, the series falls flat on the subject of race. In this panel, we'll explore—"

"Like a series from the 1960s needs all that PC crap!" yells a voice from the back of the room. It's Con Bro, his pale face red in a way that suggests the day-drinking began early this morning.

"Don't feed the troll," I whisper to Benji, but his knuckles tighten around the mic.

"On the contrary, it's important to examine why a series that borrowed so much from cultures around the globe failed in depicting actual people of color on the page," Benji argues. "For example, author C. H. Nortman admitted that he drew inspiration for the elven race from the Akan people of Ghana, yet there isn't a single dark-skinned elf in all thirteen books—"

"The Blarvins are dark-skinned."

"Ah yes, the race of bloodthirsty, warmongering monsters are the only explicitly Black-coded people in the entire realm. Even you have to see the issue with that, right?"

Con Bro snorts, which probably increases the amount of methane in this room by at least 60 percent. "Blarvins aren't real. If you want to pretend they're Black, then maybe you're the racist one, not Nortman."

Benji grits his teeth, and even though we're on shaky ground right now, seeing him upset causes fur to curl up under my right jacket sleeve. All my instincts scream *defend him*, but my dad's voice rings in my ears: *A man who can't control his emotions isn't a man at all*. Reluctantly, I follow Benji's cue as he turns back to the wider audience and tries to continue on with the panel.

This works for about two minutes before it becomes clear Con Bro is not going to let us speak in peace. He loudly contradicts everything Benji says, interrupting him literally midsentence to tell him how wrong he is. The people sitting around the man are all clearly uncomfortable, but no one makes any moves to stop him. After the fifth interruption in as many minutes, I rise from my chair and storm over.

"It's time for you to go," I demand.

I grab Con Bro by the arm. He grunts, clearly surprised I'm not nearly as much of a scrawny weakling as I look. He turns to Benji and yells, "Hey, tell your boyfriend to get his grubby paws off of me!"

"He's not my boyfriend!" Benji snaps.

Everything goes red. The "paws" comment or Benji's rejection alone I could handle, but the two together rips past the small semblance of control I have left.

It happens quicker than a heartbeat. One second Con Bro is in front of me bellowing like a whale.

The next he's on the ground, blood leaking down the side of his face and dripping down my now claw-tipped arm. The world seems to halt as I lock eyes with a terrified Benji, whose mouth has fallen open into an adorable little O as he stares at me.

That's the last thing I see before the wolf takes me over.

My limbs elongate, the muscles twining and growing. Our senses meld together, the canine instincts bringing a heightened awareness to my surroundings. I try to explain to Benji what's happening, but only a howl comes out. He backs away, and someone yells to call the police. I have to get out of here now.

I race from the room, my body ungainly on four legs instead of two. It's my first full transformation, and everything feels wrong, my body an arrow I can't control. The con goers part like the Red Sea in my mad dash, and to my surprise, a few of them even cheer—they think this is a show, that I'm wearing an extremely elaborate cosplay. But the ones closest to me can see the hunger in my eyes, feel the heat coursing off my body in a way no fursuit can replicate.

I crash into the dealers room, enamel pins, plushies, and posters flying everywhere. A yell cuts through my terror; four officers run toward me, each of them holding one of those long poles with a wire loop at the end that people use to seize rabid animals. Images of my broken, mangled wolf body in police custody overlap with images of my broken, mangled Black body in police custody until I can't tell one from the other.

One officer lunges for me, and actually manages to loop his wire around my neck. The bite of it burns against my flesh, and in a panic, I swipe for him, snapping the pole clean in two and knocking the officer into a display full of ceramic dwarves. I kick out with my back legs to take out two more of the officers, then headbutt the fourth.

After seeing how easily the officers were subdued, no one else tries to stop me as I rush from the dealers room. A pungent smell catches my attention. The trash room. Perfect. I barrel for the room and quite literally throw myself into the garbage. I burrow down, letting the bags roll on top of me for better coverage.

My heart beats triple time as footsteps pound into the trash room.

One heartbeat passes.

And then another.

And then one more.

The boots leave the room, and I sense them heading down the hallway in pursuit of a wolf they can't believe simply vanished.

It takes another fifteen minutes for me to calm down enough to shift back into my human body, which no longer feels like my body—it's too small, too vulnerable, too weak compared to the beast I was before.

I also lost my clothes during the transformation, because that may as well happen too. You'd think one of my cousins would've mentioned this little detail. Tears brim in my eyes as I realize, in less than twelve hours, I went from kissing Benji to shivering naked and alone in literal garbage.

I can't get back to the hotel room like this. I dig through the bags until I find a torn raincoat and wrap myself in it. But even though I need to get out of here, my legs don't want to move. To go back in there—to face Benji—

I can't . . . I can't do it.

There's an office to the side of the trash room, and in my first stroke of good luck all day, it's empty. A bright red landline phone waits for me inside. My first instinct is to call Cat, only to remember I don't have her number memorized. The only numbers in this world I know by heart are Benji's (yeah, not happening), 911 (hardly any better), our local taco place because of this ridiculously catchy jingle they play in their ads, and my house. I dial the last one, praying my sister picks up.

"Hello?" comes my dad's deep voice.

"Um, hi, Dad, it's me," I squeak out, then cough to make my voice sound more normal.

"Oh, hey. Why aren't you calling from your phone?"

"It died," I lie. "Is Cat there? I left something at home and need her to bring it to me."

"No, she's out with that little boy of hers, won't be back until tomorrow. What do you need? I can bring it to you."

I didn't realize how hard I was holding onto the hope of Cat getting me out of this mess until the possibility is gone. Tears blur my vision, and after several seconds of awkward silence, he goes, "You okay, D-man?"

"The wolf's out, Dad. I transformed all the way, right here at the con."

And just like that, the whole story comes out between sobs. I don't know what's worse—crying in front of my dad, or crying in front of my dad after I fucked up my family's biggest secret. By the time I'm done, I'm just hiccupping into the phone, and the seconds before Dad speaks again are some of the longest, most agonizing of my life.

"Wait right there. I'm coming to get you."

Forty minutes later, Dad pulls up to the road behind the garbage room with a pair of clean clothes and a bag of Wendy's. It's the single most beautiful meal I've ever eaten in my entire life.

"So, my boy has finally gone full wolf for the first time," he exclaims. "You didn't tell me you were experiencing the change! Who triggered it?"

The heat rushes through my body at the question I've been dreading more than anything. "It was Benji," I whisper. "It's always been Benji."

I spent years agonizing about what it would mean to come out. How it could change the way my family saw me, the way the world saw me. But what no one warned me is that you don't just come out once—it's a thousand different times, a thousand different ways, sometimes with the same people again and again and again. I don't realize until that moment, as I watch the truth of me and Benji's closeness settle over his face, that it actually isn't enough for me that his acceptance looks like silence. I *want* him to deal with me, all of me, on every level. In every way.

"Why didn't you tell me the wolf had started coming out around Benji?" Dad asks, disapproval creeping up in his voice. "If I'd known, I would've told you this con was a stupid idea from the get-go."

"Because we don't talk, Dad!" The words explode out of me, fueled not by the wolf or the curse but years of something I've been too scared to put into words. "About who I'm into, about my life, any of it!"

Of all the idiotic things I've done today, yelling at my Black father is most definitely the one that is going to get me killed. But I can't stop now; I won't stop. It's not like there's any reason to hold back, not when I've messed things up with Benji forever. Who'd want to date a boy who could maul them at any moment?

"I'm not like you or Granddad or Uncle Frances. It's so easy for you to keep your wolves contained, but I struggle against mine every moment of every day. I'm going to end up like Uncle Eddie, I'm going to lose control and hurt someone and I don't know how to stop it. I can't stop it—"

To my complete and utter humiliation, tears spill down over my cheeks. I wait for the inevitable "Don't cry. Martins men don't cry." I flinch back as a muscle twitches in my dad's jaw and his fingers clench around the steering wheel.

And then they unclench, moving instead to reach into the glove box and clumsily offer me a wad of crumpled napkins.

"This is all my fault," he says, his voice hoarse. I don't move, hardly daring to breathe. "We don't talk, and it's all on me."

I hold the napkins limply in my hands.

"When I was your age, I was so mad at my dad for always giving me the silent treatment. It felt like my problems didn't matter enough to him to even get a reaction. And now I'm doing the same to you." He lifts his hands like he's going to reach for me, then thinks better of it and drops them in his lap. "It's just, ever since you came out I'm—it's—you hear all those news stories about kids like you who get bullied or who hurt themselves because the people around them said the wrong thing. And I've been so terrified of saying the wrong thing that I say nothing."

"But that's not an excuse. I'm sorry you felt like you couldn't come to me, and I'm sorry I wasn't there today when you needed me."

Now Dad is looking misty-eyed, and I'm fairly certain Granddad would whoop both our butts if he could see us like this. A part of me still wants to turn away on instinct, but when he reaches an arm toward me, I quietly slip into his embrace.

"You're not going to be Uncle Eddie. You're not going to be me or Granddad either. You're *you*, and what the wolf means to you is going to be different than what it means to any of us. And that's okay."

We stay like that for several quiet seconds before the sharp cut of the seat belts make it impossible to hold on any longer.

"So," he says, drawing out the syllable into a full-on question. He revs up the engine and starts pulling out of the parking lot. "Benji, huh?"

I squish down in my seat, half to avoid the sudden burst of bright light that comes from us exiting the parking garage, half in response to the foreign, yet not unpleasant feeling that comes from actually talking about my crush with my father. It brings a sense of rightness, like the two sides of myself—the wolf and the lovestruck boy—aren't enemies but rather two halves of the same coin. "Yes, Benji."

He flicks the turn signal on, and just like that, the convention center becomes nothing more than another building in the rearview, getting smaller and smaller by the second.

"I wouldn't have guessed he was your type, but yeah, I can see it," he says with a grin. "Tell me about him."

So I do.

Several days later, Benji and I sit cross-legged across from each other in my fenced-in backyard. We're alone, but I can sense my nosy-ass family watching from their little hidey-holes to see how the big confrontation finally goes down. I haven't gone full wolf since the con, but now that my crush is no longer a secret, it's easier to draw on the wolf's powers without feeling like he's going to consume me.

Benji eyes me warily, as if expecting a giant dog to burst out of my rib cage at any moment and eat him.

Which, honestly, isn't impossible.

But it won't happen. Because right now, the wolf isn't in control.

I am.

Benji's arms are crossed over his chest, but he's here. I called and he came, which gives me hope that maybe everything isn't completely over between us, that whatever I broke isn't unfixable.

"You won best cosplay, by the way," he says dully when I don't speak. "The con committee will be mailing you your prize in the next week."

I nod. "And what about Con Bro?"

"He's fine—his wound bled a lot, but it wasn't bad. And he was so drunk, he couldn't recall exactly what he saw, so your secret's safe with him." He pauses. "There's a lot we need to talk about. The wolf thing, obviously, but the night before the panel . . . yeah."

I lift an eyebrow. "Oh, so now you remember. Is that a good 'yeah' or a bad 'yeah'?"

"A good yeah. The best yeah."

He nudges my shoulder, and I know deep in my gut in a way that has nothing to do with my powers that we're going to be okay. "But before we get to that, can you explain what your whole *Wolfman* deal is about? Because this is literally the coolest thing that's ever happened to me and likely ever will, and I'm low-key, high-key pissed that you kept it to yourself all this time."

I take a deep breath, and within it, I feel each of the Martins men lying in wait, tails swishing, ready to let me into the pack. And for the first time, I feel like I belong in it.

The corner of my mouth twitches up, revealing a single, gleaming canine.

"It'd be easier to just show you."

THE HERO'S JOURNEY
BY TOCHI ONYEBUCHI

The mountains were red all around them, sharp craggy things that scratched the sky bloody. The ground rumbled. Though the wind was soundless, it blew red dust into swirls between Okami and his opponent. Okami glared across the expanse of the empty battlefield at his mirror, his reflection in shadow. A flowing black cloak where Okami's was white, scars patterned in straight lines around the eyes and down the left cheek, whereas Okami's patterning was swirling and circular around his right.

"At long last," Okami said. Though he spoke in a low growl, he could be heard on the other side of the Red Plains, a voice both soft as a feather and heavy as lightning. "I have tracked you across the Lands, every village you have laid to waste, every kingdom you have toppled, Agent of Chaos. When the stars dot the night and I close my eyes in sleep, I hear their cries." With a flick of his wrist, a sword of light flashed to life in Okami's hand. The blade glowed red and electricity shot out and snapped at the ground and the air like the crack of a dozen whips. Then, the sword ceased its writhing. "Your path of destruction ends today!"

Across the plain, a grin split Imako's face. Even though he too spoke in a low growl—a growl tinged with a rasp that spoke to his unhinged nature—his words could be heard across the plain. "You hear their cries and how do you react? You weep for them. You think you are their hero, but look at how they have scorned you. Is there a single village you can call your home? A single kingdom to which you belong? No, you have been cast out of every place, just like I. And yet you refuse to understand that if you want change, YOU HAVE TO MAKE IT YOURSELF." Imako raised his arms and fissures ran through the earth. A section of mountaintop separated from its base. The ground quaked. Clouds darkened the sky, shot through with forks of dirty lightning. "THEY WILL NEVER CHANGE, BROTHER. WE MUST DESTROY AND REBUILD!"

"Never!" Okami shouted over the roaring earth.

The mountaintop drew closer. The wind howled around Okami. His Greater Sense pulsed through his body, radiating outward, allowing him to draw from his inner power. Gate after gate unlocked to allow the energy to flow through him. And at the very last moment, his sword blazed forth, up and down with blinding speed such that the very air it cut through hissed and smoked and spoke of its passage. A crack split the moving mountaintop. Just as it would have crashed into Okami, it SHATTERED into a million pieces.

His eyes still closed, Okami smiled, then whirled around and swung, his blade catching Imako's. As the shattered ruins of the mountain swirled around them, Imako grunted, broke away and charged again, swinging and swinging, Okami dodging and parrying until a cut sliced through his shoulder. He grunted and stepped back, but Imako kept up the assault. Okami grit his teeth. Imako only seemed to be getting more powerful. Until suddenly, Imako broke away, and the two of them stood dozens of meters apart, shoulders heaving with the effort. Okami held his wounded arm.

Imako was untouched. "Why do you fight, brother?"

Okami struggled to move his arm but it was useless. When he closed his eyes, his power was nowhere to be found. "What?" he gasped. But before he could move, the ground rose and swallowed him up to the waist. He struggled and struggled but it was futile. Even when he banged the hilt of his sword against the stone that enclosed him, nothing.

Imako stepped forward, drawing close. He flipped his sword upside down, drove the tip into the earth, and propped his hands and chin on the handle. "For real, though. Like, what's your motivation?"

"What are you talking about? We were fated to meet on the field of battle. You're, like, my evil twin and this is just how it's supposed to go."

"But, like, is it 'cause you're the Light and I'm the Darkness or whatever? Like, is there a deeper reason? Did I kill your gf?"

Okami looked away, shamefacedly. "I *wish* I had a gf."

"You need a motivation, bro. Something that's specific to *you*." Imako picked up his sword, pointed it at Okami and jabbed it when he said *you*. Then he waved it around as he continued, "None of this general 'I'm a good person' or 'I'm the hero' or 'I'm the good guy' type of nonsense." His sword vanished from his hand. He snapped his fingers, and the ground encasing Okami turned to rubble. Imako then turned and started walking away.

"Hold on!" Okami shouted, sounding less like the warrior he was and more like a fourteen-year-old weeb. "Where are you going?"

Imako turned to look over his shoulder. "I'm gonna go find a worthier opponent." He crouched, then launched himself into the sky, shooting a hole through the clouds and becoming a winking star before vanishing.

Okami's mouth hung open as he watched the sky turn from red back to blue.

At his computer, Dayo buried his face in his hands, let out a loud "Ugh!" and hit backspace.

Even though the bullets pinged against metal staircases and pieces of the shuttle station leagues below [OUTLAW CHARACTER NAME], [OUTLAW] could hear those bullets as though they were deflecting right off his headrest. His fingers blazed over the console while the shuttle spaceship grumbled to life around him. It was supposed to be a stealth mission—like stealth was ever Outlaw's thing!—his employer should've known who he was getting for this job. And, as always, things just hadn't gone according to plan. Because that's how it always goes. And now, there was some wolf lady with infinite ammo blasting away while clinging to a ladder that led up to the entry socket of the cockpit; Outlaw Character's little buddy Kyle who, constantly pulling back his oversized jacket sleeves, had his fingers blazing over the console; and some sort of cosmic golden treasure map the shape of a compass and as big as his head stuffed in a cooling suitcase at his feet.

"[OUTLAW CHARACTER NAME]!" Kyle shouted (I really need to come up with a name for him), "enemy heat signatures closing in on our location!"

It only took Outlaw the quickest of glances at the screens surrounding him to see footage of the soldiers and facility security storming like a phalanx up the railways.

"I see that!" Outlaw shouted back through gritted teeth (somehow). "Hey, Wolf Lady!" he yelled into the comms device at his cheek. "What's your status?"

Her voice came back a little garbled, but shrieky nonetheless. "I swear if you call me Wolf Lady again, there won't be enough of you left to put on a slice of bread! The name's Asuka!"

Suddenly, he couldn't hear any return fire from her. "Asuka!" he screamed into his comms. "Asuka, your status! Gimme your status!" He shot a worried look at Kyle. "Dammit," he hissed beneath his breath. He took a moment, but he knew what he needed to do, and he leaped out of his seat and ran back down the cockpit.

"[OUTLAW CHARACTER NAME], what are you doing?! What about the treasure?" shouted Kyle. "We got a job to do!"

"I'm not leaving her behind!" OUTLAW (this is getting ridiculous what do I call him) shouted, pulling his blasters out of his shoulder holster and kicking open the hatch at the back of the cockpit.

It opened out onto a walkway so high that if you fell from it, you could count three full minutes before hitting the ground, and even then, you'd probably be consumed by the fires nearby rockets belched well before impact.

The ladder was gone, broken off at the halfway point and swinging from a single hinge. Below that were the remains of a platform that looked like it'd seen the business end of a grenade launcher.

Outlaw leaped onto the platform, then onto another that led to the station. His bootsteps clanged against the metal as he leaped over the staircase railings. Even as he took the steps four at a time or leaped down ladders and darted through enclosed walkways, he had enough time to think about how ridiculous this all was. How reckless. This Asuka lady, for example. This morning, he had no idea she even existed. They were strangers. Then he goes to pick up a suitcase—a pretty heavy suitcase, it turns out—only to have her come from out of nowhere and kick him so hard in the face, he was seeing silver stars for the next fifteen minutes. Then had come the brief gun battle before folks with bigger guns came along, and half a day and a lot of bullets later, here he was risking his life AND HIS PAYDAY for this lady who was probably gonna blast his head off first chance she got anyway once all the smoke had cleared.

With each hall he went through, the walls got bloodier, and more and more spent laser cartridges littered the floor. "Asuka!"

The smoke got thicker. He coughed, but still kept his blasters at the ready. Another door whisked open, then another. Until a bullet PINGED by his face and he lunged for cover against the wall.

"Asuka!" he yelled through the smoke. "Asuka, it's me!"

"Oh, great!" she snarked, but Outlaw could hear the pain in it. "Captain's come to rescue the damsel in distress."

"You're hurt."

"You should see the other guy."

PING. PING.

The blasting turned into a fusillade, and this time Outlaw heard Asuka send a few more shots back, but they were weak, paltry things compared to the bullets and laser beams that chewed up chunks of her hiding place.

"I'm gonna try to make it to you."

"Don't even think about it, [OUTLAW]. Second group starts firing as soon as the first group starts reloading. There's no break." She had some fight left in her voice, even as each word taxed her.

"Ain't no breaks but the ones we make for ourselves," Outlaw said before he slipped his favorite lighter out of his breast pocket. It was an antique silver thing with a dragon insignia, all curls and sharp edges, fangs and flames. He turned it over in his gloved fingers for a quiet moment. Then he let out a sigh and said, "I'm gonna miss you, ol' buddy," before kissing it, tossing it behind him, and without looking, firing directly at it.

The explosion filled the entire hallway and the sound of lasers cut off completely only to be replaced by screams and bloodcurdling cries.

"That's our cue!" Outlaw grabbed Asuka by the wrist and hauled her to her feet. She stumbled and that's when he saw the wound in her side.

They passed through one corridor and found a walkway where the smoke had thinned. Asuka groaned.

"Almost there."

Asuka groaned again, louder.

"Pretty soon we can get you all bandaged up and—"

"I'm not groaning 'cause I'm hurt. I'm groaning because this is so

BORING! I've been here a million times before. YOU'VE been here a million times before."

"What?"

She pushed off of him and stood up straight, all of a sudden unaffected by her gunshot wound. Hands on her hips, feet shoulder width apart, she stared him down. "We get in your shuttle and we go into space. Why?"

"Why?" Outlaw stepped back in shock. "What do you mean, 'Why?' To get out of here! To get away from the guys that shot you, by the way, hello!"

Asuka poked at her wound. "Oh, this?" Then shrugged. "What's that got to do with *you*, though?" And she jabbed a finger at him when she said *you*.

"I . . . Hey, I'm saving your life."

"You don't even have a flashback moment prepared! We're gonna get on that ship and go God knows where and you're not even gonna have a specific traumatic memory to power your story."

"What do you mean? Of course I have traumatic memories!"

"Oh? Name one."

"Well . . . uh . . . I, uh . . . Hey! I have scars!" He reached behind his shoulder to pull the skin forward a little and reveal the tastefully patterned scar tissue lacing his back and upper arm. "See? Battle scars. That's trauma, right?"

"I swear, they must make you all in a factory these days." She turned around and plopped down on the smoke-filled walkway, chin on her palm, finger tapping her cheek.

"What are you doing? We gotta get outta here! They're gonna come barging through that door any second now to finish the job!"

She stood up and turned to face him. "Look, [OUTLAW CHARACTER NAME], this is fun and all, but"—she put a hand on his shoulder—"I'm not just some random tsundere. Until you figure out what *you* want—not what you think you should want because it's what everybody else wants—I can't go with you to outer space." She shook her head. "You don't even know who you are."

"But!"

She brandished her pistols, then turned toward the door, cocked and ready to go. "You should probably leave."

Then the doors to the station burst open.

It had happened again. He was stuck. Dayo stared at the screen, but as much as he tried to will his character forward in the story, he couldn't. It all felt so . . . false. Asuka was right. Dayo pressed backspace.

Officer Yagami vaulted over the railing, but when he went to land on the ground, it swayed beneath him, undulating like it had turned to a pond he had just splashed in. He scrambled to find purchase on the railing, but his hands passed through everything that looked like metal, which now felt like air. He fell and fell and fell, flailing and trying to catch hold of anything but also remembering the blaster at his hip and how, if he lost it, this whole thing would be for naught.

If anything, though, he could rest assured that the person he was chasing was, beyond all doubt, the suspect in the nightmares that had, for the past year, been rendering so many people in this city comatose. A hacker that could invade a person's dreams and turn them into horrors, forcing people to confront their greatest fears but on the hacker's terms and not their own. Inevitably, the victim wilted. So overcome by fear were they, that they never woke from their sleep. Their chests rose and fell with each breath they took, and their vitals came through clear whenever they were hooked to machines by their hospital beds. But whenever a doctor tried to open any of their eyes, there was only the rapid back-and-forth that told the medical personnel that the people were dreaming. Trapped in a dream was more like it, reliving horrors over and over and over again.

Only someone capable of hacking people's braincases and taking over their subconscious could be capable of this. Of turning a metal bridge into water, of turning a railing into air.

Officer Yagami splashed into a pool of concrete that started to swallow him up like quicksand. Instinct made him want to struggle and pull himself out, but he knew that if he obeyed the logic of this nightmare-land this hacker had constructed, he would lose. So he closed his eyes and told himself, "It's just a dream," and the concrete became the lip of a pool that he crawled out of. "Just a dream," he said, closing his eyes and listening for a sound, any sound, that might tell him where the hacker was.

"There." And he ran forward. Instantly, a skyscraper rose from the ground in front of him, and without missing a beat, he sprinted up its walls and windows, racing it to the sky, running as it rose, until he crested the lip and flipped over. A stone pathway, suspended in midair, sprung to life before him and he bounded along each step, calling forth the stone pathway with his mind so that he could swerve around buildings as they sprouted from the ground, trying to impale him.

"You really think you're in charge?" came a voice from nowhere and everywhere at the same time.

Lightning struck from the sky and clipped him on the right. He spun out of control, then crashed onto the hard floor of a dark alleyway.

Slowly, he came to his feet.

"Oh, Officer Yagami," the hacker said, again, from everywhere and nowhere. Then they made a tut-tut sound. "So foolish. I'd merely invited you here for a friendly chat, and this is how you react."

"Invited me into my own dream?" Officer Yagami shouted at the sky. "You barged in here just like you always do! Just like you've done with every one of your victims!"

"Why, that's rude. I would never! I only go where I'm invited. You see, the people of this city are blind, all of them. So afraid. And because of that fear, they cloak themselves in the illusion that all is well, that all is taken care of, that they needn't worry. They are *satisfied*. How can we reach greatness as a species if we are always *satisfied*?"

Sharp pain shot through Officer Yagami's side, and he gritted his teeth against it. That fall had done a number on him. "What's wrong with happiness?" he hissed.

"Oh, Officer Yagami. This isn't happiness. This is a prison. A prison of complacency. I'm here to free you. It's what you've always wanted. That's why you called to me, even when you didn't realize you were doing it."

"I never called to you."

"Why, yes, you did. Don't you remember when you . . . when you . . . hmm, what was that moment?"

Officer Yagami blinked. What was happening?

"Definitely a moment of personal weakness, but what on earth could have been happening?"

The air swirled before Officer Yagami to reveal the form of a skinny young man with wild, spiky white hair who had his fingers to his chin and who paced back and forth. But he seemed entirely made of smoke, more a silhouette than a man.

"You definitely called to me. It was a scene wherein a special connection between us was unearthed. Not established, because it's always been there according to your character arc, but . . . hmm, what were you thinking about? Help me out."

"Um . . . my love that you killed?"

"Nope. Not that."

"Um, my parents?"

"Ugh, so generic. No, it was something else."

"Were we separated at birth? No, wait, I got it. We grew up together as best friends, but then tragedy struck our neighborhood and you went evil while I became police, and we were fated to meet, which is why I've tracked you down. AND it explains why you'd gotten sloppy in your latest attacks. You *wanted* me to catch you."

The pacing figure stopped. He sighed, then said, "I'm tired of this."

The wind shifted behind Officer Yagami. He tried to spin around but was too late. The blade had pierced his back, running all the way through his chest, its point dripping blood on the floor.

"Omae wa mou shindeiru," the hacker said as light engulfed Officer Yagami's world, first appearing at the corners of his vision before growing larger and larger until his whole world was that on-the-verge-of-death blinding blaze.

Maybe it *was* always supposed to be like this. A kid like him never wins anyway.

Why would it be any different here?

A thin strip of blood ran down the side of his mouth, a single drop dripping from his chin. "Yame . . . ro."

Dayo gave up. This time, he didn't even bother to erase the part of the Word document where his character had started talking directly to him. If he couldn't figure out Officer Yagami's goal, his purpose, then what was the point of telling this story?

Dayo opened up a new Word document. This time, there would be no notes. No outline. He would just write. Inhale. Exhale. He began to type.

Water woke him up.

Or, rather, water sloshing against the side of his face woke him up. The sound of the surf covering, then backing away from, the sand was the most soothing sound in the world. Not even the gulls overhead, cawing or making whatever noise it is they made, could disrupt the serenity.

He wanted to lie there for all eternity, the sand soft as a bedsheet beneath him, the water lapping against his cheek like a caress.

"O-LA-DAY-O!"

The call came like a shot from a cannon, a thunderclap that tore open the sky, but when he opened his eyes, the sky was a tranquil azure. No clouds threatening rain. He propped himself up on his elbows, but then stopped, frozen. Several blinks later, the sight was still there. Even after he wiped his eyes, what he was looking at had not vanished. No. Not what—*who*.

"Auntie?"

The silver threaded in her argentate blouse and patterned purple wrapper made her glow like an otherworldly being in the sunlight. A moment later, the glare diminished, but only slightly. She raised a feathered hand fan and slowly waved over a face that didn't seem to sweat at all.

"Auntie, is that you?"

A grin and a chuckle. "Who were you expecting?"

He came to his feet and brushed the beach sand out of his shirt and pants, then patted his hair and scrubbed his arms clean. "I don't know. I . . . where are we?"

"Ah-ah! Don't you know? This is your flashback!"

"Wait, what?"

"Oladayo, you know exactly where we are."

"The beach?" He blinked as the thought hit him with the force of a Spirit Bomb. "Is this a beach episode too?"

"We don't have a lot of time, so I had to squeeze a few things together. Your stories are already going long. If I had the time, I would teach you how to properly get to the point and not waste our time with excessive battles or overdescribing things I do not care about."

"Wait, Auntie! You read my stories?!" He shook his head, realizing that she had also just insulted his writing. "I don't overwrite! Okay, maybe a little."

A portal opened up behind Auntie and she tugged him through. They landed on a pitch laden with bright green grass, white lines spray-painted in a clear pattern over it.

"Where are w—"

A dozen bodies crashed together around them, grunting and colliding and shouting. Dayo flinched, then dove to the ground, noticing only after a moment that the hands and feet of the people battling around him were passing through his body. He was not really here. He looked up to find Auntie standing by the sidelines and, after a cautious glance to make sure the storm had passed, he scurried to her.

On the sidelines, he stood beside her in silence, waiting for whatever lesson he was supposed to be learning, when he noticed something strange on the field. It was a game of rugby, that much was clear. He guessed that was something they played in England. This must be a moment from Auntie's past. Dayo turned to look in the stands. Maybe her younger self was sitting there cheering on her boyfriend or something, but there was no one.

A smack on the head stole his attention. "Baaaaka. Pay attention to the game."

Rubbing the back of his head, he squinted at the game that was taking place. "Wait." The players were . . . women. He stopped himself from wondering out loud how women played rugby, realizing how backward a thought that was to say. He couldn't imagine the way Auntie would pummel him for letting a question like that escape his lips. So he watched and squinted some more and noticed that, among the bodies colliding and tossing the rugby ball about, among the bodies leaping and swerving and dodging, one Black woman stood out. Auntie. But . . . younger. He gasped. Auntie had played rugby.

"Is this your first time seeing a Black woman playing rugby?"

His mouth hung open, dumbfounded at the revelation.

"Well, it was certainly *my* first time seeing a Black woman playing rugby. There was no end to people telling me that people like me didn't play rugby. A Nigerian woman like me just breaking my body all jagga-jagga. On purpose! We didn't do such things. That's what everyone told me. But I remember watching those games, and the envy I felt? Chai! Eventually, I asked the coach if I could join the club league. And she said yes." Auntie turned to smile at Dayo. "Your auntie even competed in New Zealand."

Right when she said that, Auntie's younger self tucked the rugby ball in the crook of her arm, checked an opponent backward so hard, the other player went horizontal with the ground, spun through another opponent's tackle, then dove across the goal line. The way she moved, Oladayo imagined sparks of energy flaring from her, speed lines speaking to how she cut through the air, how the wind moved around her. He imagined that time slowed for her, that she was powering up and this was her finishing move.

Auntie had performed a finishing move.

Tears sprang to his eyes. He scrubbed them away with his knuckles, but they kept coming. "Kusssso."

"Ah! Why are you crying?"

"*Of course* you're a hero, Auntie. You and Mom and the rest of the grownups. But I'm just a kid with a name I've never heard an anime character say."

Auntie knelt in front of him and put a hand on his shoulder. When she smiled, her teeth twinkled like Guy-sensei's. "We share blood, my nephew. The power that runs through me runs through you as well. *Dattebayo.*"

The flow of tears slowed, then stopped. Dayo sniffed away a sob. "Thank you, Auntie."

"Of course."

She started to shimmer. Slowly, she turned to dust whisked away on the wind.

"Wait. Auntie! How do you know all of this?"

As she faded away, her words became softer and softer. "I was always . . . watching." Then she was gone.

A portal opened up where she had been.

Oladayo gathered himself, a determined frown knitting his brow, and stepped through.

The concrete pressed against his cheek was suddenly the coldest thing he'd ever felt in his life. But he knew instantly what that meant. He was alive. His eyes shot open. The pool of blood beneath him was still wet, still steaming with newness. But he pushed himself to his feet. The laughter he'd been hearing stopped. In the neon glow of the alleyway and in his reflection in the puddles of water at his feet, he saw his form change. His skin grew darker, his eye color morphed. His hair began to kink.

The hacker stood before him, then started to shiver, to come apart, until suddenly the hacker snapped back to normal, his form concrete again. Tangible. Conquerable.

"I know my truth now." A pair of handcuffs appeared in Officer Yagami's—no, Oladayo's—outstretched hand and dangled dramatically. "You're under arrest."

Imako sat placidly on the stone bench outside of his cottage, munching on a mango, surveying the landscape he was preparing to lay waste to. He could take his time, and he enjoyed being leisurely about it. A part of him missed being chased, having a foil, but a larger part of him thrilled at winning. There was no one to oppose him now.

He finished the mango and tossed the leavings away, then stood and stretched. Destroying villages was so delicious, and a veritable feast awaited him.

He took a step forward before the ground exploded before him, chunks of earth shooting into the sky as though he'd stood on a volcano.

The smoke still obscured his visitor, but then energy pulsed like lightning caught in the bellies of clouds. Dust and ash parted to reveal a portion of the stranger's face: a brown-irised eye shot through with flecks of morning, sable skin along cheek and jawline. Then: hair kinked in an afro.

Imako stepped back in shock. "That energy . . ." Unabated, the waves of power emanated like a storm front from this figure. "Who . . . ?"

The smoke cleared. Fire burst to life around the figure's fists. "I'm that worthier opponent you were looking for."

Imako cowered backward.

Oladayo grinned.

Asuka crouched on her haunches behind the barricade she'd made of the fallen file cabinets and support beams. Explosions sounded around her as the security forces emptied cartridge after cartridge of laser blasts. She had no grenades left and was down to her last clip. Pretty soon, she would have nothing left but her superhuman reflexes and a dwindling supply of luck. Another BOOM sounded. She let out a sigh. This was the life she had chosen. The ceiling creaked above her. Before long, it would collapse, burying her and everyone else in this corridor. Death from blaster or death from above?

She was about to rise, but a hand gripped her shoulder and pulled her back down. "Wait, you?!"

"My name is Dayo," the outlaw said, out of breath. "I'm an outlaw who takes jobs no one else will because I secretly hope one of them will change my life and Kyle's, and I've had a crush on you since right after you kicked me in the face, and I know our trope says that we're going to fall for each other two-thirds of the way into this story, but I'm being real when I tell you that I want you to come to space with me."

Her gaze softened.

"And why am I going to space? Well . . ." Even though the gunfire grew louder, his voice lowered, almost as though he were talking to himself more than to her. "It's strange. And new. And different. Before, I didn't know I could even go to a place like the stars. I never imagined it. I never thought I *could* imagine it. I couldn't . . . I couldn't *see* it. But space is all about possibility. All you need is a ship." He reached his hand out to her. "And a friend."

She kissed him, then smacked his hand away, trying not to smile—"Fine. All right. You've convinced me"—but failing. "I'll go to space with you."

Dayo grinned at his screen, then started to write the next chapter.

ABYSS
BY AMERIE

In the chill of the abandoned tower, surrounded by a multitude of candles, the boys sit in shock and the girl watches from the shadows. The tower stands in a far corner of campus, and at a time like this—the middle of a thunderstorm that heaves enough rain onto the university that already paths have been flooded over—no one will have heard the boys' hoarse curses and shouts.

The girl remains hidden because despite the fact that things have gone horribly sideways, she mustn't be discovered. She peers at them through a spacious nook behind messy columns of stacked trunks and before a mirror draped over in velvet; on her left side sits a cloth-covered chaise piled high with broken crates filled with ancient books and brass instruments that look like compasses but aren't; on her right, a jumble of wooden chairs, one of which sports a broken leg that juts toward her ribs but is far enough away to not snag her university-issued cardigan. She's been here for a half hour.

The two boys sit before the open side of the Box, thin blankets beneath their knees. It really was kind of Catch to make her friends comfortable, and before either of them arrived, as she watched Catch fold each blanket just so, the girl allowed herself to pretend one of the blankets had been laid for her.

The atmosphere in the tower feels electric and heavy, and she wonders if it's the Box. The ancient artifact is an enormous cube with its front face shorn off. Its smooth, matte exterior is dark as midnight, with gold etchings that resemble Egyptian hieroglyphics and inlaid jewels that form constellations of stars, none of which have ever been seen on Earth.

She didn't have much time with the Box before hearing Catch come up the tower stairs—far too early—leaving her scrambling to hide.

And now . . . disaster.

She sits in the shadows, and there, in the tower's illuminated center and encircled by the dancing flames of tinned candles: Ingram Toussaint and Malcolm Porter. The second-years stare silently at the young prodigy in the Box, she who gathered them here tonight—Catch Jones—she who had promised wonders but now sits slumped against the Box's interior, appearing quite dead.

There hangs in the air an unmistakable whiff of burnt hair; probably some of Catch's long locs have gotten singed.

This was unforeseen, but the girl had been rushed.

She wonders if she got the spell wrong.

Ingram works an incantation to check Catch's pulse. There isn't one.

Well, he says, this was unexpected.

Malcolm rises to his feet and releases staccato curses into the cool, damp air.

Careful, Ingram says with an arched brow. You don't want to wake her.

Leave it to Ingram Toussaint to say the least empathetic thing.

Of the golden brown and slender young man, on campus there exists a collective impression: that through his round, wire-rimmed glasses, Ingram literally looks down his nose at the world. His features are bone sharp, and there is something off-puttingly patrician about his general air—a bougie-ass, she once overheard Malcolm saying about Ingram in the cafeteria. At the time, Ingram was just outside the series of half-stained Gothic windows, leaned nonchalantly against a balustrade smoking a nonregulation cigarette he didn't bother to hide. She hadn't heard Catch's response; desperate to escape notice, she'd hugged her notebook and sped to the buffet line. In truth, she admires Ingram despite his insouciance, because he never tries to avoid taking up space; instead, he carries his wealth, and hence his whole being, like he carries his cigarettes: laissez-faire with a core of contradictory challenge.

You got jokes? Malcolm says now. That supposed to be your version of a coping mechanism?

Life is absurd, Ingram replies. What else would you call it?

Come on, man, is Malcolm's only offering, which feels utterly insufficient considering the situation and also sums it up thoroughly. He sits with his brown, calloused hands on his knees in his impeccable school uniform; extra-tall, fitted, and starched to fanatical precision. He exhales and runs a hand over his tightly-waved fade, the waves shiny and flat and in flawless formation. Waves such as these just don't come about without a great deal of discipline and consistency and so, considering the late hour, it is of no surprise to see the end of a black durag peeking from the stiff edge of Malcolm's pants pocket.

Catch has been lying there a full minute, and for the second time, Ingram works a spell to check her pulse. His shoulders sag.

A roll of thunder sends vibrations through the old stone tower and rain taps harder against the leaded glass of the arched windows.

We should get her out, says Malcolm as he gets to his feet.

No, Ingram says sternly.

The thing is, one has to be wary of bodies belonging to those who have died by magickal means. You can never know if there is some bad arcane energy lingering about. The best they can do is pull Catch out with one of the blankets upon which they've been sitting.

Catch, though, is not completely dead. Yet there's no way for them to know this unless the girl tells them, which would require she reveal herself, which she will not.

Some of Catch's locs are draped across her round face; she looks as if she is sleeping.

She won't die, she won't die.

There is a creeping of doubt but the girl closes her eyes and takes a slow breath, the way in which she's trained herself when she feels the permeable barrier between what is and isn't real go translucent.

sunlight zone

They had an auspicious beginning. A couple of weeks into their second year, the girl was caught out in Nico Quad when the sky cracked open. Weighed down by her backpack and an armload of books, she shuffled across the uneven pathway because of course she'd forgotten to pack her mini umbrella. A week into a magickal fast and already she was tempted to cast a quick spell, but the societies had upperclassmen keeping an eye out for that, ready to pounce on anyone trying to cheat their way out of hazing. She quickened her steps only to slip in a puddle, watching in horror as her books and several loose pages of notes grew soggy on the stones. She was tearfully scrambling to get them together when an ebony hand reached down benevolently as if from the skies. Catch Jones. The girl knew her from Philosophy of Magickal Transcendence, one of the overenrolled lectures, and a few times she'd watched Catch and her friends laze about the main lawn. Catch smiled at the girl before rescuing a book, and another, and another, and said, You okay?

And then Catch saw it. The book was small and slender and bound in red leather so dark as to be nearly black, and her hand lingered over it just long enough to reveal that, though facedown, she knew what it was. Catch snatched it from the stones and hesitated before relinquishing it. A unicorn, that book, she said, and the girl pretended not to know that really what Catch was asking was where she'd acquired it, this book that would mean instantaneous expulsion.

As they walked, Catch smiled conspiratorially and the girl's heart quickened. She'd left high school the way she'd left junior high: a creep, a weirdo, a nobody; yet here, at a school in which there were so many faces it was easy to not recognize someone whom you'd sat near for an entire semester, perhaps she'd finally found what had always proven elusive: a kindred spirit.

In a breath's span they reached the girl's dormitory entrance. Catch asked, Blasian, right? Black and . . . Vietnamese? and the girl gave a tiny nod and amended, Black and Korean. Catch was several paces away when the girl called out a belated Thanks and Catch spun and gave a bow and replied, Your friend on call. A line from a disgraced magician's obscure memoir. It was both a test and an invitation, and the girl caught it with both hands.

Your friend.

The girl dropped out of the hazing that very afternoon, because being in a magickal secret society was her mother's dream, not hers, and now she had Catch, and she'd have her friends too. Catch, Malcolm, Ingram, herself. They would become a foursome, even if the girl was the only one to know it.

It's our fault, Malcolm says.

It isn't anyone's fault, says Ingram. Except maybe Catch's.

Malcolm looks back at him as if he wants to stab him with a blunt object.

If they leave the tower, the girl can step into the open and wait for them to return—or better yet, she can play it out the way she'd planned: she'll arrive Hey sorry I'm late didn't she tell you I was coming oh no what happened but look I know something that can bring her back.

She flexes her tingly feet. She's been huddled in the same awkward position, yet the entirety of the turret's interior feels somehow smaller . . .

She shakes away the claustrophobia and watches Malcolm stare down at Catch with thick, furrowed brows, his full mouth puffed in contemplation.

Is he thinking of all the hours the friends spent in the darker recesses of the library, debating in hushed tones the veracity of the rumors regarding reverse magick or the literal keys to immortality? In the shadows nearby, the girl would sit unnoticed, muttering the names of out-of-print books or discredited theories the friends kept overlooking, and grinning when Catch managed to fit sacred geometry into this or that magickal theory. On Wednesday nights, Ingram almost always brought coffee—the good stuff, not the dishwater you two are used to drinking—and they would congratulate Malcolm's latest exploits on the basketball court as they laughed over vegan BLT-bagel sandwiches, which she, too, brought, complete with a cup of Ingram's favorite coffee, as she pretended their trio was her quartet.

A stab to the ribs sends her whirling.

The jagged edges of the broken chair leg that once sat a foot away are pressed so firmly into her side that several threads of her cardigan have been ripped loose. An alarm blares somewhere in the recesses of her mind . . .

An electric tang zips across her tongue.

The walls.

The room.

The furniture.

Closer.

The tower has grown much smaller, and a thought she hardly dares to think to completion: the unrelenting suspicion that the mirror, the plethora of lost and forgotten objects, and the walls themselves have not only drawn close . . .

But are in fact *actively listening.*

The last thing the girl would have ever expected was for her to show up at the door.

And yet there Catch was, two weeks ago, with that bright grin and earnest look in her eyes. Hey, she said, her voice cheerful but precipitously so. I need a solid.

The girl didn't answer, still trying to figure out how she'd found her.

So, Catch went on, I stumbled onto something.

Okay.

Yeah. But I don't know how to use it. And I need to know but . . . Catch shook her head. The thing is, it's . . .

Off the books?

That grin again. I knew you'd understand, said Catch. You still have it, right? The— As if the word itself was too dangerous to utter, with her hands she pantomimed the opening of a book.

But the girl said nothing. *Spells Unforgivable and Illicit, Vol. III* was her secret.

Catch took her silence for assent and dropped into a chair. I found one, she said. A Box.

Overwhelmed, the girl lowered herself onto the edge of her bed.

Box magick was hardly more than a cipher—and all theory, no action. The idea was that one step into a Box, murmur an incantation, and wait for the portal door to appear—never in the Box itself, but somewhere off to the side. Once opened, a portal door had to be entered by its creator in a finite amount of time, else one risked the very painful process of being deconstructed, molecule after molecule, by the Origin. It was rumored to have actually happened a couple of hundred years ago, this death by deconstruction, to an entire body of Nonagon Society initiates, after which the Semreh Academy of the Arcane put a moratorium on Box magick discussion of any substantial depth.

Yet even a cursory internet search could tell you that, once numbering seven, two Boxes were destroyed, with rumored locations of four: the International Institute of Esoteria; the French Alps in the Blue School of Small Magick; China, high atop Mount Tai in the House of Tranquility; the Congo, in the constantly disappearing and reappearing Institute of Three. And the fate of one Box: unknown.

The fifth Box exists, Catch whispered. And it's right here on campus.

Where? How did you find it?

Catch waved a hand. None of it matters if I can't use it.

There was such instruction in the book. Yet thrilled as she was to possess something Catch so desperately desired, the girl did not rush to retrieve the book because she felt another, stronger sentiment: anger. Catch had never taken notice of her after the day in the rain, despite the girl having been with her and Malcolm and Ingram for months, despite their having done so many things together.

Where are you going? the girl asked, inherent in her question that Catch must tell her before she'd allow even a glimpse of the book. The girl had sampled her first taste of power and she never felt so brash, so cocky. She liked it.

To the beginning, Catch said simply.

Catch was playing coy, but there was no need to be excessively domineering, and anyway, the girl would know soon enough. She remained silent.

An interesting expression fell upon Catch's face, an incongruent look of recognition, as if she hadn't truly seen the girl until that moment. And then: You can come.

Even as her heart raced, the girl forced a noncommittal shrug.

Later, when they were huddled over the book, contemplating how Box magick did and did not work, and after they determined the most favorable celestial timing, Catch said, This'll be special. You'll see.

I don't want to come.

Catch looked surprised but said nothing more, just bent back over the book, over her notes.

The girl knew Catch and her friends better than they could guess. The impervious clique of three wouldn't respect her coming along as some interloper, some nobody who was just tagging along and happy to be present. No. She would have a proper introduction to the group and that would require another entrance. It would require that they *need* her.

So she made other plans.

The walls have grown worryingly close.

Do Ingram and Malcolm notice?

It doesn't seem so. They are too focused on Catch, who lies at their feet like someone's twisted idea of a sacrifice.

It isn't raining anymore and the hush and chill of midnight cloak the abandoned tower, and for a moment she wishes she hadn't come, that Catch had never sought her out in search of the book, had never helped her in the rain. But if none of it had happened, what a sad alternative that would be, the girl in her dorm room alone, staring out the window waiting to exist.

If you're not going to say it, I will, Ingram says, his voice a cruel slice through the silence. We have to get rid of her body.

The girl starts in shock. *She isn't dead!* she wants to shout. She should stop them before they unknowingly commit murder. Shouldn't she?

No, Malcolm says. Whatever you're thinking, we'll be able to handle it— we can explain.

Thank you for that assessment, Porter, Ingram says drily. It's clear a basketball's not going to get you—us—out of this one. *This* will require a brain.

Malcom's hands tighten into fists.

What's that? Ingram says arrogantly as he holds a finger to his ear. Oh, just that I'm right, per usual?

Malcolm's jaw looks soldered tight but he manages to grind out, We go to the dean.

Yes, she thinks from the shadows. *Go!* Alone, she can fix this.

Because the woman's going to do what? Ingram continues, as if speaking to a child.

I don't know! sputters Malcolm. She'll—

She can't fix her, Ingram says harshly. She can't fix *this*. Catch is gone and we're here and unless you're fine with spending the rest of your life sleeping in a bed an arm's length from a toilet, I suggest we get to it.

Lightning fills the tower with white light and harsh shadows. The air is traced with something dangerously acidic.

Malcolm scowls at Ingram and Ingram stares back, unperturbed.

If the boys unwittingly kill Catch, is it the girl's fault? *She* left her alive. Between states, certainly, but alive still. But she won't betray herself.

Something heavy lumbers onto her shoulders—

She pitches to the side, twisting in panic. She's smothered in velvet and whips around to see a brown-skinned girl with wavy dark hair and darker eyes so close they are nearly nose to nose.

A phantom, trapped in the tower—

She leaps forward with a scream, bulldozing her way through trunks, sending them cascading to the hardwood with a series of crashes.

When she tumbles forward, she lands on her knees, barely a foot from Catch's body.

twilight zone

Beneath their gazes, she's a crustacean with a crushed shell. She turns back. There is no ghost. Just the mirror.

Malcolm stares down at her with open unease. He glances at Catch, at Ingram, back down at the girl, likely trying to figure what she's doing here and how this is going to play out.

Badly.

Ingram tilts his head. I've seen you before.

I don't know if you've noticed, she says quaveringly, but the tower is shrinking.

Lightning flashes and pulls her attention to one of the turret windows. As she walks toward it, she senses a hitch somewhere, a snag in the fabric of the night. Her final step, she falters. The stormy night sky still rages; rain pelts the window.

But she can't hear it hitting the glass.

It occurs to her that this might be her fault, that when she placed the spell upon the Box, and hence interfered with Catch's incantations, she set something off kilter.

Ingram appears at her side to take a look. He mutters, What the hell.

She's never been so close to him. He smells of sweet tobacco, vanilla, and wood—with a hint of bourbon. Such a warm scent for a cold personality.

What are you doing? Ingram asks stiffly.

What?

Were you just sniffing?

No.

You were.

She stares at him.

He looks back at her dubiously and turns away. All right. Let's grab Catch and get out of here. Whatever's happening, we need to clear the tower.

But why is the tower shrinking? Malcolm asks nervously.

I'm guessing a side effect of Catch's failed experiment, Ingram answers. We should get going.

She could say something now. She could say that she magicked the Box, or more specifically, conjured a spell that would interfere with *Catch* magicking the Box, and that she can fix it all. But she hasn't figured out a way to say it without bringing to attention the fact that, up to now, she's been squirreled away, wasting precious time.

She says nothing.

In moments they're carrying the blanket with Catch's body toward the door.

Where was Catch trying to go? says Malcolm. She wouldn't say.

A noted silence as Ingram pretends not to have heard the question. And then: Fine, she told me, okay?

When Malcolm speaks his voice is brittle. All right, so where?

Ingram straightens and says, The Origin.

The girl feels a lurching in her gut. Catch told her she wanted to go *to the beginning*.

The Origin, says Malcolm, as in . . . ?

As in all of it, says Ingram. Magick, life, death. Everything.

The temperature in the tower plummets.

This changes things.

What is it? Ingram asks.

What?

You were about to say something.

No.

You were.

She doesn't reply. If it's true that Catch was trying to get to the Origin, and why in the name of everything living would she want to do that, God only knows what she may have opened up. The silent rain, the shrinking tower—it could all be due to Catch's attempt and nothing to do with the girl's spell having gone wrong.

Which means reawakening her might be impossible.

Catch obviously made a mistake, the girl blurts, but what if her being asleep is keeping something worse from happening?

Asleep? You think she isn't dead? Malcolm asks.

I—I know she isn't.

Malcolm lowers his edge of the blanket to bring Catch's leg to the floor, and the girl and Ingram follow suit. How do you know this? I mean, look at her. And we checked her pulse.

She sighs. I can just tell, okay? She adds a lie: I've seen this before. And I know a way to wake her up. I'm just not sure if . . . it's safe to.

Why the hell didn't you say this before? Ingram says.

I've been thinking about it and just figured it out.

He looks as if he doesn't believe her.

She explains the blood rite, and when she finishes, Ingram's gaze is sharp.

Williamson, he says. Yeong He Williamson. Right?

He's spoken her name.

None of them have ever spoken her name, not even Catch, with whom she'd spent an entire evening poring over *Spells Unforgivable and Illicit*. And now Ingram Toussaint has spoken her name and it's as if she and all that she has ever been to the group has been made real.

DMPM, he says with recognition.

Every second-year is required to take Dark Matter, Paradoxes, and Magickwork, and like her, Ingram took it first semester.

You wrote a paper, he says, on how every spell affects the seen and unseen, matter and dark matter, and you weren't even in our class but Professor King laid in on the rest of us. Congratulations.

It's unclear whether he's being sarcastic. His perpetually dry delivery makes it almost impossible to ever tell.

We'll be bonded over this, he says. And this isn't theory—you really know how to do it.

He makes it sound like an accusation. Or is it a challenge? She shrugs with feigned confidence—something he would do—and turns away to dig into her backpack.

You have a knife? Ingram muses. How fortunate for us. A real Girl Scout.

We don't know what might happen if we wake her, she warns.

In the silence is the implication that they will try anyway.

In moments, the three are standing over Catch's body, bleeding from the crooks of their elbows, their fingertips dripping blood onto her sleeping face. Yeong He mumbles the incantation in the Original language, the so-called Language of Babes known to every human baby before they forget and before they learn to speak.

They wait.

Nothing happens.

Catch does not stir.

Malcolm curses and it's as if Catch has died all over again.

Ingram doesn't bother hemming. So is she dead or not?

Yeong He presses her lips into a hard line.

Without another word, Ingram bends to lift his side of the blanket and soon they're all lifting Catch toward the door. Yeong He doesn't dare tell them to wait or reconsider because she knows she will be blamed if Catch isn't saved. Clutching the blanket, she hopes the downpour will wash away most of the blood from Catch's face, from their hands.

Wait, she says. She turns back to the room, which has grown so small, the covered furniture sits just a couple of feet from the circle of candles.

Ingram follows her gaze and grouses an incantation with barely mustered patience. In an instant, the candles extinguish. Right. Can you get the door?

Distantly, she hears Malcolm ask, Y'all's watches stopped?

She reaches for the doorknob but misses. She tries again, slower.

But her hand does not wrap around the ball of aged brass. Neither does it miss.

It falls through, as if her fingers are as insubstantial as air.

midnight zone

After they set down Catch's body, Yeong He relights the candles. There has to be a way to open the door, she says shakily as she turns to Ingram.

I didn't major in locksmith, he says flatly.

What about a gravitational spell? Malcolm says. I think it only works on physical objects, but maybe something strange shows up. Like the portal?

Ingram claps obnoxiously and snipes, See there? Basketball not required.

No one sees the punch coming, least of all Ingram, who takes the full brunt of it in the jaw and is sent sprawling. Immediately Malcolm's glower dims, leaving him sheepish and rubbing his knuckles.

Ingram rises and stands chest to chest with Malcolm, as if there exists even one scenario in which after a fistfight with the athlete, Ingram would emerge with only his ego out of shape.

The tower isn't getting any bigger, Yeong He says as she hurries across the ancient floorboards, making her way toward a tangle of broken furniture and a standing globe with unrecognizable landmasses.

I've got something, says Ingram. It won't keep the walls from closing in, but it'll shrink us down and buy us more time.

Wait! Yeong He shouts. We can't throw spells around if we don't know what's changed. (She won't tell them that her spell on the Box may have altered things in addition to Catch's own incantations because why draw more heat?) I don't think it's related to a physical object, she continues. Wasn't there something in DMPM about that?

Ingram frowns thoughtfully. Theory of Exponential Collapse, he says. Right. Good save, Williamson.

The question is, Yeong He says, if it isn't physical, what is it? Something dimensional?

Yeah, yeah, says Malcolm. Could be a dimension split.

Yeong He rummages through a series of nesting baskets before moving them aside to step behind a large set of armoires. I'm guessing we'll know it when we see it, she says, like shimmering air or a visible tear in space, or maybe—

She halts.

What can only be described as floating voids hover in a loose circle. They aren't random bits of emptiness, but rather silhouettes: an upside-down table . . . an upside-down set of stairs . . . an octagon-ish bulk, among other familiar and unfamiliar shapes.

Yeong He calls the boys over. They're three-dimensional, she says.

Ingram points downward.

Flat against the hardwood, a circular black void. She crouches and peers inside. The blackness is unyielding, dizzying . . . and she can swear she feels a pulling. Soon, Ingram and Malcolm, too, are bent over the bizarre nothing.

She asks, mostly to herself, Could it be a portal?

You think it's the portal Catch was trying to open? says Malcolm, sounding like he's hoping it's exactly not that.

No, says Ingram. Look at it. If it were a portal, we'd be able to see the other side.

Hence Yeong He's uncertainty. Looking through a portal should be as if looking through a window—to a verdant knoll, windswept dunes, a foreign cityscape. This is like looking into death.

Ingram steps away.

I think it *is* a portal, Yeong He whispers. I think it's a portal to exactly where Catch was trying to go.

Malcolm makes a strangled noise. You telling us we're looking at the Origin?

Ingram strides forward and pitches a tinned candle into the void. The moment the tin passes through the barrier between worlds, it bursts into flame. And in a single blink, it is lost to the darkness.

This, Ingram says, is very bad. But.

Malcolm and Yeong He turn to him.

But, he repeats, we can use it.

What do you mean? Malcolm says. You just said—

It's the perfect size.

A silence falls over them. Yeong He rubs the length of her arms and asks, Perfect size?

Ingram blinks. For a body.

■ ■ ■

Whatever Catch did with the box, Ingram says, it set things off-balance. We're stuck in a tower that's literally closing in around us, and frankly, this might be our only chance to get rid of her body, our only chance to set things right.

You don't know if that will fix it! Malcolm says.

And you don't know that it won't. But if we do nothing, we die. Do either of you argue with that?

Neither Malcolm nor Yeong He reply but Malcolm has to see that it's true, that they risk more by trying to wake Catch than . . . doing what Ingram suggests.

Yeong He avoids looking down at Catch, avoids snagging her sight line on anyone's gaze, because isn't it her own fault? It was Yeong He's spell that made it so Catch would fall into the in-between state. If it's true that the portal demands magickal restitution, if they do this thing and Catch isn't enough, will Yeong He have to throw herself into the portal too?

Tentatively, she side-longs Malcolm, who stares down at Catch with game-day concentration. He doesn't appear ready to murder his best friend . . . but he looks as if he's mulling it over.

There are obvious things to say but no one says a word.

They're making silent considerations.

Self-preservation.

The voice is snide and familiar, having lived with her for as long as she can remember, echoing the whispers that trailed her through school corridors. Yet, for nearly a year, until this very moment, it had been silent, without judgment as she followed these three people to and from classes, hovered over them in stairwells, eavesdropped in the cafeteria, lurked in the library.

Now it has an opinion: *Survive this.*

We have to decide together, right? Yeong He asks, looking to each of them. But are we supposed to pretend this never happened, that she never invited us here? People are going to ask us if we saw her, *when* we saw her. And her family will be wondering—

She doesn't have family, Ingram says sharply.

Malcolm shakes his head sadly. We don't know that. She only said they were gone.

What they are all thinking but no one says: no one outside this tower will mourn her.

Yeong He studies Catch's beautiful face, her dense curly lashes, her perfectly smooth dark skin. And her mind, her potential . . . She deserved better than her friends. She deserved better than this.

All they can do now is try to not make things worse, which might be defined as destabilizing this portal to the Origin or doing something that lands them all in prison.

Malcolm sighs heavily. Nah. We can't put her in there. Hell no.

You keep saying that, Ingram says, his gaze locked on Catch, yet here you are, standing over her like the rest of us.

Malcolm doesn't reply.

After a time, Ingram draws a deep breath: We do this. We tell no one. Not even ourselves.

Yeong He swallows.

Ingram stares at Malcolm before turning his attention to Yeong He, and at his uncharacteristically open expression, she starts, after which she is embarrassed for the slight lifting of her heart. For being included in the count, as if she is one of them. For finally belonging. She would wither in self-disgust if she weren't so heartened at the same time.

■ ■ ■

If the heart is an ocean, it is one of impenetrable depths, increasingly crushing in force

the farther

one

falls.

You want to believe that, facing down what is good, what is evil, you know what you'll do when put to the test. But you can't know. Because beneath it all is the singular drive to survive. Throw it all to the fire if it means putting space between you and an unthinkable future, an unbearable consequence.

But it's the knowledge that you can't actually know

the depths of your own heart,

that there lies within

an unexplored

abyss,

that

is

most

frightening

of

all

.

abyss

Yeong He whispers: Agreed.

Malcolm, with great reluctance: Agreed.

Ingram's response is more breath than word: It's agreed.

At their feet, Catch's body jerks.

Her blood-covered face contorts and she lets out a great gasp, as if she's been struggling to take a breath she can only manage to take this very moment. Her eyes fly open, wide and unseeing, and they stagger back from her, from this inconceivable fact:

Catch Jones is very much alive.

She smiles. It is not a nice smile.

Catch's gaze homes in on Yeong He. You made it after all.

Yeong He nods as she feels herself shrink.

Catch's eyes narrow. You got here before I did. You tampered with the Box.

Yeong He feels everyone turning to her. I—I made an adjustment. And then she adds a lie: It was meant to keep you safe.

Catch cracks an unexpected grin, crooked and assured even as she lies with her back pressed against the thin blanket. I was conscious but I couldn't move, she says, couldn't breathe. But I recognized your voice. It's good you're here. Backup.

Backup.

Malcolm demands, Yeong He is backup for what?

Catch places her arms onto her knees and clasps her hands. For the ritual.

You never mentioned no ritual, says Malcolm.

I didn't tell you the specifics, Catch says, her voice gone hard, but you wanted in.

Yeong He looks around to see that the oversized furniture and the trunks and the arcane instruments are practically on top of them; whatever is happening, it isn't stopping because Catch is awake.

Wanted in on what? says Malcolm.

On knowledge, Catch says, and is that a glint of cold amusement in her eye? Come on, she continues, you know it's true. I knew something you didn't and you would never forgive yourself for being shut out.

Yeong He thinks there must be something that can hold the walls back long enough. Perhaps Catch might have a suggestion. But it's as if Catch hasn't even noticed.

No, says Ingram. You needed us. And you still do, don't you?

Catch stares back at Ingram with assessment, the way one would an opponent. At this point, she says, it's safe to say we need each other.

Just admit it, Ingram says, his voice as chilled as Catch's. You lured us here to make whatever you're trying to do work. Oh, we saw what happens when anything goes through that nightmarish portal.

Catch rises slowly to her feet, only a bit unsteady. And you're so high and mighty? Were you *not* about to throw my body into that void like it was a trash chute? And you knew where I wanted to go. And here you are.

Ingram has no answer for that.

Whatever you needed, says Yeong He, I don't think it matters now. The tower is collapsing or shrinking and we can't even touch the door. But I guess you heard that too.

Why isn't Catch worried?

The tower, Catch says, is collapsing. But not *the* tower, exactly. Just the version we're in now. Just the version in this half-space.

What do you mean? Yeong He asks.

What I mean is that I put a little hot sauce on the conjuring. When I worked the Box. I didn't know there was already spellwork on it to make me fall out—she pierces Yeong He with a pointed glance—but I added something to give us more time.

More time—stop playing games! says Malcolm.

The portal's open, Catch says, but only halfway.

If what Catch says is true, probably the same rule to portals and Box magick applies. Yeong He says, We go through or face—

Deconstruction, et cetera, finishes Ingram, who has been observing this exchange with all the excitement of watching water boil. But it must be feigned; even he can't be genuinely nonchalant about obliteration.

You made a trap, Malcolm says. You made it so we'd get stuck in some half-dimension where the walls close in on us—for what? Why?

No, says Catch, I made it so we wouldn't all be dead in seconds. I bought us time.

But you set us up in the first place, Malcolm counters.

Catch shrugs and says, To open a portal to the Origin, you need three people. I did the first part to show you that it was possible, that it was real and we could get there. But to fully open the portal, to not light up like a firework, four people need to go in at the same time.

Yeong He is angry and frightened, but also she is curious. The four of us? she asks. In the Box?

A perfect fit, Catch says, and for a moment they're back in the dorm room, intoxicated on magickal postulates and theories. She points to Malcolm, Ingram, and Yeong He, and says, Three people to form the three points of a triangle. She points to herself and adds, And one person in the center, as the Eye.

Inviting Yeong He as backup—

No. Never backup.

You knew I'd come, Yeong He says softly. Is her hunger so obvious?

Catch smirks and says, A girl with that book in her possession? Of course you'd come. Glad you didn't disappoint.

Even as Yeong He seethes, she appreciates Catch's bold intelligence.

You manipulated us, Malcolm says, and now you're saying we're trapped?

I'm saying, Catch says, that you don't have to be. Trapped. But the only way out is through. We do the ritual and the portal opens up fully, and we're in and back out before you know it. Only this time with power you can hardly begin to imagine. We won't even need a Box to get back. *That's* the kind of power I'm talking about.

Ingram stares at Catch, a sly smile on his own face. You have a cruel streak. I'm impressed.

Everyone does, Catch says easily. Have a little something vicious inside.

Yeong He shifts, feeling too seen.

Catch looks back at them with a good-natured grin. Ingram wears a smug smile, as if his beliefs regarding humanity have been confirmed; Malcolm still frowns, his eyes shiny with fury and betrayal. Over them all, a veil of precariousness. But no one's punching anyone, so there's that.

Why? Ingram says abruptly. What's there? Immense power, fine. But it's more than that. Why risk it all—risk us—to get to the Origin?

Catch doesn't answer.

Ingram tilts his chin a fraction. Your family.

No, Catch says, too quickly.

You think they're in there? Because if they were, I'm sorry, but—

They're not dead!

What happened to them? Malcolm asks.

Catch steps back. We're running out of time.

As if the point needs illustrating, she reaches to push over one of the stacks of trunks. At the beginning of the night, they sat nearly fifteen feet away.

We'll never be right after this, Malcolm laments.

We'll be better than right, Catch says. We'll be real.

She strides toward the Box, kicking strewn blankets from her path, looking hardly the same girl who, an hour earlier, so carefully laid them out for her friends. When she reaches the Box, she turns.

Are you in? she asks.

Perhaps Catch saw it in Yeong He that day, on the quad, the vicious vein that runs through her, through them all. Perhaps Catch recognized it in her like she recognized the book, when she'd invited her, a famished outsider, into their midst. Until tonight, Yeong He was only ever halfway to them, half-visible in her half-existence, but now she can be fully theirs as much as they've been wholly hers.

Yeong He steps forward until she stands at the Box's edge. At the precipice of a fathomless future, she looks to Malcolm and Ingram and says the thing she needs to hear herself say, says the thing she knows they all need her to say, the way they have always, however unknowingly, needed *her* to make them complete:

We're in.

CONTRIBUTOR BIOS

AMERIE is a Grammy-nominated singer-songwriter, producer, and writer. The daughter of a Korean artist and an African American military officer, Amerie was born in Massachusetts and raised all over the world, and she graduated from Georgetown University with a bachelor's degree in English. She is the editor of the *New York Times* bestseller *Because You Love to Hate Me*, and is the founder of Amerie's Book Club, a book club that highlights diverse and unique perspectives and voices. She lives in Atlanta with her husband and son.

KALYNN BAYRON is the award-winning author of the YA fantasy novels *Cinderella Is Dead* and *This Poison Heart*. Her latest works include the YA fantasy *This Wicked Fate* and the middle grade paranormal adventure *The Vanquishers*. She is a CILIP Carnegie Medal nominee, a two-time Cybils Award nominee, and the recipient of the 2022 Randall Kenan Prize for Black LGBTQ Fiction. She is a classically trained vocalist and musical theater enthusiast. When she's not writing, you can find her watching scary movies and spending time with her kids. She currently lives in Ithaca, New York, with her family.

TERRY J. BENTON-WALKER is the author of *Blood Debts*, his magical YA contemporary fantasy debut on the way from Tor Teen in Winter 2023, and *Alex Wise vs. the End of the World*, his apocalyptic middle grade contemporary fantasy debut coming from Labyrinth Road/PRH in Fall 2023. He lives in Atlanta, Georgia.

ROSEANNE A. BROWN is an immigrant from the West African nation of Ghana and a graduate of the University of Maryland, where she completed the Jiménez-Porter Writers' House program. Her debut novel, *A Song of Wraiths and Ruin*, was an instant *New York Times* bestseller and an Indie bestseller, and received six starred reviews. She has worked with Marvel, Star Wars, and Disney, among other publishers.

ELISE BRYANT is the NAACP Image Award–nominated author of *Happily Ever Afters*, *One True Loves*, and *Reggie and Delilah's Year of Falling*. She was born and raised in Southern California. For many years, Elise had the joy of working as a special education teacher, and now she spends her days writing swoony love stories and eating dessert. She lives with her husband and two daughters in Long Beach.

TRACY DEONN is the *New York Times* bestselling and award-winning author of *Legendborn,* and its sequel *Bloodmarked.* A second-generation fangirl, she grew up in central North Carolina, where she devoured fantasy books and Southern food in equal measure. After earning her bachelor's and master's degrees in communication and performance studies from the University of North Carolina at Chapel Hill, Tracy worked in live theater, video game production, and K-12 education. When she's not writing, Tracy speaks on panels at science fiction and fantasy conventions, reads fanfic, arranges puppy playdates, and keeps an eye out for ginger-flavored everything.

DESIREE S. EVANS is an award-winning writer, scholar, and activist from the Louisiana bayou. She holds an MFA from the Michener Center for Writers at The University of Texas at Austin. She also holds a bachelor's degree in journalism from Northwestern University's Medill School of Journalism and a master's degree in international affairs from Columbia University's School of International and Public Affairs. Desiree's creative writing has been nominated for the Pushcart Prize and Best of the Net. Her writing has appeared in literary journals such as *Gulf Coast, The Offing, Nimrod International Journal, Cosmonauts Avenue,* and others. She is a 2020 winner of the Walter Dean Myers Grant awarded by We Need Diverse Books.

ISAAC FITZSIMONS writes so that every reader can see themselves reflected in literature. His debut novel, *The Passing Playbook,* received numerous accolades, including being named a Junior Library Guild Gold Standard selection, a Summer/Fall 2021 Indies Introduce title, a *Kirkus Reviews* Best Young Adult Book of 2021, and a 2022 Lambda Literary Award Finalist. A lifetime dabbler in the arts, Isaac has performed sketch comedy and can play three songs on the banjo. His dream vacation would be traveling around Europe via sleeper train to watch every top-tier soccer team play a home game. He currently lives outside Washington, DC.

LAMAR GILES writes for teens and adults across multiple genres, with work appearing on numerous Best Of lists each and every year. He is the author of acclaimed novels *Fake ID, Spin, The Last Last-Day-of-Summer,* and *Not So Pure and Simple,* as well as numerous pieces of short fiction. He is a founding member of We Need Diverse Books and resides in Virginia with his family.

JORDAN IFUEKO is the *New York Times* bestselling author of the Raybearer series. She's a Nebula Award, Ignyte Award, Audie Award, and Hugo Lodestar Award finalist, and she's been featured in *People*, NPR Best Books, NPR Pop Culture Hour, and ALA Top Ten. She writes about magic Black girls who aren't magic all the time, because honestly, they deserve a vacation.

Ifueko lives in Los Angeles with her husband, David, and their three-legged trustafarian dog, Reginald Ovahcomah.

LEAH JOHNSON is an eternal Midwesterner and author of award-winning books for children and young adults. Her bestselling debut YA novel, *You Should See Me in a Crown*, was a Stonewall Honor Book, the inaugural Reese's Book Club YA pick, and named a best book of the year by Amazon, *Kirkus Reviews*, *Marie Claire*, *Publishers Weekly*, and the New York Public Library. In 2021, *TIME* named *You Should See Me in a Crown* one of the 100 Best Young Adult Books of All Time. Leah's essays and cultural criticism can be found in *Teen Vogue*, *Harper's Bazaar*, and *Cosmopolitan*, among others. Her debut middle grade, *Ellie Engle Saves Herself*, is forthcoming from Disney-Hyperion in 2023.

AMANDA JOY is the author of the River of Royal Blood duology. She has received starred reviews from *School Library Journal*, *Kirkus Reviews*, and *Booklist*. Her debut, *A River of Royal Blood*, was a Junior Library Guild selection, and *A Queen of Gilded Horns* was named to best teen fiction list by *Kirkus Reviews*. Her work has also appeared in the anthologies *Up All Night* and *Game On*. Amanda studied writing and literature at the University of Missouri, and earned her MFA in writing for children from the New School. She currently writes and teaches in Chicago, with her dog Luna.

KWAME MBALIA is a husband, a father, a writer, a *New York Times* bestselling author, and a former pharmaceutical metrologist in that order. His debut middle grade novel, *Tristan Strong Punches a Hole in the Sky*, was awarded a Coretta Scott King Author Honor, and it—along with the sequels, *Tristan Strong Destroys the World* and *Tristan Strong Keep Punching*—is published by Rick Riordan Presents/Disney-Hyperion. He is the co-author of *Last Gate of the Emperor* with Prince Joel Makonnen, from Scholastic Books, and the editor of the #1 *New York Times* bestselling anthology *Black Boy Joy*, published by Delacorte Press. A Howard University graduate and a Midwesterner now in North Carolina, he survives on Dad jokes and Cheez-Its.

TOCHI ONYEBUCHI is the author of *Goliath*. His previous fiction includes *Riot Baby*, a finalist for the Hugo, Nebula, Locus, and NAACP Image Awards and winner of the New England Book Award for Fiction, the Ignyte Award for Best Novella, and the World Fantasy Award; the Beasts Made of Night series; and the War Girls series. His short fiction has appeared in *The Best American Science Fiction and Fantasy* and elsewhere. His nonfiction includes the book *(S)kinfolk* and has appeared in *The New York Times*, NPR, and the